PENGUIN MODERN CLASSICS

The Hand

Georges Simenon was born in Liège, Belgium in 1903. An intrepid traveller with a profound interest in people, Simenon strove on and off the page to understand, rather than to judge, the human condition in all its shades. His novels include the Inspector Maigret series and a richly varied body of wider work united by its evocative power, its economy of means, and its penetrating psychological insight. He is among the most widely read writers in the global canon. He died in 1989 in Lausanne, Switzerland, where he had lived for the latter part of his life.

Written in 1968, *The Hand* takes its setting from the years Simenon had spent living at Shadow Rock Farm, in Lakeville, Connecticut, during the early 1950s.

He wrote *Betty* in 1960 on his return from a few weeks' convalescence in Versailles.

The Blue Room was completed in 1963 and is one of the last novels Simenon wrote in Échandens Castle in Switzerland, where he lived from 1957–63. All his typescripts from this period were datelined 'Noland', his nickname for the peaceful, unassuming village that had become his home.

GEORGES SIMENON

The Hand

And Other Novels

PENGUIN BOOKS

PENGUIN CLASSICS

UK | USA | Canada | Ireland | Australia
India | New Zealand | South Africa

Penguin Classics is part of the Penguin Random House group of companies whose addresses can be found at global.penguinrandomhouse.com.

Penguin Random House UK
One Embassy Gardens, 8 Viaduct Gardens, London SW11 7BW

penguin.co.uk

The Hand first published in French as *La main* by Presses de la Cité 1968.
First published in Great Britain in Penguin Classics 2016.
Betty first published in French as *Betty* by Presses de la Cité 1961.
First published in Great Britain in Penguin Classics 2021.
The Blue Room first published in French as *La chambre bleue* by Presses de la Cité 1964.
First published in Great Britain in Penguin Classics 2015.
This selection published in Penguin Classics 2025.

001

The Hand translation copyright © Linda Coverdale, 2016
Betty translation copyright © Ros Schwartz, 2021
The Blue Room translation copyright © Linda Coverdale, 2015
Betty copyright © 1961, Georges Simenon Limited, all rights reserved
La main copyright © 1968, Georges Simenon Limited, all rights reserved
La Chambre bleue copyright © 1964, Georges Simenon Limited, all rights reserved
The Hand And Other Novels copyright © 2025, all rights reserved

GEORGES SIMENON and ® **Simenon.tm**®, all rights reserved

 original design by Maria Picassó i Piquer

The moral rights of the author and translators have been asserted

No part of this book may be used or reproduced in any manner for the purpose of training artificial intelligence technologies or systems. In accordance with Article 4(3) of the DSM Directive 2019/790, Penguin Random House expressly reserves this work from the text and data mining exception.

Set in 12.5/15pt Dante MT Std
Typeset by Six Red Marbles UK, Thetford, Norfolk
Printed and bound in Great Britain by Clays Ltd, Elcograf S.p.A.

The authorized representative in the EEA is Penguin Random House Ireland, Morrison Chambers, 32 Nassau Street, Dublin D02 YH68

A CIP catalogue record for this book is available from the British Library

ISBN: 978-0-241-78791-5

Penguin Random House is committed to a sustainable future for our business, our readers and our planet. This book is made from Forest Stewardship Council® certified paper.

Contents

The Hand 1
Betty 183
The Blue Room 331

The Hand

PART ONE

I

I was sitting on the bench, in the barn. Not only was I aware of being there, in front of the sagging door that, with each swing, let in a gust of wind and snow, but I saw myself as clearly as in a mirror, noting the incongruity of my situation.

The bench was a garden bench, painted red. We had three of them, which we put away for the winter along with the lawnmower, the garden tools and the window screens.

The barn, also of wood painted red, had been a real barn a hundred years earlier, but was now nothing more than a vast shed.

If I begin with that particular moment, it's because it was a kind of awakening. I had not slept. Yet I was emerging, abruptly, into reality. Or was it a new reality that was beginning?

But then, when does a man begin to . . . No! I will not let myself go down that slippery slope. I am a lawyer by profession and have the habit, some even say the mania, of precision.

And yet, I don't even know what time it might have been. Two o'clock? Three o'clock in the morning? At my feet, on the floor of beaten earth, the pink filament of the small flashlight was still shedding its last gleam without illuminating a thing any more. With cold, numb fingers, I was trying to strike a match to light my cigarette. I needed to smoke. It was like a sign of recovered reality.

The smell of tobacco felt reassuring to me, and I stayed there, leaning forward, elbows on my knees, staring at the huge banging door that might collapse at any moment under the onslaught of the storm.

I had been drunk. I probably still was, which has happened to me only twice in my life. I remembered everything, however, the way you remember a dream when laying scraps of it end to end.

After a trip to Canada, the Sanders had come to spend the weekend with us. Ray is one of my oldest friends. We studied law together at Yale and, later, after our marriages, we had kept up the connection.

So. That evening, Saturday 15 January, when the snow had already begun falling, I'd asked Ray:

'How do you feel about coming along with us for drinks at old Ashbridge's place?'

'Harold Ashbridge, from Boston?'

'Yes.'

'I thought he spent the winter down at his home in Florida . . .'

'Ten years ago, he bought some property about twenty miles from here to play the gentleman farmer. He's always there for Christmas and New Year's and only goes off to Florida around mid-January, after a big party.'

Ashbridge is one of the few men who impress me. As is Ray. There are others. Actually, they aren't as rare as all that. Not to mention the women. Mona, for example,

The Hand

Ray's wife, whom I always see as an exotic little animal, although as far as exotic goes, she's barely one-quarter Italian by blood.

'He doesn't know me . . .'

'At Ashbridge's, you don't need to know anybody.'

Isabel was listening without saying a word. Isabel never intervenes in such moments. She is the docile wife par excellence. She does not protest. She simply watches you and passes judgement.

At that point, there had been nothing to criticize in my behaviour. We went every year to that party at the Ashbridges', which is like a professional obligation. Isabel did not point out that the snow was falling hard and that the drive up to North Hillsdale is a difficult one. In any case, the snowplough had certainly gone by.

'What car are we taking?'

'Mine,' I said.

And at the back of my mind – it's only now that I discover this – there was a tiny ulterior motive.

Ray works on Madison Avenue. He is a partner in one of the biggest ad agencies. I see him almost every time I go to New York and am familiar with his routine.

Without being a drinker, he does need two or three double martinis before each meal, like almost all those in his profession who live on their nerves.

'If he drinks a bit too much, at the party . . .'

It's funny – or tragic – to recall those little details a few hours later. For fear that Ray might over-indulge, I was taking precautions, arranging to be the driver on the way home. Except that I was the one who had got drunk!

At first, there were at least fifty people, if not more. An immense buffet was set out in the front hall, but all the doors were open, with people coming and going, even in the upstairs bedrooms, and bottles and glasses were everywhere.

'May I introduce Mrs Ashbridge . . . Patricia, my friend Ray . . .'

Patricia is only thirty. She is Ashbridge's third wife. She's very beautiful. Not beautiful like . . . I wouldn't say like Isabel; my wife has never been truly beautiful. Besides, I always find it difficult to describe a woman and I automatically do so in relation to my wife.

Isabel is tall, with a graceful figure, regular features and a slightly condescending smile, as if those with whom she is speaking were at fault in some way.

Well, Patricia is the opposite. On the small side, like Mona. Even more of a brunette than she is, but with green eyes. And Patricia, she looks at you, fascinated, as if she desired nothing more than to learn your innermost thoughts or to confide her own to you.

Isabel never conjures up the image of a bedroom. Now, Patricia – she always makes me think of a bed.

They say . . . But I pay no attention to what people say. First of all, I don't trust hearsay. And then, I instinctively loathe indiscretion, so I hate backbiting all the more.

The Russels were there, the Dyers, the Collinses, the Greenes, the Hassbergers, the . . .

'Ted! Hello!'

'Dan! Hello!'

People talk, drink, come, go, nibble things that taste

The Hand

like fish, turkey or beef . . . I had, I remember, a serious conversation off in the morning room with Bill Hassberger, who was thinking of sending me to Chicago to settle a legal matter.

Those people are rich. For most of the year, don't ask me why, they live in our little corner of Connecticut, but they have business interests more or less throughout the country.

Compared to them, I'm a poor man. Dr Warren as well, with whom I chatted briefly. I was not drunk, far from it. I don't know exactly when it all began.

Or rather, as of a few seconds ago, I do know, because on my bench, where I'm having at least my fifth cigarette, I'm suddenly discovering in myself a curious lucidity.

I went upstairs, for no reason, like others before and after me. I pushed open a door and quickly shut it, with just time enough to see Ray and Patricia in what wasn't even a bedroom, but a bathroom, where they were making love, completely clothed.

I may be forty-five years old, but that image made such an impression that I can still see it in minute detail. Patricia saw me, I'm sure of that. I would even swear that the look in her eyes was not embarrassment, but a kind of amused defiance.

That's very important. That image has considerable importance for me.

Sitting on my bench, in the barn, I had only a presentiment of this, but later on I had plenty of time to think about it.

I'm not claiming that it's what drove me to drink, but

it was about at that moment that I began draining all the glasses within reach. Isabel caught me, and I blushed, naturally.

'It's hot,' I murmured.

She did not advise me to be careful. She said nothing. She smiled, with her terrible smile that forgives or that . . .

That what? Later. I'm not there yet. There are so many other things to work out!

One summer, I decided to clean up the barn, intending to empty it, throw things away and neatly arrange what was worth keeping. After a few hours, overwhelmed, I sheepishly gave up.

That's a little like what happens with another inventory, the one I undertook in the very same barn that night. This time, however, I'll finish the job, no matter what it costs and what I discover.

Already there's the image of Ray and Patricia to be properly filed away. And shortly afterwards, the look in old Ashbridge's eyes. He's no drunk, either, but a man who sips his drinks, especially after five in the afternoon. He's a bit portly, and his big pale eyes are always moist.

'Well, Donald?'

The two of us weren't far from the buffet, with several noisy groups around us. We could hear various conversations overlapping at the same time.

Why did I have the impression that we found ourselves suddenly isolated, he and I? Confronting each other, that's a better way to put it. For it was barely five minutes after the scene in the bathroom.

The Hand

He was looking at me calmly, but he was looking at me. I know exactly what I mean. Most of the time, especially in such encounters, you don't really look at the other person. You know the person is there. You talk. You listen. You reply. You let your gaze wander to a face, a shoulder . . .

He was looking at me, and the two words he'd just spoken took on the tenor of a question.

'Well, Donald?'

Well . . . what? Had he seen, too? Did he know that I had seen?

He was neither gloomy nor threatening. He was not smiling, either. Was he jealous?

Did he know that Patricia was in the habit of . . . I was the one who felt guilty as he continued.

'Your friend Sanders is a remarkable fellow . . .'

Some people left. We could see them, in the entryway, putting on their coats and rubber boots, which stood in a row all along a shelf. Each time the front door opened and closed it let in a gust of icy air.

Then there was the sound of the wind, monotonous at first, blustery in bursts later on, and the guests began to look questioningly at one another.

'It's still snowing?'

'Yes.'

'Well, then, we're going to get a blizzard.'

Why I kept drinking, which was so unlike me, I still don't understand. I went from one group to another; familiar faces began to seem different to me. I believe I even sneered and that Isabel saw me at it.

A kind of uneasiness began to set in. Certain guests lived rather far away, some in New York, others in Massachusetts, and had up to forty miles to cover to get home.

I was one of the last to go. I heard raised voices, exclamations whenever a group was leaving and a particularly violent blast entered the house.

'In an hour there'll be three feet of snow . . .'

I don't know who said that. Then Isabel took my arm in a relaxed way, like a good wife, quite naturally. I understood nevertheless that it was time for us to leave as well.

'Where is Mona?'

'She went to get her mink in Pat's bedroom.'

'And Ray?'

Ray was in front of me, the everyday Ray, the Ray I'd been used to for twenty-five years.

'Are we leaving?' he asked.

'I think so, yes.'

'It seems you can't see a thing in front of you.'

I did not shake Patricia's hand the way I had those other times. I admit that I made this somewhat obvious, that I took a perverse pleasure in doing so. Did old Ashbridge notice?

'Get in the car, kids . . .'

There were only three or four cars left out in the driveway. The already savage wind was blowing so much snow hard into our faces that we had to walk bent over.

The two women climbed into the rear seats. I took the wheel, without Isabel asking me if I were in a fit state to drive. I was neither depressed nor tired. On the contrary,

The Hand

I felt pleasantly elated, and the roaring of the storm made me feel like singing.

'And that's one down!'

'One what?'

'Party . . . There's still one left, next week at the Russels', after which things will be quiet until the spring.'

At times the windshield wipers jammed for a moment before starting up again. The snow streamed by in almost horizontal white stripes in front of the headlights, and I used the black line of the trees to guide me because the edges of the road were no longer visible.

Behind me I could hear, in the warmth of the car and their fur coats, the two women exchanging banal remarks.

'You weren't too bored, Mona?'

'Not at all. Patricia is charming . . . Actually, everyone was nice.'

'In three days, they'll be swimming in Florida.'

'Ray and I think we'll spend a few days in Miami next month . . .'

I had to lean forwards to see ahead of me and several times I got out of the car to scrape ice off the windshield. The third time, I felt as if I would be carried off by the blizzard.

We have them every winter, more or less powerful storms. We know the treacherous places, the snowdrift spots, the roads to avoid.

How did we get back to Brentwood? Through Copake or Great Barrington? I couldn't tell you.

'This one is a beaut, Ray ol' buddy . . .'

A beautiful snowstorm. A true blizzard. When I turned

on the radio, that was in fact the word they were using. Up by Albany, they were already talking about winds of more than sixty miles an hour, and hundreds of cars were snowed in on roads to the north.

Instead of worrying me, the news excited me, as if I were welcoming with relief a little something extraordinary into my life.

We were not talking much, Ray and I. He was staring straight ahead, frowning whenever the visibility dropped close to zero. Then, on purpose, I would drive faster.

I had no score to settle with him. He was my friend. He hadn't wronged me in any way by making love with Patricia Ashbridge. I wasn't in love with her. I wasn't in love with any woman. I was content with Isabel. What score would I have had to settle?

I had to spend a few minutes manoeuvring around a snowdrift and used one of the bags of sand we always keep in the car trunk in the winter. I had snow in my eyes, nose, ears, and some was getting in through the gaps in my clothing.

'Where are we?'

'Three more miles . . .'

It was harder and harder to make any progress. Even though we'd seen three ploughs, the snow piled up as soon as they had passed, and our windshield wipers were now useless. I kept having to leave the car to scrape the windshield.

'Are we still on the road?'

Isabel's voice was calm. She was asking the question, that's all.

The Hand

'I assume so!' I replied gaily.

The truth was, I no longer knew. It was only in crossing the small stone bridge a mile from home that I regained my bearings. Except that, after the bridge, the snow had formed an actual wall in which the front of the car embedded itself.

'That's it, folks. Everyone out . . .'

'What do you mean?'

'Everyone out. The Chrysler is not a bulldozer. We'll have to keep going on foot . . .'

Ray looked at me, wondering if I was serious. Isabel had understood, since this had happened to us twice before.

'Are you taking the flashlight?'

I removed it from the glove compartment and switched it on. It had been some months, perhaps two years, since we last used it and, as we might have expected, it produced only a yellowish gleam.

'Let's go . . .'

Things were still cheerful, at that moment. I can still see the women arm in arm, huddled forward, pressing on through the snow up ahead. I followed with the flashlight, and Ray walked silently beside me. No one said anything, actually. It was already rather hard to breathe in the blizzard without wasting more breath.

Isabel fell, got gamely to her feet. Sometimes the two women vanished into the darkness. I would shout, my hand in front of my mouth to ward off the freezing air: 'Yoo-hoo! . . . Yoo-hoo! . . .'

And a vague 'Yoo-hoo!' would echo a reply.

The flashlight beam was weakening. All of a sudden, when we must have been only three or four hundred yards from our place, it died completely.

'Yoo-hoo!'

'Yoo-hoo!'

I had to be quite close to the women, because I heard the snow crunching. I could also hear, to my right, Ray's footsteps.

My head began to spin. The energy the alcohol had given me was ebbing away, and it was more and more difficult to advance. In my chest, right where my heart was, I thought, I felt a pain that worried me.

Hadn't men my age, even strong, healthy men, died like this of heart attacks in the cold and snow?

'Yoo-hoo!'

I felt dizzy. I laboured with each step. I couldn't see a thing any more. I could hear only that aggressive uproar of the blizzard and I was covered in snow.

I don't know how long that lasted. I was paying no more attention to the others. I was still holding on, stupidly, to the dead flashlight, and was stopping every two or three steps to catch my breath.

Finally, there was a wall, a door opening.

'Come in . . .'

A gust of warmth, in the darkness of the house.

'And Ray?'

I did not understand. I wondered why the women hadn't turned on the lights. I reached for the switch.

'There's no electricity . . . Where's Ray?'

'He was close by me . . .'

The Hand

I called to him from the threshold.

'Ray! . . . Hey, Ray! . . .'

I seemed to hear a voice, but it's easy to hear voices in a blizzard.

'Ray . . .'

'Take the flashlight from the night table.'

We keep a smaller flashlight on our night table because the electricity sometimes goes off. I fumbled my way slowly through the rooms, bumping into furniture I did not recognize. Then a gleam appeared behind me, one of the red candles from the dining room.

It was strange to see Isabel emerge dimly from the darkness holding aloft one of the silver candelabras.

'You found it?'

'Yes.'

I had the flashlight in my hand, but it was hardly brighter than the one from the car had been.

'Don't we have any spare batteries?'

'Aren't there any in the drawer?'

'No . . .'

I wanted a drink to buck me up but didn't dare have one. The women said nothing to me. They did not urge me on. Even so, I felt that they were sending me out, armed with a half-dead flashlight, to search for Ray in the blizzard.

I will say everything, obviously, otherwise it would not have been worthwhile to begin. And, first of all: at no moment of the evening was I completely drunk.

If I try to define my state as accurately as possible,

I'd say that I possessed a warped lucidity. Reality existed around me, and I was in contact with it. I was aware of my actions. Taking pencil and paper, I could record almost exactly the words I spoke at the Ashbridge party, in the car afterwards and, later, at home.

Suffering from the cold on my bench, however, where I lit one cigarette after another, I was entering, I felt, a new lucidity, which made me uneasy and was beginning to frighten me.

I could sum it up in a word – in four words, rather, which I seemed to hear out loud: 'You have killed him . . .'

Perhaps not in the legal sense. But then again, isn't the refusal to help someone in danger considered a kind of crime?

When I had left the house, when the two women had sent me out to look for Ray, I had gone immediately to the right. More precisely, to fool them, in case they'd been watching me from the window and seen the glint from my flashlight, I'd first walked straight ahead for a few yards and then, safe in the darkness, I had veered right, knowing that I would find the barn about thirty yards along.

I was physically exhausted and think I can say that my morale was spent as well. This enormous storm, this world gone mad that had earlier elated me to the brink of nervous hilarity, now suddenly scared me.

Why had the women stayed in the house? Why hadn't they, too, come along to search? I thought back to Isabel, impassive, looking like a statue with her silver candelabra

The Hand

held a little higher than her shoulder. Mona, her features blurred in the shadowy light, had said nothing.

Neither of them had seemed to understand that a real tragedy was taking place and that by sending me outside they were putting me, too, in danger. My heart was beating too fast, in fits and starts. At every moment I kept losing my breath.

I was afraid, I've already said so. I called out one or two times more.

'Ray! . . .'

It would have been a miracle if he had heard me, just as it would have been if he had glimpsed the glow, way too weak, of the flashlight through the snow falling almost parallel to the ground. It wasn't falling, it was whipping, thrown forward in actual clumps that hit you in the face and smothered you.

I heard the barn door creak and rushed inside, where I collapsed on the bench.

A red bench. A garden bench. I did see the grotesque aspect of the situation: in the middle of the night, in the middle of a blizzard, a forty-five-year-old man, a lawyer and respectable citizen, sitting on a red bench lighting a first cigarette with a trembling hand as if this were going to warm him up.

'I killed him . . .'

Perhaps not yet. Doubtless he was still alive, but dying, in danger of death. He was not familiar, as I was, with the area around the house and if he veered to the right, if he was off by just a few yards, he would tumble down a small cliff into a freezing stream.

That was nothing to me. I did not have the courage to look for him, to run the slightest risk. On the contrary.

And here is where I've arrived, where I am indeed forced to end up. Here is where I was heading little by little, on that particular night, the night of 15–16 January, on my bench, in the barn: what was happening to Ray did not displease me.

Would I have been in the same frame of mind if I had not been drinking at the Ashbridges' party? This problem is difficult to resolve and, in the end, does not change much. Would I have felt the same perverse relief if I had not pushed open the bathroom door and surprised Ray making love with Patricia?

Now, that's different. I'm getting to the heart of my ruminations. For what I was indulging in on my bench were ruminations rather than coherent reflections.

I had the time. I was supposed to look for Ray. The longer I stayed outdoors, the more thanks I would receive.

What Ray was doing that evening in the bathroom, with a woman he had known for barely two hours, one as beautiful and desirable as Patricia, was something I'd dreamed of doing a hundred, a thousand times.

He had married Mona, who, like Patricia, makes men think of a bed.

Me, I married Isabel.

I might almost say, 'That's all there is.'

But it isn't. I had begun, God knows why, tearing off a corner from everyday truth, begun seeing myself in another kind of mirror, and now the whole of the old, more or less comfortable truth was falling to pieces.

The Hand

This went back to Yale. This went back to before Yale, before I knew Ray. This went back, in the end, to my childhood. I would have liked . . . Where are words when you need them! . . . I would have liked to do everything, be everything, be daring in every way, to look people in the eye, to tell them . . .

To look at people the way old Ashbridge does, for example, before whom, earlier that evening, I had felt like a little boy.

He didn't bother to speak, to strike an attitude. He didn't try to communicate. I was in front of him. Was he perhaps looking straight through my head? I was of no importance.

He was seventy years old and had never been handsome. He drank his little drinks that gave his eyes that glazed look, and dozens of guests had invaded his house.

Did he worry about what they thought of him? He provided them with food, drink, armchairs, open bedrooms, as well as the bathroom where Patricia . . . Did he know that his wife was cheating on him? Did he suffer because of it? Did he, on the contrary, despise poor Ray, who had merely followed so many others and who, within five minutes, would no longer matter, who already no longer mattered, whom Patricia would perhaps, that very evening, replace with a successor in the same or some other room?

I didn't admire Ashbridge simply because he was rich and had interests in fifty different business ventures, from commercial shipping to television stations.

When he had moved into the area ten years earlier,

I would have liked to have had him as a client, to have acquired just a tiny part of his affairs to look after.

'One of these days, I'll have to have a talk with you,' he'd told me.

The years had passed, and he had never had that talk. I did not resent him for that.

With Ray, it was different, because Ray and I were the same age, had almost the same background; we'd studied the same things, and at Yale I'd been more brilliant than he was and he'd become an important figure on Madison Avenue, whereas I was just a plucky little lawyer in Brentwood, Connecticut.

Ray was taller than I was, stronger than I was. At twenty, he could already look at people the way old Ashbridge did.

I've met other men of their kind. I have some for clients. My attitude towards them varies depending on the day and my mood. At times I'm convinced that it's admiration. At other moments I admit to a certain envy.

Well, I knew this now, I'd just discovered it on my bench: it was hatred.

They frightened me. They were too strong for me, or I was the one too weak for them.

I remember the evening when Ray introduced me to Mona, who was wearing a little black silk dress, underneath which you could sense her body, alive in its smallest recesses.

'Why not me?'

For me, Isabel. For him, Mona.

And, if I chose Isabel, isn't that precisely because I never dared to speak to a Mona, to a Patricia, to all the

The Hand

women whom I've desired to the point of clenching my fists in rage?

The wind was blowing so violently that I expected to see the roof fly off the barn. Its upper hinge broken, the door now sagged crookedly, which did not prevent it from striking muffled blows against the wall.

The snow whirling inside the barn almost reached my feet, and I kept thinking in a kind of delirium, a cold delirium, a lucid delirium.

'I killed you, Ray . . .'

And what if I went to tell them this, those two women nice and warm in the house, in the candlelight?

'I killed Ray . . .'

They would not believe me. I was not even the man to kill Ray, or to kill anyone.

I had just done so, however, and this flooded me with a sense of physical joy, as if I had just cheered myself up with a potent drink.

I stood up. After all, I was not supposed to spend hours outside. Besides, I was frozen stiff and was scared about my heart. I have always been afraid that my heart would suddenly stop beating.

I plunged out into the snow that was hitting my face, my chest, enveloping my legs. I had to make an effort to hoist out one foot, then the other.

'Ray!'

I had to make sure I did not make a mistake and stray from the path. The house was invisible. I had taken my bearings when I'd left the barn. All I had to do now was walk straight ahead.

And what if I found Ray in front of the living-room fireplace with the two women? I imagined them, watching me enter like a ghost, smiling and saying, 'Why did you stay out so long?'

That frightened me so much that I managed to walk faster, so that I bumped into the wall of the house. I felt my way along to the door. No one had heard me arrive. I turned the knob and saw first the logs burning in the fireplace, then someone, in an armchair, wearing Isabel's light blue peignoir. It wasn't Isabel. It was Mona.

'Where is she?'

'Isabel? . . . She went to fix something to eat. But . . . Donald!'

It was almost a shout: 'Donald!'

She did not rise from her armchair. She did not look at me. She stared at the flames in the hearth. Her face reflected no feeling; she looked stunned.

In a low voice she added, 'You didn't find him?'

'No.'

'Watching the time go by . . .'

Yes, seeing the time pass, she had begun to understand.

'Still, he's a strong man,' I said, 'more vigorous than I am . . . Perhaps . . .'

'Perhaps what?'

How to lie? And how could Ray have oriented himself in that ocean of snow and ice?

Isabel arrived, candelabra in one hand, a plate of sandwiches in the other. She looked at me; her face became paler, her features more rigid.

'Eat, Mona.'

The Hand

How long does it take to die, buried in snow? Another three or four hours, and day would begin to break.

'Did you try telephoning?' I asked.

'The lines are dead.'

She looked pointedly at a small transistor.

'We've been getting the news every fifteen minutes . . . It seems the storm stretches from the Canadian border to New York. Almost everywhere, out in the countryside, the phone and electricity are cut.'

In a dull voice she added:

'Ray should have held on to your arm, the way Mona and I were walking . . .'

'He was at my right, not far from me . . .'

Mona wasn't crying. She was holding a sandwich and finally took a bite.

'Have you anything to drink, Isabel?'

'Some beer? Spirits? I can't fix you anything hot, because the stove is electric.'

'Some whisky . . .'

'You ought to take a bath, too, Donald. Later, there won't be any more hot water.'

It's true, the oil burner shuts down. Everything is electric, even the clocks, except for the little one in our bedroom.

Now I understood why Mona was wearing Isabel's bathrobe. My wife had made her take a bath, to relax as well as warm her.

'Did you go as far as the car?'

'Yes.'

Again, I felt a rush of fear. What if, while zigzagging

in the snow, Ray had wound up back at the car? The smartest thing would then have been to shelter inside it, muffling up there as best he could to wait for daylight.

Our house, Yellow Rock Farm, is not on the road. We have a private access road of more than half a mile. As for the neighbours, they're about a mile away.

'From what I know of Ray . . .' my wife began.

I waited for the rest with curiosity.

'. . . he'll have pulled through . . .'

Not me, but him. Because it's Ray. Because it's someone other than Donald Dodd.

'Aren't you going to have a bath? . . . Take the candle . . . We'd best not waste them, and light only one at a time. Here, we have the fireplace flames.'

The radiators were going to grow cold. They were cooling already. In a few hours, there would be no more heat except in the living room. We'd be forced to huddle there, all three of us, as close as possible to the hearth.

It was my turn to carry the candelabra to find my way to our bedroom. I began wanting a drink again. Retracing my steps, I found Isabel pouring Mona a whisky.

I took a glass from the cupboard, picked up the bottle in turn and understood my wife's look. Still no reproach. Not even a mute warning. It was different. It had been going on for years, doubtless for as long as we'd known each other. A sort of official record.

She noticed things, without commentary, as if without passing judgement – and even forbidding herself to do so. The facts were nevertheless all there, in columns, perfectly organized, one after the other.

The Hand

There must have been thousands, tens of thousands of them. Seventeen years of life together, not counting a one-year engagement!

I served myself generously on purpose, pouring the double – if not the triple – of my usual amount.

'Cheers, Mona . . .'

A silly thing to say, but she didn't seem to hear. I drank greedily. The warmth spread through me, and only then did I realize how cold my body was.

The bathroom reminded me of the one at the Ashbridges' house, and a thought of humiliating vulgarity occurred to me.

'At least he will have had one last pleasure . . .'

Why was I so sure that Ray was dead? The hypothesis about the car was plausible. Perhaps Isabel was right. She had no idea that I hadn't gone that far. He might also have reached, although that was more difficult, one of the surrounding houses. Since the telephone was out of order, it was impossible for him to let us know.

'I killed him . . .'

Mona had the same impression as I did; I'd seen that in her attitude. Does she really love Ray? Are there people who go on loving one another after a certain number of years?

Ray and Mona have no children. Us, we've got two, two girls, who are at Adams, one of the best boarding schools in Connecticut, in Litchfield, run by Miss Jenkins.

Did they have light, in Litchfield?

Mildred is fifteen, Cecilia twelve, and every two weeks

they come and spend the weekend at the house. Luckily this had not been one of their weekends.

The water was running in the bathtub. I put my hand under the faucet in time to notice that the water was now cold, and I had to settle for a third of the bathtub.

It was an odd feeling, that night, to be an honourable man, one of the two partners of the firm of Higgins and Dodd, married, the father of two girls, the owner of Yellow Rock Farm, one of the oldest and most pleasant houses in Brentwood, and to think about having just killed a man.

By omission, true! By having failed to look for him.

Who knows? If I had spent hours with my dying flashlight, wandering in the snow, it is possible, even probable, that I would not have found him.

In my mind, then? That was closer to it. I had not searched. As soon as I could not be seen from the house, I had veered off towards the barn to take shelter.

Would Mona be in despair? Did she know that Ray was having sex with other women whenever he got the chance?

Who knows if she wasn't like Patricia? Perhaps Ray and Mona weren't jealous and told each other about their adventures?

I promised myself to look into that. If anyone ought to profit from that, it was I . . .

I almost fell asleep in my bath and was careful not to slip getting out of the tub, because I did not feel too sure of my movements.

What would we do, all three of us? Going to bed wasn't likely. Do you go to bed when the husband of a guest . . .

The Hand

No. We wouldn't go to bed. Besides, the rooms were growing chilly, and I was shivering in my bathrobe. I chose some grey flannel pants and a thick pullover I usually wore only to shovel snow along the driveway.

One of the two candles was finished, so I lit the second one and put on my slippers to head for the living room.

'Do you know if there's more wood in the cellar?'

We hardly ever used any. We only had a fire in the fireplace when we had friends over. To get to the cellar we raised a trapdoor and went down a ladder, which complicated the fetching of any logs.

'I think we still have some . . .'

I looked automatically at the bottle of Scotch. When I'd left the two women, the bottle had been half full. Now it was almost empty.

Isabel had followed my glance, evidently, and – again evidently – had understood.

With another look, she gave me the answer, gazing at Mona asleep in her armchair, her face crimson. Her peignoir, in falling slightly open, had uncovered a bare knee.

2

When I half-opened my eyes, I was lying on the couch in the living room, where someone had covered me with the red, blue and yellow plaid throw blanket. The sun was up, but its light shone only weakly through windowpanes thick with frozen snow.

What first struck me, and had perhaps awakened me, was the familiar odour of ordinary mornings: the smell of coffee. Memories of the previous evening and night returned. I wondered if the electricity was back on. Turning my head a little, I caught sight of Isabel on her knees at the hearth.

I had a really bad headache and was not pleased at having to tackle the reality of a new day. I would have liked to fall back asleep but, before I had time to close my eyes again, my wife asked:

'Did you get some rest?'

'I think so . . . Yes.'

I got up and realized that I had been drunker than I'd thought. My whole body hurt, and I felt dizzy.

'Coffee will be ready in a minute.'

It was my turn to ask.

'Did you sleep?'

'I dozed . . .'

Well, no. She had watched over the both of us,

The Hand

Mona and me. She had been magnificent, as always. It was in her nature to behave perfectly, whatever the circumstances.

I imagined her, sitting up straight in her armchair, looking from one to the other of us, sometimes rising quietly to stoke the fire.

Then, at the first glimmer of dawn, snuffing out the precious candle and going to the kitchen to look for the pot with the longest handle. While we were sleeping, she had thought of the coffee.

'Where is Mona?'

'She went to get dressed.'

In the guest room, at the end of the corridor, with windows that looked out over the pond. I remembered the two blue leather suitcases that Ray had carried in the previous day, before the evening at the Ashbridges' house.

'How is she?'

'It hasn't sunk in yet . . .'

I was listening to the storm, still as strong as when I had fallen asleep. Isabel poured me coffee in my usual cup; we each had our own cups, and mine was a little larger, because I drink lots of coffee.

'We'll have to bring up some wood.'

There were no more logs in the basket to the right of the fireplace, and those burning there would soon crumble to ash.

'I'll go.'

'You don't want me to help you?'

'No, no . . .'

I understood. She'd glanced at me two or three times

and knew I had a hangover. She knew everything. Why bother trying to deceive her?

I finished my coffee, lit a cigarette, went into the little room next to the living room, the one we call the library because one wall is covered with books. Folding back the oval carpet, I uncovered the trapdoor; I lifted it and only then remembered that I would need a candle.

All this is confused, unreal.

'How many candles are left?'

'Five. Just now, I got Hartford on the radio.'

It's the nearest big city.

'Most of the countryside is in the same fix we are. They're working everywhere to repair the lines, but there are still places they can't get to.'

I imagined the men, outside in the blizzard, climbing the poles, and the tow trucks making their way through the ever-thicker snow.

I descended the ladder, holding my candle, and went towards the back of the cellar carved out of the bedrock, the yellow rock that had given its name to the former farm. I was tempted to sit down to be alone, so that I could think.

But think about what? It was over. There was nothing more to think.

Now I had to bring up some wood.

My memory of that morning is vaguely sinister, like certain Sundays of my childhood, when rain kept me inside and I didn't know what to do with myself. Then I would feel that people and things were not where they should

The Hand

be, that sounds were different, both those in the street and those inside. I felt at a loss, with a small knot of anguish in the deepest part of me.

That reminds me of a silly detail. My father would lie in bed longer than on other days, and sometimes I'd see him shave. He came and went, wearing an old bathrobe, and his smell was different, like the smell of my parents' bedroom, perhaps because it was tidied up only later in the day.

'Good morning, Donald . . . Did you manage to sleep a little?'

'Yes, thanks. And you?'

'Me, you know . . .'

She was wearing black slacks and a yellow sweater. Hair and make-up just so, she was smoking a cigarette with a weary air while stirring her spoon in her cup.

'What are we going to do?'

She was just making conversation, carelessly, watching the flames.

'I think, at a pinch, that I can fix you some fried eggs. There are eggs in the fridge . . .'

'I'm not hungry.'

'Neither am I. If there's any more coffee . . .'

Coffee, cigarettes: as far as I was concerned, that was all I wanted. I went to peek out the door, which I had to hold tightly against the blowing snow, and could barely recognize our surroundings.

The snow formed waves more than a yard high. It was still falling, as heavily as during the night, and you could hardly see the red mass of the barn.

'You think we could try?' Isabel asked me.

Try what? Going to look for Ray?

'I'll put on my boots and sheepskin jacket . . .'

'I'll go with you.'

'Me too.'

All this made no sense, and I knew it. I felt like telling them quietly: 'It's useless to look for Ray. I killed him.'

Because I remembered having killed him. I remembered everything that had happened on the bench, everything I had thought. Why was my wife constantly darting glances at me?

In her eyes, I'd done some drinking, of course. That's not a crime. A man has the right, twice in his life, to get drunk. I had picked the wrong evening, but I'd had no way of knowing that.

Besides, it was Ray's fault. If he hadn't dragged Patricia into the upstairs bathroom . . .

Tough luck! I was going to pretend again. I put on my boots. I put on my sheepskin jacket. Isabel did the same, telling Mona:

'No, no, you stay here. Someone has to keep the fire going.'

We walked side by side, basically pushing ourselves through the snow, which piled up in front of us as we tried to advance. The cold stiffened our faces. My head was spinning, and I was afraid every instant that I would collapse, worn out. I didn't want to be the first to give up.

'It's useless,' Isabel finally decided.

Before going inside, we scraped clear one of the windows so we would now have some view of the outdoors.

The Hand

Mona had returned to her place by the fire and asked us no questions.

She was listening to the radio. Hartford was announcing that roofs had been torn off, that hundreds of drivers were trapped on the roads. They mentioned the places most affected, but Brentwood was not among them.

'We still have to eat . . .'

Making up her mind, Isabel went off to the kitchen, and we were left side by side, Mona and I. I wonder if that was really the first time that we'd found ourselves alone in a room. Anyway, I thought it was, and that gave me an uneasy pleasure.

How old was she? Thirty-five? Older? She had done some theatre, a while back, and a bit of television. Her father was a playwright. He wrote successful musical comedies and had had a rather tumultuous life until his death three or four years back.

What was mysterious about Mona? Nothing. She was a woman like any other. Before marrying Ray, she must have had some affairs.

'All this seems so unreal to me, Donald . . .'

I looked at her and found her touching. I would have liked to take her in my arms, hold her close, stroke her hair. Were those the actions of a Donald Dodd?

'It seems that way to me, too.'

'You risked your life, last night, leaving to look for him . . .'

I kept quiet. I wasn't ashamed. Deep down, I was enjoying this moment of intimacy.

'Ray was a great guy,' she murmured a little later.

She was speaking of him as if he were someone already far away, with, I thought, a sort of detachment.

After a fairly long silence, she added, 'We got along well, the two of us . . .'

Isabel returned with a pan and some eggs.

'This is the easiest thing to prepare. There's some ham in the fridge, for whoever wants some.'

As she had in the morning, she knelt down before the hearth, where she managed to settle the pan on an even keel.

What were people doing in the other houses? The same thing, probably. Except that not everyone had a fireplace, or wood. The Ashbridges would definitely be obliged to postpone their departure for Florida.

And the girls, off at Adams? Did they have anything to heat with, up there? I reassured myself: Litchfield was a rather important town, and there had been no mention of power outages in the towns.

'The most powerful blizzard in seventy-two years . . .'

After the news, the radio went back to singing, and I turned the dial.

We had to eat quite close to the fire because at a few yards away you could already feel the bitter cold.

Why Isabel? . . . For as long as we've known each other, as I've said, she has constantly looked at me in a certain way, but it seemed to me that on that morning there was something different.

I even had the feeling, at one point, that her look meant: 'I know.'

The Hand

Without anger. Not like an accusation. Like a simple observation.

'I know you and I know.'

It's true that my hangover was not going away and that at least twice I almost went off to throw up my lunch. I was anxious to drink something to get me back on my feet. I didn't dare.

Why? Always questions. I've spent my life asking myself questions – not many, a few, some rather idiotic – without ever finding satisfactory answers.

I'm a man. Isabel had found it normal, the previous evening, to see about fifty men and women drink beyond all measure. Well, I had almost felt that I should sneak those glasses I was grabbing from the tables and draining on the fly.

Why?

She had been the first, when we arrived home, to pour a Scotch for Mona, even though she was a woman, while I had waited a long time before daring to get myself one.

What was preventing me, now, from opening the liquor cabinet, taking out a bottle and fetching a glass from the kitchen? I needed a drink. I was literally staggering. I had no desire to get drunk, wanted only to steady my nerves.

It took me more than half an hour and even then, I cheated.

'Wouldn't you like a Scotch, Mona?'

She looked at Isabel as if to ask permission, as if my offer didn't count.

'Perhaps it would do me some good?'

'How about you, Isabel?'

'No, thanks.'

Outside of the evenings we spend at parties or giving one at our house, I usually drink only a single whisky a day, after getting home from the office for dinner. Isabel often has one with me, quite a weak one, it's true.

She is not a puritan. She does not criticize either people who drink or those of our friends who lead more or less irregular lives.

So, why that fear, for God's sake? Because anyone might have thought that I was afraid of her. Afraid of what? Of a reproach? She had never reproached me for anything. What then? Afraid of a look? The way I was scared, as a child, of the look in my mother's eyes?

Isabel is not my mother. I am her husband, and we have had two children together. She never undertakes anything without asking my advice.

She is nothing like the pushy, dominating woman so many husbands complain about and when we are with other people, she always leaves the talking to me.

She is calm, quite simply. Serene. Wouldn't that word explain everything?

'Cheers, Mona . . .'

'Cheers, Donald . . . And to you, Isabel . . .'

Mona wasn't trying to put on a show of grief. Perhaps she was suffering, but it must not have been a wrenching sorrow. She had said, as if truly from her heart: 'Ray was a great guy.'

Was that not revealing? A fellow something like a pal, a good friend with whom one has travelled a while through life in as pleasant a way as possible.

The Hand

That was also what was attracting me. For a long time, I had had a sense of that peaceful and indulgent understanding between them.

Ray had wanted Patricia Ashbridge and he had taken her, without worrying – I'm sure of that now – about whether his wife would learn of it or not.

'I think the wind is dying down . . .'

Our ears were so used to the noise of the storm that we noticed the slightest change. It was true: we were still a long way from silence, but the intensity of the sound had dropped, and, looking out of the window we'd tried to scrape clear, I thought the flakes were falling almost vertically, although just as thickly.

Emergency teams were working all over the area to clear the roads, and ambulances were trying to get through to reportedly dozens of dead and injured.

'I wonder what will happen . . .'

It was Mona talking, as if asking herself the question. The snow would not melt for several weeks. Once the roads were cleared, they would deal with our access road. Then crews would undoubtedly come to look for Ray's body.

And after that? Ray and Mona had a handsome apartment in one of the most pleasant and elegant neighbourhoods of Manhattan, in Sutton Place by the East River.

Would she return to live there alone? Would she try to get work again in the theatre, in television?

She had been right, a little earlier. It was all unreal, incomprehensible. And I, during my meditation on the bench in the barn, I had not thought for one instant about Mona's future.

I had killed Ray, so be it. I had taken revenge in a rather foul and cowardly way, without worrying about the consequences.

In reality, I had not killed anyone. It was useless to boast. I could have floundered around in the snow for the rest of the night with absolutely no chance of finding my friend.

I had killed in thought. In intention. Not even in intention, because that would have required a cold-bloodedness I had not possessed at that moment.

'Maybe we should bring mattresses in front of the fire and try to sleep?' suggested Isabel. 'Not you, Mona. Let Donald and me do it.'

We went to the guest bedroom for that mattress, and then upstairs to get the two girls' mattresses, which were narrow and light.

I wondered somewhat foolishly if we were going to place them side by side, thus making a kind of huge bed on which all three of us would sleep, and I'm sure Isabel guessed what I was thinking.

She left about the same space between the mattresses that usually separates twin beds, and then she went to get some blankets.

I could be mistaken. I probably am. During the short time in which we were again alone, Mona looked at me, then at the mattresses. Was she wondering which would be hers and which mine? Was there, I won't say a temptation, but some vague notion in the back of her mind?

The Hand

After Isabel had returned and spread out the blankets, we hesitated for a second. And, this time, I am certain of what I am saying. Isabel did not just happen to choose the mattress on the right, leaving me the one in the middle, and saving the one on the left for Mona.

She was putting me, on purpose, between the two of them. This meant: 'You see! I have confidence . . .'

In me or in Mona?

True, it might also mean: 'I'm leaving you free. I have always left you free.'

Or even: 'You really wouldn't dare . . .'

It was just past noon, and we all three tried to get some sleep. The last thing I remember was Mona's hand, on the parquet floor, between our two mattresses. That morning, in my sleepy state, was taking on an extraordinary significance. For a long while, I wondered if I would dare reach out my hand to touch her as if by accident.

I was not in love. It was the gesture that counted, the audacity of the gesture. I felt that it would be a deliverance. But my mind must already have been fogging over because the image of the hand turned into that of a dog I recognized, the dog owned by one of our neighbours when I was twelve.

I must have been asleep.

The electricity came back on shortly after ten o'clock that evening, and it was a curious sight to see all the lamps in the house suddenly turn on by themselves while the candle kept burning, almost ridiculous with its reddish flame.

We looked at one another, relieved, as if it were the end of all our problems, all our sorrows.

I went down into the cellar to turn the heat back on; when I came upstairs again, Isabel was trying out the telephone.

'Is it working?'

'Not yet.'

Once more I imagined the men outside, climbing the telephone poles with those strange metal half-circles on their feet that enable them to clamber up like monkeys. I've often dreamed of climbing poles like that.

'Where are we sleeping?' asked Mona.

'The bedrooms will take a while to heat up. We'll have to wait at least two or three hours.'

We did not talk much, that Sunday, neither during the day nor in the evening. If I were to write out the string of words we said, it wouldn't make three pages.

No one tried to read. It was even more out of the question to play any kind of game. Luckily there were the flames dancing in the fireplace, and we spent most of our time gazing at them.

We went to bed fully dressed, in the same places as that afternoon, but I did not see Mona's hand on the floor. At one point, I heard movements around me. I saw Isabel, standing in front of the fireplace, folding a blanket.

I didn't need to ask her what was happening. She had read the question in my eyes.

'It's six o'clock. The bedrooms are warm. It would be better to finish the night in our beds.'

Mona was kneeling on her mattress, her face flushed, her eyes dazed with sleep.

The Hand

I helped Isabel carry Mona's mattress off to the guest room, where the two women remade the bed. I went to undress in our bedroom, then put on pyjamas and was in bed when my wife arrived.

'She's taking it quite calmly,' she said.

Isabel was speaking calmly herself, as if mentioning something of little importance. Later, she touched my shoulder.

'The telephone, Donald.'

At first I thought that someone had called us, that the telephone had rung and I thought immediately of Ray. Isabel had simply wanted to indicate that the telephone was working. The old clock on the chest of drawers said 7.30.

I got up. I went to drink a glass of water in the bathroom and ran a comb through my hair while I was there. Then, sitting on the side of my bed, I called the police in Canaan.

Busy . . . Still busy . . . Ten times, twenty times, the busy signal . . . Finally, a tired voice . . .

'This is Donald Dodd, in Brentwood . . . Dodd, yes . . . The lawyer . . .'

'I know you, Mister Dodd . . .'

'To whom am I speaking?'

'Sergeant Tomasi . . . What's wrong at your place?'

'Lieutenant Olsen isn't there?'

'He spent the night here, like the rest of us . . . Would you like me to put him on the line?'

'Yes, please, Tomasi . . . Hello? . . . Lieutenant Olsen?'

'Olsen here, yes . . .'

'This is Dodd.'

'How are you?'

Isabel could not see my face, since my back was to her, but I was sure that she was looking at my neck, my shoulders, and that she was reading me as well as if she were facing me.

'I have to inform you about a missing person . . . Yesterday evening . . . No, it was the evening before that one . . .'

The notion of time had already gone awry.

'Saturday evening, we went with two friends from New York to a party at the Ashbridges' . . .'

'I know about it.'

Olsen was a tall, blond man with an impassive face, high colouring, a crew cut. I have never seen him with a speck of dust or a crease wrong on his uniform. I have never seen him tired, either, or impatient.

'On the way home, late that night, we were stopped by the snow a few hundred yards from my house. The flashlight was going out . . . There were four of us, the two women in front, my friend and I behind them, trying to reach the house . . .'

Silence at the other end of the phone, as if the line had been cut again. It was irritating, and I could still feel Isabel's eyes on me.

'Are you there?'

'I'm listening, Mr Dodd.'

'The two women arrived safely. I finally reached the house as well, and it was only then that I realized that my friend was no longer beside me.'

The Hand

'Who is it?'

'Ray Sanders, of the firm of Miller, Miller and Sanders, the advertising agency on Madison Avenue . . .'

'You haven't found him?'

'I went out looking for him, basically without any light . . . I floundered around in the snow shouting his name . . .'

'With the blizzard, he would have had to be very close to you to hear you.'

'Yes . . . When I felt my strength going, I went back inside . . . Yesterday morning . . . Yes, on Sunday, yesterday, we tried to go outside, my wife and I, but the snow was too deep.'

'Have you phoned your closest neighbours?'

'Not yet . . . I assume that if he were with any of them, he would already have called me.'

'That's likely. Listen, I'll try to send a crew over to you . . . It isn't snowploughs we need, but bulldozers . . . Only one section of the road is more or less clear. Call me if there's anything new . . .'

In short, we had done what we could. I'd put myself in a good position with the authorities.

'They're coming?' asked my wife evenly.

'Only one section of the road is clear. He says that snowploughs are not what are needed, but bulldozers . . . He's going to try to send us a crew, he doesn't know when . . .'

She went to the kitchen to make coffee, while I took a shower and put on the same clothes as the day before, my grey flannel pants and my old brown sweater.

Isabel had made some bacon and eggs for the two of us, and, since Mona's place was still empty, she told me:

'She's sleeping.'

I think she was a little surprised, though, by Mona's reactions, or, rather, her lack of reactions. Would Isabel have behaved differently if I had been the one to get lost in the snow?

Incidentally, I suddenly understood the strange emptiness I'd been feeling ever since my wife had touched my shoulder to awaken me: the wind had stopped blowing. The universe had fallen silent, with a silence that seemed unnatural after the hours of horrific noise we had just experienced.

I turned on the television. I saw shredded roofs, cars entombed in snow, trees knocked down and a bus turned over, in the middle of the street, in Hartford. I also saw New York, where men were trying to clear the streets, and a few dark figures were getting bogged down in the sidewalk snowdrifts.

There had been no news from several ships at sea. One house blown away by the wind. Another leaning crookedly, held up by a mountain of snow.

Snow: we had more than three feet of it at our own door and could do nothing but wait.

I made three telephone calls: to Lancaster, the electrician, whose house is a half a mile as the crow flies from ours; to Glendale, the chartered accountant; and lastly to a fellow I don't like, named Cameron, who is involved somehow in real estate.

'It's Donald Dodd . . . Sorry to bother you . . . One of

The Hand

my friends wouldn't happen to have taken shelter with you, by any chance?'

None of the three had seen Ray. Only Cameron asked, 'What's he look like?' before replying.

'Tall, brown hair, about forty . . .'

'His name?'

'Ray Sanders . . . Have you seen him?'

'No . . . I haven't seen anyone.'

When I returned to the kitchen, Mona was eating there. Unlike Isabel, she had not washed her face or brushed her hair, which was falling over her eyes. She smelled of bed. Isabel never smelled of bed; as my mother used to say, she smells clean. Mona's sloppiness and slightly animal casualness unsettled me, as did the questioning, indifferent look she gave me before asking in an artificial tone:

'When will they come?'

'As soon as they can. They're already on the way, but will have to wait for the road to be cleared . . .'

Isabel looked back and forth between us, and I cannot say what she was thinking. Although she could divine the thoughts of others, it was impossible to divine her own.

And yet, she had the most open countenance imaginable. She inspired confidence in everyone. In the projects she worked on, she was the one to whom the boring or delicate tasks were entrusted, which she accepted with her everlasting smile.

'Isabel is always there when you need her . . .'

To advise, console, assist . . . Outside of a cleaning woman, who came three hours a day and one full day a week, she took care of the house and the cooking. She was also the one who looked after our daughters until they went off to Adams, the boarding school in Litchfield, since there was no good school for them in Brentwood.

There was perhaps a certain snobbery in that. Isabel had also gone to Adams, considered one of the most exclusive institutions in Connecticut. Isabel was not a snob, however. I have lived seventeen years with her. For seventeen years, we have slept in the same bedroom. I suppose we have made love several thousand times. Yet I still cannot form a precise image of her.

I know her features, the colour of her skin, the blonde highlights of her slightly reddish hair, her broad shoulders that are becoming somewhat heavy, her placid movements, her bearing.

She wears a lot of pale blue, but the colour she prefers is a light mauve.

I know her smile, never too wide, a slightly fixed smile that still brightens up her already naturally open face.

But what does she think about, for example, all day long? What does she think of me, her husband and the father of her daughters? What are her real feelings towards me?

What does she think, at that very moment, of Mona, who is finishing her eggs?

She can't love Mona, who is too different from her and who represents slovenliness, disorder and God knows what else.

Mona's past is not simple and straightforward like her own. Some of it is rather dubious: the Broadway nights, backstage at the theatres, the actors' and actresses'

The Hand

dressing rooms, and her father, who saw nothing wrong with entrusting his daughter to one mistress or another.

Mona had not shed tears. She was not crushed. Instead she seemed like someone who feels that time is beginning to drag.

Her husband was out in the snow somewhere, one or two hundred yards from the house, a house that was not her home, which she wasn't used to and where she must have felt like a prisoner.

Now that the blizzard was over, that the snow had stopped falling, that the lights were back on, that we could communicate by phone and see the world live again on the television screen, we still had to wait for a crew to arrive from Canaan to begin moving thousands of cubic yards of snow.

'I'm out of cigarettes,' Mona announced, pushing back her plate.

I went to get her a pack from the liquor cabinet. It suddenly struck me that we had eaten in the kitchen, whereas when we have friends visiting, we always have our meals, including breakfast, in the dining room.

Even on our own, Isabel and I eat our lunch and dinner in the dining room as well.

We'd carried the girls' mattresses upstairs to the bedrooms, and the dirty glasses had disappeared.

'I'll give you a hand . . .'

Mona was wearing her black slacks, her canary-yellow sweater. She was helping my wife do the dishes, and I didn't know what to do with myself. I was thinking too much. I was asking myself too many upsetting questions.

Those questions could not all have sprung from the time I'd spent on the bench in the barn. Seventeen years had not passed without me asking myself some of them.

How was it possible that, until now, they hadn't troubled me? I must have answered them, automatically, with the appropriate responses, the ones you learn starting in school. Father. Mother. Children. Love. Marriage. Fidelity. Goodness. Kindness. Devotion . . .

It's true that I had lived like that. Even as a citizen, I took my duties as seriously as Isabel did.

Is it possible that I never realized that I was lying to myself and that in my heart I never believed in those edifying images?

In our office, it's my associate, Higgins (whom I always call old Higgins, even though he's only sixty), who takes care of the buying and selling of property, the mortgages, the company incorporations and, in general, all the technical business.

He's a chubby, crafty fellow who in other times could have sold quack medicines at country fairs. He's sort of grubby and untidy, and I suspect him of exaggerating the vulgarity of his behaviour the better to fool those around him.

He doesn't believe in anything or anybody and often shocks me with his cynicism.

As for me, my domain is more personal, because I deal with wills, inheritances and divorces. I have taken care of hundreds of them, because our clientele extends rather far beyond Brentwood, and many rich people live in the area.

I am not talking about criminal cases. I don't think I've

had to appear before a jury more than ten times. I ought to know men. Men and women. I thought I knew them and yet, in my private life, I was behaving and thinking the way they do in what are called edifying books.

Basically, I was still a Boy Scout.

It's on the bench that . . .

I don't know where the two women are; probably in the guest room, and I'm wandering around alone in the living room and library, brooding over thoughts I'm not proud of.

And I had considered myself someone with a precise mind! The sight of a man and woman making love in a bathroom had been enough . . .

Because that was really the starting point. Apparently, at least. There must have been other causes, earlier ones, which I would discover only later on. It was on the red bench, in the barn where the door was banging, that a truth occurred to me and changed everything.

'I hate him . . .'

I hate him and I let him die. I hate him and I kill him. I hate him because he is stronger than I am, because he has a wife more desirable than mine, because he lives a life like the one I would have liked to lead, because he goes through life without bothering about those he bumps aside as he goes by . . .

I am not a weakling. I am not a failure, either. My life? I am the one who chose it, as I chose Isabel.

For example, had I known Mona at the time, it would never have occurred to me to marry her. Or to join a Madison Avenue ad agency.

Such choices I made through neither cowardice nor laziness.

All that is becoming much more complicated. I'm reaching an area where I suspect I will make unpleasant discoveries.

Let's take Isabel. I met her at a dance, in Litchfield, as it happens, where she lived with her parents. Her father was Irving Whitaker, a surgeon who was often called to Boston and elsewhere for difficult cases. As for her mother, she was a Clayburn, of the *Mayflower* Clayburns.

It was neither her father's reputation nor her mother's family name that influenced me. It was not her beauty, either, or her physical attractiveness.

I wanted other girls much more than I wanted her.

Her calm, that kind of serenity she already possessed? Her gentleness? Her forbearance?

But why would I have been seeking forbearance when I was doing nothing wrong?

In short, I'd needed to have things all compatible and well organized around me.

Whereas I feel raging desire for a woman like Mona, who is the complete opposite!

'The important thing,' my father used to say, 'is to make the right choice to begin with . . .'

He was talking about choosing not only a wife but a profession, a way of life, a way of thinking.

I thought I had chosen. I have done my best. I have worn myself out doing my best.

And, little by little, I have wound up hoping to see approval in Isabel's eyes.

The Hand

What I had chosen, in the end, was a witness, a benevolent witness, someone who, with a glance, would let me understand that I was keeping myself on the right path.

All that had just cracked apart in one night. What I was envying in Ray, as in an Ashbridge, was their having need of no one, of no one's approval.

Ashbridge did not care if people mocked him because three wives in a row had cheated on him. He picked them young, beautiful, sensual, and he knew in advance what to expect.

Did he really not care at all?

And did Ray love Mona? Was it all the same to him that before he knew her she had been in the arms of so many men?

Were they the strong men and I the weak one, because I had chosen to live in peace with myself?

Well, that peace, I had not found it. I had pretended. I had spent seventeen years of my life pretending.

I could hear a rumble still in the distance, and when I opened the door, it grew louder. I realized that the snow-removal machines were approaching and I even thought I faintly heard men's voices.

Would they find Ray today? That was unlikely. Mona would be spending at least one more night with us, and I was sorry that it would not be, as on the first night, on a mattress in the living room.

I could see her hand again on the floor, that hand I had so longed to touch, as if it had become a symbol.

I was trying to escape. But to escape what?

For just over twenty-four hours now I had known that

in reality I was cruel, capable of taking pleasure in the death of a man I had always considered my best friend and capable, if necessary, of provoking that death.

'You're going to freeze us . . .'

I swiftly closed the door and saw that the two women had got dressed. Mona was in a red dress, my wife in a pale blue one. They looked as if they were trying to get back to everyday life.

All that was still only a sham.

3

Towards four o'clock that afternoon, we noticed through the window that the machines were slowly attacking the snow, cutting a trench there with walls as crisp as cliffs. It was fascinating. We said nothing. We watched without thinking. I wasn't thinking, in any case. Ever since Saturday evening, I had been outside my ordinary life and as if outside of life itself.

What I remember best was the presence of a female in the house. You would have thought that I could smell her, like a dog, that I went looking for her as soon as she left my sight, that I prowled around her, awaiting an occasion to touch her.

I had an insane, irrational, animal desire to touch her. Did Mona realize this? She didn't talk about Ray; two or three times, if that. I wonder if she, too, was not looking for some sort of physical release.

And there was Isabel's gaze, following both of us, without anxiety, with only a touch of astonishment. She was so used to the man I had been for so many years that she had almost lost the need to look at me.

Now, she sensed the change. She could not help sensing it. And she could not understand it all immediately, either.

I can still see the immense snow-removal machine

appearing a few yards from the house, coming at us as if it were going to plough right through the living room. The beast stopped in time. I opened the door.

'Come in and have a drink.'

There were three of them. Two others were in a machine behind them. All five of them came in, stiff in their sheepskin jackets, their huge boots, and one of them had a frozen moustache. Simply their presence chilled the room. Isabel had gone to fetch the glasses and some whisky. They looked around, surprised by the intimate calm of the house. Then they looked at Mona. Not Isabel, but Mona. Did they, too, fresh from their silent battle with the snow, sense the warmth of a female?

'Cheers . . . And thank you for coming to our rescue.'

'The lieutenant will be along . . . He's been told that the road is open.'

They were the kind of people who pop up only on rare occasions, like chimney sweeps, and who live God knows where the rest of the time. There was only one face I knew, but I couldn't remember where I'd seen it.

'Well, thank you, too. This warms us up . . .'

'A refill?'

'We wouldn't say no, but we've still work to do . . .'

The monsters lumbered out, surrounded by white powder, and soon, as night began to fall, we saw the pale headlights of a car at the far end of the trench.

Two men in uniform got out, Lieutenant Olsen and a policeman I did not know. I was the one who opened the door, while the two women remained seated in their armchairs.

The Hand

'Good evening, lieutenant. I'm sorry to have caused you this trouble . . .'

'You've had no news of your friend?'

He went over to bow slightly to Isabel, whom he had met several times. I introduced him to Mona.

'The wife of my friend Ray Sanders.'

He accepted the chair brought forward for him. His companion, a very young man, sat down as well.

'If you don't mind, Mrs Sanders?'

He pulled a pen and notebook from his pocket.

'Ray Sanders, you say . . . What address?'

'We live in Sutton Place, in Manhattan.'

'What is your husband's profession?'

'He's the managing director of an advertising agency on Madison Avenue: Miller, Miller and Sanders.'

'Been there a long time?'

'At first he was the Millers' attorney and for the past three years he has been their associate partner . . .'

'Attorney . . .' repeated Olsen, as if to himself.

'Ray and I, we studied at Yale together,' I added. 'He was my oldest friend.'

There was no point to all this.

'You were just passing through?' he asked Mona.

I was the one who answered.

'Ray and his wife came to visit us on their way back from Canada. They were to have stayed here this weekend.'

'Do they come often?'

The question threw me off balance, because I couldn't see the point of it. Mona replied instead.

'Two or three times a year . . .'

He looked at her attentively, as if her appearance were important.

'When did you and your husband arrive?'

'Saturday, at around two in the afternoon.'

'On your way here, did you have any trouble with the snow?'

'A little. We drove slowly.'

'You told me, Mr Dodd, that you took your friends along to the Ashbridges'?'

'That's correct.'

'Do they know one another?'

'No. As you must know, when old Ashbridge gives a party, he doesn't mind if there are one or two extra faces . . .'

A slight smile appeared on the lips of the lieutenant, who seemed to know a great deal about the Ashbridge parties.

'Did your husband have a lot to drink?' he asked Mona.

'I wasn't with him the whole time . . . I think he was drinking hard, yes . . .'

I had the feeling that Olsen had already made inquiries, doubtless through a few phone calls.

'And you, Mr Dodd?'

'I was drinking, yes . . .'

Isabel was watching me, her hands crossed in her lap.

'More than usual?'

'Much more than usual, I confess . . .'

'Were you drunk?'

'Not completely, but I was beyond my usual state.'

The Hand

Why did I feel compelled to add: 'That has only happened to me twice in my life.'

A need for sincerity? Defiance?

'Twice!' exclaimed Olsen. 'That's really not a lot.'

'No.'

'Did you have a reason to drink that much?'

'No . . . I began with two or three whiskies, to put me in the mood, then I began emptying all the glasses I could get my hands on . . . You know how it goes . . .'

Very much the lawyer, I was furnishing precise details.

'Was your friend Ray drinking with you?'

'We ran into each other a few times . . . We'd exchange a few words, happen to be in the same group, then be separated again. The Ashbridge house is big, and there were guests everywhere . . .'

'And you, Mrs Sanders?'

She looked at me as if for advice, then at Isabel.

'I was drinking, too . . .' she admitted.

'A lot?'

'I think so . . . I stayed with Isabel for a while . . .'

'And your husband?'

'I only saw him, at a distance, two or three times.'

'Whom was he with?'

'With different people whom I don't know . . . He had a somewhat long discussion with Mr Ashbridge, I remember, and the two of them went off into a corner to talk . . .'

'In short, your husband behaved as he usually did on such occasions?'

'Yes . . . Why?'

She looked at me again, amazed.

'I am obliged to ask you these questions because they are routine when someone goes missing.'

'But it's an accident . . .'

'I don't doubt that, madam. Your husband had no reason to kill himself, correct?'

'None.'

Her eyes grew wide.

'Or to disappear without a trace?'

'Why would he have wanted to disappear?'

'Do you have any children?'

'No.'

'Have you been married a long time?'

'Twelve years . . .'

'Your husband, at the Ashbridges', did he run into any old acquaintances?'

I was beginning to feel uneasy.

'Not that I know of.'

'A woman?'

'I saw him with several women . . . He's always quite popular . . .'

'No arguments? Nothing eventful that springs to mind?'

Mona blushed slightly, and I'm convinced that she knows what happened between Ray and Patricia. Did she, as I did, start to open the bathroom door? Did she see them leave that room?

'You were among the last to go?'

Now it was obvious that the lieutenant had made inquiries.

The Hand

'After us, there were only half a dozen people . . .'

'Who was at the wheel?'

'I was.'

'I have to admit that, given the weather, you managed very well. Four hundred yards more and you would have made it home.'

'After the little bridge, there are always drifts . . .'

'I know.'

For a few minutes I had been hearing a new rumbling outside. Turning towards the windows, I caught sight of a bulldozer in the now complete darkness, working in the beam of a floodlight.

Olsen understood my unspoken question.

'Just in case, I ordered the search to begin despite the darkness . . . You never know . . .'

Know what? If Ray was still alive?

'Once out of the car, you walked in the dark . . .'

'The flashlight was almost dead. I preferred to have the two women walking up ahead.'

'That was prudent.'

Sitting still on her chair, Isabel looked from one to the other of us, following the answers on each person's lips, almost as if she were knitting with her eyes. She was knitting the images that, one day, would perhaps form a perfectly organized whole.

'We two were holding tightly to each other,' she said.

'Were the men far behind you?'

'Quite close . . . The wind was so loud that we could hardly hear them when they called to us . . .'

'You didn't have any trouble finding the house?'

'Frankly, I wasn't exactly sure where I was . . . I believe I made it here on instinct.'

'When you turned around, could you see the light?'

'At the beginning, a little . . . It quickly faded, then vanished.'

'How long after you got home did your husband arrive?'

She looked at me as if questioningly. She wasn't uneasy, and she did not seem to find these questions rather bizarre, either, under the circumstances.

'Perhaps a minute? I tried to turn on the lights and found that the electricity was off. I asked Mona if she had any matches. I went towards the dining room to light a candle in one of the candelabras, and Donald came in . . .'

What notes could the lieutenant be taking and what purpose could they serve for him? He was addressing me, now.

'Did you find the house easily?'

'I literally bumped into it when I still thought myself a certain distance away. I was wondering if I mightn't have got lost . . .'

'And your friend?'

'I assumed he was next to me . . . Meaning a few yards away . . . Now and then I would call: "Hey! Hey!" . . .'

'He would answer?'

'Several times, I thought I heard him, but the storm was so loud . . .'

'Then?'

'When I saw that Ray wasn't coming . . .'

'How long did you wait?'

'About five minutes?'

The Hand

'Did you have another flashlight in the house?'

'In our bedroom, yes. Since we hardly ever use it, we don't check the batteries, and they were dead.'

'Did you go out alone?'

'My wife and Mona were exhausted.'

'And you?'

'I was too.'

'How did you find your way?'

'As best I could. My idea was to go around, making bigger and bigger circles . . .'

'You weren't afraid of slipping down to the bottom of the cliff?'

'I felt I could avoid it. When you live someplace for fifteen years . . . Several times, I fell to my knees.'

'Did you get as far as your car?'

I looked at the two women. I no longer remembered what I had told them about that. I had a sort of blank. I took a big chance.

'I reached it by accident.'

'It was empty, of course . . .'

'Yes. I rested there for a moment, out of the wind.'

'And the barn? Did you check to see that he wasn't in the barn?'

For the first time since this unexpected interrogation had begun, I was afraid. It was as if Olsen knew something, something I myself did not know, as if he were setting traps for me, looking innocent and scribbling in his notebook.

'I found it because the door was banging . . . I called Ray's name and heard nothing.'

'You went inside?'

'I must have taken two or three steps . . .'

'I see . . .'

He finally closed his notebook and stood up, like a soldier.

'My thanks to all three of you, and I'm sorry to have disturbed you. The work will continue through the night, weather permitting.'

And, to Mona:

'I suppose, madam, that you are staying here?'

'But . . . Of course . . .'

Where would she have gone, while they were searching for her husband's body in mountains of snow?

We had dinner. I remember that Isabel heated up some canned spaghetti with meatballs.

What day was it? Monday. I had done nothing all day but drag around. I had not gone to the office, which would have been impossible, but I felt guilty anyway.

In the morning, I am usually the one who goes to pick up the mail at the post office. My days followed a well-defined routine I had grown attached to. There was a time for each thing, almost for each action.

I still *felt* Mona's presence and wondered if it would happen. Not here, probably . . .

And why not? She had just lost her husband, whose body the dark forms and their machines were searching for outside.

'Ray was a great guy . . .'

Ever since Saturday night the three of us had been living on our nerves, Mona most of all. Isn't that the

The Hand

moment when you feel the need to throw yourself into someone's arms?

At war, men get rid of their fears through explosions of sexuality.

If we were to find ourselves alone in a room for long enough, safe in the knowledge that Isabel would not show up to disturb us . . .

Nothing happened. We went to the window to watch the bulldozer, and I barely found a way to brush against Mona's elbow.

We went to bed, Mona by herself, Isabel and I in our bedroom.

'What do you think of Olsen?'

The question startled me, because it showed which way my wife was thinking. And I happened to be thinking of Olsen as well.

'He's quite a good sort. People say he knows his job.'

I thought the conversation would continue, but Isabel left things there, without revealing whatever else was on her mind.

It was only later, when we were about to turn the lights off, that she murmured, 'I don't think Mona is suffering much . . .'

'There's no way to tell,' I replied evasively.

'They seemed much attached to each other . . .'

That word struck me. Attached! It's a common expression, I know, but I suppose people who use it have wound up forgetting its meaning. Human beings, two of them 'attached to each other'.

Why not 'chained'?

'Good night, Isabel.'

'Good night, Donald.'

She heaved a sigh, as on every evening, to mark the end of her day and the beginning of a night's rest. She was asleep almost immediately, whereas I would often try for more than an hour to drift off.

Mona was alone in the guest room. What was she thinking about? How was she lying in bed? I could hear the clanking sounds of the machines and I imagined the men somehow passing the snow through a gravel screen.

I woke up with a start in the middle of the night and, hearing nothing any more, I thought perhaps they'd found Ray. Why, in that case, had they not come to tell us?

I didn't move. I wonder if, in her sleep, perhaps sensing that I was awake, Isabel might have begun to listen as well. She did not stir, but her breathing became quieter. Everything was quiet, except an engine running, far away, over by the post office.

I was anxious, for no reason. This sudden peacefulness seemed like a threat to me, and I was relieved when I heard the machine abruptly start up again.

Had it broken down? Had they adjusted or greased it? Or had the men simply needed to take a swig of something?

I fell back asleep, and when I opened my eyes it was day. There was no aroma yet of bacon and eggs, but the smell of coffee already filled the house.

I got up. I put on my bathrobe, brushed my teeth, combed my hair and went down in my slippers to an

The Hand

empty kitchen. There was no one in the dining room either, or in the living room.

Assuming that Isabel was with Mona, I watched the machine at work; it had gone around the cliff and was now at the base of it.

A figure appeared at the side of the barn, and I was stunned to recognize my wife. She had put on my sheepskin jacket and her boots and was managing to make her way through the deep snow.

Did she catch sight of me in the window? The living room was in half-light, and I had not turned on the lamps. I don't know why I preferred not to be there when she came back inside. That visit to the barn had something secretive about it and was evidently linked to either the questions the lieutenant had asked me or my replies.

I retreated, went back to our room and ran my bath water.

I was hoping, without expecting much, that Isabel would come and join me, because I was eager to see if anything in her eyes had changed.

She had heard the water running. She had probably also heard Mona getting up, for when I walked into the kitchen, bacon and eggs for the three of us were on the stove, and the table was set in the dining room.

'Good morning, Mona.'

Today she was wearing a very clinging little black dress and, perhaps because her face looked tired, she was wearing more make-up than she had before, especially around the eyes, which gave her a different look.

'Good morning, Donald.'

I kissed my wife's cheek.

'Good morning, Isabel.'

She did not kiss me back. That was a tradition. I don't know when or how it started. It reminded me of my mother, who never kissed me and would automatically offer me her cheek or forehead.

I realized right away that Isabel had understood. I had also known, since Lieutenant Olsen's interrogation the previous day, what mistake I had made.

During the entire time I had been in the barn, on my red-painted bench, I had smoked cigarette after cigarette, lighting them one after another, simply dropping the butts to the dirt floor and rubbing them out with my boot toes. I'd smoked at least ten.

That's what Isabel had gone to get in the barn, while I was still asleep: the proof of my stay, of my sheltering there so long while I was supposed to be looking for Ray.

She knew. There was no hint of accusation in her blue eyes, however, no new harshness. Only astonishment, curiosity.

She did not look at me as a stranger because of what I had done, either, but I had become someone else, someone she had known for a long time without intuiting his true personality.

While we ate we could hear the men working at the base of the cliff. Mona, intrigued by the quality of our silence, looked from one to the other of us and wondered, perhaps, if my wife might be jealous.

The Hand

This showed in a short remark: 'I'm ashamed to be imposing myself for so long . . .'

'Don't be silly, Mona. You know perfectly well that we think of you and Ray as family . . .'

I felt uncomfortable and ate quickly. As I stood up I announced, 'I'm going to see if I can go and get the car.'

I put on my boots, my jacket, my fur hat. I had the feeling that Mona was going to offer to go with me, for a change of air, but she did not dare to.

Below the cliff the men were working more carefully, having reached the place where they were most likely to find the body.

I followed the trench, where the frozen pathway had become slippery, and I felt liberated at being outdoors in the fresh air, once again recognizing my changed but still familiar surroundings.

The men had pushed my car, still covered with snow, up against the side of the trench. I had to clear the windshield. I wasn't sure if the engine would start. It seemed as if a long time had passed and that major difficulties must have ensued.

Well, the Chrysler purred immediately into action, and I drove it, carefully, to our garage. This was a small wooden building painted white, facing the barn. I had to clear some space with a shovel to open the garage door and inside I saw the Lincoln convertible Ray and Mona had driven down from Canada on Saturday afternoon.

A few minutes later, I entered the barn; the big door

had collapsed outside the building. There was a large patch of snow, but it did not reach the area around the bench. I looked at the ground.

The cigarette butts were gone.

When I went back inside, I looked immediately into her eyes, and she did not turn away but looked back openly, calmly. What could I read there?

'So! . . . I know! . . . I had suspected it . . . When you answered Olsen about the barn, I understood . . . I went to see and arranged things so that others wouldn't know . . .'

Wouldn't know that I was a coward? Did she think it was because of physical cowardice, because I was afraid of getting lost in the blizzard, that I had taken refuge in the barn?

Why, then, was there no contempt in her eyes? No pity, either. No anger. Nothing.

Wait, yes! Curiosity.

'You didn't have any trouble with the car?' she asked, a little too brightly.

'No.'

'Aren't you going to the office?'

'I'll call Helen to have her get the mail . . . There shouldn't be any, because the delivery trucks have probably been unable to make their rounds . . .'

We were talking to no purpose. She had seen me go inside the barn. So I had to know that she had removed the cigarette butts.

The dishes were already done. We looked at one

The Hand

another, all three of us, not knowing where to go or what to do. Mona felt even more strongly that something was happening and announced uncertainly:

'I'm going to straighten up my room.'

The cleaning lady had not come. She lived beyond the hill, and the road that led through the woods to the village was probably not clear.

'Actually, I will go in, as far as the office.'

It was unbearable to be shut up like that, waiting for the men to find the body. I got out the car I had just put away moments before.

Once off the property, I found the road clearer, with signs that several cars had already passed that way. The main road looked almost normal, except for the height of the snow piled at either side.

Most of the shopkeepers were busy with shovels, cutting paths to their stores. The post office was open, and I went in, waving to the cashier as usual, as if nothing had happened. In our post office box I found only a few letters and a handful of brochures. Then I went to the office.

Here as well, nothing had changed. Higgins was in his room and looked up at me in some surprise.

'So, they finally found him?'

I frowned.

'Your friend Sanders . . . Are they still rummaging in the snow?'

Five years earlier, we had built an attractive building of pink brick and white stone window surrounds on the site of the old offices. The door was white. The well-kept surrounding lawn was not visible for the moment, of course, but every year the grass sprang up into the sunlight by the middle or end of March.

Helen, our secretary, was typing in her office and did not stop work to greet me.

Everything was calm, orderly; my law books were in place in the mahogany bookcases. The hands of the electric clock advanced silently. I sat down in my chair and opened the envelopes one by one.

'Helen . . .'

'Yes, Mr Dodd . . .'

She was twenty-five and rather pretty. She was the daughter of one of our clients, a building contractor, and she had got married six months earlier.

Would she stay with us if she had a child? She claimed that she would. I wasn't so sure of that and I anticipated having to find someone to replace her.

I dictated three unimportant letters.

'The others are for Higgins.'

Had Isabel been shocked? Was our life going to be disturbed because of this? I wondered, without knowing if I desired that or not. The exaltation of the night in the barn had died down, yet something still remained of it.

My wife was right to look at me curiously. I was no longer the same man. Higgins had not noticed this. Neither had my secretary. Sooner or later, they would discover the transformation.

I checked the time as if I had an appointment. And I did have one, in fact. Only, it had no appointed time. I was eager to have done with the search out at Yellow Rock

The Hand

Farm, eager to have Ray's body found. I was eager to be rid of it.

What would they do with it when they finally found it? That was not my business. That was Mona's concern. She was busy making her bed, tidying her room.

There were no newspapers. The New York train had not arrived. Much quicker than I had expected, Helen brought me my three letters to sign.

'I'm going home. If something comes up, just call me.'

I walked past Higgins' office and shook his hand.

Outside, I decided that it wouldn't be a bad idea to buy some meat and I went to the supermarket.

'Have they found your friend, Mr Dodd?'

'Not yet.'

'When you think that such things happen right next to us and we don't even notice! . . . Did you have any damage?'

'Only the barn door.'

'A house was blown away, in Cresthill . . . It's a miracle that no one was killed.'

Cresthill is where our cleaning lady lived.

Even though I was talking, looking around, going through the everyday motions, I was constantly asking myself: 'What does she think?'

From what I knew of her, she would not talk to me about it. Life would go on as always, with this secret between us. Now and then, I would feel her gaze on me, doubtless reflecting the same astonishment.

Turning left toward our drive, I noticed that the machines were no longer running and a few moments later I saw from a distance the two women leaving the house in boots and heavy jackets. At the base of the cliff, men were standing around a form lying on the ground.

They had found Ray. I put the car in the garage. I was calm. I felt no remorse. I experienced, on the contrary, immense relief.

The women waited for me before going down the slope. I gave each of them a hand, which didn't prevent us from slipping, and the machine operators had to help us up.

Ray seemed to be smiling under the fine sprinkling of snow that still covered his face and whitened his hair. His right leg was twisted, and one of the men told us it was broken.

I wondered what Mona would do. She did not throw herself on the body. Perhaps she had wanted to for a moment, because she took two or three steps forward; then she stopped, staring and shivering. My wife was on her right, I was to her left. It was to me she turned ever so slightly, just enough to touch my shoulder and side, as if she'd needed my warmth. Then, looking at Isabel, I put my arm around her shoulders.

'Be brave, Mona . . .'

It was a natural thing to do. She was the wife of my best friend. The men around us seemed completely unfazed. Far from being offended, Mona seemed to press even closer to me.

Only I felt it necessary to shoot Isabel a look of defiance.

The Hand

It represented another step, as if, with this apparently simple gesture, I were assuring her of my emancipation.

She did not flinch and turned again to the body, which she contemplated with clasped hands, as one considers a coffin descending into the grave.

'Do you want to move him into the house?'

The crew chief stepped forward.

'The lieutenant advised us not to do anything until he arrived.'

'Did you telephone him?'

'Yes. I had instructions.'

We couldn't stay there in the cold, standing deep in the snow, waiting for the lieutenant to arrive from Canaan.

'Mona, come . . .'

I thought she was going to protest, but she allowed herself to be led away, and we had to climb the hill. I no longer had my arm around her shoulders, but I had done it. It was a victory.

'I suppose he slipped,' she said, once we were back up. 'Poor Ray . . .'

The three of us were walking, three dark figures in the white scenery, and I felt that this must be grotesque. Below, the men started up their machine again to disengage it and probably go and work somewhere else.

'Would you make some coffee, Isabel?'

We followed her into the kitchen, where she set water to boil. She was the one who asked the question.

'What are you going to do, Mona?'

'I don't know.'

'Does he still have any family?'

'A brother who's an embassy attaché in Germany . . .'
'Didn't he ever tell you anything?'
'About what?'
'The arrangements to make in the event . . .'
Calmly, she searched for the words and found them.
'. . . in the event of an accident.'
'He never talked about that.'
'The thing is, there are arrangements to be made,' continued Isabel, thus taking on the most unpleasant tasks. 'Do you think he left a will?'

Mona and I said no at the same time.

'If Ray had drawn up a will,' I explained, 'he would have done it with me and left it with me as well.'

'Do you think, Mona, that he would have preferred cremation?'

'I don't know . . .'

We each took our cup of coffee into the living room; out the window we could see the police car arrive and the lieutenant and another officer go down to the base of the cliff.

Within ten minutes, the lieutenant appeared alone at the door and removed his cap.

'May I offer you my condolences, Mrs Sanders . . .'
'Thank you.'
'It's just what you thought, Mr Dodd. He swerved over towards the cliff and slipped, fracturing a leg in his fall . . .'

Had I said that to him? I no longer remembered. I think he, too, was looking at me in a different way.

'I'll have the body taken to the funeral home, and you will merely have to give them their instructions.'

'Yes,' murmured Mona, who did not seem to understand what was expected of her.

'Where do you intend to have him buried?'

'I don't know . . .'

'At Pleasantville,' I suggested.

It was the large cemetery in New York.

'Probably . . .'

'Is there any family?'

'A brother, in Germany . . .'

We began again. Words. Lips moving. But I was not listening to the words. I was watching the eyes. I think that I have always watched the eyes. Or, rather, that I have always been a little afraid of them.

There were Isabel's eyes. Those I was familiar with. I had known since that morning what astonishment they expressed.

Yet she was the one carefully watching the lieutenant. She had realized that he was glancing at me from time to time, as if something about this business were bothering him.

I am convinced that if the lieutenant had attacked me, she would have come to my rescue. You'd have thought she was waiting only for that moment.

As for Mona, it was towards me that she turned whenever she was asked a question, as if I had naturally become her chief support. This was so apparent, and her attitude revealed such confidence and surrender, that Olsen must have thought we were bound by some intimate relationship.

Was that why he was less cordial towards me? A trifle contemptuous, I thought.

'I will leave you to do what is needed. As far as we're concerned, the case is closed. I regret, Mrs Sanders, that this tragedy took place here in our town.'

He rose, bowed to the two women and finally held out his hand to me. In good faith? I'm not so sure.

I suspect that he's hiding something. Either his men found something suspicious that puts me in a tricky position, or else Olsen, believing me to be the lover of my best friend's wife, despises me.

Would he suspect me of taking advantage of the chance to push Ray off the cliff?

I hadn't thought of that before. It was so plausible, so easy! And why, first of all, did I have the two women walking ahead, when I carried the only – albeit feeble – flashlight we possessed?

I was the one most familiar with the cliff, since it's on my property, in front of my windows. I could hold Ray by the arm, lead him off to the right, push him at the proper moment . . .

I was scared to think that Olsen might have found the cigarette butts in front of the bench in the barn. Would he have come to the same conclusions as Isabel?

Exactly what were Isabel's conclusions? What proved to me that she did not, in fact, believe that I had pushed Ray?

In which case, her silence became a kind of complicity . . . The defence of her home, our two children . . .

She kept her eyes on me when I opened the liquor cabinet.

'A drink will do you good, Mona. Would you like one too, Isabel?'

The Hand

'No, thanks.'

I went to get the glasses and ice from the kitchen. Holding her drink out to Mona, I said:

'Courage, my dear Mona . . .'

As if I were staking my claim. This time, Isabel noticed and for a moment seemed startled. I had never called her that: my dear Mona . . .

'I'm going to telephone the funeral parlour,' announced Isabel, heading for the library to use one of our two telephones.

Was it to leave us alone?

After taking a swallow, Mona turned to me, smiling a little sadly.

'You're a nice man, Donald.'

Then, after a glance where Isabel had just gone, she seemed about to add something, but in the end said nothing.

4

The funeral took place Thursday morning and did not proceed as I had envisioned when the three of us were still off alone in our house.

There must be some catastrophes that are like illnesses. You think that it will take a long time to get well, that life will no longer be the same, and then you see that daily routine takes over again.

At ten o'clock, there were more than twenty cars in front of the Fred Dowling Funeral Home, barely a hundred yards from my office, and two of them had brought reporters and photographers from New York.

Some of them had come to the house the previous day. They had insisted that Mona pose at the spot where Ray's body had been found.

Bob Sanders had arrived the day before from Bonn. Isabel had offered him one of the girls' bedrooms for the night, but he had already reserved a room at the Turley Hotel.

He was taller, thinner, more nonchalant than Ray. He was even more casual in his behaviour than his brother was, and I did not like the self-satisfaction of his smile.

I had met him a few times when we were students, but he was much younger than Ray and I were, and I had barely paid attention to him.

The Hand

He did not show much consideration to Mona.

'How did it happen? He'd been drinking?'

'Not more than usual . . .'

'Had he started to drink a lot?'

Ray was five years older than he was, and he spoke of him rather like a judge preparing to deliver a verdict.

'No . . . Two or three martinis before meals . . .'

The brother was born near New Haven and he knew about our climate. He must have experienced blizzards, not as fierce as the one last Saturday, but still just as disruptive.

'How come they didn't find him sooner?'

'In some places the snow was more than six feet deep . . .'

'What arrangements have you made?'

He didn't like me, either. He frowned at me now and then, perhaps finding that I had been very quick to take Mona under my protection.

Because I was doing that, openly, on purpose. I kept close to her. I was the one who answered most of the questions and I could tell that it exasperated Bob Sanders.

'Whom have you told about this?'

'His associates, of course . . .'

'Were you the one who informed the newspapers?'

'No. That must have been someone in the village, maybe one of the policemen . . . A Scotch?'

'No, thanks. I don't drink.'

He had rented himself a car at the airport. He was married. His wife and three children lived in Bonn with him. He had come over alone. I'm fairly sure he had not seen Ray for several years.

As for the Miller brothers, they did not bother stopping by the house. It was only at the funeral parlour that they went over to Mona to offer their condolences.

I knew one of them, Samuel, having lunched with him and Ray once in New York: a man of about sixty, bald and jovial.

He approached me to ask quietly, 'Do you know who's handling the estate?'

'That is Mona's business.'

'She hasn't talked to you about it?'

'Not yet . . .'

He went to speak to the brother as well, whom he must have asked the same question, because Bob Sanders shook his head.

Mona was driving her own car, since she would be going directly on from Pleasantville to New York. Although I had suggested that Isabel drive, Mona had said no to that, but had welcomed her company.

Behind the two women came the brother's car, then mine, then the chauffeured limousine belonging to the Miller brothers, who looked like twins. Other Madison Avenue people followed, including Ray's secretary, a tall, statuesque redhead who seemed more grief-stricken than Mona.

Many people whom I did not know. No announcements had been sent out, but the time and place of the funeral had been published in the papers.

I was familiar with the road, which was still bordered by mounds of snow, and the sun came out after only a few miles.

The Hand

Mona had confided something strange to me the previous day; we had been alone in the living room while Isabel was out running some errands.

'You're the only one I can tell this to, Donald . . . I'm wondering if Ray didn't do it on purpose . . .'

Nothing she could have said would have surprised me more.

'You mean that he might have committed suicide?'

'I don't like that word. He might have helped fate along . . .'

'He had problems?'

'Not in business . . . In that department, he was succeeding beyond his hopes . . .'

'In his private life?'

'Not there, either . . . We were great pals, the two of us . . . He told me everything . . . Or almost everything. We didn't show off or play-act in front of each other . . .'

I was struck by those words. So, there were some people who could behave naturally, face to face? Was that what Isabel had been seeking in my eyes for so many years? That I reveal myself? That I confess to her for once what was weighing on my mind?

'Affairs . . . He had a lot of them. Starting with his secretary, that tall redhead, Hilda.'

She was the woman who had followed in one of the cars.

'It's hard to explain, Donald . . . I wonder if he didn't envy you . . .'

'Me?'

'You studied the same things . . . He could have become a lawyer, that was his ambition when he started

83

out in New York. Then he became legal counsel in that ad agency . . . He began to earn money and realized that he'd make more by selling contracts.

'You see what I mean? He became a businessman. We rented one of the most beautiful apartments in Sutton Place and we gave parties there or went out every evening . . .

'In the end, he was heartsick . . .'

'He told you that?'

'One evening when he'd been drinking, he confessed that some day he would be fed up with being just a puppet . . . You know how his father finished . . .'

Of course I knew. I had known Herbert Sanders well, having often spent the weekend at his home when I was at Yale.

Ray's father was a bookseller, one of a rather special kind. He did not have a bookstore in the city. He lived in a house of the purest New England style on the road to Ansonia, and on the ground floor the walls of every room were entirely lined with books.

People came to see him not only from New Haven, but from Boston, New York, even farther away, in addition to which he received many mail orders.

He was in correspondence with most countries in the world, keeping abreast of everything being written in the fields of palaeontology, archaeology and the arts, in particular the area of prehistoric art.

He had two other obsessions: works on Venice and books on gastronomy, and he prided himself on having more than 160 such titles on his shelves.

The Hand

A curious man, whom I can still see: young, distinguished, with a smile both ironic and kind.

His first wife, the mother of his two sons, had left him to marry a wealthy landowner in Texas. He had lived alone for a few years, acquiring the reputation of a skirt-chaser.

Then, suddenly, he had married a Polish woman whom no one knew, a gorgeous twenty-eight-year-old.

He was fifty-five. Three months after his marriage, one evening when his wife was out, he had shot himself in the head, among all his books, leaving no note, no explanation.

'Now do you see what I mean?' said Mona.

I refused to accept that revelation. Ray had to remain the man I had imagined, hard on himself and on others, cold and ambitious, the strong man on whom I had taken revenge against all the strong men on this earth.

I did not want a Ray disgusted with money and success.

'You must be mistaken, Mona . . . I'm sure that Ray was happy . . . When people have a few drinks, you know, they tend to dramatize things . . .'

She looked at me as though debating whether to believe me or not.

'He was starting to have had enough,' she insisted. 'That's why he was drinking more and more. I began drinking with him . . .'

She added, hesitantly, 'Here, I didn't dare, on account of Isabel . . .'

She bit her lip, as if afraid she had wounded me.

'You find Isabel forbidding?'

'Don't you? Ray thought so, too. He admired you . . .'

'He admired me, you say?'

'He said you'd chosen your life wisely and well, that you had no need to numb yourself, to go out every evening, to let yourself get carried away in affairs . . .'

'He wasn't making fun of me?'

I was dumbfounded. The reversal was complete.

'According to him, a man able to marry Isabel, to live with her day after day . . .'

'Why? Did he tell you why?'

'Don't you understand?'

She was amazed by my innocence, and I abruptly understood Mona's attitude towards me during those past few days. For her, the strong man was not Ray, it was me.

And, quite naturally, it was my protection she had sought. When she looked at me, from deep in her armchair, when she brushed me with her shoulder, it was not simply a sensual thing.

'I've often observed the two of you, Donald . . . With Isabel, you cannot cheat. You can't behave beneath yourself, either, not even for a moment. She's an extraordinary woman, and you have to be extraordinary to live by her side . . .'

I was so confused and upset that it took me more than two hours to fall asleep later that night.

'Ray, he had his ups and downs, like everyone . . . Say, you're not going to drop me, are you, now that he's gone?'

'But Mona, on the contrary, I ask only . . .'

I almost jumped up to rush over and take her in my arms. I was troubled, elated, beside myself.

The Hand

'Shh . . . She's coming . . .'

Out in the snow we could see the little Volkswagen I had bought my wife for running her local errands. From a distance, I watched Isabel come out of the garage, carrying her bag of groceries: serene, clear complexion with always a touch of pink at the cheekbones, and the blue eyes, those eyes that refused all lying, all cheating.

I would have to rethink everything. Ray had admired me. That was the most staggering news.

Mona admired me, too; she had just admitted it in her own way. And I, poor fool, who that first night had not dared to reach out over the floor to touch the hand that held me so tightly!

What Mona did not know, when she was talking about my relationship with Isabel, was that I had been released. I, too, had admired my wife. I had even been afraid of her, afraid of a frown, of a passing shadow in her limpid eyes, of a mute judgement.

Because she has never said anything unpleasant to me. She has never reproached me.

I must have had occasion to be disagreeable, unjust, ridiculous, what have you, towards her or our children.

Not one word. Her smile never faded. There were only her eyes. And no one would have seen anything there. Her eyes remained as serene and clear as ever.

What would Mona have thought if I had confessed: 'It's not a woman I married, it's a judge . . .'

Wasn't that what Ray had felt, and hadn't he pitied more than admired me? Unless he had been completely fooled.

He'd believed that I had married Isabel because I was a strong man, capable of accepting the challenge.

On the contrary. With her, I kept living in my mother's skirts. I was still a schoolboy. I remained a Boy Scout.

Too bad for Ray. I did not regret a thing, except that he was depriving me of some guilt. I wanted to have killed him, to have desired his death and helped fate along insofar as I could.

If Ray hadn't even struggled, if he had accepted death with relief, the tragedy I had experienced that night on my bench, in the barn, no longer made any sense.

I needed my revolt to remain total, of my own free will.

I was not a sheep, as people thought. I was cruel, cynical, capable of allowing my best friend to die without holding out my hand to him.

And while he was dying quietly in the snow, with one leg twisted, I was smoking cigarettes and thinking of all the times he had unwittingly humiliated me . . . And not just him! . . . There was Isabel, too . . . The two images blended together a little in my mind . . .

The funeral procession had to slow down two or three times. I tried to see Mona's car, beyond the ones between us.

Was I in love with Mona? I was now able to consider questions frankly, without lying to myself, without cheating.

The answer was no. Not in love. Even if it had suddenly become possible, I would not have married her. I did not want to live with her day and night, either, to link my life with hers.

The Hand

What I wanted, what would happen soon, was to make love with her.

Not tenderly. Not passionately. Who knows? Perhaps standing up, like Ray and Patricia at old Ashbridge's house.

I wanted to take a female, like that, in passing, and in my eyes, Mona was a real female.

We arrived at the cemetery. The cars followed a number of paths in that metropolis for the dead until we reached a new section, on the hill.

There was snow everywhere. The evergreens looked like Christmas trees. No one was wearing boots, so we were all stomping our feet while the coffin was brought up.

The minister was brief. There were no other speeches. The Miller brothers slipped into the first row, because of the photographers; going closer to Mona, I lightly supported her elbow.

Bob Sanders noticed. He was a head taller than I and so looked down on me, with what I took to be haughty disdain.

A few days earlier I would have been ashamed, crushed. That day, I didn't care. Neither did I care that my wife was watching me in some surprise, doubtless caught off guard by the audacity of my gesture.

We headed for the cars. I was walking next to Mona, whose arm I still supported as if she needed it, whereas she was perfectly calm. Bob Sanders strode up to catch her, ignoring my presence.

'I must say goodbye now, because my plane leaves in

less than two hours . . . If you need anything at all, if there are formalities to complete, here is my address in Bonn.'

He handed her a card he'd had ready, which she slipped into her purse.

'Take care of yourself, then . . .'

He shook her hand almost militarily and went on ahead. His car was the first to leave the cemetery.

'He doesn't seem to like you . . .'

He had avoided acknowledging me.

'No . . . I suppose he's imagining things.'

Isabel came up to us.

'Are you going back to New York alone, Mona?'

'Why wouldn't I?'

'Won't it be too painful for you to return to an empty apartment?'

'The maid, Janet, is waiting for me . . .'

Isabel looked at me. It was as if she had given me a hint. I could have offered to accompany Mona and come home that evening by train.

I did not even invite her to have a bite to eat with us. On the other hand, just when she was about to get into her Lincoln, I kissed her on both cheeks, gripping her arms rather hard.

'Goodbye, Mona.'

'Goodbye, Donald. Thank you . . . I suppose I'm going to need you for the formalities, the questions about the estate, and so on?'

'Simply call me at my office.'

'Goodbye, Isabel . . . Thank you, too . . . Without you, I don't know what would have become of me.'

The Hand

They kissed. One of the Miller brothers rejoined me after Mona's car had driven away.

'You're her lawyer?'

'I suppose so . . .'

'There'll be complicated questions to answer. Might I have your telephone number?'

I handed him one of my cards.

Isabel and I found ourselves alone in the Chrysler.

'Were you thinking of having lunch along the way?'

'No. I'm not hungry.'

'Neither am I.'

I was at the wheel, she was beside me, as usual, and her three-quarter profile was at the right edge of my vision.

We drove for a good fifteen minutes in silence before Isabel spoke.

'How do you think it all went?'

'The burial?'

'Yes . . . I don't know what was bothering me . . . It was as if there were no cohesion, no order . . . I didn't feel any emotion. I don't think anyone did, not even Mona . . . It's true that it hasn't sunk in yet . . .'

Lighting a cigarette, I said nothing.

'The hardest moment will be when she gets home . . .'

I still kept quiet. Now she was the one who felt the need to break the silence.

'I wondered if you should have gone along with her . . .'

'She'll get along just fine on her own.'

'Will you be taking care of the estate?'

'She asked me to. The Millers want to be in touch with me as well.'

'Do you think she'll have enough to live on?'

'More than enough, I'm sure.'

Was I strong? Was I weak? Was I clever? Was I naive? Was I cruel? Was I cowardly? They were the ones trying to find out, even Isabel, who no longer understood and had to puzzle over why, after the business with the cigarette butts, I was not acting more humble, if not scared.

At the house, we settled for a sandwich in the kitchen. It was three o'clock.

'Are you going out?' I asked.

'I'll be leaving soon to do my shopping.'

I, at least, found it a little odd to be alone together in the house. In so few days, I had lost that habit and wondered how we would behave living in tandem.

I went to the office. Higgins was waiting for me.

'I hope you snagged the Sanders estate?'

'I will certainly help Mona Sanders with my advice, but in a private capacity and without charge.'

Higgins made a face.

'Too bad . . . That must be a big haul . . .'

'I have no idea. On the other hand, it's possible that the Miller brothers will engage me to dissolve the company, and that would be different.'

'Everything went well?'

'The way it usually does . . .'

I would have been hard put to describe what had happened at the cemetery, for the good reason that I'd been distracted by my thoughts, preoccupied only with Mona. Once in my office, I almost picked up the phone to call

The Hand

her to ask if she had arrived home all right, mostly to hear her voice.

And yet, once again, I was not in love. I know that is hard to understand, but maybe I'll manage to explain myself.

I worked for two full hours, on an estate, as it happened. The *de cujus* – the dear departed – had taken such careful precautions to avoid taxes that it was almost impossible to establish the value of the assets and divide them among the heirs. I had been studying the file for several weeks.

I dictated several letters to Helen while asking myself why, before her marriage, I had not thought of flirting with her. I looked at pretty girls, of course, including the wives of certain of my friends. Occasionally I desired them. But that desire remained, so to speak, theoretical.

It was forbidden. By what? By whom? I didn't ask myself the question.

I was married. There was Isabel, with her eyes of such limpid blue and her bearing, so calm and relaxed.

Isabel and our daughters. I was fond of our girls, Mildred and Cecilia, and when Mildred was the first to leave us for boarding school, I had missed going to kiss her goodnight in her bed.

Now, except for two weekends a month, I had no more occasion to go upstairs. Mildred was fifteen.

If she were to marry young, in three or four years, five at the most, it would mean the first bedroom to remain empty in the house.

Cecilia's turn would follow, for time was passing ever

more quickly. The last five years, for example, seemed shorter to me than a single year when I was between ten and twenty.

Is that because the recent ones were less full?

I dictated. I thought. I looked at Helen, debating whether she was already pregnant and if, in that case, we would find a replacement. Ray had slept with his secretary. He'd slept with all the women who came within reach.

And he was the one Mona felt sorry for. Not finding what he had hoped for in life had demoralized him. So he drank and chased women . . . Poor Ray!

Did Helen realize that it was a new man she had before her? Did Higgins? Would all those I would be meeting discern that they were looking at a new Donald Dodd?

My actions, my attitudes, had not changed. Nor had my voice, of course. But the look in my eyes? Was it possible that my eyes had remained the same?

I went to stand before the bathroom mirror. My eyes are blue, too, a darker blue than Isabel's, with brown flecks, while hers are really the colour of a springtime sky when there is no humidity in the air.

I made fun of myself.

'Well, that did you a lot of good! What are you going to do now?'

Nothing, keep going. Sleep with Mona, of course, without that making any real difference.

Saturday morning, or Friday evening, Isabel or I, or both of us, would go and pick up the girls in Litchfield. We would present, in the car, the image of a united family.

The Hand

Except that I no longer believed in the family. I no longer believed in anything. Not in myself, not in other people. Basically, I no longer believed in mankind and I was beginning to understand why Ray's father had shot himself in the head.

Who knows if that might not happen to me some day? It was a comfort to have a revolver in the night-table drawer.

On the day when I will have had enough of struggling in the void, one squeeze of the trigger – and it's over.

Isabel would manage quite well with the girls, and they would receive a handsome insurance payout.

No one could read those thoughts on my face. You get so used to people that you keep seeing them the way you saw them for the first time.

Did I, for example, notice that Isabel was past forty and that her hair was starting to turn grey? I had to make an effort to convince myself that we had both passed the midpoint in life and would swiftly become old folks.

Wasn't I already an old man to my daughters? Would they ever have imagined that I wanted to make love to a woman like Mona? I bet they told themselves that we no longer made love, their mother and I, and that that's why they don't have a whole bunch of brothers and sisters.

I went home and found Isabel busy cooking. She was looking down, and I touched her cheek with my lips, as usual, then went to change my jacket for an old one I wear at home, of soft tweed with leather elbow patches.

I opened the liquor cabinet and yelled, 'Do you want one?'

She knew what that meant.

'No, thanks . . . Or, just a weak one . . .'

I made a weak Scotch for her and poured one a lot stronger for myself.

She joined me in the living room. She was wearing the flowered housedress she had adopted for domestic chores.

'I haven't changed, yet.'

I held out her glass.

'Here's to you . . .'

'And here's to you, Donald . . .'

I thought I heard a special solemnity in her voice, a kind of message.

I preferred not to look at her eyes, for fear of seeing something different there. I went to sit in my armchair in the library, and she went back to work.

What had she thought when she found the cigarette butts? When she had gone out to the barn, didn't she know that she would find them, or at least some trace of me?

What had made her suspect that when I'd left the house to look for Ray I'd had no intention of battling against the blizzard?

She hadn't seen me change course, the night had been too dark. She would not have been able to hear me shouting because of the wind.

At the moment when I stepped outside, even I was uncertain . . . I had only veered off after taking a few steps.

Did she know that I had been a coward? Because that's

The Hand

what it was, at the beginning. An insuperable physical cowardice. I had been at the end of my strength and needed to escape that ordeal at any cost.

Could she have guessed that? Only on the bench did I understand that I was glad that Ray had disappeared and would probably die, unless he found his way again through some miracle.

Had she also understood? And if so, what were her feelings towards me? Contempt? Pity? I'd seen nothing like that in her eyes. Nothing but curiosity.

Another, wilder idea occurred to me. Isabel had read Olsen's mind, which explained some of her questions, but Olsen didn't really know me and thought like a policeman.

The lieutenant had looked at us in turn, Mona and me, asking himself if there were any ties between us. Of that I'm certain. I would bet that he made discreet inquiries. Well, during the Ashbridges' party it so happened that I was never near Mona.

Does Isabel imagine that Mona and I meet secretly?

I go to New York about once a week and spend the day there. Sometimes I spend the night. Ray was often off travelling, because his agency has offices in Los Angeles and Las Vegas.

When she saw me come back to the house alone, did my wife think, even for an instant, that I had taken advantage of that nightmarish storm to get rid of Ray?

Now that I think back coolly, it doesn't seem impossible. I truly believe that if she were to learn that I had killed a man, she would not show any more reaction but would go on living with me and looking at me as she does: with curiosity, hoping to understand.

We ate alone together in the dining room with the two silver candelabras on the table as usual, each with its two red candles. It's a tradition with her. Her father, the surgeon, was somewhat fond of display.

In my home, above the printing press and the offices of the *Citizen*, we lived much more simply.

Speaking of which, my father had not called me to ask for details about Ray's accident, even though he still published the weekly paper in Torrington, one of the oldest newspapers in New England, having lasted over a hundred years.

He'd lived alone since the death of my mother. He had returned to his bachelor habits and when not eating at the restaurant across the street, where he had his table, he liked to fix his own meals. The woman who cleaned the offices every morning would go upstairs to tidy things there and make his bed.

We lived only around thirty miles from each other, yet I hardly went to see him more than once every two or three months. I would enter his glass-walled office, where he worked in his shirt-sleeves. He would look up from his papers, appearing surprised to see me.

'Hello, Son . . .'

'Hello, Father . . .'

He would continue writing, or correcting proofs, or telephoning. I would sit in the only available armchair, which had been in the same place when I was a child.

The Hand

'Are you content?'

'Everything's fine, yes . . .'

'Isabel?'

He had a soft spot for her, even though she intimidated him a little. Several times, he had joked to me:

'You didn't deserve a woman like her . . .'

To which he invariably added, dutifully:

'No more than I deserved your mother . . .'

She had died three years earlier.

'Your girls?'

He was never really sure about their ages and thought of them as much younger than they were.

He was seventy-nine. He was tall and thin, stooped. He'd been stooped, skinny, with a true gleam of malice in his little grey eyes for as long as I'd known him.

'The office?'

'I'm not complaining . . .'

He looked out of the window.

'Say! You've got a new car . . .'

He'd kept his for more than ten years. True, he hardly used it. He edited the *Citizen* practically by himself, and his rare collaborators were volunteers.

A woman in her sixties, Mrs Fuchs, whom I had known for ever as well, took care of soliciting advertising.

My father printed business cards, announcements, prospectuses, catalogues for the local stores. He had never sought to expand his business, which was, on the contrary, slowly shrinking.

'What are you thinking about?'

I looked up, as if caught out. Force of habit!

Georges Simenon

'My father . . . It occurred to me that he hasn't called us . . .'

Isabel no longer had her father or mother, only two brothers, both living in Boston, and one married sister in California.

'I'll have to go and see him one of these mornings.'

'You haven't been there in over a month . . .'

I resolved to go to Torrington. It would interest me to see my father and our house again, with my new eyes.

Back in the library, I hesitated between my paper and the television. I finally opened the paper and fifteen minutes later, while I listened to the hum of the dishwasher, Isabel joined me.

'Don't you think you should call Mona?'

Was it a trap? She seemed sincere, as always. Would she have been capable of insincerity?

'Why?'

'You were her husband's best friend. She probably doesn't have any real friends in New York, and Bob Sanders flew home without bothering to stay a single day more . . .'

'Bob is like that.'

'She must feel lonely in that big apartment. Will she be able to keep such a big place?'

'I don't know.'

'Did Ray have money?'

'He earned lots of it . . .'

'He also spent lots of it, didn't he?'

'I suppose . . . His share of Miller and Miller must represent a tidy sum.'

The Hand

'When do you plan to go and see her?'

It was not an interrogation. She was speaking unaffectedly, as a woman would to her husband.

'Give her a call. Believe me, it will do her good . . .'

I knew Ray's number by heart because I used to see him now and then when I was in the city. I dialled the number and listened to the phone ring a rather long time.

'I don't think there's anyone home.'

'Unless she's gone to bed . . .'

At the same instant, I heard Mona's voice.

'Hello . . . Who's calling?'

'Donald.'

'It's kind of you to call me, Donald. If you knew how lost I feel here . . .'

'That's why I phoned. It was Isabel's idea.'

'Be sure to thank her for me.'

I thought I heard a hint of sarcasm in her voice.

'If you weren't so far away, I'd ask you to come and spend the evening with me . . . Good old Janet does what she can . . . I wander around from room to room without knowing where to go . . . Has that ever happened to you?'

'No.'

'You're lucky . . . This morning was awful. The procession that took for ever, then those people, at the cemetery . . . If you hadn't been there . . .'

So, she had noticed that he had taken her arm.

'I could have just collapsed in a heap, from weariness . . . And that big pompous Bob who greeted me so ceremoniously before dashing off to the airport . . .'

'I know.'

'Did the Millers speak to you?'

'They asked me if I would be handling your affairs.'

'What did you tell them?'

'That I would help you insofar as I could . . . You should understand, Mona, that I don't want to impose myself. I'm only a small-town lawyer . . .'

'Ray considered you a first-rate attorney.'

'There are a lot more clever ones than I in New York . . .'

'I'd like it to be you . . . Unless Isabel . . .'

'No. She would not see any problem, on the contrary.'

'Are you free Monday?'

'What time?'

'Whenever you want. You'll have two hours of driving . . . Would eleven o'clock be all right?'

'I'll be there . . .'

'Now I'm going to do what I already wanted to do at five o'clock this afternoon: swallow two sleeping pills and go to bed. If only I could sleep for two days . . .'

'Goodnight, Mona.'

'Goodnight, Donald. Until Monday . . . Thank Isabel again for me.'

'I will, right away.'

I hung up.

'Mona says thank you.'

'What for?'

'First off, for everything you did for her. Then, for letting me handle the estate.'

'Why ever would I oppose that? Have I ever objected to you handling some business matter?'

It was true. I had to laugh. That wasn't like her. She

The Hand

never allowed herself to express an opinion. At most, from time to time, in certain cases, a look of approval or, on the contrary, a slightly vague look, which in itself constituted sufficient warning.

'You're going to New York on Monday?'

'Yes.'

'By car?'

'That will depend on the weather. If they forecast more snow, I'll take the earliest train . . .'

There. It was simple. We were chatting like a normal couple, quietly, with ordinary words. Anyone looking on and listening would have taken ours for a model marriage.

Well, Isabel considered me a coward or a murderer, take your pick. And I – I had decided that on Monday, I would cheat on her with Mona.

The house was purring along as usual, because it was a living thing, perhaps because it was very old and had sheltered so many human lives. The rooms, with time, had grown larger. Windows had been changed into doors. Dividing walls had been built, others torn down. Barely six yards from our bedroom, a swimming pool had been cut into the rock.

The house breathed. Now and then the furnace could be heard starting up in the basement. At times a radiator clanked; at others, the wood panelling of a room or one of the beams would creak. Until December, we'd had a cricket chirping in the fireplace.

Isabel opened her paper and wiped off her glasses, because for several years she has needed glasses to read.

They made her eyes different, less sure of themselves, not as clear, as if they were frightened.

'How is Higgins?'

'He's fine.'

'Has his wife recovered from the flu?'

'I didn't ask him . . .'

We were gently webbing ourselves in for the rest of the evening, and I had lived like this for seventeen years.

5

It happened, just as I had expected, and I don't think Mona was surprised. I'm even almost sure that she was expecting it, that she was hoping for it, which doesn't mean that she is in love with me.

Before that, Isabel and I had had the traditional weekend with our daughters.

The two of us had gone to get them in Litchfield, without dodging the fifteen-minute conversation with Miss Jenkins, who has small, glittering black eyes and who sputters when she talks.

'If only all our pupils could be like your Mildred . . .'

To be honest, I detest schools and especially all those occasions when parents are reunited with their children. First of all, you see yourself again at every age, which already creates a certain uneasiness. Then you remember, in spite of yourself, the first pregnancy, the infant's first cry, the first baby clothes and finally the day when you take the child to nursery school and leave by yourself.

The years are marked, like stages, with the distribution of prizes, with vacations; traditions are created, which you imagine are immutable. Another child is born, who goes through the same rites, has the same teachers.

You find yourself with a daughter of fifteen, another of twelve, and you've become a man on the decline.

As in that song about Little Jimmy Brown: the bells of birth, the bells of marriage, the bells of burial. Then it starts again with others.

Mildred had hardly got into the car before asking:

'Can I spend the night at Sonia's, Mommy?'

It's always their mother they ask for permission, as if I didn't count. Sonia is the daughter of Charles Brawton, a neighbour who is vaguely our friend.

'Did she invite you?'

'Yes. There's a little party, tomorrow evening, and she insisted that I should sleep over . . .'

Mildred has a face so delicious looking that you'd like to eat it right up. Her complexion is fair like her mother's, but sprinkled with freckles on her nose and under her eyes. She's in despair over them, when they are what give her such charm. Her features are still rather childlike, and her body as well, which resembles a doll's.

'What do you think, Donald?'

I must admit that Isabel never fails to ask my advice. But if I had the misfortune to refuse, I'd set the children against me, so I've always said yes.

'Then what about me!' exclaimed Cecilia. 'I'm going to be left alone in the house?'

Because being there with us, that's being alone! Everyone praises the family, togetherness among parents and children. Cecilia is twelve and is already talking about solitude.

It's true. I was like that at her age. I remember dreary, interminable Sundays with my parents, especially when it rained.

The Hand

'We'll invite one of your friends over . . .'

So, we parents call one another up. We arrange exchanges.

'Could Mabel come and spend the weekend at our house?'

Sunday morning at eleven, the four of us gathered together again to attend church. There as well, you can see people growing older from year to year.

'Is it true that your friend Ray died in our garden?'

'It's true, dear.'

'Will you show me the place?'

We did not show it to her. With children, we act as if death did not exist, as if only other people, strangers, those outside the family or the small circle of friends, pass away from life into death.

No matter. All that isn't important. What's odder is that Cecilia suddenly said, while we were having Sunday breakfast, 'Are you sad, Mommy?'

'Not at all . . .'

'Is it because of what happened to Ray?'

'No, dear . . . I'm the same as always.'

Both girls look more like their mother than like me, but Cecilia has something different about her. Her hair is almost brown, her eyes are hazel, and, when she was still quite little, she was already saying things that surprised us.

She must think a lot, have an inner life we don't suspect.

'Are you both taking us back?'

'Ask your father . . .'

I said yes. We drove them back Sunday night. We had hardly seen them, in the end.

I watched television. I'd be hard put to say what Isabel did. She is always busy.

Our cleaning lady came back to work. Her name is Dawling. Her husband is the local drunk, the true, complete drunk, who gets into fights every Saturday night in bars and is found sleeping on a sidewalk or next to a road.

He has tried every kind of job and been fired from every one of them. For a short time, he has been raising pigs in a hut he built from old planks at the bottom of his property. The municipality is trying to stop him, because everyone complains about it.

They have eight children, all boys, who all resemble their father and are the terror of the local countryside. People call them the Redheads, without distinguishing one from another, and most of them go around in pairs, because Mrs Dawling almost always has twins.

Those folks form a band, a clan that lives on the outskirts of the community, which allows only poor Mrs Dawling in, as a cleaning lady. She rarely speaks. Her lips are thin, and she looks at everyone with a contemptuous eye. She's willing to work for hire, but she still has her doubts.

'Do you think you'll stay overnight in New York? Do you want me to pack you a suitcase?'

'No ... I'll almost certainly be through before evening ...'

Her eyes are beginning to irritate me. I no longer

The Hand

know exactly what they mean. It isn't irony, yet they seem to say:

'I know you, ha! . . . I know everything. Try as you may, you'll not hide a thing from me . . .'

On the other hand, there is curiosity as well in her gaze. It's as if she were constantly speculating about how I will react, what I will do.

She has before her a different man and is perhaps not certain of having explored all his possibilities.

She knows I'm going to New York to see Mona. Didn't my wife sense, while she was here with us, that I wanted her? Doesn't she suspect what is going to happen?

She is careful not to show any jealousy. She is the one who advised me, Thursday evening, to call Sutton Place. She is the one, this Sunday evening, who offered to pack my things, as if it were understood that I would spend the night in New York.

Sometimes I wonder if she isn't pushing me. But why? To keep me from rebelling? To save whatever is still left to save?

She definitely knows that for a week now we have been strangers. Strangers who live together, eat at the same table, undress in front of each other and sleep in the same room. Strangers who talk together as husband and wife.

Would I still be able to make love with her? I don't think so.

Why? Something broke while I was on the red bench in the barn, smoking cigarettes.

Mona has nothing to do with it, no matter what Isabel believes.

Georges Simenon

The sky was overcast, Sunday night.

'I'll take the train,' I announced.

I rose at six on Monday morning. The sky was a little clearer, but I thought the air smelled like snow.

'Do you want me to drive you to the station?'

She took me there in the Chrysler. The Millerton station is a small wooden building where there are never more than three or four people waiting for the train, a train on which all the passengers know one another by sight. I was greeted by our shoemaker, who was also going to the city.

'Don't bother waiting, you can go on home. I'll call to let you know what train I'll be taking back.'

It did not snow. On the contrary, as we approached New York, the weather cheered up, and the skyscrapers appeared against the purest blue, with a few golden clouds.

I went to have a coffee. It was too soon to go to Mona's place, and after leaving the station I walked along Park Avenue. I, too, could have lived in the city, had an office in one of those glass buildings, lunched with clients or friends, had a cocktail, my day over, in an intimate and dimly lit bar. We could have, in the evening, gone to the theatre, or dancing in a nightclub . . .

We could have . . .

What was it that Mona had said on that point, exactly? That Ray envied me, that I was the stronger of the two, that I had made my choice wisely! A Ray for whom everything had been a success and who talked about blowing his brains out!

The Hand

Rubbish!

Were passers-by really looking at me? I always feel as if people are looking at me, as if I had a birthmark in the middle of my face or were wearing something ridiculous. This feeling was so strong that when I was a child, and then a young man, I would stop in front of shop windows to make certain that I looked completely normal.

At 10.30, I hailed a taxi and went to Sutton Place. I knew the building, the orange marquee, the doorman with the gold-laced coat, the lobby with a few leather armchairs and, to the right, the receptionist's desk.

That man knew me as well.

'For Mrs Sanders, Mr Dodd? . . . Would you like me to announce you?'

'Don't bother, she's expecting me.'

The elevator boy was wearing white cotton gloves. He took me to the twenty-first floor, and I knew at which of the three mahogany doors I should ring.

Janet came to let me in. She's a delectable girl in her black silk uniform, with a pretty embroidered apron, and her face is usually sunny.

I suppose she felt she should wear an expression suitable for the occasion, and she murmured something like, 'Who would ever have believed it . . .'

Relieved of my hat and coat, I was escorted by her into the living room, where I feel almost dizzy every time. It's a vast place, all white, with two bay windows overlooking the East River. I'd known Ray long enough to be certain that the décor did not reflect his own taste.

This room was defiant. He had wanted it to be rich,

modern, astounding. The furniture, the paintings on the wall, the sculptures on their pedestals seemed to have been chosen for a film set rather than a place to live in, and the room's dimensions precluded any idea of intimacy.

A door opened in a small room called the boudoir, from which Mona called out:

'Over here, Donald . . .'

I hesitated over whether to bring my briefcase; in the end I left it on the armchair where I'd placed it.

I walked towards her. She was almost ten yards away. She was standing in the doorway, wearing dark-blue. She was waiting, watching me approach.

She let me by without holding out her hand and closed the door behind her.

Only then, face to face, did we look into each other's eyes, hesitating. I put my hands on her shoulders and began by kissing her on the cheeks, as in Ray's time. Then, abruptly, without waiting any longer, I crushed her lips with mine, hugging her tightly.

She did not protest, did not stiffen. I saw her eyes staring at me with a certain amazement.

Didn't she know that would happen? Was she surprised at how quickly it had? Or was it my emotion, my clumsiness that were astonishing her?

My entire being began to tremble. I could not take my mouth from hers, my eyes from hers.

I think that deep down I felt like crying.

The blue garment was a peignoir of very supple silk, and I could feel that there was nothing under it but her.

The Hand

Had she done this on purpose? Had she not had time to dress because I'd arrived ten minutes early?

I murmured, 'Mona . . .'

And she said, 'Come . . .'

We were still in each other's arms as she led me to a couch, on to which we fell at the same moment.

I literally plunged into her, all of a sudden, violently, almost viciously, and for a second there was fear in her eyes.

When I stood up again, she rose swiftly, retying the belt of her peignoir.

'Please forgive me, Mona . . .'

'There is nothing to forgive . . .'

She was smiling at me, still with joy in her eyes but, on her cupid's-bow lips, a hint of melancholy.

'I wanted to so much!'

'I know . . . What can I get you, Donald?'

A small bar was housed in a Louis XV piece. As for the huge bar in the living room, that one didn't hide away at all.

'Whatever you're having . . .'

'Then it will be Scotch . . . Some ice?'

'Please . . .'

'Isabel said nothing?'

'About what?'

'About your trip and our meeting . . .'

'On the contrary . . . She is the one who advised me to call you.'

It was a strange feeling, one I'd never had before. We had just made love savagely and Mona's face still showed some signs of this. Perhaps mine did as well?

Yet the moment we both stood up again we were talking like old friends. We were quite at ease, in mind and body. My eyes must have been shining with delight.

'To us, Donald . . .'

'To us . . .'

'She's an unusual woman . . . I still find her somewhat forbidding . . . It's true that, for a long time, you scared me a little, too . . .'

'Me?'

'That startles you? With most people, you know how to deal with them . . . You quickly discover their weak point . . . You, you don't have one.'

'I've just proved otherwise to you . . .'

'You call that a weak point?'

'Yes, perhaps . . . You know, the night when we slept on the floor, on mattresses, I was hypnotized by your hand, lying on the parquet . . . I had an insane desire to touch it, to seize it. I wonder what would have happened if I had done so . . .'

'In front of Isabel?'

'In front of the whole world, if need be . . . You don't call that a weak point?'

She sat down in an upholstered French armchair and thought for a good while. The peignoir had fallen open over almost all of one thigh, but without bothering either of us. We paid no attention.

'No,' she finally announced.

'I didn't shock you by my brusqueness?'

'I admit that I was disconcerted . . .'

We could talk about it without any fuss, without

The Hand

affection, like old comrades, like accomplices admitting their weaknesses to each other.

'It had to happen, or we would have spent a ridiculous day thinking of nothing else.'

'Do you feel a bit of affection for me, Donald?'

'A lot.'

'I will need that. I don't want to play the weeping widow, and anyway, that would be distasteful at this moment. I was very fond of Ray, you know that. We had become a couple of true friends . . .'

I was sitting in front of her; here, too, the bay window looked out over the East River, bathed in sunlight.

'When I arrived home Thursday, I almost phoned you . . . The apartment seemed ten times bigger than it actually is and I felt lost in it . . . I was pacing around, touching the furniture, objects, as if trying to reassure myself that they were real . . . I began to drink . . . When you phoned me, that evening, could you tell from my voice that I'd been drinking?'

'I was too keyed up to notice anything. Isabel was watching me . . .'

Mona was watching me as well, silently at first, and then as she said: 'I will never understand her.'

She was smoking, with a dreamy air.

'Do you understand her yourself?'

'No.'

'Do you think she can suffer, that there must be something that could get to her?'

'I don't know, Mona. For seventeen years I've never asked myself that question.'

'And now?'

'I've been pondering it for more than a week.'

'Doesn't she scare you a little?'

'I was used to it . . . I thought it was quite simple . . .'

'You don't think so any more?'

'She watches me live, knows my slightest reactions and doubtless my least little thought . . . She never says a word that might suggest that. She remains quiet and serene.'

'Even now?'

'Why do you ask that?'

'Because she has understood. A woman doesn't make such mistakes.'

'Has understood what?'

'That what just happened would happen sooner or later. You were talking about the night spent on the mattresses. She put you between us on purpose.'

'So as not to seem jealous?'

'No . . . For a test . . . It's even subtler than that, I'd swear . . . To tempt you. To unsettle you.'

I was trying to understand, to see Isabel in this new role.

'At least twice she arranged to leave us alone together and she knew of my desire to throw myself into your arms . . . I needed comfort, to feel someone solid pressed against me.'

'I was no help to you.'

'No . . . At first I thought you were afraid of her . . .'

That's the wrong word. I have never been afraid of Isabel. Only afraid of hurting her, of disappointing her, of appearing inferior to the idea she had formed of me.

The Hand

As long as my mother was alive, I was afraid of hurting her, and even now, if I feel uncomfortable in my father's printing offices, in Torrington, it's because I wouldn't want him to sense my pity.

He is just a shadow of his former self, as they say. He digs in, through bravado, publishing his paper that no longer has much readership, no matter what the cost.

He keeps up the ironic front that was his hallmark all his life, but he well knows that some day or other he'll have to be taken to the hospital, unless he falls dead in his bedroom or his office.

Can I let him see my fears? And see that each time I leave him I wonder if I'll see him alive again?

Mona checked the time on a small gilt clock.

'I'd bet that by now she knows exactly what just happened . . .'

She kept coming back to Isabel, who preoccupied her, and I asked myself why.

If it had been anyone else, I would have thought that she was hoping to see me get a divorce in order to marry her. That idea put a small knot in my throat, and I rose to top up the glasses.

'I didn't shock you, did I, Donald?'

'No.'

'You still love her, right?'

'No.'

'But you did love her very much?'

'I don't think so.'

She drank her Scotch in smaller sips than the first one, still watching me.

'I feel like kissing you,' she murmured finally, as she rose.

I stood up as well. I put one arm around her and, instead of leaning in for a kiss, I put my cheek against hers, staying like that a long time, watching the landscape outside the windows.

I was very sad.

Then that sadness changed into a gentler emotion, in which only a vague bitterness remained.

Leaving my embrace, she said, 'I'd really better get dressed before lunch . . .'

I watched her move towards what I knew was the bedroom. I was resigning myself to sitting with the paper while waiting for her, and my disappointment must have shown on my face because she added, in a perfectly natural way:

'If you'd rather come along . . .'

I followed her into the room, where one of the beds was unmade. The door to the bathroom was open, and some water on the tile floor told me she had taken her bath shortly before my arrival. She sat down at the dressing table and began by brushing her hair before applying make-up.

I followed her movements, the light reflected on her skin, with wonderment. I know that we had just made love, but it was almost more precious to be admitted like this into her feminine intimacy.

'You amuse me, Donald . . .'

'Why?'

'One would think this was the first time you'd ever watched a woman at her dressing table.'

The Hand

'It is . . .'

'But Isabel . . .'

'That's not the same thing.'

I have rarely seen Isabel sitting at hers, which holds only essential things instead of all the small bottles and jars I saw on Mona's.

'You won't mind lunching here with me? I've asked Janet to prepare us a nice little meal.'

I remember two young lions, at the Zoo, who were rolling around gently together with perfect confidence. That was about the feeling I had there with Mona.

When she rose, it was to get some underwear from a wardrobe. She did not hide to take off her peignoir and when naked she was not provocative either. She dressed as naturally as if she had been alone, and I did not miss a single one of her movements, her positions.

Was it still true that I was not in love with her? I think so. I had no thought of living with her, of joining my fate to hers the way I once had with Isabel.

I saw Ray's untouched bed without discomfort; it evoked no disagreeable image for me.

There were two other bedrooms in the apartment, I knew. I had once slept in the guest room when I had missed my train, and Janet used the other, smaller one, closer to the kitchen.

Strangely, there was no dining room, doubtless because all possible space had been devoted to the living room.

'Is this all right? I'm not overdressed?'

She had selected a black dress of delicate woollen

material, which she had perked up with a belt of silver braid. She must have known that black was becoming to her.

'You're perfect, Mona . . .'

'Later, we'll have to talk seriously. I can't imagine what I would do if you weren't here, with all the problems cropping up . . .'

Janet had set a small table near one of the bay windows, and there was a long-necked bottle of Riesling in an ice bucket.

'I must move, find a smaller apartment . . . Actually, neither of us liked this one. For Ray, it was all smoke and mirrors, to impress his clients . . . I also think it amused him to invite people over, see a crowd around him, intrigues forming, guests gradually forgetting their dignity . . .'

She looked at me, suddenly serious.

'By the way, I've never seen you drunk, Donald . . .'

'Yet I was so in your presence: Saturday evening, at the Ashbridges' party . . .'

'You were drunk?'

'You didn't notice?'

She paused.

'Not at the time . . .'

'When?'

'I don't know . . . I'm not sure . . . Don't be angry if I'm mistaken . . . When you returned after going to look for Ray, I thought you seemed . . . different.'

A lobster and some cold meats had been set out on a pedestal table for us to serve ourselves. I'd just felt a rush of blood to my head.

The Hand

'It was not inebriation,' I said.

'What was it?'

Too bad. My mind was made up.

'The truth is, I never went to look for Ray. I was too exhausted. I was winded from the storm, with the feeling that at any moment my heart would stop beating. I had no chance of finding him in the darkness, with the snow whipping my face and closing my eyes.

'So, I headed to the barn . . .'

She had stopped eating and was looking at me in such amazement that I almost regretted my frankness.

'I sat down on a bench we store there during the winter and I lit a cigarette . . .'

'Did you stay there the entire time?'

'Yes. The cigarette butts were on the ground, by my feet. I smoked at least ten . . .'

She was troubled, but not angry at me. In the end, she reached for my hand.

'Thank you, Donald.'

'For what?'

'For trusting me . . . For telling me the truth. I felt that something had happened, but I didn't know what . . . I even asked myself at one point if you might not have had an argument with Ray.'

'Why would I have argued with him?'

'Because of that woman . . .'

'What woman do you mean?'

'Mrs Ashbridge . . . Patricia . . . When Ray went off with her, you seemed jealous . . .'

I was stunned to learn that she knew all about it.

'Did you catch them?' I asked.

'Just when they were coming out . . . I wasn't following them, it was pure chance that I saw them . . . Weren't you jealous of Ray?'

'Not because of her . . .'

'Because of me?'

She was asking the question without any flirtatiousness. We were really both speaking from the heart. It was not, as with Isabel, a battle fought with our eyes.

'Because of everything. I actually pushed open that door through which you saw them leave . . . I wasn't thinking of anything, I'd drunk more than usual . . . I surprised them at it . . .

'And then, abruptly, like a hot flash goes to your head, I felt terribly jealous of Ray . . .

'At Yale, I was a grind considered much more brilliant than he was, forgive me for saying so myself.

'When he decided to set himself up in New York, I told him that he risked vegetating there a long time . . .

'I went to ground in Brentwood, barely thirty miles from my father's house, as if I feared losing that protection . . . And almost immediately, as if to protect myself further, I married Isabel.'

She listened, bewildered, and raised her glass, pointing to mine.

'Drink . . .'

'I've told you everything. You'll guess the rest, my other thoughts that Saturday . . . Ray got you, became a partner at Miller and Miller . . . And along the way, he could pick up women like Patricia, casually . . .'

The Hand

She spoke slowly:

'And he was the one who envied you!'

'Do I disappoint you, Mona?'

'On the contrary . . .'

She was moved. Her upper lip was quivering.

'How did you summon the courage to tell me all that?'

'You're the only person to whom I can talk . . .'

'You hated Ray, didn't you?'

'That night, on my bench, yes.'

'And before?'

'I considered him my best friend . . . But I discovered on that bench that I'd been lying to myself.'

'And if you could have saved him?'

'I don't know. I probably would have, unwillingly . . . I'm no longer sure of anything, Mona. You see, in one night, I changed a great deal . . .'

'I'd noticed. Isabel did, too.'

'She figured things out so well that she went to the barn and found the cigarette butts.'

'Did she mention them to you?'

'No. She disposed of them. For fear, I'm sure, that Lieutenant Olsen would discover them.'

'Doesn't Isabel believe that you . . . that you did something else?'

I preferred to speak bluntly.

'That I pushed Ray off the cliff? . . . I don't know. For the last week she's been looking at me as if she didn't recognize me, as if she were trying to understand . . . And you? Do you understand?'

'I think so . . .'

'Aren't you disappointed?'

'On the contrary, Donald.'

That was the first time I'd ever felt as if bathed in a warm feminine gaze.

'I was wondering if you were going to speak to me about it . . . I would have been a little sad if you hadn't . . . That took courage.'

'Given where I am now, you know . . .'

'And where is that?'

'I've drawn a line through seventeen years – no, what am I saying, forty-five years of life . . . Everything is in the past . . . Yesterday, in front of my daughters, I was ashamed, because I felt like a stranger. And yet, I will continue to go through the same motions, to say the same things . . .'

'Is that necessary?'

I looked at her. I hesitated. It would have been easy. Since I had erased everything, didn't I have the right to start over differently? Mona was in front of me, solemn, trembling.

That minute was decisive. We were eating, we were drinking Riesling, we had the view of the East River flowing at our feet.

'Yes,' I murmured. 'It is necessary.'

I do not know why. That 'yes', I said it with my throat choked up, looking intently at Mona. I was on the point of . . . No, not yet, but I could have, very quickly, begun to love her. I could have moved to New York as well . . . We could have . . . I don't know if she was wounded. She did not show it.

The Hand

'Thank you, Donald . . .'

She stood up, shaking the crumbs from her dress.

'Will you have some coffee?'

'Please . . .'

She rang for Janet.

'Where would you like to have it? Here or in the boudoir?'

'In the boudoir.'

This time, I brought my briefcase. Then I walked beside her, slowly, one hand on her shoulder.

'You understand me, Mona, don't you? You feel, as well, that it couldn't work . . .'

She raised her hand to take hold of mine, and again I saw that hand on the floor of our living room, in the light of the flames on the hearth.

I felt relaxed. A little later, I sat down at a small antique table on which I had placed pencil and paper.

'First of all, do you know what your situation is?'

'I don't know a thing. Ray did not talk to me about his business.'

'Do you have any ready money?'

'We have a joint bank account.'

'Do you know how much is in it?'

'No.'

'Did Ray have any insurance?'

'Yes.'

'Do you know what his arrangements were with the Millers?'

'He was a partner, but not a full partner, if I've understood correctly . . . Every year, his percentage share increased.'

'Did he leave a will?'

'Not that I know of.'

'Did you look through his papers?'

'Yes.'

I went with her to the office Ray had set up for himself, and we went through his papers together. We were perfectly at ease with each other, without any reservations. The insurance policy, with Mona as the beneficiary, was for 200,000 dollars.

'Have you informed the insurance company?'

'Not yet.'

'Or the bank?'

'No. I've hardly left the apartment since Thursday. Sunday morning only, I went out to walk up and down the sidewalk for some fresh air.'

'May I make a few phone calls?'

I was back in my role as a lawyer and notary. She listened to my calls, impressed by the way things were being so easily arranged.

'Would you like me to go to see the Miller brothers on your behalf?'

'Yes, do that, will you?'

I telephoned the Millers and told them I would be coming over.

'I'll be back to see you in a little while,' I told Mona.

I took my briefcase. In the living room, I turned to her and, quite unselfconsciously, as I expected, she came into my arms and kissed me.

The offices of the Miller brothers comprise two entire floors of one of Madison Avenue's new buildings, near

The Hand

the archbishop's drab grey mansion. In one immense room alone, more than fifty employees were working, each at a desk, with one or two telephones within reach, and I had glimpsed in passing the same bustling scene in the creative department.

They were both there waiting for me, David and Bill, short and fat, so alike that people who did not know them well could not tell them apart.

'We are glad, Mr Dodd, that Mrs Sanders chose you to represent her. If she had not, we would have chosen you, as I told you at the cemetery.'

The office was vast, luxurious, just solemn enough for a consultation this important.

'What can I offer you? Scotch?'

A mahogany panel concealed a bar.

'I suppose you are, loosely speaking, abreast of the situation? Here is our partnership contract, as it was drawn up five years ago.'

It consisted of about ten pages; I simply skimmed through it. A first glance indicated that Ray's share might come to around half a million dollars.

'Here are the latest statements . . . You'll have time to study these documents at leisure and contact us again. When are you going back to Brentwood?'

'Probably tomorrow.'

'Might we have lunch together?'

'I'll phone you in the morning.'

'Before you leave, I would like you to have a look in the office of our poor friend and see if there might not be some papers or personal objects to take with you . . .'

Ray's office was almost as impressive as the one I'd just left, and his beautiful red-haired secretary was working at a table. She rose to shake my hand, although I had the impression that she did not appreciate my visit.

I knew her from having stopped by now and then to pick up Ray at his office.

'Do you know, Miss Tyler, if Ray had any personal papers here?'

'That depends on what you would call personal . . . Take a look . . .'

She opened the drawers, leaving me the task of flipping through the files. On the desk sat a silver-framed photograph of Mona.

'I'd best take that with me, don't you think?'

'I suppose . . .'

'I'll be back tomorrow. If you'd be kind enough to collect his small personal effects . . .'

'There's even a coat in the closet.'

'Thank you.'

I had myself driven to the bank, then to the headquarters of the insurance company. I was liquidating, not only a man's past, but the man himself. I was legally erasing him, the way the Miller brothers were erasing him from their corporate name.

It was six o'clock when I arrived at Sutton Place. Mona opened the door to me, and we kissed as if this had become a ritual.

'Not too tired?'

'No . . . I still have lots to do tomorrow . . . It would be better if you came to the Millers' office with me.'

The Hand

Without asking, she was pouring our drinks.

'Or do you want . . .'

She was going to ask me again if I preferred the living room or the boudoir.

'You know perfectly well . . .'

We began drinking, both of us, without much talk.

'You're rich, my dear Mona . . . Including the insurance, you're going to find yourself sitting on seven hundred thousand dollars.'

'As much as that?'

She was astonished, but you could tell that the figure meant nothing specific to her.

'May I call home?'

Isabel answered right away.

'You were right . . . I won't be able to come home to Brentwood tonight . . . I saw the Millers, yes, and I have to study the documents they gave me for tomorrow's meeting.'

'Are you at Mona's?'

'Yes, I just got back.'

'Are you planning on staying at the Algonquin?'

That's the old hotel we used when we spent the night in the city. It's in the theatre district, and I was eight the first time I went there with my father.

'I don't know yet.'

'I understand.'

'Is everything fine at the house?'

'There's nothing new . . .'

'Goodnight, Isabel.'

Goodnight, Donald . . . Give my regards to Mona.'

I repeated aloud, turning towards her, 'My wife sends you her regards.'

'Thank her and give her mine . . .'

After I'd hung up, she looked at me questioningly.

I understood that she was thinking of the Algonquin.

'Because of Janet,' I said softly.

'You think that Janet doesn't already know?'

She looked over at the couch.

'Why don't we have dinner in a little restaurant off the beaten track and then come back here to bed?'

She filled the glasses.

'I'll have to get used to drinking less. I drink way too much, Donald.'

Then, after some thought, as if struck by an idea:

'Aren't you afraid Isabel will call you back at the Algonquin?'

I replied with a smile.

'You think she doesn't know, too?'

I wondered if I'd be obliged to sleep in Ray's bed. In the end, we both squeezed into Mona's bed, next to the one left empty.

PART TWO

I

Isabel continues to watch me. Nothing else. She does not ask me any questions. She does not reproach me. She does not cry. She does not play the victim.

Life goes on as in the past. We still sleep in the same room, use the same bathtub, eat together and, in the evening, when I haven't brought home work, we read or watch television.

Every two weeks, the girls come for the weekend, and I believe that they don't notice a thing. True, they are more preoccupied by their own personal lives than by ours.

Basically, they have already lost interest in us, at least where Mildred is concerned. The twenty-year-old brother of one of her friends claims a greater share of her attention than we do.

Every day, morning, noon and night, Isabel looks at me with her pale-blue eyes, and it feels like a collision. I wind up no longer knowing what those eyes are saying.

Do they contain a message? Sometimes I wonder.

'Careful, my poor Donald . . .'

No. They don't show enough warmth for that.

'If you think I don't understand what's going on . . .'

She certainly wants to show me that she is lucid, that nothing escapes her, has ever escaped her.

Georges Simenon

'You're going through a crisis typical of almost all men your age...'

If she thinks that, she's mistaken. I know myself. It isn't the infatuation of a man growing old. Besides, I am not in love. Neither am I plunging into some kind of pathological sexuality.

I remain composed, attentive to what is happening inside me and around me and am alone, no doubt, in knowing that there is nothing new in my innermost thoughts, except that I have finally dared to look at them in the light of day.

So, what is it those eyes want to say?

'I pity you...'

That is more likely. She has always harboured a need to protect me, or to seem to protect me, just as she imagines that she protects our daughters, that she is the driving force in all the projects she undertakes.

Modest, self-effacing, she is actually the most arrogant woman I have ever met. She never allows the slightest fault to show, none of our little human weaknesses.

'I will always be here, Donald...'

That is also there in her eyes: the faithful companion who sacrifices herself to the very end! But in the end, there is something else.

'You imagine that you have freed yourself... You think you are a new man... In reality, you remain the little boy who needs me and you will never free yourself.'

I don't know any more. I lean now towards one hypothesis, now towards another. I live under her gaze, like a microbe under the microscope, and sometimes I hate her.

The Hand

Three months have passed since the bench in the barn. The bench is gone, back in its place in the garden, near the cliff, as it happens, from which Ray fell. The last scraps of snow have been absorbed by the warming earth, and the jonquils are sprinkling their yellow accents everywhere.

The first month, I went to New York up to twice a week, staying overnight almost every time, because Ray's estate and the incumbent formalities required much time and effort.

'Where should I call you in the evening if something urgent comes up?'

'At Mona's.'

I'm not hiding away. I am, on the contrary, behaving rather brazenly and when I return from New York I'm glad to smell Mona's scent on my skin.

Bad weather no longer forces me to take the train. I drive my car. There is a parking lot across from her building. Or rather, there was, because as of two weeks ago Mona no longer lives in Sutton Place.

Through friends, she found an apartment on 56th Street, between Madison and Fifth Avenues, in one of those narrow row houses in the Dutch style that are so charming.

The ground floor tenant is a French restaurant that makes a savoury coq au vin. Her apartment is on the fourth floor, much smaller, of course, than the old one.

Warmer and more intimate as well. For the new living room, she used the furniture from the boudoir, including the couch upholstered in golden-yellow silk.

The bed is new, a vast double bed, very low, but the

dressing table and French armchair are still the same ones as before.

The dining room will not hold more than six or eight at the table, but Janet has a rather big kitchen and a pretty bedroom.

I don't know which friends found her this apartment. In Ray's time, they frequented many people, entertaining or going out almost every evening.

That is a subject that remains closed to me. As if by agreement, we do not discuss it. I have no idea whom she sees when I'm not in the city and no idea if she has one or several lovers.

It's possible. She loves to make love, without romantic illusions, I would almost say without passion, as friends.

Whenever I arrive, I find her in a peignoir and lead her in the most natural way to the couch on which I entered her for the first time.

Afterwards, she pours our drinks, carries the two glasses into the bedroom and begins her morning ritual.

'How is Isabel?'

She talks to me about her every time I visit.

'She still hasn't said anything yet?'

'She looks at me . . .'

'It's a tactic.'

'What do you mean?'

'By watching you silently, without upbraiding you, she'll wind up giving you a guilty conscience.'

'No.'

'She's counting on it.'

'Perhaps, but if so, she's wrong.'

The Hand

Mona is intrigued by Isabel and she is the one who is impressed by her personality.

As for me, this is one of the best moments of my day, of my week. She busies herself with her toilette, and I sink with delight into this intimate scene as if into a hot bath.

I know every one of her movements, each expression, the way she purses her mouth to apply lipstick.

When she takes her bath, I follow the water droplets that zigzag along her flushed skin. Because her skin is not pale and tinged with pink like Isabel's, but more golden.

She is quite petite, actually. She weighs nothing.

'Has Lowenstein made up his mind?'

Because we do discuss her business. We even pay a great deal of attention to it. Lowenstein is the decorator who made an offer to buy all the furnishings at Sutton Place, except for the few pieces Mona kept back.

Only the price was still a matter for debate. Now that's settled, and the lease has gone to an actor recently arrived from Hollywood to appear on Broadway.

The negotiations with the Miller brothers are almost completely wound up, and the name of Sanders has long since been scraped off the glass panels where it appeared after Miller and Miller. Only a few details remain to be dealt with.

I never asked Mona what she did with Ray's clothing, his golf clubs, a certain number of personal belongings I no longer see anywhere.

We often go down to the little ground-floor restaurant, where we always choose the same corner. The owner comes over to shake hands. We are treated like a couple, and it amuses us. In the afternoon, I almost always have to rush around everywhere, either for Mona's business or for mine. We arrange to meet later in a bar. We drink martinis because, for the evening cocktail, we have adopted the extra-dry martini.

We do enough drinking, perhaps too much, but without ever being drunk.

'Where shall we have dinner?'

We wander at random, on foot, and sometimes Mona, perched on her high heels, takes my arm. Once, we encountered Justin Greene, from Canaan, one of old Ashbridge's guests, in fact, who was present at that memorable evening. He hesitated to acknowledge us. I turned around at the same moment he did, and he seemed embarrassed.

By now, all Brentwood – indeed, the whole area – must know that I'm conducting an affair in New York. Did he recognize Mona? It's possible, although improbable, because it was the first time she had ever been to that house, and she had hardly made herself conspicuous.

'Was that one of your clients?'

'An acquaintance . . . He lives in Canaan . . .'

'Doesn't it bother you that he saw us?'

'No . . .'

On the contrary! I'd finished with all those people. One day they would certainly realize that although I was still pretending to play the game, I no longer believed in it.

One Saturday, I went to Torrington. It's a placid little

The Hand

town, with only two commercial streets, surrounded by residential neighbourhoods.

To the west, there's a bit of industry, but it's almost artisanal, a watch factory, for example, and another plant, brand new, where they manufacture minuscule components for electronic instruments.

The house where I was born is on the main street, at the corner of a dead end, with a sign saying the *Citizen* in gothic letters. Most of the workers in the printing shop have been with my father for more than thirty years. Everything is antiquated, including the machines that entranced me when I was a child.

Because it was Saturday, the print shop was closed. Nevertheless, my father was in his glass cage and could be seen, in his usual shirt-sleeves, from the street.

He had always worked in that spot, as if to proclaim that the newspaper had nothing to hide.

The door was not locked. I went in. I sat down on the other side of the desk and waited for my father to look up.

'It's you?'

'I'm sorry for not having come by lately . . .'

'It means that you had something else to do. So there's no need to apologize . . .'

That's my father's style. I don't believe he has ever kissed me, not even when I was little. In the evening he would simply offer his forehead, like Isabel. I never saw him kiss my mother, either.

'You're in good health?'

I replied yes, just as it dawned on me that my father had

aged a lot in the last few weeks. His neck was so thin that the tendons showed, and his eyes looked a little faded.

'Your wife came by a few days back.'

She had not mentioned that to me.

'She'd come to do some errands, to buy some dishes, I think, from that old thief Tibbits . . .'

A shop that existed already in my day, selling china and silverware. I had known old Tibbits and then his son, now old himself.

When we got married, we bought our set of dishes from Tibbits, and when too many pieces had been broken, Isabel would come to Torrington to replace them.

'Are you still content?'

The relationship between my father and me was so reserved that I never knew how to interpret his questions. He would often ask me if I was content, the way he asked me for news about the health of Isabel and the girls.

But, this time, didn't the question go deeper? Hadn't my wife spoken to him? Hadn't any rumours reached him?

He continued to run his eyes over the proofs, striking out a word and replacing it, in the margin, with another.

Had we ever had anything to say to each other? I stayed there, looking at him, sometimes turning to the street, where the traffic had changed since my childhood. Once, passing cars had been rare, and you could park anywhere.

'How old are you, by the way?'

'Forty-five.'

He nodded, murmuring as if to himself, 'That's young, of course . . .'

The Hand

He was about to turn eighty. He had married late, after the death of his father, who was already running the *Citizen*. He had begun his career in Hartford and had worked, for only a few months, on a daily paper in New York.

I had a brother, Stuart, who would most likely have taken over the business if he had not been killed in the war. He was more like my father than I was, and I have the impression that the two of them got along well together.

My father and I got along well, too, but without intimacy.

'It's your life, after all . . .'

He was muttering. I hadn't necessarily heard him. Was it better to let the matter drop, to talk about something else?

'Are you referring to Mona?'

My father pushed his glasses back up on his nose and looked at me.

'I didn't know her name was Mona.'

'Isabel didn't tell you?'

'Isabel did not tell me anything . . . She's not a woman who talks about her business, even to her father-in-law.'

There was obvious admiration in his voice. You might have thought that he and Isabel were cut from the same cloth.

'So, who told you that I had a mistress?'

'Everybody, more or less . . . There's talk . . . It seems she's the widow of your friend Ray . . .'

'That's true.'

'The one who had the accident, at your house, the night of the blizzard, right?'

I flushed, because I sensed a vague accusation behind those words.

'I'm not the one putting the two things together, Son . . . It's other people.'

'Which people?'

'Your friends in Brentwood, Canaan, Lakeville . . . Some of them wonder if you'll get divorced and go to live in New York.'

'Certainly not.'

'I'm not asking you the question, but others have asked me, and I've told them that it's none of my business.'

He wasn't reproaching me, either. He seemed not to have any hidden agenda, again like Isabel. He filled his old curved pipe with the burned bowl and lit it slowly.

'Did you come to tell me something?'

'No . . .'

'Did you have anything to do in Torrington?'

'Again, no . . . I just wanted to see you.'

'Would you like to go upstairs?'

He had understood that it was not only him I had come to see, but the house as well, that I was there, in short, to come face to face with my youth.

It's true that I would have liked to go upstairs, to see once more the apartment of former days, where I'd crawled around before I could stand up, and where my mother had seemed like an immense being.

I can just see her eternal apron with tiny checks, the kind they still wore in those days.

No. I could no longer go up there. Not after what my father had just told me.

The Hand

I could no longer make contact with him as I had obscurely hoped to do, either.

In fact, what had I come to do?

'You know, it must be rather a mess up there, because the cleaning lady doesn't come on Saturday and Sunday . . .'

I imagined the old man alone in the apartment where the four of us had lived. He drew slowly on his pipe, which made a familiar gurgle.

'Time passes, Sonny . . . For everyone, you see. You've gone more than halfway along the path . . . Me, I'm beginning to catch sight of the end . . .'

He was not waxing sentimental about himself, which would not have been in his character. I sensed that he was speaking for me, that he was trying to show me his thoughts.

'Isabel was sitting where you are now . . . When you introduced her to us, your mother and I did not much like her.'

I couldn't help smiling. She was from Litchfield, and in our part of the world those people were considered snobs who thought themselves a cut above the rest of us.

Wide boulevards, lots of greenery, lovely houses and, especially in the morning, men and women out riding horses.

Isabel had had her horse.

'You can be mistaken about people, you see, even when you think you know them. She's a fine woman.'

When my father called someone fine, that was his highest compliment.

'Again, it's your business . . .'

'I am not in love with Mona, and we have no plans for the future.'

He coughed. He had had chronic bronchitis for a few years now and occasionally had painful fits of coughing.

'Please excuse me.'

His physical decline humiliated him. He hated making a spectacle of it before others. I think that's why he would have preferred that we no longer visit him.

'What were you saying? . . . Ah, yes . . .'

He relit his pipe and, while puffing on it, announced, slowly and distinctly:

'In that case, it's even worse.'

I was wrong to have visited my father. I'm certain that I disappointed him. And I was disappointed as well. There was no connection between us, whereas, from the little he told me, I realize that he and Isabel have been keeping up some kind of relationship. When I got into my car, I saw, through the window, that he was watching me leave and probably thinking, as I did, that we had perhaps seen each other for the last time.

During the entire drive home, I kept seeing his worn-out face, his melancholy dignity, and I asked myself questions. Has he really kept his faith to the end and, at the moment of leaving, does he still harbour illusions?

Does he believe in the usefulness of this little newspaper, which fought against injustice a hundred or even sixty years ago but which no longer does anything but

The Hand

flatter people's vanity by reporting on engagements, weddings, parties and other unimportant local events?

He has devoted his life to the *Citizen* as seriously as if he had been fighting for a great cause and he is clinging to the paper until his last breath.

It's what would have happened to my brother if he hadn't died at the front. With small differences, isn't that what happened to me as well, until, on the bench in the barn, I lit a first cigarette?

After a while, I drove more slowly. Lately I've been subject at times to sudden sensations of vertigo. I am not ill. It isn't fatigue, either, because I'm not working any harder than usual.

Age? It's true that I am now conscious of my age, which I'd never thought about, and the sight of my father has reinforced this.

I would have liked to explain something to him, about Mona. I tried. Did he understand that to me she is above all a symbol?

We are not in love. I am not sure that I believe in love, or in any case, in a love that lasts a lifetime.

We join together because it reassures us to feel skin against skin, to live in the same rhythm. That's still the closest, in the union of two beings, that one can be.

We need someone. I needed Isabel, not in the same way. I needed her as a witness, as a guard rail, I'm not sure what, exactly. It's all so far in the past that I myself no longer understand what I was seeking in her and am beginning to hate her.

Her gaze exasperates me. It has become an obsession.

When I arrived home, without having mentioned either Torrington or my father, she asked:

'How is he?'

It's easy to figure out, I admit. There are clues. But I constantly feel myself at the end of a string. Wherever I go, whatever I do, it's a little as if she were keeping her eyes fixed on me.

I only go once a week to New York now, because the estate has been taken care of and, even with regard to Mona, I did need an excuse. I must not lapse back into what I was. I could not bear that any more. When you've made certain wrenching discoveries, it's impossible to go backwards.

I need Mona, which is to say her presence, an animal intimacy. I love it when, naked or half naked, she goes about her morning routine without paying attention to me. I love, in bed, feeling her skin against mine.

As for the rest, though, hasn't our experiment been a failure? I've talked about the restaurants where we'd have lunch and dinner, the little bars where we'd have our two late-afternoon martinis.

We were still good friends, of course. We were perfectly at ease with each other. But to tell the truth, I did not feel in communication with her and at times I had to look for something to say. It was the same for her.

Nevertheless, she is everything that I did not possess during those forty-five years, everything I shied away from, out of fear.

The girls have been back. I've been observing Mildred a lot. I love her complexion, the colour of warm bread, and the way she crinkles her nostrils when she smiles. She has

The Hand

begun to wear make-up, not at school, of course, where that must be forbidden, but at home.

Does she imagine that we don't notice? She spent last Sunday afternoon with her friend, the girl who has the twenty-year-old brother. Who will probably be what she'll later call her first love. She has no idea that the memory of those furtive glances, those blushes, those hands brushing against each other as if by chance will pursue her all her life.

She will not be pretty in the usual sense of the word. She isn't beautiful, either.

What kind of man will she meet and what life will she live with him?

I see her as a housewife, one of the women whom I class among those who smell like pastry.

As for Cecilia, I don't know. She remains an enigma, and I would not be surprised if she possesses quite a strong personality. She watches us live, and I'm almost convinced that she does not approve of us, that the only thing she feels for us is a certain disdain.

It's really odd! For years you're so preoccupied with the children that they become the reason for everything you do. The house is arranged for them, along with Sundays, vacations, and one fine day you find yourself face to face, strangers to each other, like my father and me.

I repeat that I was wrong to go and see him. That visit has reinforced a pessimism I'm only too inclined to indulge in when I'm not in New York. And even when I am there, actually, aside from certain moments that could be counted in minutes.

It wouldn't take much to get me talking about a

conspiracy. Isabel and my father, for a start! Why did she go to Torrington? Was it so important to replace a few plates, when most of the time there are only two of us at the table? It has been six months since we've invited anyone to the house.

My father claims that Isabel did not talk to him about Mona or me. Fine! I have to believe him. But he, didn't he speak to her about us? Even if he didn't, all they had to do was look at each other.

'So, what's Donald up to?'

She must have smiled, with a smile as pale as the sun after a rain.

'Don't worry about him . . .'

Wasn't she watching over me? Doesn't she keep an eye on me every day, at every hour?

Now here were the locals getting involved, whispering as I pass. They've finally got some disreputable gossip to spread around . . . Donald Dodd, you know, the lawyer whose office is almost directly across from the post office . . . The partner of old Higgins, yes . . . The one who has such a nice, sweet, devoted wife . . . Well, he's carrying on an affair in New York!

Higgins joins in. When I tell him that I'll be going to New York the following day he asks:

'Will you be there for two days?'

'Not this time, no . . .'

Higgins ought to be satisfied, though, because the Miller brothers paid us handsomely indeed for the work I did. I would have done it for nothing, to help Mona. They are the ones who insisted on it.

The Hand

Warren, our doctor, came to see me at my office to ask me a question about his taxes, because I handle his affairs. He studied me closely while we were chatting, and I suspected that his story about the taxes was simply a pretext.

Wouldn't Isabel have been capable of calling him? Of telling him, for example:

'Listen, Warren . . . I'm worried. For some time now, Donald hasn't been the same . . . His moods have changed. He seems very strange.'

I abruptly looked Warren right in the eye. He's an old friend. He was at the Ashbridges' on 15 January.

'You find me very strange as well, do you?'

He was so startled that he had to catch his glasses.

'What do you mean?'

'Just what I said. For a while now, when I go by, people have tended to turn around and whisper . . . Isabel looks at me as if she were wondering what's happening to me, and I strongly suspect her of having sent you here.'

'Donald, I assure you . . .'

'Am I very strange, yes or no? . . . Do I seem like a man in full possession of his wits?'

'You're joking, aren't you?'

'Not in the least . . . Get this: sometimes, in New York, I meet a woman friend with whom I have sexual relations . . .'

I spoke those words with sarcastic emphasis.

'Does that surprise you?'

'Why would it surprise me?'

'Did you know that?'

'I'd heard it mentioned . . .'

'You see! . . . And what else have you heard?'

He must have been sorry he'd come, he felt so embarrassed.

'I don't really know . . . That you might make certain decisions . . .'

'For example?'

'To go and live in New York . . .'

'To get divorced?'

'Perhaps.'

'Did Isabel talk to you about it as well?'

'No.'

'Have you seen her recently?'

'That depends on what you mean by recently.'

'Within the past month?'

'I believe so . . .'

'Did she go to see you at your office?'

'You're forgetting patient confidentiality, Donald.'

He tried to smile while saying those words as casually as possible. He was getting to his feet, but I did not set him free yet.

'If she went to see you, it wasn't because of her health. She went to talk to you about me, to tell you that she was worried, that I wasn't myself any more.'

'I don't like the turn this conversation is taking.'

'Neither do I, but I'm beginning to be fed up with being an object of curiosity . . . I did not go looking for you. You are the one who came here, under a poor pretext, to peer up my nose, take my temperature . . .

'Are there some tests you'd like me to have? . . . Have you seen enough to reassure my wife? . . . Do I seem

The Hand

very strange to you as well, because I start telling people what's bothering me?

'You're much more Isabel's friend than you are mine . . . All our friends are in the same boat. Isabel is an extraordinary woman, of exemplary devotion, of boundless goodness . . .

'Well, my dear Warren, one doesn't sleep with devotion and goodness. I've been doing that for too long not to be fed up with it. I will go to New York or elsewhere, when I please, no matter what the honourable citizens of this county think of that . . .

'As for Isabel, if she's worried, reassure her: I have no intention of divorcing and of remaking my life elsewhere . . . I will continue to work in this office and go home obediently to the house . . .

'So, do you still find me very strange?'

He shook his head sadly.

'I don't know what's come over you, Donald . . . Have you been drinking?'

'Not yet . . . I'm going to in a moment . . .'

I was beside myself. I don't know why I suddenly became so furious. Especially with poor Warren, who is truly the last person with whom I could be angry. The pill-doctor, as the children call him. In his visits, he lugs along a Gladstone bag that looks like a travelling salesman's case. All one side is kitted out with tubes and flasks and, after listening to his patient's chest, he looks over his collection, selects a flask, takes from it (according to need) two, four, six pills, which he slips into a little envelope.

He has pills of every colour: reds, greens, yellows and rainbow-tinted ones my daughters, when younger, naturally preferred above all others.

'Here . . . You'll take one fifteen minutes before dinner and another before bed. Tomorrow morning . . .'

Poor Warren! I had dumbfounded him, and my anger vanished as quickly as it had come.

'I apologize, Warren . . . If you were in my place, you would understand. As for my mental state, I don't think you need to worry yet. Do you agree?'

'I did not think for an instant that . . .'

'Yes, well, but others have thought so for you. Reassure Isabel . . . Don't tell her that I said to . . .'

'You're really not angry with me?'

'No.'

I wasn't angry with him, but I was troubled, because I wondered if I hadn't just discovered the reason why there was anxiety in my wife's eyes.

She had always been so sure of me, so sure of what she must have considered my equanimity, that she could not believe that I had deliberately changed.

I kept coming back to the cigarette butts she had disposed of. Was it possible that she'd believed that I had pushed Ray?

My trips to New York, my intimacy with Mona, paraded almost cynically after my friend's death – did they not seem like proof to her?

In which case, I had to be of unsound mind. That was the only way for her to explain my attitude.

I had just spoken of drinking. Indeed, I went to have

The Hand

a Scotch in the bar across the way, frequented mostly by truck drivers, where I almost never go.

'Another, please . . .'

Here as well people looked at me, of course, and if Lieutenant Olsen had come in, my attitude would have given him something to think about.

Another one who had his doubts. I was surprised that he hadn't tried again. Was he convinced Ray's death was due to a simple accident?

He must have heard that I was Mona's lover and that we could be seen in New York walking arm in arm.

I did not have a third drink, although I wanted one. I went back across the street to the office.

'Are you going to New York, this week?'

'Why do you ask?'

'Because if you go, I'd ask you to do something for me there . . . What neighbourhood will you be in?'

'Around Fifty-sixth Street . . .'

'It's a document to be registered at the Belgian Consulate, in Rockefeller Center . . .'

'I might be going in on Thursday.'

'Say, you really shook him up, that poor Warren . . . It wasn't my fault, I couldn't help overhearing . . .'

'Do you find me strange, too?'

'Strange, no, but you have changed. To the point that I wondered if you would stay here and if I ought to look for a partner . . . For me, that would be a catastrophe. Do you see me, at my age, training up some youngster? . . . Didn't the Millers offer to bring you in with them?'

'No.'

'Now that surprises me . . .'

I wasn't telling the truth. No, they had not made me a direct offer. They had, however, asked me about my plans, my life in Brentwood, and I had understood where they were going.

They, too, were mistaken about my relationship with Mona. They thought it was a great love affair and imagined that in a few weeks I would be settling in New York to live with her and get married.

Then I would really have stepped into Ray's shoes!

'Anyway, I'm glad you're staying . . .'

From his office, which faces the street, he'd seen me head over to the bar, which wasn't one of my habits.

What does he think, this old fox who looks more like a wily horse trader than a lawyer?

Too bad! Let them think what they want, the whole lot of them, Isabel included, of course, Isabel first of all.

When I got home, she welcomed me with a simpering smile, as if I were unhappy or ill.

It's a game that is beginning to grate on me, and I'll have to get used to it. I ought to decide once and for all to pay no more attention to her expressions.

She plays them like cards, deliberately. They're her secret weapon. She knows I'm trying to understand, that it makes me uneasy, eats away at my assurance.

She deploys an entire range of looks like precision instruments. I might reply to words, but you cannot reply to eyes.

If I asked her, 'Why are you looking at me that way?'

The Hand

she would answer with another question: 'In what way am I looking at you?'

In every way. It changes with the days, the hours. Sometimes her eyes are empty, and that's perhaps the most disconcerting look. She's there. We are eating. I say a few words, to avoid a painful silence.

And she looks at me with absent eyes. She watches my lips move the way one watches the lips of a fish open and close in its bowl.

At other times, on the contrary, her pupils contract, and she stares at me as if asking an anguished question.

What question? Did she still have any, after seventeen years of marriage?

Her attitudes, her poses, her way of holding her head tilted to the left, the hint of a smile hovering about her lips, all that never changed, remained immutable. A statue.

Unfortunately, that particular statue was my wife, and she had eyes.

The most curious thing was, morning and evening, when I leaned down to brush her forehead or cheek with my lips: she did not move, not a twitch.

'Good Morning, Isabel . . .'

'Good morning, Donald . . .'

I might just as well have been putting a dime into the slot of a collection box in church.

I tried not to undress in front of her any longer. It bothered me, just as it bothered me to see her half naked.

For her part, she kept doing it. She did it on purpose.

Not immodestly, she had always been very modest. But like an acquired right.

There were only two men in the world before whom she had the right to undress: her husband and her doctor.

Had Warren, after our encounter, called her up? Had he reassured her? Had he told her what had happened?

There were moments when I wanted to make a commotion, like that morning in the office. I restrained myself. I did not want to give her that satisfaction. Because she would have been satisfied.

Not only was she intelligent, good, devoted, indulgent, what-have-you, but I would have handed her the palm of martyrdom besides!

I really hated her. And I realized that it was not so much her fault, or mine, either. In short, she represented everything I had suffered, the stifling of my whole life, that humility I had imposed on myself.

'Don't put your fingers in your nose . . .'

'You must respect old people . . .'

'Go wash your hands, Donald . . .'

'We don't put our elbows on the table . . .'

Those words, it wasn't Isabel who said them. It was my mother. But for seventeen years, Isabel's eyes had told me exactly the same thing.

I knew I had only myself to blame, since I had chosen her.

And the best part is that I had chosen her on purpose.

To keep an eye on me? To judge me? To prevent me from committing too many stupid blunders?

It's possible. It's hard for me to remember what I was thinking when I met her. I was hesitating, at the time, over joining Ray in New York. I'd also been approached about a job in Los Angeles, and I had been tempted.

What might I have become? What would I have become, without Isabel? Would I have married a Mona?

Would I, like Ray, have earned a lot of money while despising myself to the point of talking about suicide?

I haven't any idea. I prefer not to know, not to ask myself any further questions. I would have liked to draw up a well-organized, neat dossier, without any smudges.

I haven't come close.

And I continue, at my age, to spy on my wife's eyes!

2

The Easter vacation was painful. The weather was splendid: every day the same still-youthful sun and a few gilded clouds in the sky. Beneath the living-room windows, the rock garden was crowded with flowers and humming with bees.

In spite of the cool air, the girls swam in the pool, and their mother took two or three dips there. We went on a trip to Cape Cod, where we walked barefoot for a long time on the sand by an almost-unruffled sea.

Deep inside me, I no longer felt like a husband or father. I wasn't anything any more. An empty carcass. An automaton. Even my profession as a lawyer no longer interested me, and I saw too clearly the crookedness of my clients.

I was no better than they were. I hadn't made any attempt to keep Ray from dying in the snow at the foot of the cliff. The question was not to determine if my intervention would have changed his fate. Baldly put, the fact was that I had gone to sit on the red bench in the barn.

And gradually, smoking cigarettes and sheltering from the blizzard, I had felt a physical satisfaction, a warmth in my chest, at the idea that he was dead or dying.

That night, I had discovered that for the entire time I had known him I had never stopped envying and hating him.

The Hand

I was not the friend and neither was I the husband, the father, the citizen whose roles I had played. It was just a façade. The whited sepulchre of the scriptures.

What was left?

All through this vacation, which left me no escape, Isabel seized the chance to watch me more closely than ever.

It's as if my dismay delights her. It would never occur to her to help me. On the contrary, she manages diabolically to shove my head underwater.

For example, I tried two or three times to strike up a conversation with Mildred. She is beginning to be of an age to tackle serious subjects. Each time, Isabel's look immobilized me.

It seemed to say: 'Poor Donald . . . So, you don't see that you won't get anywhere, that your daughters have no connection with you?'

That connection, they'd had it when they were little. They had turned more readily to me than to their mother.

What image do they have of me now? I don't count any more. When they ask my advice, they don't wait for my answer.

I'm the fellow who spends his days in an office to earn the necessary money, a fellow who's growing old, whose face is beginning to look gaunt, who no longer knows how to laugh or play.

Does Isabel realize that she's running a risk? It's possible. I admit that I no longer know. I've had just about enough of interpreting her looks and seeing her staring at me.

With the children, she is playful, full of bright ideas. Every morning, she was the one who came up with an agreeable activity for the day. Agreeable for her and the girls, of course.

We made several excursions, including two hikes in the mountains. I hate excursions, picnics, long walks in Indian file during which you automatically pull up wild flowers along the path.

Isabel is radiant. At least when she's talking to our daughters. As soon as it's me she's looking at, me she's talking to, she turns back into a wall.

Does she intend to push me to the breaking point? She seems to want to go to the very limit and then, perhaps, she'll hold out her hand to me, murmuring:

'Poor Donald . . .'

I am not poor Donald. I am a man, fully a man, but that is something she will never admit.

The children must have noticed that tension. I sensed a certain wariness, a certain disapproval in my daughters, especially when I pour myself a drink.

And now, each time I offer Isabel a Scotch, she just happens to reply primly:

'No, thanks.'

I'm obliged to drink alone. I did not overdo it a single time. There has never been the slightest slippage in my behaviour. No stumbling over words, no nervous excitement.

My daughters still look at me, when I have a glass in my hand, as if I were committing a sin.

This is new. They've often seen us have a drink or

The Hand

two, their mother and I. Has Isabel said something to them?

There's a kind of complicity among them, the same complicity as between Isabel and my father. She has the gift of being sympathetic, of provoking admiration, confidence.

She is so good, so understanding!

She'd be better advised to take care, because one of these days I might reach my limit. I have set myself a course of conduct and am sticking to it, but I'm beginning to grit my teeth.

I did not drive the girls back to Litchfield, leaving this chore to my wife. On purpose. So that she could cook up her schemes with them at her leisure. I defied her, basically.

'You mustn't pay attention to your father's strange behaviour, children. He's going through a difficult phase . . . Ray's accident really shook him, and his nerves have not recovered yet . . .'

'Why does he drink, Mommy?'

She could tell them that I don't drink more than any of our friends. She definitely doesn't do that.

'Because of his nerves, as I said. To steady himself.'

'Sometimes, he looks at us as if he barely knows us . . .'

'I know. He shuts himself up inside . . . I spoke to Dr Warren about that, and he went to see him.'

'Dad is sick?'

'It's not an illness, properly speaking . . . It's in his mind. He gets these ideas . . .'

'Is it what they call a nervous breakdown?'

'Perhaps . . . It's like that. It happens often, at his age . . .'

Is that how all three of them talk about me? I'd swear to it. I can just hear them. Isabel's soft, indulgent voice as she bestows upon the children the limpidity of her gaze . . .

How reassuring it is to be looked at like that! You feel as if you were diving into a fresh, cool and generous soul that is immune to the passing years.

I'm furious. At the office, my secretary is beginning to watch me uneasily as well. If this continues, everyone will start feeling sorry for me.

Sorry, or afraid?

I can feel Higgins' confusion. For this old rogue, life is simple. It's every man for himself. Anything goes, as long as it's legal. And there are a thousand normal ways of getting around the law.

It's his job. He practises law with a quiet effrontery, without any qualms of conscience.

Lieutenant Olsen passed me at the wheel of his police car when I was on my way to the post office, and he gave me a desultory wave. Does what happened to Ray still bother him? His kind, when they get an idea in their heads . . .

Fine! So what! I telephoned Mona, from the office. Openly. My secretary and even Higgins could hear what I was saying, because except when someone is with a client we usually leave our doors open.

At first, since the phone rang a long time, I was afraid that she hadn't come back from Long Island, where she had gone to spend a few days with friends who have a

The Hand

place out there, with horses and a yacht. I don't know them. She didn't tell me their name, and I didn't ask.

They had many friends, she and Ray. She'd already had lots of them before meeting him. Often, when we were walking in the streets, people would greet her more or less familiarly, some of them calling out:

'Mona, hello!'

Since I am with her, I also wave, clumsily, without asking any questions. Occasionally she'll tell me, as if it explained everything, 'That's Harris . . .' or else, 'That's Helen . . .'

Harris who? Helen who? People known, probably, in the worlds of theatre, film or television. Ray spent much of his time, with the Millers, on budgets for television shows. It had become his specialty and was probably the reason why he asked his wife not to do such work any more, which would have put him in an awkward position.

But now? Won't Mona feel like working again? She hasn't spoken to me about it. Our intimacy belongs to a different domain. There is a whole part of her life that is unknown to me.

'Hello, Mona? . . . It's Donald, yes.'

'How was your vacation?'

'Not good . . . And you? . . . On Long Island?'

'A little crazy . . . I didn't have a moment to myself . . . Every day, more friends would arrive, even ten or twenty at a time . . .'

'Did you go out riding?'

'I even took a tumble, luckily without hurting myself.'

'Any sailing?'

'Twice, I'm all tanned . . .'

'Are you free tomorrow?'

'Wait, what day is it? . . .'

'Wednesday.'

'Eleven o'clock?'

'I'll be at your place at eleven.'

That was our hour, when she was at her toilette, the time I enjoyed the most, with a feeling of abandon, of complete intimacy.

The next day the sky was clear, a lavender-blue, with those golden clouds, over the mountains, that seem to have been put there once and for all, as if in a painting. Only on certain evenings do those clouds disappear or stretch out in long, almost red bands.

I drove along happily.

'You'll be back this evening?'

'Probably . . .'

Does Isabel wonder why I stay overnight in New York less and less frequently? Does she suppose that something has changed between Mona and me?

Or else that I'm beginning to get a grip on myself, to avoid compromising myself any further?

I hate her.

I looked for a parking place for a long time before entering the building on 56th Street. I hurried to the elevator. I rang the doorbell. The door opened immediately, and there was Mona in a lightweight tailored suit of emerald green, as well as a little white hat tilted over her left ear.

The Hand

I was speechless. She was surprised, as if she hadn't expected to produce such an effect.

'My poor Donald...'

I don't like being poor Donald, even for her. I could only take her in my arms when she welcomed me in her peignoir.

'Disappointed?'

Still, we kissed. It's true that her face was tanned, which helps to change her.

'This morning I felt like taking a walk with you in Central Park... Do you mind?'

My face cleared. It was a nice idea. The weather was just right. We had not yet celebrated spring together.

'Would you like to drink something before we go?'

'No...'

She turned towards the kitchen.

'I won't be back for lunch, Janet...'

'Fine, madam...'

'If anyone phones for me, I'll be back at around two or three o'clock.'

It wasn't the first time we had strolled along the sidewalks, but the air was lighter than usual, the sunshine quite cheerful, the sky of an astonishing purity behind the skyscrapers.

In front of the Plaza, we saw the scattering of carriages that await tourists and lovers. For one second, I thought about climbing into one of them. Mona was paying no attention. Her hand was resting on my arm, lightly, without insistence.

'How are Mildred and Cecilia?'

'Quite well. They spent their vacation with us. We took several hikes and even went to Cape Cod . . .'

We were heading slowly towards the lake where Ray and I used to skate in the winter when we were students, treating ourselves to a night in New York.

I felt a stronger pressure on my arm from the white-gloved hand.

'I must speak to you, Donald . . .'

It's funny. It wasn't in my back, but in my head that I felt a cold rush and I said, in a voice I hardly recognized:

'Yes?'

'We're old pals, aren't we? You're the best pal I've ever had . . .'

Mothers were watching over children toddling about. A ragged man, who had nothing more to hope for, was sleeping on a bench, so wretched that you had to look away.

We were walking slowly. Head down, I was looking at the gravel passing by under my shoes.

'Do you know John Falk?'

I'd read his name somewhere. He was familiar enough, but at that moment I couldn't place him. I did not try. I awaited the verdict. Because all this was going to end in a verdict, sure as fate.

'He's the producer of the three best series on CBS.'

I had nothing to say. I could hear the noises in the park, the birds, the children's voices, the traffic along Fifth Avenue. I saw ducks smoothing their feathers on the lawn and others swimming, tracing triangular wakes.

The Hand

'We've known each other for a long time, he and I . . . He's forty . . . He's been divorced for three years and has a little girl . . .'

She added quickly, to get it over with: 'We intend to get married, Donald . . .'

I said nothing. I couldn't have said a thing.

'Are you sad?'

I almost laughed, because of that word. Sad? I was utterly crushed. I was . . . It was beyond explanation. There was nothing left any more, that's all.

Up until then, I had had something left, I had Mona left, even though our liaison wasn't a real one, even though there was no question of love between us.

I saw the boudoir again, the movement of her lips towards the red lipstick, the peignoir she'd let drop down behind her . . .

'Please forgive me . . .'

'For what?'

'For hurting you . . . I can tell I'm hurting you . . .'

'A little,' I said finally, using a ridiculously feeble word myself.

'I should have talked to you about it earlier . . . I've been hesitating for a month now . . . I didn't know what to decide. It even occurred to me to have you meet John and to ask your advice . . .'

We did not look at each other. She had thought of that. That's why she had led me into the park. Walking among others out for a stroll, you're obliged to control yourself.

'When do you plan on . . .'

'Oh! Not right away . . . There are the legal delays to observe . . . We'll also have to find another apartment, because Monique will live with us.'

So, the little girl was named Monique.

'Her father obtained custody of her. He absolutely adores her . . .'

Of course! Of course! And in the meantime, was this John Falk, since that was his name, already sleeping in the big bed at 56th Street?

Probably. Like friends, as Mona says. No: those two, not like friends, since they were going to be married.

'I'm dreadfully sorry, Donald . . . We'll stay good friends, won't we?'

And then what?

'I spoke to John about you.'

'Did you tell him the truth?'

'Why not? He doesn't take me for a virgin . . .'

The word shocked me, spoken aloud, suddenly, in the middle of the sunny park. I am not in love with Mona, I swear it. No one will believe me, and yet it is the truth.

It isn't only 'woman' that she represents to me, it's . . .

It's just everything! And it's nothing! It must be nothing, since she could cut the thread so easily.

She was going to go back to television work. I would see her on my screen, back there in Brentwood, sitting next to Isabel in the library.

'I thought that we might lunch together somewhere, wherever you like . . .'

'Is he the one who'll be calling between two and three?'

'Yes.'
'He knows I'm in town?'
'Yes.'
'He knows you've taken me to Central Park?'
'No . . . I thought of that while getting dressed.'
Not while getting dressed in front of me, with her quiet immodesty. While getting dressed alone. In Janet's company, rather.
'It's going to be difficult, Janet . . .'
'He'll understand, madam.'
'Of course he'll understand, but I'm still going to make him suffer . . .'
'If we had to give up everything that makes others suffer . . .'
Mona lit a cigarette, glancing at me out of the corner of her eye, and I smiled at her. Well, it was meant to be a smile.
'You'll come to see me?'
'I don't know . . .'
That was no. I had nothing in common with Mr and Mrs Falk. Nor with the little girl named Monique.
Girls, I had two of them.
The sun seemed to me to be shining harder than in previous days. We went inside the bar at the Plaza.
'Two double martinis . . .'
I hadn't asked her what she was having. Perhaps, with Falk, she drank something else? For the last time, I observed our tradition.
'Cheers, Donald . . .'
'Cheers, Mona . . .'

That was the hardest part. Saying her name, I almost, stupidly, burst into tears. Those two syllables . . .

What's the point of trying to explain? I saw myself in the mirror, between the bottles.

'Where would you like to have lunch?'

She left the choice to me. It was my day. My last day. So it was important that everything go as well as possible.

'We can go to our little French restaurant . . .'

I shook my head. I preferred a crowd, a place without memories.

We had lunch at the Plaza, and the main room was full. I suggested foie gras, almost derisively, and she agreed. Then lobster. A gala luncheon!

'Would you like crêpes Suzette?'

'Why not?'

She thought to please me by accepting. I knew that she was checking the clock from time to time.

I didn't hold it against her. She had given me what she could give me, kindly, with a warm, animal tenderness, and I was the one left in her debt.

At one point, I saw her hand flat on the tablecloth just as I had seen it on the parquet, that January night, and I felt the same desire to reach for that hand . . .

'Be brave, Donald . . .'

She had guessed.

'If you knew how this hurts me . . .' she sighed.

Then we walked to her place. I wanted to stammer, 'One last time, yes?'

It seemed to me it would be easier, afterwards . . .

The Hand

I looked up at the windows of the fourth-floor apartment; I entered the lobby.

'Goodbye, Donald . . .'

'Farewell, Mona . . .'

She threw herself into my arms and with no thought of her make-up gave me a very long, very deep kiss.

'I'll never forget,' she panted.

Then, very quickly, feverishly, she opened the elevator door.

3

That was one month ago, and my hatred of Isabel has only grown. As was to be expected, she understood right away, seeing me come home. I wasn't even drunk. I hadn't felt the need to drink.

Driving home along the Taconic Parkway, I was drawing a kind of mental picture of the life awaiting me, from waking to bedtime, with the movements, the comings and goings from one room to another, the post office, my office, my secretary, who would soon be leaving us, lunch, my office, my clients, the mail, the glass of Scotch before dinner, the meal together, the television, a newspaper or a book . . .

I did not omit a single detail. On the contrary, I itemized them carefully, as if in Indian ink.

It was an engraving, an album of engravings, the day of a man named Donald Dodd.

Isabel said nothing, I'd known that in advance. I had also foreseen that she would feel no pity and I would not have wanted any. She did manage, however, to hide her triumph, to keep her eyes impassive.

Then, over the following days, she went back to observing me, the way one observes a patient, wondering if he will die or recover.

I was not dying. My mechanism functioned without a hitch. I had been well trained. My movements remained

The Hand

the same, as did the words I spoke, my behaviour at the table, the office, in my armchair in the evening.

Why was she continuing to spy on me? What was she hoping for?

She wasn't satisfied, I could feel that. She needed something else. My complete annihilation?

I was not annihilated. The following week, Higgins was surprised not to see me go off to New York. My secretary as well.

The week after that, he was relieved, understanding that what he must have called my affair was over.

And so, I was going to re-enter the world of upright, normal people. I had had a kind of moral flu from which I was quite slowly recovering.

Higgins behaved kindly towards me, encouragingly, coming several times a day to my office to speak to me about matters he would once have reported to me with a few words in passing.

Did not my interest in life require rekindling? I met Warren, too, at the post office, where lots of people come to pick up their morning mail. Remembering the reception I'd given him the last time, he hesitated to come over but finally made up his mind.

'You're looking well, Donald . . .'

Of course!

I avoided going to New York, even when it was useful. I tried to arrange everything on the phone and through correspondence. One day, when my presence there was indispensable, I asked Higgins to go instead, and he hastened to accept.

That meant that I was cured, or almost.

If they could have known, every last one of them, how I hated her! But she was the only one who knew.

For I had understood. I had sought the meaning of her look for a long time. I had made various suppositions without thinking of the quite simple truth.

I had detached myself from her. I had broken the circle. I was out of her reach.

For that, she would never forgive me. I was her possession, like the house, the girls, Brentwood and our daily routine.

I had escaped and I was looking at her from outside, I was looking at her with hatred, because she had possessed me for too long, because she had suffocated me, because she had kept me from living.

All right! I had chosen her. I have admitted that and I repeat it. That was not reason enough. But she was still the living image, there, right next to me, in the bed next to mine, of all that I had begun to hate.

I could not take it out on the whole world and its institutions. I could not spit their truths and mine into the faces of millions of human beings.

She was there.

As Mona had been there, for a moment, to do her best representing life.

Isabel knew all that. The qualities attributed to her by others either did exist or they didn't, but there is one that she had to the supreme degree: the ability to rummage through the souls of others, and mine in particular.

The Hand

She was now doing so to her heart's content, searching all day long, sensing that there was nothing left but a façade and that if this cracked, there would be nothing left.

To see me reduced to nothing! What a marvellous feeling! What matchless revenge.

'It was so good of Isabel . . .'

To live with a man like me, obviously. To put up with what she's had to put up with these past months.

'He didn't bother to hide . . .'

In the evening, I was having more and more trouble getting to sleep and, after an hour lying motionless, I sometimes went into the bathroom to take a sleeping pill.

She knew this. I'm convinced that she avoided falling asleep before I did to enjoy my insomnia, to hear the mysterious rustling of my thoughts.

It wasn't so much Mona's face that haunted me, and I'm not sure if Isabel had guessed that. It was the bench. The red-painted bench. The din of the storm and the door banging in a steady rhythm, the snow that, each time, blew a little farther into the barn.

Ray, with Patricia, in the bathroom. I would have liked to be in his place. I wanted Patricia. One day, when the Ashbridges came back from Florida . . .

Ray was dead. His apartment in Sutton Place that had cost him so much, with its aggressive luxury he had flaunted so ironically, had been dismantled and was now inhabited by a film star.

His wife, Mona, was going to become Mrs Falk. A friend of his. A producer with whom he'd done business.

He had thought about suicide, and death had arrived without him having to lift a finger.

The lucky stiff!

My father kept publishing his *Citizen* and writing articles for two or three dozen elderly readers.

Had Isabel told him that it was over with Mona? Had he been glad like the others, telling himself that I was returning at last to the fold?

I could not bear her eyes any more. I would sometimes look away. I had already stopped brushing her cheek in the morning and evening. She had not mentioned it. I may be wrong, but I think there might have been a glimmer of hope in her eyes.

If I was reacting like that, wasn't it because I'd been affected? Indifferent, I would have continued the routine without noticing anything, without finding it painful.

It was practically a declaration of war. I was becoming her enemy, an enemy who lived in the house, next to her, ate at the same table, slept in the same room.

The month of May had begun gloriously, with days as warm as summertime. I was already wearing my cotton suit, my straw hat.

At the office, the air conditioning was on. Mornings, before I went there, I would dive into the pool and I did the same after coming home in the evening.

Isabel had adopted other hours; not once had she been in the pool at the same time as I was.

'Have you a lot of work?'

'Enough to keep me busy and pay our bills . . .'

The house, which we owned, was worth around 60,000

The Hand

dollars. Many years earlier, I had taken out life insurance for 100,000 dollars, which had seemed an enormous sum at the time, because I was only just starting out.

Every year, I bought a few stocks.

If I were to go off alone, without saying anything, to melt into the anonymous swarm, neither my wife nor my daughters would find themselves in financial difficulties.

Go where? At night, in my bed, I sometimes thought of the man in Central Park, the one sleeping on a bench at noon, his mouth open, in view of passers-by.

He needed no one. Nor did he need to pretend. He did not worry about people's opinions, good manners, what must be done or not done.

And whenever the police picked him up, he could go back to his snoring.

I wasn't obliged to take such a deep plunge. I could have . . .

But why? I had already escaped, *in situ*, in a way. I had cut the strings. The marionette was still moving, but no one was manipulating it any longer.

Except Isabel. She was there, lying on her back in her bed, silent, listening to my breathing, guessing at my phantoms. She was waiting for the moment when, giving up, I would get up to go and take my two sleeping tablets. These days, I needed two. Soon, I would need three. Was it more serious than drinking?

I had been tempted to drink. Sometimes, when I looked at the liquor cabinet, I wanted to grab the first bottle at hand and drink straight from it, no doubt like the guy in Central Park.

Exactly what was she waiting for? For me to begin screaming with rage? Or pain? Or . . .

I was not screaming, and so she provoked me. When I would get up to take my tablets, she might ask me in a soft voice, as if speaking to a child or a sick person:

'You're not sleeping, Donald?'

She could see that I wasn't sleeping, right? I wasn't a sleepwalker. So, why ask me that question?

'Maybe you should go and see Warren . . .'

Oh sure! Sure! She was trying to convince me that I was ill. She must have been convincing others, too.

'He's going through a difficult period, I don't know why . . . Dr Warren doesn't understand at all . . . He believes that it's a mental problem . . .'

The guy who has a mental illness . . .

I could get the picture perfectly, in people's minds, the sympathetic faces. I had already been the guy who had a mistress and might soon get divorced. Now I was the husband who is getting weird.

'Just yesterday, I passed him in the street, and he didn't recognize me . . .'

As if I tried to recognize the faceless people who go by!

She was depraved. I'm not the one who is busy drawing up a dossier. She is. Patiently, in minute detail, the way you weave a tapestry. She does sometimes do exactly that. Two of the living-room chairs are upholstered in her handiwork.

She weaves . . . She weaves . . .

The Hand

And she watches me ferociously while waiting for me to crack up.
Isn't she afraid?

4

I am calm, with a lucidity that I believe few men have attained. This is not a speech for the defence. I am not looking to exonerate myself. I am not writing this for anyone in particular.

It is three o'clock in the morning. Today is 27 May, and the day was stiflingly hot. Nothing out of the ordinary happened. I had a lot of work at the office and I completed it conscientiously. By the way, I now know that my secretary is pregnant; after a few months' leave, however, she intends to come back to work.

That is no longer of any importance to me, but it will be to Higgins.

Last night, as soon as I went to bed, my sheets became damp, because we don't have air conditioning. The complicated arrangement of the rooms in the house makes it almost impossible to install.

At half past midnight I was not asleep and went to take my two tablets. She did not speak to me but she followed me with her wide-open eyes. She literally caught me right when I got out of bed, watched me head for the bathroom and, when I came out, there were her eyes, waiting to lead me back to bed.

Sleep did not come. The tablets have lost their power.

The Hand

I don't dare increase the dose without Warren's advice, and I'm not eager to see Warren at the moment.

She is lying on her back. So am I. My eyes are open, because it's even worse when I close them and I can hear my heart beat.

I could, if I listened hard, hear hers.

Two hours have passed. It's unbelievable how many images can scroll through a brain in two hours. The one I saw most again was the hand, on the living-room floor.

I wonder why that hand has taken on such importance. I have held the entire body in my arms. I know it in its most minute details, in all kinds of light.

No! It's the hand that comes back to me, on the floor, near my mattress. I turned on the bedside lamp, got up and went to the bathroom.

'Don't you feel well, Donald?'

Because I don't usually get up twice.

I swallowed another tablet, then one more, to have done with this insomnia.

When I went back into the bedroom, she was sitting on her bed and looking at me.

Hadn't she almost reached her goal? Hadn't she just heard the first crack?

I did not think anything over. The action was spontaneous, and I performed it calmly. Opening the night-table drawer, I grabbed the revolver.

She was still looking at me, without frowning. She was still defying me.

Wasn't my first thought to point the gun at myself, as Ray had been tempted to do?

Probably. I wouldn't dare swear to it.

She looked at the short barrel, then at my face. What I am sure of is this: a smile flickered over her face, and there was, in her blue eyes, a gleam of triumph.

I shot at the chest and felt no emotion. The eyes were still staring at me, motionless, so then I fired two more shots.

In those eyes.

I will telephone Lieutenant Olsen to tell him what has happened. People will talk about a crime of passion, and there will certainly be questions about Mona, who has nothing to do with it.

They'll have me examined by a psychiatrist.

What difference will it make to me to be in prison, since I have been there all my life?

I've just called Olsen. He did not seem too surprised. He said, 'I'm coming right away . . .'

And he added:

'Above all, don't do anything foolish . . .'

Betty

I

'Would you like something to eat?'

She shook her head. The voice sounded unnatural, as if someone were speaking to her through a window-pane.

'Mind you, when I say something to eat, that means rabbit because, as you can see from looking around, today is rabbit day. Too bad if you don't like it. When it's cod day, there's only cod . . .'

It was strange hearing the syllables follow on from one another, connecting, forming words, sentences, rather like yarn that gradually transforms itself into lace, or wool into a knitted sock.

That image of a knitted sock, half-finished, dangling from its three needles, made her smile. It was surprising to think of such a common object here, opposite a man who visibly prided himself on his sophistication and who constructed his sentences so meticulously. He was dressed in grey. He was all grey: his eyes, his hair, his skin, even his tie and shirt. There wasn't a dash of colour. And, listening to him, she had just imagined a sock, not grey but black, because she had only ever seen black socks being knitted, a very long time ago, in the Vendée, when she was not yet fourteen. And now she was twenty-eight . . .

'One gets used to it.'

She almost asked him:

'Used to what?'

Because her mind was wandering in several directions at once. She couldn't grasp the connection between what one needed to get used to and the woollen sock, forgetting that the sock was in her memory and not in that of her companion. All the same, the man must have been able to read the question on her face because he continued undeterred, with touching diligence:

'Liking or not liking.'

Liking what? She had forgotten the rabbit and the cod. Once again, her eyes met those of an American officer sitting on a stool at the bar. He kept staring at her and she wondered where she had seen him before.

'Wednesday is cassoulet day, although it would be more accurate to say cassoulet night.'

From her companion's wan smile she guessed that there was a subtle distinction and she wished she could comprehend what he meant.

'Are you partial to it?'

Partial? This conversation, which she no longer understood at all, was becoming increasingly absurd. Everything was confused. But too bad. She said solemnly:

'Yes.'

She had no idea what he was talking about exactly, but she didn't wish to be rude. She didn't know this overdressed man with a fascinatingly penetrating gaze. She wasn't aware of his name. Even so, she was actually closer to him than she had ever been to anyone else, because, apart from him, there was nothing left in the world.

Unbelievable as it seemed, that was the way things

were. This would last as long as it would last – an hour or a night, or longer. And that thought made her smile. A smile which, for the time being, was without bitterness. He was very polite. In the car, he hadn't tried to fondle her and he hadn't asked her a single question.

Because she remembered the car, the soft, cool leather of the seats and the rain on the windscreen, and the misted-up windows on which she idly drew pictures with her fingertips. In the city, she recalled the lights concentrated into each drop of water, then the headlamps on the motorway. She could have described in the minutest detail everything that had happened since, as if before an investigating magistrate or a doctor . . .

Since when? Since the bar in Rue de Ponthieu, in any case. Casting her mind back further was too unpleasant and she refused to do so. She didn't want to ruin something that had been so difficult to achieve and was even more difficult to hold on to: that state of precise balance, or rather of perfect vacillation, which was hers for the time being, a pleasant floating feeling, relaxing, almost blissful.

Not blissful in the usual sense of the word, naturally. She didn't feel like laughing or dancing or telling stories. The thrilling thing was that she knew nothing, nothing of what would come next, not that night, or tomorrow or the following days, and she didn't care one bit.

'I'm surprised that people who eat animals every day don't wonder . . .'

She listened, gazing at the face of the man, which she saw as if through a magnifying glass, but, despite her efforts, other thoughts were going round inside her head.

Before leaving Rue de Ponthieu, she should have asked her companion to wait for her for a moment so she could go down to the toilet, where the attendant would probably have had a pair of stockings to sell her. Most of them do.

It upset her to have a ladder on each leg. For the first time in her life, she hadn't changed her stockings for ages. Two days? Three days? She would rather not be reminded. Nor had she taken a bath, which would bother her later. Would there be a bathtub, and would he let her use it?

She glimpsed faces, close up or far away, hair, eyes, noses, mouths moving, and she could hear voices that didn't always come from those mouths. She tried to fathom, without much success, what kind of place she was in. Without thinking, she grabbed her glass of whisky:

'Cheers!'

There was a blonde woman, a barmaid with big breasts like she had so desperately wanted when she was a little girl. There was also an African in a white hat who would appear, smiling, sometimes through one door, sometimes through the other, whom everyone seemed to know. There was the American officer propped up at the bar, clutching his glass and still staring at her.

Some people were eating and others were simply drinking, some in groups, others alone, staring straight ahead in silence.

'Has it never occurred to you that, as a result, we are full of animals?'

She was conscious that she was drunk. She had been drunk for a long time but, for now, she was taking advantage of a promising punter. She didn't feel unwell, nor did she feel like vomiting or crying. Was her companion drunk too? Had he already been drinking before they met at Le Ponthieu?

He had simply walked in from the dark street, with raindrops on the tweed of his clothes. There too, he was a regular: you could tell from the way he looked around and greeted the bartender with a wave.

She'd been sitting on a stool and he asked permission to sit next to her.

'Be my guest.'

His hands were long and white, very dry, and he fiddled with them all the time as if they were foreign objects.

He didn't know where she had come from or what she had drunk beforehand. Maybe he hadn't noticed the ladders in her stockings? At all events, he couldn't guess that she hadn't taken a bath, that she hadn't even been able to wash after the man that afternoon.

They weren't in Rue de Ponthieu any more. She didn't know where they were. She had only recognized Avenue de Versailles, where she'd half glimpsed her mother's house, then they'd taken the motorway and turned right on to a muddy track. On alighting from the car, she caught the smell of wet leaves and jumped over a puddle. She still had water in her left shoe.

They were in a restaurant, because people were eating. It was also a bar. There was muffled music from a turntable that no one was listening to. And yet she had the impression that this wasn't an establishment like any other and that everyone was staring at her.

All those people, including the American officer, seemed to know one another, even though, and especially, because they weren't conversing, and the owner was going from one table to the next, sitting down for a moment, he too keeping his eyes on her. Her hair wasn't dishevelled. She didn't have a smudge on her nose. Her suit was more than decent. Her stockings weren't, but that happened to all women.

Maybe she should have been introduced, approved? Or maybe she had to pass some test?

'Everything all right, doctor?'

The owner, this time, but remaining on his feet, was addressing her companion, who batted his eyelids without bothering to reply and glanced again at his hands placed flat on the table. Then he began methodically to scratch the skin between his fingers.

'You're not listening to me . . .'

He was talking to her, because the owner had already moved off.

'I assure you I'm listening.'

'What was I saying?'

'That as a result of eating animals . . .'

He stared fixedly at her and she wondered if that was the correct answer. She must have annoyed him, because he rose to his feet, mumbling:

'Would you excuse me for a moment?'

He strode towards one of the doors. The owner took the opportunity to come over and collect the two empty glasses.

'The same again?'

Betty

She had the feeling she'd seen him before as well. It was a fixation, this evening. Not only when it came to people, but also things. All this reminded her of something. But when? Where?

'Is this the first time you've been to Le Trou?'

'Yes.'

She didn't know that this place was called Le Trou and she wondered whether naming it 'the pit' was a prank, or a trap, and whether she'd been wrong to reply seriously.

'Have you known the doctor long?'

'No.'

'Do you not wish to eat?'

'No, thank you. I'm not hungry.'

'Make yourself at home. Everyone's at home here.'

She smiled to thank him for speaking to her and, for appearance's sake, drank half of her glass, opened her bag and powdered her nose. Her face was puffy. She preferred not to study it in the mirror of her compact, which at the same time reflected a very dark-haired, and above all very tall, woman sitting behind her.

'When you know the place better, you won't be able to stay away.'

Her companion, looking strangely intense, had resumed his seat opposite her.

'Forgive me for leaving you on your own.'

She tried, without any success, to hear what the people behind her were saying, convinced they were talking about her. She in turn rose, murmuring:

'Would you excuse me?'

On reaching the toilet, she found herself face to face

with the African, who stared at her and laughed a great silent laugh, as if it were funny meeting her suddenly in a narrow passage. He didn't do anything to her, however, and stepped aside, laughing even harder. She glimpsed a filthy, messy kitchen. A door that didn't close properly divided it from the toilet, whose skylight had a view over the countryside.

She was beginning to feel impatient, for no particular reason. Perhaps also a little afraid. It was time for another drink to keep herself afloat, before she was overwhelmed by anxiety or sadness.

When she went back into the restaurant, before even sitting down, she downed the rest of her whisky.

'I'm thirsty!' she sighed.

Her companion called:

'Joseph! Bring madame a drink.'

'Same again?'

She said yes.

'For you too, doctor?'

'If you like.'

Once more, she wanted things to move fast, wanted to be lying down, alone or otherwise, anywhere, and to close her eyes. She found the music and the din exhausting. She had had enough of seeing faces, eyes staring at her as if she were a freak or an interloper.

'Why do you keep scratching?'

She was definitely one step behind.

'Me?' she asked in surprise, after what felt like an age.

Perhaps she'd scratched the back of her hand without realizing. But the man seized her hand with a contained eagerness and his face suddenly lit up with childlike jubilation.

'It's here, isn't it?'

He pointed to an invisible spot.

'Yes . . . I suppose . . .'

'Under your skin?'

Now he was frightening her and again she replied yes, so as not to vex him.

'Does it crawl?'

'Does what crawl?'

'Does it move around on the surface or deep down? It's very important, because they all have their own characteristics. I know some that . . .'

'What are you talking about?'

'Worms.'

'What worms?'

'So you're not aware that you have worms under your skin, all sorts of worms, tiny ones and huge ones, fat and thin, wriggly and docile? You probably have other little creatures that are much more inconspicuous. I'll show them to you and explain their nature . . .'

She could see close up the thin, pallid face, the smooth grey hair and the eyes almost the same grey, and it suddenly dawned on her that there was something abnormal about him. She wanted to withdraw her hand; she tried, but he was gripping it firmly.

'You're going to see how I hunt down these creatures that torment us so diabolically . . .'

With his free hand, he took from his pocket a gold toothpick with a sharp point.

'Don't be afraid. I've had a lot of practice.'

A voice said:

'Leave her alone, doctor.'

He still tried to prick her skin.

'I told you to leave her alone.'

'I'm just going to remove a little worm that's bothering her and . . .'

The owner took another step forward and placed an amiable hand on the doctor's shoulder.

'Come with me for a moment.'

'In a minute. She asked me—'

'Come.'

'Why?'

'A private message.'

The grey man looked up, hesitant.

'Are you afraid I'll hurt her? You're forgetting that I . . .'

His smile was bitter, resigned, even though he was tall and the owner short and stocky. A second later, he was on his feet, toothpick in hand and, humiliated, he allowed himself to be nudged towards the back door.

Perturbed and anxious, Betty looked at her hand, drained her glass, then, with a shrug, that of her companion too. She still didn't know who he was. She knew nothing. She no longer knew anything and was beginning to feel panic-stricken. The American officer at the bar was watching her, unsmiling, morose.

'Waiter!'

'Yes, madame.'

'Give me a drink.'

This time, he didn't ask her if she wanted the same

again. She wanted it fast. The faster the better. The images became fuzzy. There was ginger hair, for example, which might have been very close to her or at the back of the room, and she didn't know if it belonged to a woman or to a man. She struggled to focus her eyes and then she saw frozen, indifferent faces that could have been wax figures.

People resented her but she couldn't understand why.

She must have done something wrong, broken the rules of the establishment.

How could she have done otherwise, since she didn't know what those rules were?

Why didn't anyone explain them to her?

It wasn't her drinking that was causing offence. The proof was that the owner himself had called Joseph the first time, and others were drinking as much if not more than her. A young woman with mousey hair on the corner of a banquette was deathly pale, her head lolling back, and her companion, who was holding her hand romantically, did not appear to be paying any attention to her.

What would happen if Betty began to shout? She was tempted to do so, to find out, to stir things up, so that someone would take notice of her, not just stare at her.

And supposing she blurted out everything she'd done over the past three days? Would those faces finally take on a human expression? Would there be compassion, or simply a flicker of interest, in all those fish eyes?

Her hand trembled as she rummaged in her bag.

'Waiter!'

'Yes, madame. The same again?'

Which proved once more that it wasn't the drinking that was the problem!

'Do you have any cigarettes?'

'One moment.'

An engine could be heard outside, a car that sounded as if its wheels were stuck in the mud. A voice said:

'Mario will drive him home.'

Betty didn't realize at first that those words were addressed to her, because they were spoken behind her back. Almost at the same time, she became aware of a woman's hand offering her a cigarette.

She half turned. The tall brunette, who had a white streak in her hair, was standing there with one hand on the chair where the doctor had sat.

'May I?' she asked.

She had a husky voice and grey pearls around her neck. Perhaps the last whisky had been one too many, because the images were becoming less and less clear, like that afternoon in the hotel room, even before the man had put his clothes back on. She hadn't seen him leave. He could have taken her handbag, her clothes. He could have strangled her, and she would have been incapable of giving his description. Of course, if she'd been strangled. But . . .

She was getting muddled. The sounds were all confused. Her body, on the chair, started swaying and she was unable to stop it. If she swayed a little harder, she would fall on to the floor amid the feet and cigarette butts. Then she would be very dirty indeed!

'Did he frighten you?'

Who? Why? It was as if she had already forgotten the man in grey.

'He's a charming fellow, a decent man, even.'

The woman had brought her glass with her.

'Cheers.'

'Cheers.'

'I hope you realized that he takes drugs? When he left you earlier, it was to get his fix, and that wasn't the first time this evening. Do you know him?'

'No.'

'His name is Bernard. He used to be a doctor in Versailles.'

Doctor in Versailles. She could still hear, still grasp the meaning of the words. What eluded her was what those words had to do with her. Why was she being told this, earnestly, as if it was important or dramatic? The woman was bound to have noticed the ladders in her stockings. Perhaps she'd also seen that she wasn't very clean under her make-up?

She had lovely brown squirrel eyes and her low, gravelly voice was comforting.

Betty tried to close her eyes so as to concentrate, but had to open them again immediately because everything began to spin.

'I'm thirsty . . .' she murmured.

The woman gave her a glass, her own or another, who cared?

'Have you eaten?'

'I think so.'

'Are you not hungry?'

'No.'

'Would you like to get some air?'

'No.'

She couldn't, because she was incapable of walking. If she tried to stand up, she was certain to fall over. She would fall over anyway, sooner or later, but she would rather it didn't happen when she was still conscious.

What did it matter where she came round, in hospital or elsewhere? And it would be even better for everyone if she didn't come round at all. She truly thought that. She wasn't sad. She had long gone beyond sadness.

'Alan has taken quite a fancy to you. He hasn't taken his eyes off you since you arrived, and he doesn't realize that he's on his eighth Scotch.'

Betty tried to smile, like a well-bred person listening politely.

'I can hear Mario coming back.'

She too heard an engine, then the slamming of a car door and the patter of rain during the short time the restaurant door remained open. In what car . . . There was a problem. If Mario had taken the doctor's car . . .

'Did you manage to get him into bed?'

'His wife helped me.'

'He didn't protest too much?'

'He's already counting the rabbits that have invaded his bedroom.'

She saw that they exchanged a glance that concerned her, and that the brunette gave a slight shrug as if to say it wasn't serious. It didn't bother her and she didn't try to guess what they were plotting.

She repeated, for no reason:

'Rabbits . . .'

And, thinking it was a question, they explained:

'When he's like this, he sees all sorts of animals around him, not to mention the little creatures teeming beneath his skin, which he tries to remove with his toothpick. When he was still practising, towards the end, he would tell his patients that all their diseases came from those invisible creepy-crawlies, which he was convinced he could rid them of . . .'

Who? What? Rid them of what? It was too late now. One drink less, or one less sip perhaps, and she could have kept up her earlier elation.

She was hurting. Nowhere! All over! She was dirty. She was miserable. And there was no one, no one in the world. She had signed. She had given them away. Not even given away: sold, because she'd taken the cheque. A document in due form, the terms of which the notary had dictated over the telephone.

I the undersigned, Élisabeth Étamble . . .

She'd had to start again on another sheet, because at first she had written Betty.

I the undersigned, Élisabeth Étamble, née Fayet, aged 28, of no known profession, residing at 22A, Avenue de Wagram, in Paris, hereby recognize that . . .

How could she not have recognized, since it was true and she had been caught red-handed?

Her glass was empty again. It was always empty. She cast around for the waiter, slightly ashamed to be ordering a drink in front of this stranger.

'I need to get sloshed,' she explained.

She added, because of the vulgar expression she'd used:

'Excuse me.'

'I know how it feels.'

She knew nothing. Never mind.

'The same again, waiter.'

And she suddenly launched into a garbled explanation, missing out syllables the way a person misses a step on a staircase:

'Actually, I'd never met him before. We were introduced earlier by friends in a bar . . .'

They hadn't been introduced, any more than the man of that afternoon, or of the previous day. Why did she feel compelled to make things up? Because it was a woman sitting opposite her?

Anyway, the woman didn't believe her, it was obvious. She nodded as if in agreement, but it was out of politeness, because she had good manners.

The pale girl was asleep in her corner of the banquette, and her companion, who had managed to free his hand, was chatting with the owner and smoking a cigarette.

For Betty, things would not be so straightforward. First of all, there was no one to hold her hand. And secondly, she was going to be sick. It was just a matter of minutes, she knew. Her upper body swayed more and more, to the point where she surreptitiously gripped the table to steady herself.

Betty

'Do you live around here?'

She shook her head, taking care not to shake it too hard.

'In Paris?'

Not in Paris either, nor elsewhere. She lived nowhere. Why was this woman persisting? If she hadn't sat down at her table, the American would probably have come over. He must have a car waiting outside. He would have taken Betty somewhere where there was a bed. He might have questioned her too, but with him she'd have said whatever came into her head and he would have been sympathetic.

Besides, perhaps with him she wouldn't have been sick, if only out of human respect, and also because at last she would have had a bath.

She didn't know what time it was. She hadn't known the time for three days and three nights; daylight and darkness no longer had any meaning. It was all a blur.

The dark-haired woman facing her was talking in a low voice, and it sounded the same as prayers in a church.

'To your left, the bald man smoking a cigar is an English lord who has an estate in Louveciennes. Every night . . .'

This woman had to be twenty years older than her. She seemed to have lived a lot, known all sorts of people, especially strange characters.

'Madame!' she suddenly blurted out.

She hadn't planned it. She'd wanted to shout to her for help, say to her, for example:

'Hold me! . . . Do something . . .'

If only it could stop! If only she could stop thinking! If someone could hold her hand, make her sleep, watch over her while she slept, if only someone, some human being, could be there when she opened her eyes again.

Had she really spoken? Had sounds come out of her throat? She was almost certain she'd said:

'Madame!'

But no one asked any questions. No one asked anything. There was no surprise, no curiosity on the face opposite her. And yet she wasn't in a hospital or an asylum where you see patients sit up in bed to call for help, was she?

She was in a bar. Men and women were drinking. Although her vision was hazy, they were there, and the sounds of the glasses clinking, the music from the turntable and the voices were real.

Then it felt as if communication between her and the others had been cut off, that they couldn't hear her, or rather that, for some unknown reason, they didn't want to hear her.

She was among them, but her existence was no more visible than that afternoon, when she had been walking the streets. People just passed her by. Some brushed against her, sometimes jostling her, but not a single person noticed that she was a living being.

'Do you understand?'

She had written the letter, all the words that had been dictated to her. She had signed. She made an effort to write Élisabeth instead of Betty. She'd stuffed the cheque into her bag and it was probably still there. She had . . .

It was too much. She couldn't go on. Her hand groped for the glass on the table. Clumsily, she knocked it on to the floor and it shattered on the red tiles.

She began:

'I'm so . . .'

She wanted to say:

'I'm sorry.'

Instead, she clenched her fists and howled:

'No! No! No! And no!'

It was over. O-ver! There's a limit to everything. She was conscious that everyone was looking at her now, but she could see no one in particular, nothing but a sea of expressionless faces.

'You don't care, do you?'

She tried to laugh, but was sobbing at the same time. She attempted to stand up and fell over, but she didn't shatter like the glass. There was a table leg an inch from her nose, chair legs all around her, men's and women's feet.

She was ashamed of behaving badly and, if she'd had the strength, she would have apologized. She knew that it was not done, that she was sozzled, that she shouldn't have had that last drink.

The table and chairs were moving away from her. She was being held by the shoulders. Her feet were dragging and she recognized the piles of dirty plates in the kitchen. She was sure that the African was there. She tried to spot him, but couldn't.

Someone was speaking, but she didn't attempt to understand what they were saying. She moaned softly, because she really was in pain.

'Have you got a gauze bandage?'

'There must be one up there in the dresser drawer.'

'What do we do with her?'

'What do you think?'
'I'll take her with me.'
'You?'
'Why not?'
'To the Carlton?'

She felt a sharper pain in her hand when someone disinfected the cut from a shard of glass.

'Do you think she needs a doctor?'
'What for?'
'Are you fit to drive?'
'Just carry her to my car.'

She thought she was unconscious. She didn't realize that she was taking everything in, that she would discover the words in her memory, with the inflections, the noises from the restaurant, the kitchen, even the smell of the rabbit mingled with that of alcohol and cigarettes.

She was aware of the taste of rain on her lips, of odours – the smell of the car, of her damp hair, the whiff of cows coming from somewhere.

'Watch out when you reverse.'
'Yes.'
'You can go another two metres . . . Go . . . Stop! . . .'

The car gave a violent lurch and the dark-haired woman lit her cigarette with one hand.

Rain. Trees. Lights. Cobblestones.

Then a gate with tall white columns and two men in blue uniforms who came rushing over.

'Give number 53 to my friend, who isn't very well.'

Her head lolled, inert, as she was carried, and a lift gently began to ascend.

2

Her eyelashes fluttered but her eyelids wouldn't open wide enough for her to see anything. At the same time, the pout disappeared from her lips and her hand, with a lazy, vague movement, brushed back her hair, which was covering almost her entire face, tickling her cheek.

Refusing to waken, she curled up, seeking the comfort of her own warmth, her smell, the blood flowing through her veins, the regular intake of breath in her nostrils, which narrowed with each inhalation.

Unwittingly she had adopted the foetal position, as if to offer less of a purchase, to form a closed entity, perfectly unified, unassailable.

She already knew many things that she did not really want to know and she was deliberately putting them out of her mind, into what was once called limbo.

As a child, she used to play an amusing, sometimes sensual game that helped her achieve that floating feeling, especially when confined to bed with flu or a slight fever.

Today, maintaining that state of quasi-innocence felt like a need, a vital necessity.

She had a headache, not too bad, not as bad as she might have expected, a dull pain, the intensity and nature of which she could alter by burrowing further into the pillow.

She was thirsty. Maybe there was some water on the bedside table, but to drink it she would have had to emerge from her torpor, open her eyes and face reality.

She preferred to stay thirsty. There was an aftertaste in her mouth that reminded her of the first time she gave birth, when she'd been so frightened and had been given injections to numb her. Now too, all her mucous membranes were sensitive, almost painful, and there were moments when she had the impression they were swelling, that her entire body was swelling, becoming so light that it was floating in space.

She'd been given an injection last night, she remembered very clearly.

'You may leave us, Lucien.'

'Are you sure you don't need anything? Would you like me to send in the chambermaid?'

The room she was in hadn't been aired for several days and it smelled fusty. Not the bland fustiness of a town, but the damp-hay smell of the countryside. When, a little earlier, the concierge and the porter had wanted to turn the lights on, the dark-haired woman had said:

'No! She mustn't have too much light. Leave me alone with her. Just open the communicating door into my room.'

The men's footsteps had faded away. Betty was lying on a bed, on top of the covers. The woman had gone off into the adjoining room where, from the noises she made, it sounded as if she was making herself comfortable. Was she afraid that Betty might throw up over her dress or tear it, clutching on to her?

Betty had tried to cheat and open her eyes for a second.

Betty

She hadn't done so and perhaps, after all, she would have been incapable of it. The dark-haired woman came back, undressed her with expert hands, removing everything, her slip, her bra, her stockings and then, after hesitating, her skimpy sheer nylon panties.

She went into the bathroom and turned on the tap and, with the deftness of a nurse, ran a soapy washing mitt over Betty's face and body, then rinsed it off with warm water and a splash of eau de Cologne.

She said nothing, didn't talk to herself but, from time to time, she absent-mindedly hummed snatches of a tune that had been playing on the turntable most of the evening.

'There you are, my dear!' she sighed at last. 'Now we're going to try to rest and not think about anything.'

Without moving her, she managed to pull back the covers and slide Betty's body between the fresh, lightly starched sheets.

Did she know that Betty was taking everything in and that she would remember? What was the expression on her face as the woman stared at her for a long while in the light from a single little lamp at the other end of the room?

Betty had not dreamed all that. Nor had she dreamed the words that came back into her head, with their precise intonation, the sounds and smells that went with them:

'What do you think?'

'I'll take her with me.'

'You?'

'Why not?'

It was Mario, the owner of Le Trou, and the dark-haired

woman who were talking. Betty had been struck by their familiar manner and how they didn't need to spell things out to understand one another.

'Are you in a fit state to drive?'

Mario was common, energetic, slightly cheeky. He exuded a quiet strength and, when he sat down at the customers' tables, he seemed to be taking them under his wing. Had he not appeared at the exact moment when the doctor with his worms was becoming disagreeable and possibly dangerous?

He hadn't grown angry, hadn't raised his voice. Firmly, but without violence, he had rid the young woman of him. He'd gone to the trouble of driving him home.

'Did you manage to get him into bed?'

'His wife helped me.'

There was no irony in his voice, only a hint of amused mockery when he added:

'He's counting the rabbits that have invaded his room.'

Betty looked half-dead. She thought she'd plumbed the depths of despair and yet, at that moment, she wondered whether Mario was the dark-haired woman's lover or just her friend.

Other images came back to her, clearer, more detailed than when she had seen them in real life, the blonde barmaid, for example, the one with the provocative breasts, who had a huge beauty spot on her cheek and was constantly smoothing her hands over her thighs as if to stop her girdle from riding up. She probably had one of those delicate, milky skins that showed red marks from the elastic and fasteners of her clothes when she undressed.

Betty

At one point, the light went out. There was just a faint glow in the room, because the communicating door was open and the dark-haired woman hadn't switched her light off yet. She came and went, smoking. The smell of her cigarette was sharp, different from the usual odour. Water was running into a bathtub.

Betty was genuinely unwell. Her heart thumped irregularly and at times she feared it would not resume its normal rhythm. What would happen then? Would she die? Abruptly, from one moment to the next, before she could realize? She did not call out. She had made up her mind not to call out, to die alone if necessary, and she was glad to know that her body was clean at last. Not completely. Almost. The woman had even run the moist mitt between her toes.

Had she been lying there long? She groaned, was aware of groaning, despite herself, and hoped that it was quiet enough not to be heard.

Especially since the lady was asleep. It was pitch dark. Betty didn't trust her senses any more. Did she really hear slippers gliding over the floor, the breathing of someone coming towards her. Did a warm hand seize her wrist? Did a voice, hers, say:

'*I'm scared . . .*'

'*Shhh! . . . No need to fret, my dear . . .*'

Someone was taking her pulse. She could tell that someone was taking her pulse. Not just once, but at least twice, perhaps three times, with intervals of stillness and silence, as at the bedsides of the very sick.

There were no sounds in the hotel, no sounds outside,

other than the patter of rain on the louvred shutters, which rattled every so often in the wind. She didn't dare ask for the lamp to be switched on.

A little later, there was some light, not in her room but next door where, for some mysterious reason, a spirit lamp was being lit. She recognized the smell. Her father used to sell methylated spirits. He was a hardware dealer. He was a redhead. He was full of life and would make fun of his customers, imitating them behind their backs. He invented cleaning products. A pity the Germans had shot him at the end of the war. No one had ever known why.

A hand drew back the blanket. Betty felt a needle prick her hip and a liquid seep slowly into her.

Like the first time she'd given birth. The second time, she'd refused. Perhaps it was the same substance. Almost immediately she felt a sense of well-being, a numbness that still left some regions of her brain alert.

Someone was holding her hand. Her pulse was taken again. She must be perspiring because she could hear the tap running and, a little later, a cold towel was placed on her forehead and over her eyes.

She would have liked to say thank you but, if her lips moved – and she wasn't certain they did – no sound came out.

After that, there was nothing. Then, much later, again there was something that was maybe true and maybe not. It was impossible to decide, because she had a lot of dreams. Why, if it wasn't true, would she have remembered just the one dream, retaining of the others only a painful feeling with no images?

Betty

It was towards morning. It must have been morning, because she could hear, in the corridor, the bellhop delivering breakfast to the rooms.

She could have sworn that she'd smelled the aroma of coffee and, when she had opened her eyes – if she had opened them – she'd seen strips of light between the curtains. The day was dawning, or had already dawned.

A noise she tried to identify reached her ears from the next room, whose door was still half-open, dramatic heavy breathing, and she rose to go and see. She had taken a few steps, her head suddenly aching, when, on a bed, she saw two naked bodies making love.

Was it possible that they hadn't heard her, hadn't noticed her, and that she could have tiptoed back to bed and gone back to sleep almost at once?

She couldn't decide. In her mind, the man was Mario and he had a very hairy body. Had that been long ago? Was it already late in the day?

She didn't want to think about it and she tried to sink back into her numbed state and oblivion. Two or three times she saw her father, in his paint-stained white overalls, in the backroom of his shop on Avenue de Versailles, which was cluttered with barrels and gas bottles and reeked of oil and acids.

She had spent her childhood surrounded by that smell, which rose up to their apartment on the first floor and clung to the folds of her father's clothes and his flaming hair.

At school, when she was in her first year, the girl she sat next to, who had a lisp, had asked to move, saying:

'She stinks.'

Her breath resumed a slower, more regular rhythm. Her lips parted over her small teeth, which her mother used to call mouse teeth. Her hand had gradually slid down her belly and, like when she was a little girl, almost without realizing it, she caressed herself, perhaps to put an even greater distance between herself and the outside world, so that there was nothing but the universe of her warm flesh and her sensations.

She had long since fallen asleep again when a creaking sound made her open her eyes and, this time, she didn't ask herself if she should open them or not. Standing between the door and the bed, she saw the dark-haired woman, in her dressing-gown. She looked even taller than the previous evening.

Had Betty actually seen her standing up, the previous evening? She had just appeared and sat at her table and, later, Betty, her eyes closed, had been incapable of . . .

'Did I wake you?'

'I don't know.'

'I came to see if you needed anything. How are you feeling?'

'Fine.'

It was true. Her headache had gone. She was weary, in a pleasant sort of way, with just an emptiness in her chest.

'I think I'm hungry.'

'What would you like to eat?'

She fancied eggs and bacon, perhaps because, whenever she stayed in a hotel, she had eggs and bacon for breakfast. She would never have thought of doing so at home. And besides, her husband . . .

She mustn't think about him yet.

'Do you think I can?'

'Why not? I'll call the bellhop.'

'Have you had something to eat?'

'Ages ago.'

'Is it late?'

'Four o'clock.'

'In the afternoon?'

It was a stupid question.

'How do you like your eggs? Well done?'

'Yes.'

'Tea? Coffee?'

'Coffee.'

'With milk?'

'Black.'

The lady went to the door to give the order to the bellhop.

'Would you like me to open the shutters?'

She drew the curtains and leaned forward to push open the shutters, and the rain could be seen falling on to the foliage.

'You gave me an injection, didn't you?'

'Did you feel it? Don't be afraid. My husband was a doctor and, during the twenty-eight years I spent with him, I often acted as his nurse.'

'Last night I was convinced I was dying.'

She didn't say that to make the woman feel sorry for her but because she suddenly remembered. It was true. She could have died. Then she would no longer have existed. They would have had to look for her identity card in her bag to find out her name and address. They'd have telephoned Guy. Would he have taken charge of the funeral in spite of everything, or would he have got his brother to deal with it? What would they have told Charlotte?

Instead of that, here she was lying in a plush room with pale blue walls and a bust of Marie-Antoinette on its white marble mantelpiece.

'Would you like to have a bath before you eat? Knowing Jules, it will take him a good twenty minutes to bring your breakfast. Don't get up right away. I'll run your bath.'

She smoked, using a long cigarette holder which Betty hadn't seen her with the previous night. Her dressing-gown was red velvet, like her slippers, her hair was done and she had her make-up on.

While the bathtub filled, she disappeared into her bedroom for a moment, and came back holding a glass.

'May I? You won't be disgusted if I drink in front of you?'

'Go ahead.'

'It's the hour when I begin to crave it. I'm like poor Bernard with his hypodermic needles. The moment comes when we can't do without.'

Betty wondered if she was talking like this to make her feel at ease, so that she wouldn't be ashamed of what had happened the night before. She also wondered whether she'd dreamed the scene in the bed, and was increasingly certain that she hadn't.

'Your bath is ready. If it bothers you that—'

'No . . .'

Hadn't she undressed her and washed her? And yet, as she got out of bed, she felt a certain shame, because she had the impression that her body was giving off a masculine smell.

Her companion, standing by the window, didn't look at her, didn't follow her into the bathroom, spoke from a distance, like an actor on the stage speaking to the audience in general.

'The water's not too hot?'

'Just right.'

'You're not feeling dizzy?'

'A tiny bit.'

She wasn't quite as in good shape as she'd thought. So long as she had lain still, she hadn't felt any pain, but once on her feet, she'd felt giddy, as well as a sharp pain on one side of her head.

'Do you need anything?'

'No, thank you. I feel bad putting you to all this trouble.'

'Not at all. I'm so . . .'

She had nearly said:

'I'm so used to it . . .'

She preferred to leave those words unsaid. It was only a little later that she went on:

'I'm so experienced! And with my husband, I saw it all. I hope you're not falling asleep in the water?'

'No.'

'I've put a new toothbrush and toothpaste on the shelf. I always have some. Because, even though this is a hotel, it's my second home. I've been living at the Carlton for three years now. Don't worry about your underwear. I had Louisette, the chambermaid, wash it and she'll bring it to you in a minute.'

There was a knock at the door.

'Put the table here, Jules. And while you're about it, bring me up a large bottle of Perrier.'

Betty wrapped herself in a towelling bathrobe, ran her hands through her hair and went barefoot into the bedroom.

'Wait while I bring you a pair of slippers.'

She felt dizzy and, now that the eggs and bacon were in front of her, she wondered whether she would be able to stomach them.

'Here, put your feet in these. They're too big, but that doesn't matter.'

'Thank you. I feel awkward not knowing what to call you. It's as if I've known you for a long time already. What's your name?'

'Laure. My name is Laure Lavancher. My husband was a professor at the Lyon School of Medicine. When he died, four years ago, I tried to live alone in our apartment and I thought I would soon go mad. I eventually came here, planning to have a rest for two or three weeks. And here I still am.'

'I'm called Betty.'

'Enjoy your breakfast, Betty.'

She tried to smile.

'I'm not sure I've got an appetite. I thought I was hungry but now . . .'

'Eat anyway. My husband wouldn't have allowed you

to have anything today, but I know from experience that the doctors . . .'

Betty overcame her revulsion, but even the coffee didn't have the pleasant taste she had hoped for.

'I was very drunk, wasn't I?'

'More to the point, you were unwell.'

'No! I was dead drunk and I behaved outrageously.'

'It's obvious you don't know Le Trou yet. If you think people even notice these incidents!'

The bellhop returned with the bottle of sparkling water and Laure went to fetch a decanter of whisky from her room.

'Later, you'll be allowed some too, as long as your pulse doesn't start racing again.'

'Was it fast?'

'One hundred and forty-three.'

She said the number with a smile, as if in her view it was of no importance. She had given her name, simply, without vanity, more out of politeness and to put the young woman at ease. She had told her why she was there and explained as discreetly as possible her need to drink. On the other hand, she hadn't asked Betty's surname and hadn't asked her any questions about herself yet.

Betty had a strange intuition. She could have sworn that it wasn't from lack of curiosity that Laure acted in this way, but because she knew. Not the details, for sure, because she couldn't know about her particular situation. But, all the same, she had understood.

And she avoided coddling her, pitying her, reassuring her.

'If my cigarette makes you feel sick . . .'

'It doesn't bother me at all.'

'Aren't you eating any more?'

'I can't swallow another mouthful.'

'Would you like me to leave you alone for a moment, to make a phone call maybe, or to write?'

'No.'

'Do your belongings need picking up from somewhere?'

How could she have thought of that? She hadn't said her luggage, but her belongings, as if she'd guessed that this was permanent.

'I'll leave you on your own.'

Betty almost shouted:

'No!'

And, at the same time, she thought she was going to be sick.

'Is something wrong?'

'I don't feel too good.'

'Nausea?'

'Yes.'

'If you're like me, a sip of pure spirits will set you back to rights. Have you ever tried?'

She nodded.

'Do you want some?'

Laure poured her a thimbleful of whisky, which she downed in one go, and it almost turned her stomach. She sat still, tense, ready to rush into the bathroom, while a warm glow gradually spread within her chest and relaxed her.

Betty

'Do you feel better?'

She gave a long sigh.

'Whew! I thought I wouldn't even have time to get next door.'

'Do you know where we are?'

'In Versailles. At the Carlton.'

Laure didn't ask her how she'd found out or what else she knew.

'Do you want to stay for a few days and rest?'

'I don't want anything.'

It was true. Betty didn't ask herself any questions. Before her, there was only a void, and she had no reason to be here rather than elsewhere.

'Listen, Betty. May I call you that instead of saying "madame"?'

Betty glanced instinctively at her wedding ring, which she hadn't thought to remove.

'And you can call me Laure, like everyone else. Besides, at Le Trou, everyone is on first-name terms, and after a certain hour, there are no formalities.'

Was that her way of explaining why she and Mario had been so familiar with each other in the car when they were driving Betty to the hotel? Was she trying to imply that there was nothing between them?

Betty blushed to have had such thoughts, to have recalled the bed scene, real or imagined, that was so vivid in her mind's eye.

'I am open with you as I am with everyone. Last night, I could see you didn't know where to turn and I brought you here because you needed a bed. Don't say anything. Let me finish. For twenty-eight years, I was a happy woman, a respectable middle-class woman from Lyon, whose husband and home were her world. Had I been fortunate enough to have children, I wouldn't be here.'

Betty had no idea how many drinks Laure had had. She spoke without getting carried away, without complacency, and with a conviction that was perhaps slightly over-emphatic, as she herself did after two or three whiskies.

'Now, I consider that my life is over and I no longer exist. Either I'm mistaken about you, or you understand me. I could have shut myself up in my apartment with dignity and waited for it to be over.

'I tried. I drank even more than here and, at one point, I almost lost my mind.

'What I do now, what I experience, what happens to me, no longer matters. Tourists come and go in the hotel, couples hole up here for a few days, old people and convalescents come for a breath of country air and every afternoon they go for their routine little stroll in the grounds.

'I don't notice them any more. A few, seeing me again after several months, greet me as if they know me, or because they assume I'm a member of staff.

'I rarely go down to the dining room and, if I have a drink at the bar to have a chat with Henri, it's usually when there's no one else there.

'I had you put in the room next to mine because I thought you might need looking after—'

'I did need looking after,' broke in Betty timidly.

She was as intimidated as a schoolgirl in front of a new teacher.

'I am not trying to persuade you either way. If you have to go somewhere else, then do go. If you want to stay another night, or a few more days, or longer, then stay without giving it a second thought and, if you'd prefer a different room . . .'

'No.'

'Tonight, like last night, like every other night, I'll be going to Le Trou.'

A suspicion occurred to Betty: was Laure talking like this to stop her thinking about her own problems? Since she'd given her an injection, she had become in her eyes a sort of doctor, and doctors sometimes have tricks like that.

'Was it your first time there?'

'Yes.'

'Did anything strike you?'

'In the condition I was in!'

She didn't dare ask for another drink, although she wanted one. The effect of the whisky had worn off and she needed another boost.

'When Mario talks about his customers, he often describes them as oddballs, and he's not so wrong. Shall I tell you the story of Mario and Le Trou?'

She said yes, still thinking about the whisky she was keen to earn, and Laure thought of it too.

'Do you need one?'

'I think so.'

'Right now?'

'Do you think it will do me any harm?'

Laure refilled her glass.

'You probably noticed that Mario acts the gangster, the tough guy, and a lot of the regulars imagine that he's done several stints in prison. That idea excites them, especially the women.

'The truth is that he was a bartender, then a taxi driver in Toulon. You mustn't mention it, because he'll be annoyed with me. He prefers to say that he was a sailor, like all the bad boys of the Riviera.

'He looks like a brute, but actually he's a softie at heart, and is even shy, strange as that might seem.

'One day, in Toulon, years ago, he met a South American woman who was a passenger in his taxi. Her husband, who had just died of an embolism in Monte Carlo, had been a wealthy Colombian cocoa plantation owner.

'Was she an oddball, as Mario claims? At any rate, she took him on as a chauffeur and manservant. For more than a year they drove around in a Rolls-Royce, spending time in Cannes and Deauville, Paris and Biarritz, Venice and Megève.

'I'm not boring you?'

'On the contrary.'

Betty could still picture the two bodies on the bed and now she was certain that it hadn't been a dream. But wasn't all of it a dream? The room with its pale-blue panelling and the bust of Marie-Antoinette on the mantelpiece. And, outside, the rain falling monotonously on the darkening leaves?

Betty

The light was fading. The lamps, in their little pleated-silk lampshades, grew brighter, and Betty hugged her naked body inside her damp bathrobe.

The dark-haired woman in front of her, too tall, even when sitting down, knew she lacked charm and did not try to pretend otherwise. She chain-smoked, occasionally taking a sip from her glass and jiggling one of the slippers dangling from her toes.

If there were other guests at the hotel and staff coming and going in the corridors, there was not the slightest sound of them.

'The rest of the story is probably a mixture of hearsay and reality, and I can't claim to be able to tell which is which. The Columbian lady was called Maria Urruti and was said to belong to one of the oldest families in her country. Since the death of her husband, this family had been urging her to return, bombarding her with letters and telegrams, threatening to cut off her resources until, one fine day, penniless, she found herself forced to make the voyage.

'*"They want me to go back there because they're going to kill me!"* she told Mario. *"They hate me"* – which she pronounced as 'ate – *"It's to kill me, or to lock me away in an asylum that they want me to return. Mario, you're strong. You have to come with me to stop them from harming me."*

'The pair of them left, by boat, because she was afraid of flying. The family lives in a city called Cali, at the foot of the Andes, on the Pacific side, and to get there you have to disembark at Buenaventura.'

Betty watched the treetops gradually being engulfed by fog, and stared between the branches at a distant light that looked like a star. She wasn't thinking. She wasn't listening. The words flowed smoothly into her, like running water.

'Mario didn't have the opportunity to use his strength. The ship had barely docked when several black-haired men, relatives of Maria Urruti, came on board, accompanied by police officers, and Maria was spirited away while the other passengers were still waiting to complete the disembarkation formalities.

'As for him, he got off the boat a little later, stony broke, to find himself on a foreign quayside.

'He claims he has practised every trade, and hints that some of them were highly illegal. He'll show you the scar at the corner of his eye, which you might not have noticed.

'It's best to pretend to believe him. As far as I'm concerned, I wouldn't be surprised if the family had paid him handsomely to be rid of him.

'He roamed around Venezuela, Panama and Cuba for a while. When he returned to France, he had the idea of opening a bar close to the Allied Powers HQ, counting on a clientele of American officers.

'That's Le Trou, which you've seen. But apart from a few rare exceptions, the Americans haven't come, perhaps because it's too close to their base, or they prefer the air in Paris.

'Those who have come, to Mario's surprise, are people whose existence he'd never suspected, the ones you saw last night, the oddballs, as he calls them, foreigners or French people who live around Versailles and Saint-Germain, Marly, Louveciennes or Bougival. Some come from even further afield, the owners of big houses or estates, who often have a wife and children, and who . . .'

She tailed off mid-sentence to grab her glass, and seemed to be inviting Betty to do likewise.

'Oddballs! Like me! People who no longer have . . .'

She began to drink, leaving her thought hanging between them, and Betty shivered, not just because of the damp bathrobe.

3

'How do you like the cannelloni, Betty?'

Mario's voice was cheerful, familiar, comforting.

'They're very good,' she replied with a grateful look.

'Admit that it's not bad here.'

'It's so nice that I feel as if I'm already a regular.'

At the beginning of the evening she had been daunted, because she felt like the newcomer and was convinced that, at the sight of her, everyone would remember her episode of the previous evening. Her embarrassment soon passed, especially when she realized that being in Laure's company acted as a sort of guarantee, and they saw her as one of them.

One detail was proof enough. When a regular came and leaned over Laure to say a few words to her, as happened from time to time, he didn't feel he had to lower his voice.

On the table between them was a huge dish of cannelloni and a carafe of Chianti. The red wine in the glasses was dark, almost black, with a lighter, pink patch in the centre. Outside, a cold wind lashed rain in the faces of the people alighting from cars, soaking their clothes, and when they wanted to leave, they found their vehicles stuck in the mud.

The buxom barmaid was at her post, and there were

more people at the bar than the evening before but few in the restaurant, perhaps because it wasn't as late.

Everything was as she remembered it, the red walls hung with etchings illustrating English hunting scenes. The previous night, despite her inebriated state, she had taken it all in, and now she had the confirmation and was amazed.

She had appeared to be totally wrapped up in herself, her drama, her self-disgust. On top of that, she had been so drunk that she'd fallen off her chair. Everything was shaky, in her life and around her, and yet she had noticed minor details like the postcards slipped inside the mirror frame behind the bottles at the bar. She was certain that one of them depicted the bay of Naples, another the temples of Angkor Wat.

The room seemed a little bigger today. She discovered that in fact there were two rooms and that the second one, which was also a restaurant, was darker than the first, illuminated with candles in bottles on the tables.

Was this section reserved for insiders, long-standing customers or lovers? Was Le Trou a haunt for real lovers?

'How's that stomach of yours behaving?' inquired Laure.

'Very well, for the time being.'

She ate heartily. Her eyes, she could feel, were shining, her expression lively and, at the slightest provocation, her lips parted in a smile that was barely hesitant.

She was like a convalescent, and it was enjoyable. She was aware that this sense of well-being was transient, superficial, that nothing had changed, that she was still the same, in fact, with all the problems she had accumulated and to which there was no solution.

Did Laure realize how precarious, how artificial, her mood was? Did she know that from one minute to the next it would all probably begin again, like the previous evening? A little alcohol kept her going, as did having dinner in the company of someone who was taking care of her. But the night before, too, sitting opposite the doctor, she had been similarly relaxed. It had only taken a couple of drinks.

There was no point worrying in advance. It was like being abroad, when, in a different clime and a foreign city, people forget their cares and lose their self-consciousness.

Laure knew her surname now. When they had gone down to the hotel lobby together, the receptionist had asked Betty:

'Would you kindly fill in this form?'

And, on reading her details, the man had commented:

'Étamble, like the general?'

'I'm his daughter-in-law.'

She added:

'Is it possible to have luggage collected from Paris?'

'Just give your instructions to the concierge.'

Laure tactfully kept her distance. Betty explained to the liveried employee that there were a number of suitcases, perhaps a trunk, to be collected from 22A, Avenue de Wagram.

'Do you know how many items?'

'No.'

'Do you think they will all fit into a car?'

'Probably. I'm almost certain.'

'It might be best if you wrote a note in case there's a problem.'

She scribbled on a notepad:

Please give my belongings to the bearer of this note. Thank you.

This time, she signed 'Betty'. It wasn't an official document. She added nothing. She had nothing to add.

'Can we go there this evening?'

'I think so.'

'Will there be someone at home?'

'There's always someone.'

How could there be no one in the apartment? The nanny at least would be there, since Anne-Marie was only nineteen months old.

She was back in Laure's car and had recognized it from its smell, the rough feel of the seats. General Étamble had died in Lyon the year before. He had lived there for many years. His wife was from Lyon and belonged to the same social circle as Laure, and so it was likely that the two women knew each other.

Laure didn't mention it, remained unruffled, capable of keeping quiet for a long time without the silence becoming awkward, then suddenly, for no apparent reason, launching into a long anecdote.

'Did you recognize John?' she asked while eating, perhaps to stop Betty's mind from wandering.

And since Betty didn't understand straight away:

'The English lord I told you about yesterday. He's

sitting to the left of the bar in the company of a girl with mousey hair wearing a leopard-skin coat.'

It was the bald man, tall and burly, a little portly, with a painter's brush moustache. He was sitting bolt upright on the banquette like a retired officer and looking straight ahead, without paying the slightest attention to his companion, who looked like some sort of starlet.

With his ruddy complexion and rosacea cheeks, he still cut a fine figure.

'He's going to sit there like that, without saying a word, for two or three hours. He doesn't drink whisky but brandy. What's going through his mind while the alcohol gradually soaks in, no one knows, and it is possible that he himself doesn't either.

'At one point, you'll see him stand up and head over towards the door, with a barely faltering step. He realizes, to the minute, when he's had enough and we have never seen him unsteady on his feet. The woman will follow him – today, the blonde, tomorrow or next week a different one, because they never last long.

'His driver waits for him in his Bentley. Within a few minutes, he'll be home at his estate in Louveciennes where he breeds Great Danes.

'I learned from Jeanine, the barmaid with a hairy mole on her cheek, what happens next, because she went there one night when he didn't have a companion, or rather, one night when his companion had become ill and they'd had to . . .'

She didn't bite her tongue. But it came down to the same thing.

Betty

'Like me, last night,' said Betty quite cheerfully.

'She was in a much worse state and she had to be taken to hospital. Jeanine stepped in, as it were, and I have reason to believe that at his place it's always the same scenario.

'First of all, in the hallway, he offered her a drink, like a man of the world being a dutiful host. Then he led her to his bedroom where he changed into a dressing-gown and sat in an armchair.

'He didn't say a word to Jeanine, who ended up taking her clothes off while he, seemingly satisfied, sat there watching her, like at the theatre.

'He pointed to the bed and she got into it, waiting for something to happen, anything. Apparently, after a while, in the silence of the room and the house, she began to feel scared.

'Still in his armchair, he stared at her the way he's now staring at the face in front of him. Within reach, on a pedestal table, was a crystal decanter containing brandy. The only movement he made was to fill his glass, cup it in his palm to warm it and take the occasional sip.

'Jeanine thought she was doing the right thing in trying to start a conversation. When she saw that this upset him and he looked annoyed, she kept quiet.

'This went on for a long time, more than an hour, and, in the end, she saw that John was asleep, still holding his empty glass.'

Laure was not laughing. Nor was Betty.

'People say that he married one of the most beautiful women in England. She still lives in her house in London and her country estate in Sussex. They're not divorced or separated. They're still good friends and see each other from time to time. When he found out he was impotent as the result of a war wound, he simply faded into the background, giving her her freedom. That was twenty years ago and, for the past twenty years, he has sat in his armchair, drink in hand, in front of a naked woman.'

Betty didn't dare turn to look over towards the corner where the Englishman was sitting, and Laure concluded:

' "An oddball", as our friend Mario would say.'

At the bar, two women in their thirties, in slacks and jumpers, were fishing gherkin after gherkin out of a huge jar; the African, Louis, came over at almost regular intervals to show his laughing face as if in a comedy act, and Betty was beginning to wonder whether all this wasn't rigged, if it wasn't staged, whether the characters were genuine or not.

'What became of Maria?' she asked abruptly.

It was Laure's turn to be bemused.

'Maria?'

Betty was in the habit of asking this sort of question. When she was young, her family used to make fun of her, and one of her childhood phrases had become a private joke in the house in Avenue de Versailles. It was before the war, when her father was still alive.

'What happened to the frog?'

Her parents had read a story from a picture book about a frog and other animals. When the story ended, her little voice had rung out in the silence:

'What happened to the frog?'

Betty

Her father and mother had caught each other's eye, not knowing what to reply. In the book, the story had ended. There was no reason to take any further interest in the frog.

After that, whenever she opened her mouth to ask a question, her father would interrupt her, laughing:

'*What happened to the frog?*'

Was it not a bit like that with the South American woman?

'Do you mean Maria Urruti?'

'Yes. I wonder whether they locked her up.'

'Mario never heard from her.'

'How old was she?'

'Around thirty. When he told me about her, I initially thought she was a mature older woman, especially since her husband was nearly seventy when he died in Monte-Carlo.'

Betty too looked around thirty. She said nothing, ate her cheese – brie – but with no appetite. She had to force herself not to look over at the Englishman's corner and, catching sight of Jeanine who was joking with the two women in slacks, she pictured her on the bed, a four-poster bed in her imagination, lying still and silent under the fixed gaze of the man clutching his drink.

In Buenaventura, the family had boarded the boat, most likely brothers, brothers-in-law, cousins. She saw them as a compact, solid block. They had the authorities on their side.

'How are you doing, ladies?'

'Fine, Mario. We're eating.'

'That's good. There aren't many oddballs this evening. Anyone would think they're afraid of getting wet.'

He glanced briefly at Betty, to check what state she was in, then, before walking off, pressed his hand on Laure's shoulder for a moment in an almost marital gesture.

'The fact is,' said Laure, 'he loves his customers, and when they don't come, he's not happy.'

But Betty had sensed for a few seconds that, for Mario, she wasn't a customer like any other and that, sooner or later, there would be something else. Did Laure suspect it? Was she jealous? Was she content with what he gave her?

Betty had begun to float once more and was in search of a solid footing. She hadn't drunk a lot. She was determined to stop in time, not wanting to be unwell and make a spectacle of herself again.

Even so, she felt a little nostalgic for the previous night, when, inert, she hadn't needed to worry about herself and nothing had mattered any more.

What mattered right now? She had sent for her belongings. The concierge at the Carlton must have dispatched a driver, perhaps accompanied by a porter. Guy would be sitting in the drawing room with his mother, and probably his brother and sister-in-law too.

The two brothers, the two households, lived in the same apartment block, Guy on the third floor and Antoine on the fourth. Antoine was the eldest. He was thirty-eight and had gone into the military, following in his father's footsteps. One day he would be a general. An artillery commander, seconded to the Ministry of Defence, he had an office in Rue Saint-Dominique.

His wife, Marcelle, was an officer's daughter, the sister of officers. They had two boys, Paul and Henri, who were at the lycée.

Why, since Antoine was the eldest, did they all gather at Guy's in the evenings? They had never made a conscious decision to do so. It had just happened of its own accord, and no one had questioned it.

Sometimes, Antoine would drop in alone, wearing a smoking jacket, and join Guy in his little study. Other times, Marcelle came down with him and Betty had to keep her company.

There was a log fire in winter, a big standard lamp with a cracked parchment lampshade. The children would be asleep, the two boys on the fourth floor and the girls on the third. At around ten o'clock, Elda, the governess, a Swiss woman from the Valais, would appear in the doorway and ask:

'May I go to bed, madame?'

Because Betty was madame. She had a household. Two children, a husband, a brother-in-law, a sister-in-law and, in Lyon, a mother-in-law who wrote to her sons every week. Every couple of months or so, she would come and spend a few days in Paris.

When the general had been alive, she and her husband used to stay at a hotel on the Left Bank where they were regulars. Since his death, Madame Étamble stayed at Avenue de Wagram, on the fourth floor, with her eldest.

She may not have liked Betty but she was not unpleasant towards her, contenting herself with looking at her as if trying to understand.

'Why her?' she seemed to be wondering, as she then glanced at her son.

Betty asked herself the same question. The general's widow was not wrong. Ultimately, no one was wrong. Guy neither, and Betty was convinced he had loved her, that he still loved her and that, most likely, he was deeply hurt.

She had nothing to complain about. At thirty-five, Guy had heavy responsibilities, grave concerns, because, having graduated among the top of his year at the École Polytechnique, he had a key post at the Union des Mines, Boulevard Malesherbes, an imposing fortress of a building, where banking operations of national importance were performed.

He was handsome, better-looking than Antoine, more striking, as his mother liked to say. Fair-haired with regular features, he dressed with the utmost elegance; not in dark colours, like a businessman afraid of not being taken seriously, but, on the contrary, most often in light colours, choosing pastel shades and soft, supple fabrics. He played tennis. His car was a sports model.

He had a cheerful nature and could make Charlotte laugh for an hour without her becoming bored and without tiring himself. He was the one who had put her to bed each night when she was a baby, and he continued the tradition with Anne-Marie.

Did Laure know the Étamble family?

Betty imagined them all in the drawing room, this evening, when the driver or the porter had shown them her note.

Betty

Where had they put her belongings? Who had taken her dresses from their hangers in the wardrobes, gathered her underwear, her shoes, her personal knick-knacks, emptied the drawers of the dressing table and her little Louis XV writing desk?

Olga, the maid, who had always looked at her even more harshly than her mother-in-law and who had strong masculine hands? Elda?

Which suitcases had they used? There were no 'his' and 'her' suitcases. They all belonged to both of them. Had they debated the question as they brought the big trunk down from the attic?

It was three days, four now, since she'd left, and they had probably been expecting her to send someone for her things straight away, the next morning in any case, as she had only the clothes she had been wearing.

Had they not been a little concerned at not hearing from her? Had they imagined that she had thrown herself into the Seine or swallowed a bottle of sleeping pills?

If she telephoned the Carlton, she could have found out whether the driver had returned, if the family had handed over her suitcases, whom he had seen and what they'd said to him.

Perhaps her mother-in-law's illness had been more serious than the previous ones? She had a heart complaint, that was for certain. She'd been receiving treatment for a long time. Even if she exaggerated her dizzy spells to arouse sympathy, she was still sick and, when Antoine had come to their apartment, he had been very frightened at the sight of his mother, whose lips had turned blue.

'May I ask you what you're thinking about? Am I being indiscreet?'

'About my mother-in-law. You must know her.'

'She lives three doors away from me, on Quai de Tilsitt. Because I've kept my apartment in Lyon and I make a pilgrimage there every so often so as not to lose touch.'

Lose touch with what? With her former life, her social connections? With the memory of her husband? Although she didn't spell it out, Betty was almost certain she understood.

'I used to meet them quite frequently in the past, her and the general, at ceremonies and official dinners we were required to attend. Apart from those obligations, my husband and I had a very small circle made up of doctors, two lawyers and a musician no one has heard of.'

Was there also, in a secluded drawing room, a standard lamp with a parchment lampshade, a piano and a sofa where the ladies sat side by side? Was there a clock that showed the minutes that were longer than anywhere else and, outside, night and day, like a reminder of another life, the noisy rumble of passing cars?

'She's in Paris,' said Betty.

She didn't want to talk about her and yet she was incapable of keeping quiet. She made herself believe that she would stop when she wanted to, that she wouldn't go any further than she herself had decided.

'She's been there for three days,' she added. 'Four now! It's funny, I always count one day less.'

It only made sense to her. For Laure it would doubtless sound baffling.

'I married one of her sons, Guy, the youngest.'

It was Laure who went on:

'The one who didn't go into the army, much to the general's despair.'

'His brother Antoine is at the Ministry of Defence.'

'And he married a Mademoiselle Fleury. I used to know her elder sister. Although the Fleurys aren't from Lyon, they have family there, vaguely related to mine. As for the general's wife, she's a Gouvieux. Her father owned a chemicals plant which the sons took over, except one, Hector, who's a doctor and is head of ophthalmology at the Broussais hospital, where my husband was also head of his department.'

She smiled with a hint of irony.

'You see! I'm talking as if in a Lyon drawing room. I also know that the Étambles have an estate in the Chassagne forest, near Chalamont, not far from the place where my brother-in-law goes duck-shooting.'

'I've been there.'

'Often?'

'Every year in the six years I've been married. The entire family spends the month of August there – the general, when he was still alive, his wife, the two brothers, their wives, their children . . .'

She didn't know why her eyes filled with tears. It wasn't nostalgia. She had always hated that month of August spent at the estate, the vast mansion with its useless turrets, the bedrooms with creaky floorboards, the iron beds they assembled for the children, the damp mattresses, the squelchy grounds.

She dreamed of the sea, a beach in the sun, salt water splashing her face, her body relaxed in a swimsuit. She dreamed of music on the terraces of outdoor restaurants, shellfish with white wine, of a motorized speedboat bouncing over the waves.

For hours on end, Guy would play tennis with his brother, sometimes with neighbours. Some days, the two wives were invited to play mixed doubles, and Betty missed every serve through trying too hard.

'We made a mistake,' she concluded in a leap that did not perturb Laure.

'So I'd gathered.'

Laure turned to Joseph and gave a little signal. Betty noticed. She could have said no. She didn't because it was the only solution.

She couldn't carry on talking like this, in this detached way, as if they were relatives reminiscing over family memories. The portrait she had just painted was false, and Laure must know it was. It wasn't a family affair. The others didn't count. The others hadn't done anything.

'I have two children,' she went on, staring fixedly.

Laure waited in silence for her to go on.

'Last month, Charlotte blew out the four candles on her birthday cake. Anne-Marie is nineteen months, and is beginning to talk like a proper little person.'

Joseph brought the whisky and soda. Why didn't Laure stop her, prevent her from drinking? Was she unaware, she who knew so many things, that it was likely to happen again, that it was inevitably going to happen again?

Was she doing it on purpose, so that Betty would

confide in her, because she needed to know people's secrets? She had said:

'Mario calls them his oddballs. You'll see!'

And hadn't she displayed a certain delight in telling the story of Maria Urruti?

When, earlier, she had disclosed John's disability, Betty had had the impression that she was undressing him in public, that she was also undressing the buxom barmaid and even the mousey starlet – all the women who had followed the Englishman to his mansion in Louveciennes, and now Betty was embarrassed to look at him.

Would Laure do the same with her? Would she not relish telling, one day, as impassive and impersonal as her husband describing a clinical case, the story of the young Étamble woman?

What had they said last night, or rather at dawn, when Mario had come to join her in her room?

'Is she asleep?'

'I knocked her out with a jab.'

'Didn't she put up a struggle! Did you undress her?'

Had Laure described her every detail to her companion? Had she added that she was dirty? Had they both come to look at her while she was asleep?

'Where do you think she's come from?'

'Bernard picked her up in a bar.'

Perhaps Laure had mentioned that her suit came from one of the best couturiers in Paris, that her underwear came from Rue Saint-Honoré? Who knew whether they'd searched her handbag?

It would have been quite natural to look inside, even

without malicious intent, without unhealthy curiosity. They'd gathered her up off the floor of Le Trou, like a sick animal. No one knew where she hailed from, not even the doctor who, in the meantime, was chasing imaginary rabbits around his bedroom.

Her pulse rate was a hundred and forty-three. She could be taken ill and neither Laure nor Mario would know who to inform, other than the police.

Had they found the cheque? For a moment she wondered whether it wasn't because of the cheque for one million that . . .

She didn't want to! She wasn't as exhausted as she had been the night before. She had slept. She'd been cared for. She'd had a bath. She had become almost a normal person again, like the four who had just come in and brought a smile to everyone's faces.

Betty couldn't help smiling as well, and yet they were normal people and her own father, for instance, coming in here with his family, would probably have behaved in the same way.

The man could be anything by profession – an industrialist, a lawyer, a civil servant, a local doctor – he was a middle-aged man, comfortable, self-assured, not necessarily naive.

It wasn't his fault if his wife had grown fat and had a candy-pink complexion. Elsewhere, as a mother, she wouldn't have looked ridiculous either.

True, there were the twins, two tall girls of seventeen or eighteen, as pudgy and pink as their mother, dressed in green to boot, identical from head to toe.

Betty

All four were hungry. They had driven a long way and were happy to have found a restaurant in the countryside.

But the minute he walked in the father had frowned on spotting Jeanine behind her bar, and he had had to slide diagonally behind the two women in slacks so as not to brush up against them.

The next moment, he saw the laughing face of the African, who appeared and disappeared like a puppet character.

He seated his wife and daughters, and then sat down himself and clapped his hands to call the waiter:

'Waiter!'

Joseph came over without hurrying.

'Whisky?'

'No, thank you.'

He turned towards the women.

'Do you fancy a little aperitif?'

They said no, as expected.

'Can I have the menu, please?'

'There is no menu, monsieur.'

Intrigued, he glanced over at the tables where people were eating.

'But this is a restaurant, isn't it?'

'Indeed it is.'

Mario broke in:

'Good evening monsieur, good evening mesdames. I presume you're going to eat some cannelloni?'

'What else do you have?'

'Cheese afterwards, a superb brie, salad and Empress rice pudding.'

'I mean as a main course . . .'

'Cannelloni.'

Under the table Laure's foot brushed that of Betty, who was forced to smile. The man gazed about him with a dawning anxiety: first the walls, the bar, Jeanine again, and lastly his eyes met John's fixed stare.

'Will you have some cannelloni?'

'Why not?'

The doctor came in and distracted Betty's attention. He was dressed as elegantly as the previous evening, in grey again, and walked with a certain stiffness. From the doorway he had recognized her and had hesitated for a moment. Now he was walking over to them.

'Good evening, Laure.'

Then he leaned over towards Betty and kissed her hand.

'I hope you have forgiven me for disappearing last night, if you missed me, that is? Laure will have explained to you . . .'

He bowed again and then went and sat on a stool at the bar.

The four had resigned themselves to cannelloni and the Chianti that had been placed peremptorily on their table. Still uncomfortable, they tried to reassure themselves by starting up a loud conversation.

'Was your aunt not surprised to see the two of you arrive unexpectedly?'

'Guess what, Papa,' replied one of the daughters in a theatrical voice, 'Aunty was in the attic having a big clear-out. You remember the attic and all those crazy objects in it?'

She was playing to the gallery and John's gaze, resting on her, seemed to excite her.

'We went up without making any noise and, all of a sudden, Laurence let out her famous moo. It really sounded as if a cow had heaved itself up to the attic, and Aunty dropped the pile of gilt-edged books she was holding . . .'

Were Guy to walk in here without being warned, would he not have felt ill at ease? Antoine, most definitely. And Marcelle! Antoine and Marcelle would have turned on their heel straight away. Hadn't Betty ended up shouting, the previous evening?

She wouldn't shout any more. She wasn't afraid any more. But on scrutinizing the faces, she still felt a vague anxiety.

She suspected that Laure had more stories to tell her, that, in a few days, in a few hours, the characters who were still anonymous would become as colourful as the doctor, the Englishman, and that Maria Urruti whom she couldn't get out of her mind.

'What happened to the frog?'

One day, someone might similarly ask, perhaps with a mix of compassion and curiosity:

'What happened to little Betty?'

Because her thoughts always returned to herself. Deep down, at the root of everything, there was a little Betty who was trying to understand herself and wished people would try to understand her.

It wasn't out of self-pity that she said 'little' in referring to herself. She really was little, slight, delicate, and had never weighed more than forty-three kilos.

Only when she was pregnant had she put on weight, but so little that the worried doctors wanted to induce birth at seven months, especially the second time.

Had the fact that she felt smaller, less robust, than other people had an influence on her behaviour? Someone had told her that it had, a medical student who, for a while, had amused himself psychoanalysing her.

She had believed him at the time. She had also believed she loved him. She tried to answer his questions honestly. Until the day she realized that these questions always revolved around the same subject and were designed to reach a foregone conclusion.

She hadn't broken off the relationship immediately. She had carried on playing the game because it excited her too. In actual fact, he was the one who tired of it first, finding perhaps that she lacked imagination and didn't vary her answers enough. He hadn't said goodbye to her. He had simply disappeared.

The four were eating. The mousey girl was waiting. From time to time the African came and poked his head through a doorway.

Bernard made his way to the toilet in a dignified manner, and Mario gazed after him. Laure sipped her drink, watching her companion over the top of her glass.

'It's not their fault,' sighed Betty, dejectedly.

She wasn't talking about the table with the twins but about the Étambles, the mother, the two sons, the sister-in-law, the boys of the brother's family and her own daughters. Her two daughters who were no longer hers!

She had to go back to the subject. It was inevitable.

She had to talk, and to talk as she needed to do, she had to drink.

But not here. She didn't want to make a spectacle of herself again, see the faces turned towards her as they were now towards the foursome, all eyes on her as they had been the previous evening.

She drained her glass in one gulp and said anxiously:

'Would you mind very much if we left?'

'Do you feel unwell?'

She didn't feel unwell, but it was best not to admit it.

'I don't know. I'd rather go home.'

She had said *go home*, as if the blue-panelled room with the bust of Marie-Antoinette was already her place.

4

'Your luggage has arrived, Madame Étamble. I'll have it taken up to your room.'

'I presume there's no message?'

'The driver didn't say anything to me. He simply asked me to give you this.'

On catching sight of an envelope from a distance, she felt a brief pang, as if she were hoping for something, whereas she wasn't really hoping for anything, didn't wish for anything coming from that quarter. She felt humiliated by her reaction, especially in front of the concierge, who had carried her blind drunk up to her room the night before and today was speaking to her with exaggerated respect, perhaps being sardonic.

The envelope contained only the keys to her suitcases, as she must have anticipated. No note. Why would they have written to her? The address was in Elda's hand.

When, a little later, Betty opened the door of number 53 and the two women saw three bulging suitcases and packages in the centre of the room, Laure turned towards the adjoining room, murmuring:

'I'll leave you to it. See you in a while.'

'Do you want to go back to your room?'

'No, but I imagine you wish to be left alone to unpack your things.'

'Would you mind staying with me?'

'Not at all. I was trying to keep out of your way. I've always loved packing and unpacking, but I've never really moved house and, when my husband was alive, the only travelling I did was when I occasionally went with him to a conference.'

A large, soft package sat at the foot of the bed, and Betty immediately tore open the blue paper.

'My mink!'

She was unable to conceal her delight, because she hadn't been certain that they would send on her fur. Her sister-in-law Marcelle, although older than her, didn't have one yet and had to make do with an astrakhan coat. When Guy had mentioned a mink, two years earlier, he had explained:

'It's not so much a gift as an investment. In our social situation, you would have to have a mink sooner or later. The longer I wait to buy you one, the more expensive it will be. And since it will last your whole life . . .'

So he might have considered it less a personal item of clothing than an asset, a family possession. He had sent it to her all the same and, had Laure not been present, she would have slipped it on at once for the pleasure of being enveloped in it, for the comforting feeling of luxury that it gave her.

'Is it wild mink?'

'We were guaranteed it was.'

'I made the stupid mistake of buying farm-raised mink and within a few years it already looked like rabbit. Shall I pour you a drink?'

Betty suddenly became considerate.

'You're always the one who pays.'

'I promise I'll let you buy the next bottle, the next two bottles if you insist. I'll even show you the place where I stock up.'

Betty tried the keys in the locks, opened the suitcases and then the wardrobe and drawers. Laure came back with two glasses just as she was raising the lid of the last suitcase, the smallest, in blue leather, which she usually kept for toiletries.

On top of the contents, clearly visible, lay two photographs: the one of Charlotte on her fourth birthday and the one of Anne-Marie, beside her parents' big bed, the Sunday she had taken her first steps.

Guy, still in his pyjamas, had rushed to grab his camera to photograph her. In a corner, you could see the striped pinafore of the nanny, ready to support the toddler.

'My daughters . . .' she muttered, gesturing to Laure to look at the photos.

'The eldest looks like you. She has your eyes. She will be very sweet.'

Laure was watching her out of the corner of her eye, thinking she was emotional, perhaps expecting her to burst into tears. But Betty was calm, more restrained than downstairs when she'd spotted the envelope, or when, from the doorway, she had caught sight of the suitcases. She grabbed the drink Laure had poured, but not to give herself a boost.

'To your health and to everything you have done for me.'

Betty

It was as if, in being reunited with her belongings, she were starting to behave in a conventional manner. True, there was irony in her voice, an irony that was at her own expense, not Laure's. Picking up the photos again and throwing them down on the bed, she said:

'In any case, they're no longer my children and I wonder whether, apart from the time I carried them in my womb, they ever were mine . . .'

Needing to keep busy, she scooped up piles of linen which she put away in the drawers, returned to the suitcases, went back to the chest of drawers or the wardrobe, talking all the while, her voice clearer, her features sharp, without taking the trouble to glance at Laure's face to gauge her reactions.

'Do you believe in maternal love?'

She was expecting the silence that greeted her question and went on:

'I was forgetting that you don't have children. So you can't know. I'm talking about maternal love like in books, as it's spoken about at school and in songs. When I got married, I thought that I would have children one day, and I liked that idea. It was part of a whole: a family, a home, holidays by the sea. Then when I was told I was pregnant, I was thrown off balance that it had happened so quickly, when I was scarcely more than a little girl myself.

'I had barely two years with my husband. Already people no longer talked about me but about the baby on the way. Or, if they did mention me, it was in connection with the child, who was more important. Before I had even given birth, I became the mother.

'You're going to think I was jealous. That's almost true. Not entirely. I had hardly begun living. I'd promised myself so much happiness for the day when I would finally have a man to myself . . .!

'My idea of marriage was to be two, and we were almost immediately going to be three.

'I didn't think like that every day, of course. At times I was moved, especially when I felt it kicking. Shortly afterwards, my health gave cause for concern, still not for me but for the unborn baby, and I was put on a strict regimen. I spent most of the time in bed.

'In the evenings, my husband would come and spend half an hour, three-quarters of an hour with me, then, unable to sit there any longer and having nothing to say to me, he would return to his study or go and join Antoine and his wife in the drawing room.

'He'd bring me flowers. Everyone brought me flowers and was nice to me, even Olga, the maid, who was already in Guy's service before I arrived. She's never stopped seeing me as an interloper.

'My mother-in-law too was pleased with me.

'"*Very good, my girl! Above all, think of the baby, of your responsibilities, and follow the doctor's orders.*"

'They secretly watched me to make sure I kept to my regimen. After all, I was so delicate!

'Was it not natural that they should worry about the future Étamble? Since Antoine, the eldest, had had two sons, no one doubted that Guy would also have boys.'

She bustled about, while Laure helped her by putting the dresses on hangers. There weren't enough in

Betty

the wardrobe, and so she went and fetched some from her room.

'I was taken to the maternity hospital too early and I stayed there waiting for forty-eight hours. I was frightened. I was convinced I was going to pay. Even now, I would find it impossible to explain what I meant by that. It was a confused notion of justice, a justice which, by the way, I didn't recognize. In giving life to a human being, I would pay one way or another, with my pain, or with my own life, or again by remaining infertile for the rest of my days.'

'I understand.'

That surprised Betty, who frowned.

'I wouldn't have thought anyone else could understand that and I've never talked about it to anyone, for fear of being laughed at. The baby was born, a girl; the family pretended to be pleased, especially my husband, who has never looked at me as tenderly as on that day.

'At the time, I was thrilled; then I understood that that tenderness wasn't for me but for the mother of his child.

'Because it was his child. Any woman could have played my part and given him one, more easily than me, without all the little woes and anxieties of those last months; and, who knows, it might have been the son he so longed for?

'The nanny, hired from a Swiss school, was at the hospital at the same time as me, ready to take possession of the baby.

' *"Rest, my darling. Elda is here to look after the baby."*

'With my flat chest, breast-feeding was out of the

question. The doctors, nurses, the family – everyone tiptoed in and out of my room, staying only a minute.

' "*You rest!*"

'And I heard them whispering and laughing in the next room.

'I'm not looking to make excuses. I am trying to understand. It is possible that the outcome would have been the same if things had been different. Perhaps I am a monster. In that case, I would swear that the same applies to thousands and thousands of women.

'I never felt the bond of blood, the bond of flesh. They showed me a little creature that I didn't even know how to hold properly and, right away, the nanny took her back as if to return her to safety.

'At Avenue de Wagram, I would go into the nursery several times a day, full of good intentions. But either the baby was asleep, and Elda would put a finger on her lips, or she was feeding, and Elda would signal to me not to distract her, or again she was being changed, and all I could do was watch.

'Everything was neat and tidy, everything was clean. In the kitchen too, and in the apartment, thanks to Olga, who didn't need me either to run a household.

'That was four years ago. Charlotte started walking and talking, and grew. She is still not my daughter.

'I don't know what they'll tell her, that I'm dead or have gone on a long journey.'

'Will you not see her again?'

She shook her head so hard that her hair tumbled over her face.

Betty

'They don't want me to,' she said in a low voice.

Then, diving into a suitcase:

'I promised.'

She straightened up, a large yellow envelope in her hand.

'Let's not talk about it any more. Where's my drink?'

'Here.'

'Thank you. If I go on, I'll end up getting you down. It's Elda who took charge of packing up my things, I recognize her ways. She thought I'd be happy to have the photos of the children and, after all, perhaps she wasn't wrong. That belongs to my past too, like this envelope that contains old photographs. I had forgotten all about it and I wonder where she found it.'

She talked effusively and, although all the lights were on, it felt to her as if the room was dark. Dark and damp.

'One day, when I was around twenty, I bought a lovely album for these photos. In my head, they would constitute a sort of story of my life.

'Look! I can see the album poking out, underneath my toiletry bag. I never stuck anything in it. It's as new as when I brought it home from the stationer's, and yet it's not that I didn't have the time. If I'd had less time . . .'

She shook herself again. Her voice changed register again.

'Do you want to see my father? I only knew him until I was eight years old, because the war broke out, the Germans invaded France and, once it became hard to find enough to eat, I was packed off to stay with an aunt in the Vendée. Already they were saying I wasn't very strong.

In the Vendée you could get all the food you wanted – butter, eggs, meat and even white bread.

'Look! Here's my father. Exactly as I always saw him. He was too proud of his filthy overalls to be photographed in his Sunday suit. His hair was always windblown.

'"*At least run a comb through your hair,*" sighed my mother, embarrassed.

'"*Why? Would you have me leave a false picture of myself?*"

'He liked practical jokes, made fun of his women customers. At the table, to make me laugh, he would mimic them and was able to imitate each of their voices.

'I have no idea what he did during the Occupation. My mother swore to me that she didn't know either. It was only much later, when he was awarded a posthumous medal and the matter of a pension arose, that she spoke of his mysterious activities.

'I don't think he belonged to a Resistance network, because he was a sort of anarchist who didn't believe in anything and had no time for either Pétain or de Gaulle, or for the Germans, the Americans or the Russians.

'Even so, the Gestapo came and arrested him a few weeks after the liberation of Paris. We had no news of him until, two years later, my mother was officially informed that he had been shot.

'We don't know where exactly. Not in a camp, or in a prison but, according to some witnesses, on a railway platform where he had been made to get off a train transporting a load of prisoners to Germany.'

In a calmer voice she stated, holding out a photo taken in front of a photographer's pearl-grey backdrop:

'My mother.'

'Don't you see her?'

'Every so often. Rarely. With my father away, she carried on the business alone for a few months, then she hired a chemist to whom, two years ago, she sold the firm, keeping for herself some rooms in the apartment above the shop.'

'She didn't remarry?'

Betty looked surprised, shocked. Her mother was an old woman, wasn't she? It suddenly occurred to her that she had been widowed at forty, when she was much younger than Laure.

'Me, at ten or twelve weeks.'

The traditional photo of a baby lying on her stomach on a bearskin.

'The only time of my life when I was chubby!'

'You're not thin.'

Hadn't Laure seen her naked?

'Not that thin. Not as thin as I look with my clothes on.'

All the same she gave a wan smile.

'Me again, at four, when I was sent to kindergarten. And at eight, the day before I left for La Pommeraye. It was my mother who took me there and, with the trains in those days, it was almost an expedition.'

She made no comment on the aunts, uncles, the old glossy photos mounted on card.

'Do you know the Vendée?'

'Not well. Only Luçon, Les Sables-d'Olonne, La Roche-sur-Yon too, having spent the night in a hotel overlooking a vast square.'

'I've never been there. La Pommeraye is at the other end of the region, in the Bocage, on the boundary with Deux-Sèvres. The Sèvre Niortaise flows through the village, which is so tiny and so remote that we only saw a handful of Germans during the entire war.

'My uncle François, who married Rachèle, my mother's sister, is the most important person in the place because he owns the only inn. He's also a grain merchant, fertilizer dealer and livestock trader.

'I don't have a photo of him. Picture a great brute of a man with a walrus moustache, shining, beady eyes that are mischievous and even a little mean, velvet breeches and leather gaiters, day in, day out, from morning till evening.

'I remember his smell, that of the dining room at the inn, the lovely musky odour of the rooms, the feather beds you sank into . . .'

She was holding a photograph that seemed to surprise her and change the course of her thoughts.

'I didn't recall having a photo of Thérèse.'

Visibly moved, she showed it to Laure, not letting go of it or taking her eyes off it.

'The smallest one, on the left, is me at eleven. Look at my skinny legs and my stiff plaits. My aunt always used to hurt me when she braided my hair . . .'

The slightly fuzzy picture was of two girls standing upright in front of the stone steps of a village church.

'Who was Thérèse?'

'The servant at the inn, a ward of state.

'She was barely more than fifteen at the time and always

wore the same black dress. It was the only one she owned and it was tight over her pointed little breasts. When I was ten, I already admired them, and I would have given anything to have breasts like hers.

'Thérèse served in the restaurant when my aunt was busy. She was also the one who cleaned the rooms, peeled the vegetables and, often, was sent to bring the two cows up from the fields.

'She never complained. Nor did she ever laugh. My aunt said she was sneaky and was on at her all day long, yelling shrilly at one door or another:

'"*Thérèse! . . . Thé-rè-se! . . .*"'

"*Yes, madame,*" Thérèse would mumble, popping up right beside her, whereas she was thought to be elsewhere.

'I wished I could have been her friend, but she was too old for me and I had to be content with hanging around her. I'd heard that she was an abandoned child and those words sounded magical to me, making Thérèse someone special. I sometimes envied her, even though I loved my father . . .'

She grabbed her glass and took it over to an armchair, into which she lowered herself, the yellow envelope on her knees and, on top of it, the little photograph, which she glanced at every so often.

'How Schwartz used to annoy me because of her! Schwartz was the medical student I told you about. He had an evening job in a bar where he washed the dishes to pay for his studies, and he lived in a garret room near Place des Ternes. That was how I met him, because he lived in the neighbourhood.'

She added with a hint of defiance:

'I was already married, of course. It was even after Charlotte. A year after. Not quite. When I lay on his bed, I could see hundreds of roofs and smoking chimney stacks.'

Laure didn't bat an eyelid.

'From being quizzed about you-can-guess-what subjects, I ended up telling him about Thérèse and he claimed that that incident affected me more than all the rest of my childhood. He made me repeat the story so often that I ended up being obsessed by it.'

'What happened with Thérèse?'

'You can imagine that, at the age of eleven, I knew as much as all girls of my age, and even more, because I lived in the country. I'd seen the animals. Close to the inn, there was a bull, and all the local cows were brought to him. We used to walk past him on our way home from school.

'I'd seen boys too. Unlike a lot of my friends, though, I'd always refused to touch them.

'Every Saturday, my aunt would go by horse and cart to the market at Saint-Mesmin, the neighbouring big village, to sell her hens, ducks and cheeses, because she made fromage blanc with skimmed milk.

'There, like everywhere in the countryside, I suppose, livestock is men's business while poultry, butter and cheese are the women's concern.

'Was it the school holidays? Was I off school for a reason I don't remember?

'I can picture myself, alone in the yard, in the garden,

then alone again in the square in front of the church, as if the village was deserted, probably because of the market in Saint-Mesmin.

'The priest walked past and waved at me. It was summer. It was hot. You could see the pebbles on the riverbed, the water dividing into thin trickles.

'At one point, I went into the café and there was no one there either. The door to the cellar was half-open. I went to close it. First of all, I glanced into the shadows, which always fascinated me, and there, just behind the door, stood my uncle, servicing Thérèse, who was leaning forward with her head against the whitewashed wall.

'I say "servicing" because it was the only word I knew at the time, the one everyone uses in those parts.

'I didn't move. It didn't occur to me to leave. I watched, fascinated, Thérèse's thin, pale thighs which my uncle penetrated with great brutal thrusts.

'He'd seen me, knew that I was still there, but he didn't stop. Breathing very heavily, he barked:

'"*You, brat, if you dare tell your aunt, I'll do the same to you!*"

'Still I didn't run away. I stepped back slowly, leaving the cellar door wide open, still watching, absolutely enthralled.

'I wanted to stay to the end, see Thérèse's face afterwards, hear her voice.

'She became more extraordinary than ever in my eyes. She didn't cry, didn't struggle. Her features were hidden from me by her hair and her folded arm, but I can still see her black stockings that stopped above her knees, her black dress hitched up over her shoulders, her knickers on the floor, around her ankles.

'I didn't dare wait for it to finish, for fear my uncle would change his mind and carry out his threat immediately, for fear he would hurt me.

'I avoided him until the evening and, as you can imagine, I said nothing to my aunt.

'I realized afterwards that she suspected the truth and chose not to take any notice.

'I hung around Thérèse more and more, unable to bring myself to ask her my questions. What bothered me the most, I think, was that she was midway between being a girl like me and a grown-up.

'I'd never considered her entirely as a grown-up and, several times, she'd asked if she could play with the doll my mother had sent me from Paris.

'Schwartz told me a lot of things about my feelings for Thérèse, some of which are probably true, others which I think are exaggerated.

'He claimed I envied her, and that is right. I might not have admitted it then, but I can see now that she aroused envy in me.

'By following the clues, I found out that it didn't happen to her just with my uncle, but that she did the same thing with other men, and I discovered too that my uncle was jealous of them.

'He spied on her and, when she was alone in the restaurant with customers, he'd suddenly appear, coming from a shed or the stables, and plant himself near the bar, a suspicious look in his eye.

'Me, I caught her at least twice. Once in the winter, before supper, after dark, lying in the grass by the roadside, between the inn and the grocer's where she'd been sent to buy something or other.

'The man was a local farmhand. I recognized him from his red rubber boots, because he was the only one with boots that colour.

'Another time, I was passing the room where a travelling salesman was staying. The door was closed. I didn't see anything, but I heard Thérèse saying:

' *"Get a move on. If I stay too long, he'll come up."*

'From the sounds I could hear, I knew they were on the bed, or on the edge of the bed.

'So, at fifteen, Thérèse was no longer a girl, like me and my friends, but a woman. Because, to me, becoming a woman was that. I didn't think that she could be enjoying it and that was precisely, according to Schwartz, what troubled me.

'In short, being a woman was to suffer, to be a victim, and in my eyes there was something pathetic about that.

'You don't find me ridiculous? Am I boring you?'

'Not at all.'

It seemed to Betty that Laure's features were blurred and she let her refill their glasses and sit down again in her armchair before continuing:

'That's about all. My uncle never touched me, despite his threat, and even though I didn't leave La Pommeraye until I was fourteen.

'Because, once the war was over, it was still hard to find food supplies in Paris and because, in my father's absence, my mother had a lot to cope with, she decided to leave me there for a while longer.

'How would I have reacted if my uncle had dragged me behind the cellar door too? I would have been scared, for certain. I don't know if I'd have screamed and, to be honest, I don't think that I would have struggled.

'I am going to go too far, perhaps scandalize you if you're a Catholic.'

'I am not.'

'My parents weren't either, my father less than anyone. Only my aunt used to go to mass, and she was the one who made me celebrate my first holy communion, unbeknown to my parents.

'I was twelve. It was after the incident of Thérèse and the cellar. When I had to confess, I didn't say anything to the priest about my uncle, or about what I'd seen, but I stammered that I often had sinful desires.

'I could tell it was bad but, at the same time, I had the feeling that what had happened to Thérèse was a bit like receiving a sacrament.

'A punishment too, just like when I gave birth, I had the vague sense I was paying for something.

'In my mind, women were made for this. To be humiliated and physically hurt by men.

'I couldn't wait to be physically hurt, to receive that consecration, and I would desperately feel my breasts, which weren't growing. I'd gaze in the mirror at my stick-thin legs and my child's narrow, rounded stomach.'

Without knowing it, she wore the same fixed smile as in the photo of her at La Pommeraye. Laure was solemn.

Betty

The radiators were on and yet they both felt as if the cold was seeping into the room.

'Everything I have done since, I have done because I wanted to. Ultimately, that is what I wanted to say to you, out of honesty, because I have always wanted to be honest. I am not a victim. I am not to be pitied. No one has hurt me, rather I am the one who has hurt others.

'That's probably the reason why Schwartz left me without a word, simply moving to a new neighbourhood and new lodgings overnight.

'I suppose he felt I was leading him on, goodness knows where.

'As for Guy, at thirty-five there he is, wifeless, with two little girls who will grow up and, unless he remarries, be an encumbrance one day.

'Oh! There's a word that comes back to me, which says more or less what I am trying to explain. As I moved slowly away from the cellar door, do you know why I was so anxious to wait for Thérèse and talk to her? To ask her:

' "*Show me your wound.*"

'The word just came back to me after all these years. I wanted to have a wound too. All my life, I've . . .'

She looked Laure in the eyes, defiantly, and ended in a hard voice:

'All my life, I've chased after my wound.'

She had sworn to herself that she wouldn't cry. She couldn't hold out any longer. Fat tears welled up behind her warm eyelids and ran down her nose, forming a salty taste in her mouth. At the same time, she was laughing.

'I'm an idiot, aren't I? Goodness what an idiot I am! I've

ruined everything, sullied everything. I've spent my time making myself dirty and I'm telling you these stories to gain sympathy. All my life, from the age of fifteen, yes, fifteen, in imitation of Thérèse, I've been nothing but a whore. A whore, do you understand?'

Unable to sit still, she leaped up and began to pace up and down the room. Laure hadn't moved from her armchair.

'It's not because my husband threw me out, because the Étambles excluded me from the clan, from the family, that I started drinking. Nor is it because I sold my children. I can recite the document by heart:

'*"I, the undersigned, Élisabeth Étamble, née Fayet . . ."*

'Because I had to write my real name. It's an official document. *Élisabeth Étamble, née Fayet,* acknowledges that she is a prostitute, that she has always had lovers, before and after her marriage, that she would pick them up in bars like a professional, that she brought them into the marital home and that she was caught making love a few metres from her children's bedroom . . .

'And here I am, sounding emotional, telling you about my memories, my girlhood memories!

'Look! When I say I sold them, I'm not lying . . .'

She grabbed her handbag, rummaged inside feverishly, and flung the cheque into Laure's lap.

'One million, an advance of course, because that would be too cheap.

'*"I don't want you to end up in the street,"* he said.

'He, that's Guy, you understand? Honest Guy, decent Guy, the son of General Étamble, who had the misfortune to fall in love with a girl and marry her without making inquiries as his mother had advised him to do.

'It was Guy who laid down the law and the others just listened, making sure he hadn't forgotten anything – Antoine, Marcelle in her dressing-gown, having been dragged out of bed for the occasion, and the General's widow, clutching her left side with both hands while waiting for the doctor.

'Perhaps it killed her.

' *"You will let me know your address as soon as you have one so that my lawyer can contact you. I'll make sure you lack for nothing, whatever happens."*

'And that's what it became, my wound, all my wounds, my hundreds of wounds, the wounds inflicted by all the men I chased after to punish myself.'

She seized the bottle with a rapid movement, as if afraid of being stopped, raised it to her lips to drink straight from it, in a wilfully dissolute gesture.

'I've been drinking in secret for years, because I couldn't live without it, because I'm incapable of being like them and, anyway, I wouldn't want to be. When I was expecting Charlotte, then Anne-Marie, I stopped drinking, because the doctor told me it could damage them.

'I was happy enough to have a whore's babies, since my husband was keen on having a family. But I had enough pride left not to bring children into the world who would be sick or deformed because of me.

'Well, when I went into hospital, I took a bottle with me, a flat bottle, hidden under my things, and a few hours after giving birth, I was already having a sip.

'An alcoholic and a whore, that's what I am!'

She raised the bottle to her lips again and Laure, who was on her feet now, tried to snatch it from her. Betty struggled, suddenly furious, scratching and lashing out. Between gritted teeth, she snarled, panting:

'You too, you're like them and I'm going to show you . . .'

She tailed off mid-sentence, abruptly letting go, and stood there, arms dangling, in the centre of the room, beneath the chandelier, so stunned that her face was expressionless.

Laure had just slapped her, calmly, without anger, but so hard that it had left a red mark on her cheek.

'And now, my dear, to bed. Get undressed.'

The strangest thing was that she obeyed, and began to remove her clothes with the gestures and eyes of a sleepwalker. A few minutes later, when she was lying between the sheets, Laure's husky voice said:

'You're freezing. I'm going to make you a hot-water bottle.'

Stepping into her room, she had made a point of taking the bottle of whisky with her.

5

She slept a dull, greyish sleep, as exhausting as walking through desert sands. She didn't dream. There was nothing, no shadows or light, no action, no people, nothing but the dragging, monotonous rhythm of her heart, which skipped the occasional beat.

Then she heard a bell, real or unreal, she didn't ask herself, she was so tired. The shrill sound pierced her skull and she hoped it would stop, as with the departure of trains and ships, for instance, but the ringing became more and more insistent and eventually she realized that it was the telephone by her bed.

She didn't want to hear anyone speak or to speak herself. She answered it purely to stop the clamour, dropping the receiver on to the pillow.

Then a voice said, distant, distorted as if from an old broken-down gramophone:

'Madame Étamble! . . . Madame Étamble! . . . Are you there? . . . Can you hear me? . . . Madame Étamble! . . . Madame Étamble! . . .'

At length she mumbled:

'Who is this?'

'The hotel switchboard, Madame Étamble. You had me worried. I've been calling you for five minutes. I was about to send someone up to your room.'

'Why?'

The previous evening, Laure had given her two sleeping pills, but it wasn't the medication that was making her body ache. Something had snapped, at a certain point when she wasn't paying attention, and now, somewhere inside her, a switch had been turned off.

'There's a call for you from Paris.'

She did not react, didn't think of her husband or of anyone who might telephone her. The room was dark, with only a wan light filtering between the slits in the shutters.

'I'll put the call through.'

She wished she could go back to sleep.

'Is that you, Betty?'

She didn't recognize the voice. She had already closed her eyes and her breathing was becoming deeper.

'This is Florent.'

She stammered reluctantly:

'Yes.'

'Can you hear me?'

'Yes.'

'I can hardly hear you. Are you well?'

'Yes.'

He was in a world of light, he was awake, washed, shaved, dressed and fully alive.

'I saw Guy early this morning. You gave him a big fright by not getting in touch. It was only last night, thanks to the driver, that he finally learned your address.'

His name was Florent Montaigne. He was a friend of Guy's, a friend of the family. He was sure of himself because he was a very successful lawyer.

'Are you certain that everything is fine?'

'Yes.'

'You're not unwell? You sound very far away. Are you still in bed?'

'Yes.'

'Can I talk to you?'

He added hesitantly:

'Are you alone?'

'Yes.'

'Guy has told me everything and has asked me to contact you. In my opinion, the sooner the better, you understand? It is my intention, if it is convenient for you, to make a quick trip to Versailles this afternoon, late afternoon preferably, and we could have dinner together.'

'Not today.'

'Tomorrow morning, then? Tomorrow afternoon I can't because I'm in court.'

'Not tomorrow.'

'When?'

'I don't know. I'll call you.'

'Are you certain that everything is all right, that you don't need any help?'

'Certain. Goodbye, Florent.'

She exerted herself to stretch out her arm and replace the receiver. The communicating door was half-open and, in the adjacent room, the curtains were drawn back, everything was bathed in daylight, life had already begun. She had the impression that the sun was shining for the first time in days and days.

Laure must have heard. She would probably come in

and ask if she needed anything, but Betty wanted neither to see nor talk to her.

It wasn't because of the slap, which she remembered as she remembered everything she had said the previous evening.

On the contrary, the slap had done her good and, had she been capable of it, she would have given it to herself, to put a stop to her outburst.

Until now, she had always avoided uncomfortable home truths. She knew what they were. She had no delusions as to her character. The slap, which was long overdue, had abruptly brought her back down to earth.

There was no longer that ambivalent inconsistency between her words and thoughts, no more fever, no more artificial heat, no more vagueness. Instead was the reality in all its rawness, in black and white, in stark, cruel lines.

And that was impossible to communicate. It was already overwhelming to think of it. It was dangerous.

She had cheated, this time like other times, instinctively, because it was her nature. Out of an innate need to protect herself?

She always found a way, afterwards, to make it bearable, for it not to be too ugly, too dreadful.

She wouldn't speak to Laure any more, or to anyone. She didn't have the energy. She felt listless and empty. All she wanted was to lie still in her bed, her eyes open, gazing at a corner of the mirror where she could glimpse a little light and a flower on the curtain.

It hadn't occurred to her to ask Florent for news of her husband and her children. For his part, he hadn't seemed surprised at what had happened and had only been concerned on finding her voice unrecognizable. Admittedly, it was a different Betty he had known.

Florent was married, and Guy was not exactly indifferent to his vivacious, sparkling wife, Odette.

Every so often, the two couples used to go out together. The previous winter, they had been to the theatre, and on leaving, had decided to have dinner in a restaurant on Place Blanche. As they got into their cars, Florent had said:

'Will you take my wife? And I'm kidnapping yours.'

The car had barely started up when the lawyer, one hand on the wheel, had begun caressing Betty with the other. There had never been anything between them. He hadn't wooed her. He hadn't said anything. He still wasn't saying anything but stared straight ahead as he weaved in and out of the traffic.

It had never entered her head that she could say no, and, docilely, as he seemed to be expecting, she had reached out her hand in turn.

The previous evening, she had told Laure that at the age of eleven, unlike some of her friends in La Pommeraye, she refused to touch boys.

It was true. As was everything she had told Laure. But it was only part of the truth, the aspect that can be communicated.

What held her back then, despite her curiosity, was the fear of sullying herself, of materially dirtying herself. Only much later had the word 'dirty' taken on another meaning, developing into an obsession, perhaps because she had heard it said too often by her mother.

'Don't touch, Betty. It's dirty!'

'Don't pick your nose, it's dirty!'

And, if she knocked over a glass of milk:

'There you go again! Making everything dirty as usual!'

She was a dirty girl. Her father too was dirty, as her mother kept telling him:

'You should change your overalls, Robert. Those are so dirty they could stand up on their own.'

There were dirty customers and clean customers.

'Madame Rochet is filthy as sin.'

While Madame Van Horn's home, on the other hand, was so clean you could have eaten off the floor.

Betty wanted to be dirty so as to be like her father. She was angry at her mother for nagging him, for talking to him as if she had rights over him, whereas he was head of the family.

'Are you coming downstairs? You're not going to spend the evening doing your filthy experiments again?'

He would laugh. He didn't get annoyed. Perhaps, alone in the back of the shop where he had set up a laboratory, he imitated his wife the way at the table he imitated his customers to make Betty laugh?

She dreamed of being older, of being her father's wife and treating him as he deserved.

She tried to go back to sleep, to stop thinking, but when she wasn't thinking, she still had the same sense of inevitability.

She had delayed the final moment as long as possible. Because of Bernard, the doctor with the hypodermic needles, who had picked her up in Rue de Ponthieu and driven her to Le Trou instead of taking her to the nearest hotel as she had expected, and then, thanks to meeting Laure, who had taken it upon herself to rescue her, everything had become a muddle.

Two or three times since, she had talked to her heart's content, going round and round the truth, taking care to avoid the crux of it.

It was both true and false that she had wanted to be dirty as a sort of mystical protestation. She would have liked to be clean too. All her life she had yearned for order and cleanliness, and that was why she had married Guy.

She had been working in an office at the time, on Boulevard Haussmann, a stone's throw from Boulevard Malesherbes and the Union des Mines. They'd met in a snack bar where Guy would grab something to eat when he didn't have time to go home for lunch.

At first, it hadn't occurred to her that the relationship could be serious. She was peeved that he didn't ask her to sleep with him, as the others did, and in the end, out of sheer frankness, she had almost demanded it.

On realizing that he loved her and wanted to make her his wife, she had been thrown into such a panic that she'd decided not to see him again.

'I have to tell you, Guy . . .'

'Tell me what? That you don't love me enough?'

'You know that's not true.'

'Then what?'

'I'd rather you didn't marry me. It's for the best.'

'For what reason, I'd like to know?'

'Because of everything. Because of me. My life.'

She intended to tell him everything, everything she'd done, everything she'd almost done.

'Look, Betty. I wasn't born yesterday. What you have been is none of my business and is no longer yours. It's wiped clean, understood? Do you love me?'

'Yes.'

She believed it. She was certain. She probably still loved him. She surely still loved him because she was continuing to hurt herself.

'In that case, say to yourself that life is just beginning, as if we were both new, and that on Saturday I'm taking you to Lyon to introduce you to my mother.'

He imagined it was easy. For him it was easy. He never looked back. He had decided on the place she would occupy and had put her in it. And so there were no problems.

'I'm not even capable of running a household.'

'Olga is there to do that, and she would hand in her apron if I were to make the mistake of marrying a woman who interfered with her household management.'

She had ended up believing in it, and, full of good intentions, she had slipped into the skin of her new character.

All that was a mistake. Not only because of her past.

It was a mistake because she and Guy didn't want the same thing. Proud and protective, he would say:

'You are my wife!'

Was that not enough? His wife! The mother of his children! The woman he came home to every evening to tell about his troubles and his hopes.

'You look a little pale today.'

'That's because I haven't been out.'

'You shouldn't spend so much time indoors. I'll have to ask Ménière to examine you.'

Their doctor. For Guy, if something was wrong, it was Ménière's business, and had she shouted at him, as she so often wanted to:

'Pay a little attention to me!'

He would have replied, in good faith:

'I do nothing but pay you attention!'

It was true that he was concerned about her health, bought her dresses and little gifts, and that he often thought to send her flowers.

'To *me*. Don't you understand that word?'

She needed him to pay attention to *her*, to her real self, to the person she truly was. Not pay attention according to his needs, but according to hers.

In short, it was out of cowardice, for his personal ease, for his peace of mind, that he hadn't allowed her to confess. She had tried several times. Each time, he had put a finger on her lips, smiling.

'What did we decide?'

It was too easy. He wanted the pleasant, convenient side of her, the one that suited his life, happy to brush aside anything that could have complicated their relationship, and in so doing, almost condoning it.

The moment something didn't exist for him, it must no longer exist for her.

'Aren't you happy with me?'

'Of course I am.'

'Why don't you go out with Marcelle more often? She's

a bit dull, but she's decent at heart, worth getting to know better.'

Only one person in the world had cared about her for who she was: her father.

When she was still only a little girl, he had understood – he the eccentric – that she was a budding woman and had treated her as such.

She had been very young when the war had separated them, and so they hadn't been able to have long conversations. Most of the time, they played and joked, and yet, with one look from her father, a squeeze of his hand, she felt that he understood her and that for him she was a human being.

Might he even have known her well enough to be worried about her future?

Schwartz, later, had almost been the second man. She had hoped so, until she realized that for him she was no more than a sort of guinea pig. He too knew her. He had dismantled her like a piece of machinery. He'd forced her to confront things that she had always refused to see. He would sometimes interrupt her, laughing:

'Careful, darling. There you go sublimating again!'

That was his word. And yet, despite his cynicism, sometimes he was moved.

'You would so like to be a heroine, my poor Betty! I'm coming to the conclusion that that's your downfall. You aim so high, you have such ideas about what you could, what you should be, that each time you fall a little lower.

'You're a born liar. You spend your life lying to yourself because you're unable to face yourself in the mirror.

'When you are bored or you feel bad about yourself, instead of going to the cinema like other people, or buying yourself new shoes or dresses, you start telling yourself lies.'

Once, overwrought as she often was with him, she had talked a great deal and he had muttered, half-joking, half-serious:

'You'll end up in the mortuary or in a psychiatric hospital.'

Had he done her harm? Had he done her good? His diagnosis was accurate, because she now found herself well and truly at the threshold of the mortuary or the hospital.

She could hear muffled footsteps. Out of tact, Laure had not joined her immediately after the telephone call. No longer hearing her voice, she had now come in to make sure that Betty had gone back to sleep.

Betty could have closed her eyes and pretended, but she was too weary to cheat.

'I thought you were asleep.'

She didn't move her head, didn't attempt to smile. This morning she didn't want any human contact, any presence. She felt as if she had gone beyond that point. She had tried. She had drunk. She had talked until she was gasping for breath. She had more or less distorted all the truths, for herself even more than for others, and on wakening, she was confronted with them despite everything.

It wasn't worth starting over again!

'I hope you haven't had bad news?'

Out of kindness rather than politeness, she shook her head.

'Are you hungry? Would you like me to order your breakfast?'

For a moment, she was tempted by the idea of eggs and bacon, but she knew that, if she gave in, she *would* have to start all over again.

Then there'd be the whisky, the elation, the need to talk and then . . . What was the point, since there was no solution?

'Not even a cup of coffee?'

Frowning, Laure grasped her wrist, staring at her watch. Her lips could be seen moving. Betty studied her as if she were seeing her for the first time and thought to herself that she had probably never been pretty. She had masculine features. Only her very soft, very warm brown eyes belied her mannish looks.

She read the numbers on her lips:

'Forty-nine . . . Fifty . . . Fifty-one . . . Fifty-two . . .'

Laure stopped, surprised.

'Does your pulse rate often slow down suddenly?'

What was the use of answering? To answer what?

'Would you rather lie in the dark?'

Her mouth opened a fraction at last to murmur:

'I don't mind.'

The atmosphere in the room must have been depressing and Laure went to draw back the curtains and open the shutters. Instead of flowers, Betty saw a patch of sky and the treetops in the mirror.

'But you didn't have a bad night, did you? I didn't hear you moving. Are you in pain?'

She indicated that she wasn't.

'A headache?'

Still no. She was impatient for it to be over, she wanted to be left alone.

'Would you mind very much if I called a doctor? I know one here, in Versailles, who looks after me and is very thorough. I promise he won't ask any awkward questions.'

She repeated, annoyed, as if she were being forced to make an effort for nothing:

'I don't mind.'

'Shall I splash a little water on your face?'

Her skin must be shiny. She was perspiring. She smelled of sweat but she still said no, no again, and Laure, anxious, understood that her presence in the room was unwelcome. She went into her own room and picked up the telephone.

'Hello, Blanche, put me through to 537 . . . Yes . . . I'll hold on . . .'

Betty could hear, even though it was happening in another world that was nothing to do with her.

'Hello . . . Mademoiselle Francine? . . . Is the doctor at home? . . . Can you put me through to him without disturbing him? . . . Hello! . . . Is that you, doctor? . . . This is Laure Lavancher . . . No, I'm very well . . . I'm not calling about myself, but for a friend who's here with me and who I'd like you to come and see . . . It's difficult to tell you . . . Last night I gave her two phenobarbital tablets and this morning her pulse rate is fifty-three. No! I don't think she has a particular drug intolerance . . . Twenty-eight years old . . . Thank you, doctor . . . I'll be expecting you . . . Come straight up to my room . . .'

She was loath to return to Betty and could be heard lighting a cigarette and walking over to the window, which she opened. She lingered over her cigarette, inhaling the fresh air from outside, before coming back through the communicating door.

'It's one o'clock. The doctor will drop by at around a quarter to two, before his surgery. Would you like to get washed and dressed? Are you sure you don't want anything to eat or drink?'

Betty merely flickered her eyelids.

'I'm going to have them send up a little something to eat. If you need anything, don't hesitate to call me.'

Laure pressed a button and a bell could be heard ringing at the far end of the corridor. While waiting for the food, she poured herself a drink, and Betty felt nauseous at the thought of the viscous yellow whisky in the glass.

She had the impression that she could smell it and she wondered how she could ever have drunk it.

If any man other than Bernard had spoken to her at Le Ponthieu, right now she would probably be in a hospital bed with rows of patients, nurses and a junior doctor doing his rounds at set times.

Was that not what she had been blindly seeking for three days and three nights? She hadn't actually considered it. She'd had so few moments of real lucidity that she'd barely given it a thought.

All she knew was that she was tearing her life apart, that she was doing so with a sort of frenzy, and that this gave her relief.

In short, it was a defiance, revenge. It was also a climax. It was an end. She was dirtying herself through and through, to the maximum, with no possible going back.

It had to come to this. It had been brewing inside her for months, and she was deliberately defying fate to provoke disaster.

Admittedly, sometime before, there had been Schwartz and the business with Florent in the car, which hadn't led anywhere because Florent had been afraid.

There had been others, and it had happened that she would sometimes, in the afternoons, go into certain inconspicuous bars in Rue de l'Étoile, for example, or Rue Brey, where there were only couples sitting in the shadows and men waiting and chatting with the bartender.

It was in one of these bars that she had met Philippe, a gangling, secretive young man who played the saxophone in a cabaret in Rue Marbeuf. Philippe didn't question her like Schwartz. He spoke little and was usually content just to gaze at her dreamily.

'What are you thinking about?' she would ask.

'About you.'

'What do you think of me?'

He would reply with a vague gesture.

'It's very complicated.'

When she lay sprawled on the bed after making love, he

would grab his saxophone and improvise tunes that were both ironic and haunting. She knew nothing about him, other than his mother was Russian and he had a sister. He rented furnished lodgings on Rue de Montenotte, where Betty would sometimes darn his socks for fun.

He knew that she was married and had children, because she had told him so, but he never asked any questions.

In the end, he had become a need. The hours spent at Avenue de Wagram were dead time, indifferent, like that wasted in a waiting room. She was impatient for the afternoons, when she would go and meet Philippe. The concierge greeted her when she arrived, calling her the lovely little lady. It was Betty who brought bottles purchased from the grocer's on Place des Ternes, and cakes and sweets.

Not yet twenty-four, he was still awkward, defenceless and unconcerned about his future. When she tried to encourage some ambition in him, he merely gave a thinly veiled smile.

'You sound like my sister.'

He appeared oblivious to the millions of people living around him, jostling one another and elbowing their way, and in the street a sort of aura of solitude clung to him.

'What would you do if I didn't come to see you?'

'I don't know, because you do come. Maybe I'd go and look for you?'

'Where?'

'At your place.'

'What about my husband?'

He didn't reply. He didn't ask himself any questions either.

'Tomorrow?'

'Tomorrow.'

But, the last tomorrow, as it happens, Betty had not been able to go to Rue de Montenotte. Guy's mother had arrived in Paris without warning, taking advantage at the last minute of a lift from a friend who had a driver. Marcelle had a dentist's appointment which she couldn't postpone, so it fell to Betty to entertain General Étamble's widow.

It was Elda's day off and she was visiting a friend in the suburbs. She wouldn't be back until the last train, just before midnight.

After lunch, when it was time to go back to his office, Guy had said to his wife:

'I'll leave Mother in your hands, and this evening, I'll take her to the theatre.'

Because her main reason for coming to Paris was to see a new play. The afternoon had dragged on endlessly, and until Marcelle came back from her dentist's, Betty hadn't had a moment alone to telephone Philippe.

'I have to be quick. Walls have ears. I can't get away this afternoon. I'll call you tonight at around nine.'

In Elda's absence, it was the servant who mainly looked after the children but, because her mother-in-law was there, Betty was forced to act the proper mother.

They had dined early, at Antoine's. Guy and his mother had left for the theatre. When Betty arrived back at the third floor, Olga was lingering in the apartment.

'You can go upstairs. I'm not moving from here.'

It was as if Olga had a suspicion, because she agreed only reluctantly to go up to her room on the seventh floor.

'Hello! Is that you?'

He replied ironically with a few notes on the saxophone.

'Are you sad?'

A musical-clown glissando.

'Answer me, Philippe. I'm a nervous wreck. If you knew what an afternoon I've had!'

'What about me!'

'Did you miss me? Listen. You know where I live. The children are asleep. It's the nanny's day off. The maid's just gone up to bed and my husband's at the theatre.'

'So?'

'Don't you understand?'

'Yes, I do.'

'You don't sound very keen.'

He hesitated.

'I've wanted to do this for ages. You'll understand better once you've been here.'

Standing by the door in her bathrobe, she'd watched out for him, wondering what was taking him so long. When at last he was beside her, she sensed that she had been in danger of losing him, and she leaned against the door for a long time, her lips glued to his.

'Come.'

She led him into the drawing room, motioning to him to walk on tiptoe and to keep his voice down.

'Are you scared?'

'No.'

'Aren't you pleased to see where I live?'

She pointed to the piano, the velvet drapes, the gilded picture frames.

'Come close to me.'

She was febrile, with a strange glint in her eyes. She wanted to see him on the family sofa where she spent so many evenings sitting beside Marcelle and where, that afternoon, her mother-in-law had seated herself.

This was revenge. She had had to persuade Philippe to come and if he hadn't, she would have been profoundly disappointed. The word 'dirty' hadn't come into her head at the time, but it was what she intended to do.

'You seem hesitant, as if you're scared.'

Jumping up, she ripped off her bathrobe, beneath which she was wearing nothing, and pretended to dance, naked for the first time in the middle of the Étambles' drawing room.

'What about the children?' he objected.

'They're here, on the other side of this door. There's a corridor, another door on the left, the one to their room. They're asleep. Wait!'

She half opened the door.

'Now, if Charlotte were to get up, we'd hear her.'

He didn't share her enthusiasm, and was still reluctant, as if he sensed that any man would have sent her into the same feverish state that night.

It was an old score she was suddenly settling, not so much with her husband as with the family, with a world, a lifestyle, a way of thinking.

Exaggerating her brazenness, she took the initiative, forcing him to take her, and he could see, up close, her eyes shining triumphantly, her clenched little teeth.

'Come in, Mother. I'll call Antoine and ask him to join us. Stretch out on—'

Neither Betty nor Philippe had heard the front door open, footsteps on the carpet in the hallway. The glazed door of the drawing room opened and the lovers remained frozen for a moment, too surprised to think of separating.

Philippe, who had not undressed, was the first on his feet and, bowing his head, he waited to see what the husband would do.

As for Guy, his gaze fixed, he was still supporting his mother, who had felt unwell at the theatre, and he signalled to the man to leave.

Betty, still naked, had to pick up her bathrobe from the centre of the room, while her mother-in-law protested in front of the sofa where they wanted to seat her:

'Not on there.'

Her son settled her in an armchair.

'Give me my drops, quickly. In my handbag. Twenty drops . . .'

He ran into the kitchen and came back with a glass of water, almost bumping into Betty in the corridor as she was heading for their bedroom.

She knew it was over, and was not sad. All she wanted now was for things to move quickly, and she dressed with clumsy movements, choosing a dark suit and a black beret.

She still hoped to leave via the back stairs, avoiding

explanations. Someone must have thought of it, because Marcelle came and knocked on the door.

'Guy is asking for you in the drawing room.'

Antoine was there too. Her mother-in-law's chest was still heaving.

Guy had become a stranger, a cold, methodical man as one imagines important bankers to be. He was talking on the telephone in his study, whose door was open.

'Thank you, Maître Aubernois. Agreed. So long as you have understood my wishes . . .'

He rose and turned to his wife, without curiosity, without visible anger, without any emotion of any kind.

'Come.'

'Where?'

'Here. Sit down. Write.'

. . . renounce my maternal rights and pledge to sign any subsequent documents which . . .

This hadn't happened on earth, in a big city, in a house where people were sleeping peacefully, but in a nightmare where movements dragged on in slow motion and toneless voices sounded like an echo.

'Here's a cheque for your initial needs. As soon as you let me know your address, I'll send your things and then my lawyer will contact you.'

Even her mother-in-law had risen, as people do in church or at solemn moments. Her hands were pressed together on her breast. Her lips trembled as if she intended to speak, but she didn't say a word.

All four stood stiffly upright as she walked through them and made her way to the door.

She hadn't asked to kiss the children goodbye. She hadn't said anything. She forgot to shut the door and one of the four – she didn't know which one – overcame their paralysis to shut it behind her.

She declined to take the lift and, once in the street, began to walk very fast in the rain, keeping close to the walls.

6

'Come in, doctor.'

Dressed in navy blue and gripping his black bag, he looked like one of those Frenchmen who march behind a flag on the Champs-Élysées, and he had thin ribbons of several colours in his buttonhole. It was clear that he took life seriously and thought about things, including the way to conduct himself in a patient's bedroom.

'So you're feeling unwell,' he stated, the way a musician tunes an instrument, still standing, looking Betty up and down. She did not even bat an eyelid in greeting. 'Let's have a look. May I wash my hands?'

He knew the way to the bathroom. He must know every room in the hotel. He came back, gently rubbing his palms, and pulled up a chair beside her bed.

'Are you in a great deal of pain?' he asked, seizing Betty's wrist and taking her pulse.

She shook her head.

'You're not hurting anywhere? No headaches? No pains in your chest or your abdomen?'

She merely replied with gestures and he turned to Laure, who made to leave the room.

'Please stay. Unless your friend objects. Her pulse is sixty now.'

He didn't seem taken aback at his patient's attitude, as

if he dealt with similar cases every day. Placing his bag on the bed, he brought out the blood-pressure monitor, which seemed to be giving him some trouble.

'Hold out your left arm . . . Not too stiff . . . Excellent . . . I'm simply checking your blood pressure . . .'

She saw him, his expression serious, gazing at the little needle on the gauge while she felt the blood pulsing in her artery. He took two, three readings.

'Nine point five. Do you know if you usually have low blood pressure?'

And, turning to Laure, as if he were no longer relying on Betty to give him any information:

'What did she take this morning? Did she have breakfast?'

'She refused to eat or drink anything.'

'Not even a cup of coffee?'

'No.'

You could almost hear his mind working, following a familiar thought pattern, like a circus horse that automatically changes step at a certain point in the ring. With the same precise, meticulous movements, he put his monitor away and picked up the stethoscope, inserting the two earpieces into his ears.

'Breathe in through your mouth . . . Good . . . Again . . . Keep going . . . Now cough . . .'

She obeyed, noticing that he had tufts of hair in his nostrils and in his ears.

'Breathe in again . . . Not so hard . . . That's fine . . . Can you sit up?'

Weary and listless, she raised herself up with more difficulty than she had expected.

'This won't take long . . .'

He applied the metal disc to two or three places on her back, lingered on one spot, the highest, as if he had found something abnormal.

'Hold your breath . . . Good . . . Breathe in . . . You can lie back down . . .'

On her chest, he returned to a point that probably corresponded to the one on her back that had concerned him. When he listened like that, his gaze became fixed and expressionless, like that of a hen.

'Do you see your doctor often?'

'Not very often.'

She had spoken without realizing it, in spite of herself, because she had promised herself to submit to this examination without taking any part in it.

'Have you had any serious illnesses?'

'Scarlet fever, when I was three.'

He wore the stethoscope around his neck and with his bare hand he felt her upper chest, pressing his fingers between her ribs.

'Does that hurt?'

'No.'

'What about here?'

'A little.'

'Like this?'

'More.'

'Do you sometimes feel pain here?'

'Not anywhere in particular. In my whole chest.'

Drawing back the covers, he felt her stomach through her nightdress.

'Have you moved your bowels this morning?'
'No.'
'What about yesterday?'
'I don't remember. No. Not yesterday either.'

Still grave, he selected another instrument, a little nickel hammer.

'Don't be afraid.'

She knew what he was going to do. This wasn't the first time she'd been examined in this way. Then he scratched the soles of her feet with a pointed object, a metal toothpick he'd taken from his waistcoat pocket and which reminded her of Bernard and his rabbits.

'Can you feel anything?'
'Yes.'
'And now?'
'Yes.'

He exchanged a glance with Laure, whom he treated rather like her mother, her elder sister or a nurse. The last thing he did before putting away his instruments was to push up her eyelids.

'Do you sometimes feel giddy?'
'I have these past few days.'
'Badly enough to lose your balance?'
'No.'
'Have you recently had an emotional shock?'

She did not reply and it was Laure who nodded.

'Besides,' added Laure, 'we both had a lot to drink. Last night I gave her two 100mg phenobarbital tablets. She slept peacefully. She was woken up by the telephone and she's been like this ever since.'

Betty

He turned to Betty and tapped her forearm.

'First of all, let me reassure you, madame, that you do not have any kind of organic illness and that your functional disorders will resolve themselves with quiet and complete rest.'

His eyes seemed to be asking for Laure's advice before continuing.

'My friend is alone here, doctor. She is going through a rough period.'

'I understand! I understand! The best thing, of course, would be a spell in hospital. Is there any reason why not?'

Without looking at him, Betty said:

'I don't want to.'

'Mind you, I'm not insisting. If you have the strength to take care of yourself, and above all to be strict with yourself, you'll recover just as well here as anywhere else. Do you receive any visits?'

'None,' replied Laure on her behalf.

'That's good. No going out either, for four or five days at least, and then, only short strolls in the hotel grounds. Nothing to eat until tomorrow morning; otherwise, this evening, perhaps a light vegetable broth.'

He had taken a notebook from his pocket and was conscientiously writing down everything he said. No visits. No outings for five days. A liquid diet until . . . He paused to remind himself of the day . . . Until Saturday morning . . .

'You're not afraid of injections?'

He was treating her like a child, or an idiot.

'I'll give you one before I leave and, tonight, you'll take

one of the tablets I'm going to prescribe. Continue every evening for three days. And, twice a day, a little dose of reserpine with your midday and evening meals.

He removed a sterilized syringe from a metal tin with sticking plaster wrapped around it and filed off the end of a vial. His movements and his voice reminded her of a ritual, a religious ceremony.

'Turn over slightly . . . That's enough . . .'

He pinched her nightdress to raise it while being careful not to uncover her lower abdomen.

'That didn't hurt too much?'

That was it. He was putting his things away.

'Madame Lavancher will telephone me, should you need me before tomorrow evening. Otherwise I'll drop by after my surgery, between six and seven o'clock.'

He cast around for his hat, which he had left in Laure's room, and all of a sudden, while he was conversing with Laure in the corridor, Betty regretted having let him leave.

He had only carried out professional procedures, spoken words she knew so well that she could have predicted what he would say next, and yet for a brief moment he had enveloped her in a world that was comforting.

For a quarter of an hour someone had taken care of her, as if she were worth it, as if her life mattered.

What was he saying to Laure? A doctor's wife, she had read on his face the hypotheses he ruled out one by one. Was she telling him what had happened to Betty, or at least what she knew of it?

Because she didn't know the whole story. She knew nothing of the worst part. Besides, in spite of everything,

Laure had belonged to *their* world. Whatever she did, she was still a little bit on their side, as was the doctor.

There would have been no point in talking because they wouldn't have understood.

'Would you like to rest?'

Her eyelids flickered again.

'I can reassure you, in all honesty. The doctor spoke to me in the corridor. At one point, when he was examining you, I could tell he was concerned. He might have feared neuro-circulatory asthenia, which, incidentally, isn't serious but is a nuisance.

'Having examined you, he is categorical. You are suffering from the repercussions of your emotional upheaval of the past few days. I'm the person who is going to take care of you, and I warn you, I'll be strict.'

Her cheeriness misfired. Betty did not react.

'You'll probably doze off for two or three hours. That's the effect of the injection. I'll instruct the kitchen staff to make you a vegetable broth. I'll leave you for the time being. See you later, Betty.'

Maybe she was wrong to refuse to go into hospital? She would have been sent to one of those convalescent homes on the outskirts of Paris where the newspapers regularly report that such-and-such a star is being treated. That sounded grey and dreary. Here too was dreary, but it was possible for her to leave without asking anyone's permission. When she felt less exhausted, she would go.

She heard the telephone ringing in the next room, Laure's hushed voice.

'Yes . . . Yes . . . No . . . She's fine . . . She's in bed, yes . . .

The doctor came . . . I'll explain . . . Not straight away . . . What? . . . Let's rather say two . . . That's right . . . See you later . . .'

Mario was on the other end of the line, she was positive. Mario wanted to come in an hour's time and Laure had asked him to wait for two, to be certain that Betty would be asleep.

But she knew that she wouldn't be asleep. The drug she'd been injected with was numbing her body, making her burning eyelids heavy, but was not inducing sleep.

She continued to think, especially in images, and all the images were of the same grey, with less contrast than that morning, less dramatic substance.

She unspooled them wearily, the way a person turns the pages of a book they have to leaf through to the end. She felt it was important, that she had a duty to face up to it.

In her mind, words didn't have their full, everyday meaning, but for her they were clear, and that was the main thing.

She had to face up to things instead of always trying to run away. But drinking to give herself the illusion of courage, then talking to Laure in a breathless voice and finally collapsing wasn't facing up to things.

She had always known instinctively that everything would end in disaster, even before meeting Guy. As a child, she would watch the other little girls as if they had something that she didn't. It is true that at other times she was happy, if not proud, to be herself, because then she had the feeling that she was the one who was the most complete.

Betty

The question no longer arose. It had happened. She had said nothing to them as she made her way to the door, all four of them standing there in the drawing room, watching her leave. Had she been ashamed? She would have liked, after the event, to have convinced herself that she hadn't been ashamed, because, if she had, it would prove that they were right and she was wrong.

She couldn't remember whether she had hung her head or whether she had looked them in the eye. She must have looked at them because she could clearly picture the expression on each of their faces.

Why had she signed without protest? Out of pride? Out of indifference?

And yet, once outside in the rain, she had started to run, keeping close to the walls of the buildings, as if seeking refuge. Then, breathless, she had gone into a lit-up bar on the corner of Avenue de Wagram and Place des Ternes.

There were a lot of people, a red-copper counter, trays laden with glasses of beer passing by her head and, at the tables, men and women eating.

'A whisky.'

'On the rocks?'

'Yes. Make it a double.'

'Soda?'

'I don't mind.'

She almost snatched it from the bartender's hands and gulped it down, and some people around her looked at her disapprovingly.

'Pour me another.'

She rummaged in her bag for some money, and the cheque almost fell into the sawdust on the floor. She caught it as it fluttered down. Would she have bent down to retrieve it from between people's legs? Perhaps not.

She drank and left, still walking hurriedly, raindrops on her face. Weaving in and out of the cars, she arrived in Rue de Montenotte, her heart thumping as she raced towards the lift.

The concierge opened the glazed door of her lodge.

'He's not there, my little lady.'

'Did he not come home?'

'I mean he came home about half an hour ago, but ten minutes later he was back down with his suitcase and his instrument. He asked me to call him a taxi. He seemed in so much of a hurry that I thought he had a train to catch.

' *"Is your sister ill?"* I asked him.

'Because I know from the letters she sends him that she lives in Rouen.'

'What did he reply?'

'He didn't reply. He looked frightened. When I inquired whether he would be away for long, he shrugged.

' *"You can dispose of the room."*

'That was it! I assume he won't be back. Seeing as the rent is paid in advance, I had no right to stop him, especially because the taxi arrived almost immediately and he gave me a generous tip.'

Betty had no idea what time it had been at that point, and from then on, for three days and three nights, she would lose track of time, of when she'd last eaten or slept.

She had cried as she walked the dark streets, without

Betty

thinking about which direction she was taking, and she sometimes talked to herself.

'It's not fair. I should have told him.'

She found herself in Avenue Mac-Mahon, then, still choosing poorly lit streets, she had reached Porte Maillot.

She had walked into a bar, the smallest and gloomiest. She ordered a whisky. There wasn't any. She drank a brandy with water and a woman with a fat behind wearing a great deal of make-up and wobbling on stiletto heels, stared at her, trying to figure her out.

She must have been getting drunk. She wasn't aware of it and was still bent on finding Philippe. She had gone in the wrong direction. She would have to retrace her steps. It didn't occur to her to take a taxi and, besides, Philippe didn't start work until midnight.

It couldn't be that late. He must have had to drop off his suitcase somewhere before going to his cabaret. He had been afraid of Guy, which was only natural.

She was impatient to reassure him. She was free now. She wouldn't impose herself on him. He was too young to saddle himself with a wife. But, all the same, he'd be able to see her whenever he wished.

She walked, trying not to lose sight of the Arc de Triomphe. She had no idea how much money she had in her bag. If Philippe needed money, there was the cheque, which she was prepared to give him.

She had had to stop somewhere else. A man had grabbed her by the arm, saying filthy words, and she had felt panic-stricken.

The nightclub where Philippe worked was called Le

Taxi. Betty had never been there and she couldn't find it. She looked at the neon signs one after the other and in the end it was the doorman from another cabaret who pointed out the sign to her – the least bright, in tiny, dark-red letters, the very last one in the street.

The atmosphere inside was suffocating. The place was smaller than the drawing room at Avenue de Wagram and full of smoke and loud music. Clusters of men stood around the bar and, a few feet from them, a woman was performing a striptease under the spotlight.

The musicians wore light-blue dinner jackets. She tried to seek out Philippe but couldn't see him.

'Is Philippe here?' she asked the bartender, rising on to her tiptoes.

'Which Philippe? The sax player?'

'Yes.'

'I don't know. I can't see him. He must have got someone to replace him.'

A man wanted to buy her a drink and already had his hand on her thigh.

Not yet. Not here. Philippe had given up his lodgings and had not come to work. That meant he had done the same as Schwartz.

Evaporated. Vanished in Paris. If she wanted to find him, over the coming days she would have to go from cabaret to cabaret, from Étoile to Montmartre and Montparnasse, and seek him in all the music venues.

'*As soon as you have an address . . .*' her husband had said.

The sensible solution was to go and book herself into a hotel before having her belongings sent. But how could she have shut herself away alone, between four walls, crawled into a bed and slept?

Another bar. She hadn't had anything to drink at Le Taxi. She needed to get drunk as fast as possible. She recalled different lightings, nearly always a mirror behind the glasses and bottles, often girls, next to her, who eyed her as if she was a threat.

'A whisky . . . A double . . .'

The word 'dirty' had come back into her mind, because of her mud-stained shoes and her wet feet.

She was beginning to be dirty. She had a growing urge to see this through to the bitter end. Since she hadn't succeeded in being the cleanest, was it not better, while she was about it, to become the dirtiest?

She didn't want to sleep. What she wanted was not to be alone.

Already, she was no longer alone. A man paid for her drink and took her by the arm, pushing her on to the pavement in a quiet street where the light of a hotel could be seen. They walked in through a glazed door. A redheaded woman, sitting at the desk, watched them go past and, raising her head, yelled up the staircase:

'Is number three free, Maria?'

'Right away, madame.'

'You can go up.'

A narrow corridor with a worn carpet. An unfamiliar smell. An open door into a room where the bed wasn't unmade but the chambermaid was hastily changing the towels.

'It's a thousand francs, excluding service.'

Betty was so drunk that, once the woman had left, she sank on to the bed fully clothed and almost fell asleep. She barely remembered the man's face. He was quite fat, with blue eyes, and he wore a big red-gold wedding ring.

'Get undressed.'

She tried, failed and relapsed into her drowsy state. He didn't stay long. Looking embarrassed, he had placed a banknote on top of Betty's handbag.

She slept at last, plunging quickly, like a lift whose cable has snapped.

Someone was shaking her shoulder.

'Get up, girl.'

She didn't understand what was wanted of her, why she was being harassed.

'Come on! Don't act the innocent. The half-hour's up.'

'I want to sleep.'

'You'll sleep somewhere else. If you don't get out right now, I'll call Monsieur Charles.'

He came, in shirtsleeves and slippers.

'What is Maria telling me? That you're refusing to leave the room?'

He stood her up, but she was swaying and her gaze was vague.

'I see what this is. I don't like that here. What's more, I bet your papers aren't even in order. I don't want any trouble and I need the room.'

In the street, she stumbled. There were big gaps in her memory. She had eaten hard-boiled eggs and drunk coffee that had a foul taste, and then thrown up in a filthy toilet.

Betty

A man almost as drunk as her, with a foreign accent. She no longer knew if it was that night or the next.

If it was the next, she was incapable of saying how the first night had ended up.

They drank together in a place where the customers were pressed up against one another and he fondled her rump and her breasts in front of everyone, with a smug air of ownership. Someone had said something to him and a fight nearly broke out.

Outside, it was still raining and they walked arm in arm. She talked to him about Philippe, trying to explain that it was a misunderstanding, that he had taken fright for nothing, because he was very young and above all very gentle.

'A poor creature, you understand? I have to find him. It's of the utmost importance, because he won't dare show himself. He reckons Guy is angry with him. Guy didn't even look at him and would be incapable of recognizing him in the street. The truth, if you want the actual truth, is that Guy already knew everything. Do you see? No fool, Guy!'

She was drunk. But she didn't think she was mistaken. Already, before, it had sometimes occurred to her. Quite early on, Guy had stopped asking her how she spent her afternoons.

Who knows whether he didn't prefer that solution? Who knows even how things would have turned out if his mother hadn't been with him when he'd returned home and caught Philippe and her on the drawing-room sofa?

There was no point asking herself these questions. He had never attached any importance to her past. He loved her in his own uncomplicated way, with a comfortable love. He didn't want to know what was going on in her head. At most, he would sometimes ask her, as if he knew the answer:

'Is everything all right? Are you happy?'

So long as she replied yes, he didn't probe any further.

She saw herself with the foreigner, bang in the middle of an avenue, with cars passing either side of them, drivers swearing at them and the man asking, suddenly suspicious:

'Where are you taking me?'

'I don't know. You're the one who's taking me.'

'Me? Where would I take you?'

They had had a confused argument.

'You don't know where we can go?'

'No.'

'You're not a thief, I hope?'

He looked her in the eyes as if to hypnotize her.

'Then we'll try my hotel. I'm not sure they'll let you in.'

They'd hailed a taxi, had asked it to stop somewhere outside a bar for a last drink. The hotel was next to Galeries Lafayette, with a marble staircase and a red carpet.

The man had drunk too much to get what he wanted. He still insisted, demanding help from his companion. Aching and dizzy, every few minutes she fell asleep, and he eventually dropped off too.

She could have slept all day and perhaps the next night too. She felt ill. She had the impression it was barely light when he forced her to get dressed because he had a flight to catch.

It was later than she thought. The streets were teeming with people, a sea of umbrellas above their heads.

She wandered through the crowd, ghost-like among the flesh and bone, and would occasionally stop in her tracks at the kerbside to watch the cars going past. She was no longer thinking about Philippe, or Guy, only sometimes about the letter, the shame of having signed a document selling her two daughters.

This became an obsession and she was muttering about it under her breath as she pushed open the door of a bar.

'Come in. Don't make a noise. I think she's asleep.'

Mario had knocked on the door so discreetly that Betty hadn't heard anything. But she could hear Laure's whispering. She knew they were kissing.

'I'll go and check.'

She closed her eyes and felt a presence by her side, someone leaning over her then walking away, taking care not to make the floorboards creak, and then pulling the door to.

She could no longer make out the words, only the kind of murmur you can hear from a confessional. A bottle was uncorked. Glasses were being filled. The tone of the conversation was calm, even, with the occasional stifled laugh from Mario.

He hadn't sat down but was pacing up and down the room, then the bed groaned lightly, as if Laure were reclining on it.

The light was fading. Laure must have talked about her, and Betty had the impression that at one point Mario came over to the door to peer through the crack.

In thousands of rooms, at that same moment, couples in the semi-darkness were chatting in the same way, smoking cigarettes and having a drink.

Why did that seem so extraordinary to Betty, lying in her bed? Mario was in the habit of visiting Laure in her room; he was her lover; they met up every evening at Le Trou where Laure always ate her dinner.

They conversed in an undertone, in a simple, relaxed manner, she sprawled on the bed, he sitting in an armchair. And if later they felt the urge to make love, nothing would stop them. It wasn't certain. It wasn't essential.

They were happy like that, confident, light-hearted.

Insidiously, envy was born in Betty. Fate was unjust. She didn't attempt to define the nature of the injustice, but she felt frustrated, as if something had been stolen from her, as if it were actually Laure who had stolen something from her.

Ultimately it was Laure who had chosen her from among all the strange characters, all the oddballs, who frequented Le Trou. The doctor with the little creatures had barely disappeared when she had come and sat down at her table, glass in hand.

Betty hadn't called out to her, wasn't even aware of her existence.

Did she not know, she who was a doctor's wife, that Betty wasn't supposed to drink, that she had already had too much, that she was physically and mentally at the end of her tether?

What had she done? She'd filled her glass, twice at least, perhaps more. She had brought her to the hotel without consulting her.

She had cared for her, of course, but she had given her more to drink, starting the next morning, so as to pump her, extract confidences from her, to add a story to her collection.

Betty lay there in the dark without moving, weak and listless, knocked out by whatever drug the doctor had injected into her. Meanwhile, next door, the pair of them were chatting away like two people who understood each other through half-spoken words.

Why did Laure deserve to be happy? Because already, before, she had been happy for twenty-eight years with her husband – she had boasted of it. She hadn't remained on her own for long, a year she'd said, and she had found Mario almost immediately.

Why her, when Betty had tried so hard? Nothing bothered Laure. She came and went in life, relaxed, considering others with indulgence.

She considered Betty with indulgence too, and indulgence was the word, the kind of indulgence Betty didn't want. What she wanted was what she was entitled to as a result of her efforts.

There was no justice. In a few days or in a few hours, room 53 would be empty, Betty elsewhere – it didn't matter where – and, in the next room, Laure and Mario would carry on meeting as evening fell.

'What else did she tell you?'

'She told me so much that I'm forgetting some of it. You see, she's a sad creature. She'll spend her life running after something without ever knowing what.'

'She has the eyes of a lost animal.'

'She might end up finding a good soul who'll give her a home, like a stray dog.'

Those weren't necessarily the words they would use, but she didn't think she was imagining things. She was convinced that it was true in substance, that that was what would happen. Laure would give Mario a smug, assured look, because, Betty gone, he was not likely to let himself take pity on her.

They fell silent now, and she soon understood why.

Would she herself still be capable of making love after what she had been through these past three days and three nights?

The two of them, flesh against flesh, saliva mingled, taking their pleasure in silence, motionless, and Betty stared at the grey sky and the black trees in the mirror, digging her nails into her skin. She wanted to scream, to make them stop, so that they would stop being happy.

She was tempted to get dressed and leave, so that, later, they would be mortified and shamefaced on seeing the empty room.

She didn't have the energy. Besides, as soon as she appeared in the lobby, wouldn't the concierge hasten to inform Laure? Had she not given instructions to that end? It was she whom the doctor had spoken to in the corridor, delegating his authority to her, in a way.

Betty

He had allowed Betty not to go into hospital on condition that she didn't leave the room, didn't move and didn't receive any visitors.

The crack in the door lit up. The bedside light had just been turned on in the next room, and Mario was saying:

'Do you think she's still asleep?'

'If you're worried, go and have a look,' replied Laure, still on the bed. 'But first, give me a light.'

'I find it strange.'

'What?'

'That she spends so much time sleeping.'

His footsteps came closer, retreated, then came closer to the door again, which he ventured to open a little wider.

He moved soundlessly, the way parents enter a child's bedroom at night, trying to make out Betty's face in the dark. To see her more clearly, he stepped forward, leaned over, saw her open eyes and the finger placed on her lips.

She smiled at him knowingly, as if she were putting her trust in him, and he smiled back, batting his eyelids to signal his agreement, and withdrew as silently as he had come, pulling the door to behind him.

'Well? Is she asleep?'

'She seems to be.'

He wasn't exactly lying, merely cheating.

'What did I tell you? Pour me a drink, will you?'

Betty had at last closed her eyes and was breathing regularly.

7

Laure hadn't spoken to her about Mario's visit. She wasn't accountable to her, of course. This was still significant, though, and Betty was quite glad to have a grievance, small as it was, against her companion.

She didn't like people who always appeared too perfect. She mistrusted them. After throwing herself on her, Laure was already beginning to feel a little weary, to long to have her own life back, especially since Betty was bedridden and the doctor had forbidden her to go out or to drink.

'Did you sleep well?'

She too was cheating when she replied that she had.

'Are you hungry?'

'I don't know.'

'I'll have your vegetable broth brought up. Which do you prefer: dim or bright light?'

She didn't care. She lay there, inert, and derived a secret pleasure from doing so. Laure lit the lamps, flitting between the two rooms. The soup arrived and Betty sat up in bed.

For both of them, it felt as if things were dragging on. Time was passing slowly this evening, as if each had something else on her mind.

Laure, in her room, got changed and didn't know what

to do with herself. Her voice was slightly different and she seemed to be fussing even more than usual.

'Was it a bit tasteless? Wait while I plump up your pillow. Would you like the chambermaid to come and make your bed? Do you want to freshen up?'

All those words, all those sentences, and finally:

'Would you mind very much if I left you alone for a couple of hours to go and have dinner out? It's not very charitable of me to say this when you're confined to bed, but I need some air, some life. If you want anything, ring the bell. I'll leave instructions for Louisette. She'll telephone me if necessary and I'll be here within a few minutes. You're not annoyed? You don't feel as if I'm abandoning you?'

On the contrary, Betty was pleased she was going. She couldn't wait to be alone and, after letting ten minutes or so go by, so as to be certain that her friend hadn't forgotten anything and wouldn't be coming back, she got up, began by closing the communicating door, for no particular reason, perhaps as a symbolic gesture, and went into the bathroom.

She wasn't feeling very strong and she took a long time to wash, do her hair and put on some discreet make-up.

While choosing a nightdress from the drawer, she found a travel alarm clock and started to wind it up.

'Hello, mademoiselle, can you tell me what time it is, please?'

'Are you better? It's half past eight. Eight thirty-two, to be precise. Do you need anything?'

'No, thank you.'

She set the hands. This was the first time since Avenue de Wagram that she had taken an interest in the time, was aware of it, and that already represented a return to some kind of life.

In spite of the doctor's orders, she would have been capable of getting dressed on her own and going out, of calling a taxi to take her to Le Trou.

Looking at herself in the mirror, she was tempted to do so, and tried to imagine Laure's reaction on seeing her walk in, and that of Mario.

She mustn't. It would be no use, quite the opposite. She switched off the lights, except the bedside lamp, and slid between the sheets.

She didn't intend to sleep. Nor did she want to dwell on depressing memories. Something was brewing, something still very vague, which it wasn't advisable to spell out, a possible solution.

Yesterday, this morning, still this afternoon, she had been convinced that there was no way out. This evening, she was in a state of expectation, fighting off the numbing drowsiness. All of a sudden, at ten to nine, her hand groped for the bell marked *Beverages*.

She needed a coffee. A few more minutes and she would have fallen asleep. Jules knocked at the door, worried, and murmured:

'I'll call the chambermaid right away.'

'It's not the chambermaid I want.'

'Madame Lavancher told me . . .'

'It doesn't matter what she told you. I want a cup of black coffee.'

'That's different.'

All the same, he was hesitant.

'I suppose I can bring you one. Are you sure it won't do you any harm?'

A little later, he brought her a filter coffee and she sat up in bed. She was waiting while the coffee strained when the telephone rang. She reached out, surprised that something had happened so soon. A man's voice said:

'Madame Étamble? I haven't woken you? I apologize for disturbing you. A Monsieur Étamble insists on speaking to you.'

'Did he give his first name?'

She thought it might be Antoine.

'No. I'll ask him.'

'Don't bother. Put him through.'

'The thing is, he's downstairs.'

Under his breath, as if he were afraid of being overheard by someone close by, he added:

'He asked me a lot of questions, demanded to know whether you were alone, if you'd had any visitors . . .'

It hadn't occurred to her for one moment that Guy might want to see her, or even, if it was Antoine who was waiting, to send his brother. Hadn't Florent, his lawyer, already contacted her?

'Send him up.'

She took a sip of coffee and snuggled between the sheets, resuming her pose of that afternoon.

The stern Jules walked ahead of the visitor along the corridor and showed him into the room. It was Guy, hat in hand, embarrassed, who was trying to accustom his eyes to the dim light.

'I'm not disturbing you?'

She waved him with a weary hand to a chair, the one at her bedside in which the doctor had sat.

'Have a seat.'

'When he spoke to you on the telephone, Florent had the impression that you weren't yourself. He said that he could barely recognize your voice. I was afraid you were ill or that something had happened to you.'

'I am simply tired. Very tired. It will pass.'

She watched him covertly. He was the same as always, a little more anxious, a little awkward. He did it on purpose, out of prudishness, to choose mundane language.

'Have you seen a doctor?'

'This afternoon.'

'What does he say?'

'That I'll be up and about in four or five days.'

'Do you have someone to take care of you?'

She automatically looked over towards the communicating door.

'A friend. She's gone out for dinner and will be back shortly.'

She felt no emotion on seeing him and she was even amazed to note that he seemed like a total stranger.

She found it hard to believe that she was his wife, that, for six years, she had lived with him, sleeping in his bed every night, that they had two children together, made from part of each of them.

Betty

Did Guy feel the same? He too gazed at her furtively as if trying to think of what to say.

She was the one who spoke.

'Are the children well?'

'Very well, except that Charlotte has a head cold and is cross at being kept indoors.'

'Has your mother returned to Lyon?'

'Not yet. She's staying with Antoine. She's better but it's preferable for her not to travel on her own at the moment. The friend she came down with had to go back. It's likely that, in two or three days, Marcelle will drive her home.'

It was almost unbelievable. They were talking as if nothing had happened, uttering the same words, even though there was no real bond left between them.

Betty still didn't understand why he had come, found it hard to believe it was simply to inquire after her health. He could have sent Florent or possibly Antoine. He could even have asked the hotel management. Which he had done, in fact. So? Why come up?

Putting his hat down on the carpet, he stood up, because he had never been able to sit still for long, especially for an important conversation, and he had to resist the urge to stride up and down as he was used to doing in his study.

'I wanted to say something to you, about the matter of the document you signed. Know that it is not my intention to use it right away.'

> . . . *I declare that I was caught by my husband and my mother-in-law, Madame Étamble, a widow, in the marital home, at 22A, Avenue de Wagram, on* . . .

Everything was there, the date, the time, the name of her accomplice, which she'd been loath to divulge. The presence of the two children in the apartment was mentioned, as well as the fact that she was stark naked.

She agreed to an at-fault divorce and relinquished in advance her maternal rights.

'I've thought very hard about it. I shan't hide the fact that having no news of you for several days worried me.'

'Florent told me.'

'It was above all to make sure that nothing had happened to you that I asked him to telephone this morning to suggest a meeting. Apparently you refused to see him.'

'I was waiting until I was better.'

'Have you had a nervous breakdown?'

'I don't know. In any case, it's not serious.'

He clasped his hands behind his back as he walked, like when he was dictating.

'I think, you see, that in a situation like ours, we shouldn't be in a rush. No one can foresee the future and we are not the only ones involved. Mother and I talked about it at length.'

Betty's forehead creased, her pupils narrowed. She listened with heightened attention.

'I don't know what you will think. It is not necessarily the best solution. I presume you realize that it would be difficult now for you to come back home.'

She couldn't believe her ears.

'On the other hand, it's not good for you to remain on your own. Because I imagine you are on your own?'

'Didn't the concierge tell you I was?'

'Yes. Besides, I thought you would be. My mother and I wondered whether we could try an experiment. You would go with her to Lyon. There's no reason why she can't stay in Paris until you're better. Two or three days won't make any difference. You'd live there with her for a while and if, afterwards . . .'

He didn't finish his sentence. He was clearly embarrassed, but full of good intentions.

'Was this your idea?'

For Betty, it was at the same time both kind and repulsive. As he paced up and down the room, this overgrown boy, Guy, was hinting that she might be able to resume her place in his home, with his children, rather as if he were beginning to forgive, as if he were promising to forget.

And it was her mother-in-law who had thought of it, who had suggested this trial period comparable to a nun's novitiate.

She would take her in under her roof, under her control. In the apartment on Quai de Tilsitt, full of the general's memorabilia, she would watch her day after day, noting her progress, probably counting on her influence.

Betty didn't laugh, didn't become indignant. She almost had tears in her eyes.

'Were you hoping I'd say yes?'

'I don't know.'

'Is it what you want?'

'I'm thinking of the children, of you.'

He felt sorry for her. He had just extended a helping hand to rescue her.

'Thank you, Guy. I am very touched by your gesture. And by your mother's. Please tell her so from me.'

'Is it no?'

'I believe it's wiser. Not so much for me as for all of you. I warned you, remember. You wouldn't listen to me.'

With one sentence, she reversed their positions. She was the one who became magnanimous, self-sacrificing and, as she spoke, she glanced at the carriage clock, wondering what was going on in Mario's restaurant.

She was afraid her husband would linger and ruin everything with his presence.

'You were right to come. It was better for us to say goodbye on a different memory.'

If Schwartz had been there, he would have said sarcastically:

'And there you go, romanticizing again!'

She hadn't expected this opportunity, this part she was being given to play, this choice that she was being offered.

'I'll telephone Florent in a few days. Go. Don't forget to thank your mother. It's not my fault if I've hurt you, believe me, but all the same I ask you to forgive me.'

She went along with it herself and, what's more, she was half sincere. It wasn't a cynical act. She felt no attachment to Guy, but, if life had been different, they might perhaps have been able to be happy. Well, he could have been happy, in any case. He could have been happy with any woman, except with her.

She had no regrets, but that didn't stop her feeling sorry for him.

'Go!'

Betty

'Are you sure?'

'Yes. Go!'

She was panic-stricken at the thought that Mario might arrive. Guy didn't realize that he represented a past world from which she had cut herself off. She was already living elsewhere. She was convinced another life was about to begin, had already begun, or almost, but it was still precarious, vague.

He picked up his hat, murmuring:

'You don't need anything?'

'Nothing.'

'Good luck, Betty.'

'Thank you. You too.'

He didn't know whether to hold out his hand. She didn't dare hold out hers. As he made his way slowly over to the door, she said again:

'Thank you.'

He didn't turn around. She heard his footsteps fade away down the long corridor and she wiped her hand over a forehead damp with sweat.

She drank the rest of the coffee, now cold, even though she was not likely to fall asleep any more. Guy's visit had perked her up, and so had the thought of Le Trou, where she already was in her mind.

She was tempted, better to put herself in the mood, to slip out of bed, go into Laure's room, look for the bottle they'd opened earlier and take a large glug.

She mustn't smell of alcohol. It was important that she should be exactly as she had been that afternoon, when Mario had tiptoed over to the bed.

Georges Simenon

She rang the bell. Even the filter and the cup on the table were in the way.

'Remove that, Jules.'

'Are you going to sleep?'

'I think so.'

She tried to calm herself down, unsuccessfully. Her nerves were taut with impatience and she found it hard to lie still in bed.

Ten o'clock . . . Half past ten . . . People were eating at Le Trou, surrounded by the red walls with English etchings . . . Jeanine, at the bar, was jiggling her big breasts as she laughed, running her hands over her hips to smooth her girdle . . . The African was popping up at one door, then another, like a benevolent genie . . . Laure had finished eating and was sipping her drink, watching the faces around her and taking in snatches of conversation . . .

Had the doctor shamefully slipped into the toilet to give himself an injection? . . . Did John have a new companion who was waiting for the moment when she would lie down on his bed while he gazed at her, his eyes bulging, a drink in his hand, sitting in his armchair, where he would eventually doze off . . .?

She was afraid of missing her chance, of losing her place, because, in her mind, it was already her place. Mario was strong, slightly brutish, a little naive. From the first moment their eyes had met, he'd been intrigued.

He had driven Maria Urruti to Buenaventura to defend her against her family and she had been kidnapped under his nose. He came every day to a quiet room at the

Betty

Carlton to chat with the widow of a professor from Lyon and give her, before leaving, the pleasure she needed, as Bernard needed his drug.

He probably had known other women of all kinds, but he had never yet encountered one like Betty.

Betty knew that she was all women rolled into one. He already suspected it. He had received her silent message and had responded.

Why wasn't he there yet? Was Laure detaining him? Did she have any inkling that they had arranged to meet almost in front of her?

The other evenings, he would go from table to table, and he sometimes jumped into his car to drive a customer home, an oddball in a bad way, as he'd done with the doctor.

He would find an excuse. He didn't need one. He didn't belong to Laure.

He had no idea that, because of him, Betty had just refused to return to Avenue de Wagram. By way of Lyon, true, as if on a trial basis.

And she had given Guy the task of thanking her mother-in-law!

But it wasn't generosity. Betty could even reconstitute her mother-in-law's thought process. Now that she was no longer in that atmosphere, she wasn't tempted to feel moved any more, but to rebel.

Not even that! No! At Le Trou, there was no question of rebellion. She had gone beyond that stage. There was no possibility of going back either.

It was the end of the line.

The end of the line for oddballs! Last stop before the asylum or the mortuary!

She had been mistaken in thinking that, for her, the time for the asylum or the mortuary had come. She hadn't known then that she still had Le Trou, still had Mario. She wanted to live. She was eager to live.

Anxiously, she looked at the clock, perfectly aware that it would be tonight or never. She didn't want to miss the opportunity. She dredged up a prayer.

'Oh Lord! Let him come.'

And, her body aching from impatience:

'Let him come quickly!'

She did not add:

'And let me succeed.'

If he came, she was certain she would. She desired it too much. She hungered for it too much. It was heartbreaking to be left in uncertainty and not be allowed to move.

It would be better if she didn't have to get up to open the door, she thought, all of a sudden. He had to come in by himself, thinking it was a surprise, a gift, and he should find her lying in the semi-darkness.

Barefoot, she hastily opened the door into the corridor a fraction, hoping that the bellhop on night duty or the chambermaid wouldn't close it as they walked past.

Instead of the bedside lamp, which was too bright, she lit the lamp on the dressing table, which was further away and dimmer.

Half past eleven . . . She wrung her arms with nervousness . . .

'Oh Lord! Please, let him . . .'

She was of a mind to make a promise, a vow, in exchange. She didn't know what to offer and was afraid it would backfire on her.

Let her just be given this chance, the last one. Was it too much to ask as a reward for all her efforts?

She had closed her eyes. Her thoughts clanged in her head and now she howled, in a voice that came from the depths of her throat:

'Mario!'

He was there, between the door and the bed, walking on tiptoe like earlier, and mischievously he placed a finger on his lips.

He had understood the message. He had come. He sat on the edge of the bed and, holding her shoulders with outstretched arms, he gazed at her for a long time before bending down to press his cheek to hers.

'You came!' she said, laughing and crying at the same time.

And, rubbing her cheek against his like an animal rubbing up against another animal:

'You're here!'

8

Someone was trying to turn the handle of the communicating door. They were trying to open it. Betty hoped that Mario couldn't hear it, because she wasn't certain enough yet.

Laure, next door, didn't insist, and the bell soon rang at the end of the corridor. She was calling the bellhop or the chambermaid. There were footsteps, a murmuring.

'Are you scared?' asked Mario, his eyes close to hers.

She hesitated, aware she was risking all she had and, trying to smile, answered:

'No.'

He clasped her more tightly to him and both stopped listening out. It was only much later that he whispered:

'I have to drop by Le Trou.'

'I'll come with you.'

'You're not allowed to. The doctor said . . .'

'The doctor knows nothing about women.'

She rushed towards the chest of drawers, towards the wardrobe.

'Would you like me to wear a dress instead of my suit, for a change? You haven't seen me in a dress yet.'

She would need a drink on arrival, because she felt dizzy.

She still managed to put her clothes on very quickly

and led him outside. Ignoring the lift, they went down the stairs hand in hand, as if they were stepping down from a town hall or a church.

'I have never felt so joyful in my life. And you?'

'I am happy.'

It wasn't yet entirely true. He must still be thinking of room 55, above them, and the forty-eight-year-old woman who found herself alone there.

'Where do you live?' asked Betty.

'Above the joint. It's a former farmhouse. The upstairs is under the eaves.'

The night concierge watched her go past in amazement.

She was alive! She had got over it! She had found a way out!

Already, she was taking ownership of the car, inhaling its smell.

'I don't want whisky tonight but champagne. Don't worry, I won't drink too much.'

The car accelerated. The concierge and the doorman exchanged glances. The bell rang on the concierge's desk.

'Yes, Madame Lavancher . . . They have just left, yes . . . They didn't speak to me . . . Sorry? . . . What? . . . At this hour? . . . But that's not possible . . . Of course, if you wish . . . Right away, Madame Lavancher . . .'

His head lowered, he went to join the doorman.

'I need you to come up with me to collect the luggage from room 55.'

'Is she leaving?'

'Apparently. I think I understand what's happening. It's that little slut she brought us a few nights ago who . . .'

Georges Simenon

What was the point of explaining? The doorman too had seen them.

'You'd better go and fetch her car.'

The receptionist emerged sleepily from the little office where he napped when things were quiet.

'What is it?'

'A departure. Number 55.'

'Madame Lavancher?'

'Yes.'

'Should I prepare her bill?'

'She didn't say anything about it.'

The receptionist, embarrassed, watched the two men enter the lift and automatically began to look for the file for room 55.

They had to go up to the room twice, and outside the sound of a car boot opening and closing could be heard, then the car doors.

'You don't have a length of rope?'

'There's one in the chef's van.'

Too bad for the chef. They'd sort it out with him in the morning.

Suitcases were strapped to the roof. Laure came down the stairs, walking a little stiffly.

'Tell Monsieur Raymond to send my bill to Lyon.'

He was the manager.

'Very good, Madame Lavancher. I hope you plan to return?'

She looked at him without replying, and shook his hand.

'Goodbye, François.'

She knew them all and called them by their first names.

The long lobby was empty, lit only by a few lamps and, at the far end, behind a glazed door, the dining room was in darkness.

'Goodbye, Charles. Goodbye, Joseph.'

They were at a loss for words. She got into the car, paused to light a cigarette, and started up the engine while the porter was still reluctant to close the door.

'Are you taking the N7?'

He had the impression that, in the dark, she was smiling at him. The door slammed. Gravel crunched under the tyres of the car as it went through the gates and vanished into the night.

It was only a week later, on leafing through *Le Progrès de Lyon*, that Guy's mother learned that one of her neighbours had been found dead in her apartment. In an emotionless voice, she said to the friend who was having tea with her:

'Did you know that Madame Lavancher is dead?'

'The professor's widow?'

'She was found dead this morning, in her bed, by her cleaning woman.'

'I thought she'd left Lyon long ago. Didn't she live in Paris?'

'In Versailles, but she'd kept on her apartment here and would come back every so often.'

'What was wrong with her?'

'The newspaper doesn't say.'

'But she wasn't old.'

'Forty-nine.'

Madame Étamble remembered something. It was to Versailles that Guy had gone to have a conversation with his wife. If Betty had been in her right mind, would she not have leaped at the chance she was being offered?

It was best this way for everyone, especially for Guy, who was still young, for Antoine and for his wife too, who would no longer have felt at home in the evenings on the third floor.

'I used to run into her from time to time. She was a tall woman, always quite pale, but I had no idea she was ill.'

How could Madame Étamble have guessed that, ultimately, Laure Lavancher had died instead of Betty?

It was one or the other.

Betty had won.

The Blue Room

I

'Did I hurt you?'
 'No.'
'Are you angry with me?'
 'No.'

It was true. At that time, everything was true, for he was living in the moment, without questioning anything, without trying to understand, without suspecting that one day he would need to understand. Not only was it all true, it was all real: himself, the room, Andrée still lying on the ravaged bed, naked, thighs spread, a thread of sperm seeping from the dark patch of her sex.

Was he happy? If anyone had asked him, he would have said 'yes' without any hesitation. It had not occurred to him to be angry at Andrée for biting his lip. That was part of it all like everything else and he stood, also naked, in front of the wash-basin mirror, dabbing at his lip with a towel moistened with cold water.

'Is your wife going to ask you any questions?'
'I don't think so.'
'Does she ever ask any?'

The words hardly mattered. They were talking for the pleasure of it, as one does after making love, bodies still flushed with sensation and minds slightly dazed.

'You have a beautiful back.'

A few pink stains dotted the towel, and in the street an empty lorry bounced over the cobblestones. On the terrace, some people were talking. A few words were audible, here and there, without making complete sentences or any real sense.

'Do you love me, Tony?'

'I think so . . .'

He spoke in jest but without smiling, because he was still patting his lower lip with the damp towel.

'You're not sure?'

He turned around to look at her and was pleased to notice that semen, his semen, in such intimacy with his companion's body.

The room was blue, 'washing-blue' he had thought one day, a blue that reminded him of his childhood, the tiny muslin sachets of blue powder his mother dissolved in the washtub water for the final rinse, right before she went to spread the laundry out on the gleaming grass of the meadow. He must have been five or six years old and often wondered through what miracle the blue colour could turn the laundry white.

Later, long after the death of his mother, whose face was already fading from his memory, he had also wondered why people as poor as they were, dressed in patched clothing, attached such importance to the whiteness of their linen.

Were those things going through his mind at that moment? He would find out only later. The blue of the room was not just washing-blue, but the sky-blue of certain hot August afternoons as well, shortly before it turns pink, then red, in the setting sun.

The Blue Room

It was August. The 2nd of August. Late in the afternoon. At five o'clock gilded clouds, as light as whipped cream, began to float up over the train station, leaving its white façade in shadow.

'Could you spend your whole life with me?'

He had hardly noticed her words; they were like the images and odours all around him. How could he have guessed that this scene was something he would relive ten times, twenty times and more – and every time in a different frame of mind, from a different angle?

For months, he would struggle to recall the slightest detail, and not always of his own free will, for sometimes others would demand it of him.

Professor Bigot, for example, the psychiatrist appointed by the examining magistrate, would keep after him about it, studying his reactions.

'Did she bite you often?'

'A few times.'

'How many?'

'All in all, we only met eight times at the Hôtel des Voyageurs.'

'Eight times in one year?'

'In eleven months . . . Yes, eleven, since it all began in September . . .'

'How many times did she bite you?'

'Maybe three or four.'

'During intercourse?'

'I think so . . . Yes . . .'

Yes . . . No . . . Today, actually, it was afterwards, when he had withdrawn from her and was lying on his side, looking at her through half-closed eyelashes. The light spilling all around them delighted him.

It was hot outside, in Place de la Gare, and hot as well in the hotel room bathed in sunshine, in a heat that seemed alive and breathing.

As he had left a gap some twenty centimetres wide when closing the shutters over the open window, they could hear the sounds of the little town; some were like the murmur of a distant choir while others, such as the voices of the customers on the terrace, were closer, crisp and distinct.

A little earlier, while they were both lost in wild love-making, those sounds had reached them and become one with their bodies, saliva, sweat, the whiteness of Andrée's belly, the darker tone of his own skin, the blue of the walls, the diamond-shaped sunbeam cutting the room in two, a shifting reflection in the mirror and the odours of the hotel, which still smelled of the countryside – of the wine and spirits served in the main room, the ragout simmering in the kitchen, even the slightly musty fibre stuffing of the mattress.

'You're handsome, Tony.'

She said this to him every time they met, always when she was still lying there while he moved around the room, looking for his cigarettes in the pocket of his trousers flung across a straw-bottomed chair.

'Are you still bleeding?'

'It's almost stopped.'

'What will you tell her, if she asks about it?'

He shrugged, couldn't see why that should worry

Andrée. Right now, nothing seemed important to him. He felt good, in tune with the universe.

'I'll tell her I bumped into something. My windshield, say, from braking too suddenly . . .'

He lit his cigarette, which had a special taste. When he reconstructed this conversation, he would remember another distinctive smell among all the others: the smell of trains. A freight train was manoeuvring behind the engine sheds, and the locomotive occasionally blew short blasts on its whistle.

Professor Bigot – short, thin, with red hair and thick, unruly eyebrows – would press him further.

'Did it never occur to you that she was biting you on purpose?'

'Why?'

Later, Maître Demarié, his lawyer, would bring it up again.

'I think we might be able to use these bites to some advantage . . .'

But again, how could he have thought about such things when he was completely caught up in experiencing them? Was he thinking of anything at all? If so, then he wasn't aware of it. He was answering Andrée off the top of his head, carelessly, in a light, teasing tone, convinced that such words had no weight and would therefore leave no lasting impression.

One afternoon, during their third or fourth assignation, after telling him that he was handsome, Andrée had added, 'You're so handsome that I'd like to make love with you in front of everyone, in the middle of Place de la Gare . . .'

He had laughed but hadn't really been surprised. When they were in each other's arms, he didn't mind keeping some slight contact with the outside world, with sounds, voices, the flickering light on the walls and even footsteps on the pavement, the clinking of glasses on the terrace tables.

One day, a brass band had marched past, and they'd had fun making love to the beat of the music. Another time, when a storm had sprung up, Andrée had insisted that he throw the window and shutters wide open.

Wasn't it a game? In any case, he had seen no harm in it. She was naked, lying across the bed in a deliberately provocative pose. She made a point of behaving as provocatively as possible as soon as she entered the room.

Sometimes, after they had undressed, she would murmur with an obviously feigned innocence that was all part of the game, 'I'm thirsty. Aren't you thirsty too?'

'No.'

'You will be later. Ring for Françoise, why don't you, and order something to drink.'

Françoise, the maid, was about thirty and had been working in cafés or hotels since she was fifteen, so nothing surprised her.

'Yes, Monsieur Tony?'

She called him Monsieur Tony because he was the brother of her employer, Vincent Falcone, whose name was painted on the front of the hotel and whose voice they could hear on the terrace.

'You never wondered if she might have behaved this way through some ulterior motive?'

The Blue Room

What he was living through – a half-hour, if that, just a few minutes of his life – would be broken down into images, detached sounds, peered at through a magnifying glass, not only by others but by himself.

Andrée was tall. That wasn't obvious, on the bed, but she was three or four centimetres taller than he was. Although she was a local girl she had the brown, almost black, hair of people in Italy or the south of France, a startling contrast with that smooth white skin gleaming in the light. She was amply proportioned, a little heavy, and her flesh was voluptuously firm, especially her breasts and thighs. At thirty-three, he had known many women. None of them had given him as much pleasure as she had, an animal pleasure, complete and wholehearted, untainted afterwards by any disgust, lassitude or regret.

On the contrary! After two hours spent seeking the maximum of pleasure from both their bodies, they would remain naked, prolonging their carnal intimacy, savouring the contentment they now felt not only with each other, but with everything around them.

Everything counted. Everything had its place in a vibrant universe, even the fly perched on Andrée's belly that she watched with a satisfied smile.

'Could you really spend your whole life with me?'

'Sure . . .'

'Really sure? Wouldn't you be a little afraid?'

'Afraid of what?'

'Can you imagine what our days would be like?'

Those words would crop up again as well, so lightly spoken today, so threatening in a few months.

'We'd get used to it in the end,' he murmured casually.
'Used to what?'
'To us.'

He was candid, innocent. Only the present mattered. A virile male, a highly sexed female had just enjoyed each other to the full, and if Tony ached a bit afterwards, the pain was healthy and satisfying.

'What do you know! The train's here . . .'

It wasn't Tony who'd spoken, but his brother, outside. Intrigued, Tony had gone automatically to the window, to the slit of blazing light between the shutters.

Could anyone see him from outside? He didn't care. Probably not, because the room must seem dark to those outdoors, and, as it was one floor up, only his torso might show.

'When I think of the years you cost me . . .'
'I cost you?' he replied playfully.
'Who was it who left? Me?'

They'd been in school together from the age of six. Only after they were both over thirty and married to others . . .

'Answer me seriously, Tony. If I became free . . .'

Was he listening? The train had arrived, invisible behind the white station, and passengers were beginning to appear through the door on the right, where a man in uniform was collecting the tickets.

'Would you free yourself too?'

Before leaving, the train blew its whistle so loudly that he couldn't hear anything else.

'What did you say?'

The Blue Room

'I'm asking if, in that case . . .'

He had turned his face halfway to the blue of the room, the whiteness of the bed and Andrée's body, but something he saw out of the corner of his eye made him look outside again. Among the anonymous figures – men, women, a baby in its mother's arms, a little girl dragged along by the hand – he had just recognized a face.

'Your husband . . .'

Tony's expression changed in an instant.

'Nicolas?'

'Yes.'

'Where is he? . . . What is he doing?'

'He's crossing the square . . .'

'He's coming here?'

'Straight here.'

'How does he seem?'

'I can't tell. He's got the sun behind him.'

'Where are you going?'

For Tony was collecting his clothes, his shoes.

'I can't stay here . . . As long as he doesn't find us together . . .'

He wasn't looking at her any more, wasn't interested any more in her, her body, what she might say or think. In a panic, he darted one last glance out of the window and ran from the room.

If Nicolas had come to Triant by train while his wife was here, it was for an important reason.

It was cooler out in the dark staircase with the worn steps. His clothes over one arm, Tony headed up one floor, then down the corridor to a half-open door at the end. Busy changing a bed in her black dress and white apron, Françoise looked him up and down and burst out laughing.

'Well, here's Monsieur Tony! . . . Did you have an argument?'

'Hush . . .'

'What's going on?'

'Her husband . . .'

'He caught you?'

'Not yet. He's coming towards the hotel . . .'

He dressed feverishly, listening hard, expecting to recognize the shuffling footsteps of Nicolas climbing the stairs.

'Go and see what he's doing then come and tell me, quick . . .'

Tony was fond of Françoise, a brisk, sturdy girl with laughing eyes, and she returned the feeling.

Half the ceiling was on a slant, the wallpaper had a pattern of pink flowers, and a black crucifix hung over the walnut bed. In the blue room as well, a smaller crucifix hung over the fireplace.

He had no tie, and his jacket was down in the van. The precautions he and Andrée had been taking for almost a year were suddenly proving useful.

Whenever they met at the Hôtel des Voyageurs, Tony left his little van in Rue des Saules, a quiet old street running parallel to Rue Gambetta, while Andrée parked her grey Citroën 2CV in Place du Marché, more than 300 metres away.

The Blue Room

Through the dormer window, he could see the hotel courtyard with stables at the end, where some hens were scratching for food. On the third Monday of every month, a livestock fair was held in front of the engine sheds, and many country folk still came to Triant in horse carts.

Françoise came back upstairs in no hurry.

'Well?'

'He's sitting on the terrace and he's just ordered a lemonade.'

'How does he seem?'

He was asking the same question Andrée had.

'He doesn't seem like anything.'

'Has he asked about his wife?'

'No. But from where he is, he can watch both exits.'

'Didn't my brother say anything to you?'

'That you should slip out the back and go through the courtyard of the garage next door.'

He knew the way. Going over a wall a metre and a half high, he would be behind the Garage Chéron, with its petrol pumps lined up on Place de la Gare, and from there an alley led to Rue des Saules, coming out between a pharmacy and the Boulangerie Patin.

'Do you know what she's doing?'

'No.'

'Did you hear any noise in the room?'

'I didn't listen for any.'

Françoise didn't much care for Andrée, perhaps because she was fond of Tony and felt jealous.

'You'd better not go through the ground floor, in case he goes to the toilet.'

Tony imagined Nicolas, with his bilious complexion and eternally sad or grumpy expression, sitting at a table on the terrace with his lemonade when he should have been behind the counter of his grocery store. He must have had to ask his mother to take his place while he was off in Triant. What reason had he given her for this unusual trip? What did he know? Who had told him?

'Did you never think, Monsieur Falcone, about the possibility of an anonymous letter?'

The question had come from the examining magistrate, Maître Diem, a man so shy it was disconcerting.

'No one in Saint-Justin knew about our affair. Or in Triant, either, aside from my brother, my sister-in-law and Françoise. Andrée and I were careful. She used to enter via the little door on Rue Gambetta, which opens on to the foot of the stairs, allowing her to head up to the room without going through the café.'

'You're sure about your brother, of course?'

Tony could only smile at that question. His brother was like another self.

'And your sister-in-law as well?'

Lucia loved him almost as much as she loved Vincent, in a different way, naturally. Like the two of them, she was of Italian parentage, and family came before everything else.

'The maid?'

Even if Françoise was in love with Tony, she would never have sent an anonymous letter.

Diem had to look away, and the sunlight gleamed in his untidy hair.

The Blue Room

'There's still someone . . .' he murmured.

'Who?'

'Don't you see? Remember the words you recalled for me during our last interview. Would you like the clerk to read them back to you?'

Tony flushed, shaking his head.

'It isn't possible that Andrée . . .'

'Why not?'

But that still lay far ahead. For the moment, Tony was following Françoise down the stairs, trying not to make the ancient steps creak, for the Hôtel des Voyageurs dated back to the days of the stagecoaches. He paused a moment in front of the blue room but couldn't hear a thing. Did that mean Andrée was still lying naked on the bed?

Françoise led him down the corridor and around a corner, pointing to a small window opening on to the sloping roof of a shed.

'There's a pile of straw, on the right. It's quite safe to jump . . .'

The hens squawked when he landed in the courtyard, and the next moment he was scaling the wall at the far end to find himself in a clutter of old vehicles and bits of machinery. A white-uniformed pump attendant was filling up a car in front of the station and never turned around.

Tony slipped away to the alley, which smelled of stagnant water at first and further on, of freshly baked bread, thanks to a ventilator behind the baker's oven.

Finally, Rue des Saules, he slid behind the steering

wheel of his lemon-yellow van, on which black letters spelled out:

Antonio Falcone
Tractors – Agricultural Machinery
Saint-Justin-du-Loup

A quarter of an hour earlier, he had felt at peace with the whole world. How to describe the deep uneasiness that had come over him? It wasn't fear, for he had had no reason to suspect anything was wrong.

'Weren't you concerned to see Nicolas walk out of the station?'

Yes . . . No . . . A little, because of the man's nature, his habits, the way he was always worrying about his health.

To avoid crossing Place de la Gare, Tony went the long way round to reach the road to Saint-Justin. Near a bridge over the Orneau, an entire family was fishing in the river, including a little girl of six who had just landed her catch without any idea how to get it off the hook. Parisians, no question. In the summer they were everywhere; there were some at his brother's hotel, and a little earlier, in the blue room, he had recognized their accent on the terrace.

The road ran past wheat fields freshly harvested two weeks back, past vines, past meadows, where the tawny cows of the region were grazing, their dark muzzles almost black.

Some three kilometres along, Saint-Séverin was just a

The Blue Room

short street with a few farms scattered around it. Then he saw, to the right, Bois de Sarelle, a small wood named after the hamlet hidden behind the trees.

In September of the previous year, it was here, a few metres from the unpaved road, that it had all started.

'Tell me about the beginning of your liaison . . .'

First the sergeant, then the lieutenant of the gendarmerie in Triant and then an inspector of the Police Judiciaire in Poitiers had asked him these same questions before he met with Diem, the thin psychiatrist, and his lawyer, Demarié, all in preparation for his interrogation by the presiding judge of the Assize Court.

The same words were repeated for weeks and months, by other voices, in other places, while spring turned into summer and summer into autumn.

'The real beginning? We first met when we were three years old, because we lived in the same village, and we went to school, then we made our First Communion together . . .'

'I'm talking about your sexual relations with Andrée Despierre. Did they begin before?'

'Before what?'

'Before she married your friend.'

'Nicolas was not my friend.'

'Let's say your classmate or, if you prefer, fellow student. Her last name was Formier, at the time, and she lived in the chateau with her mother . . .'

It was not a real chateau. There had once been a chateau there, abutting the church, but only a few outbuildings remained. For perhaps a century and a half, doubtless ever since the Revolution, people had still been calling the place the chateau.

'Did you ever, before her marriage . . .'

'No, Your Honour.'

'Not even a flirtation? Didn't you ever kiss her?'

'It would never have crossed my mind.'

'Why not?'

He almost replied, 'Because she was too tall.'

And it was true. He could not have imagined this tall, impassive girl who reminded him of a statue ever making love.

Besides, she was Mademoiselle Formier, the daughter of Dr Formier, who had died during the wartime deportations. Was this explanation enough? He couldn't think of any other reason. The two of them had not belonged to the same circles.

When they left school each afternoon with their satchels on their backs, she had only to cross the playground to be home, in the heart of the village, whereas he and two friends walked on to La Boisselle, a tiny 'three-hearth hamlet' near the Orneau bridge.

'When you came back to Saint-Justin four years ago, married and a father, and you built your house there, did you contact her again?'

'She had married Nicolas and was running the grocery store with him. I bought something there now and then, but it was more often my wife who . . .'

'Now tell me how it began.'

He was driving past the place right now, at the edge of Bois de Sarelle. It wasn't the day of the monthly cattle

The Blue Room

fair in Triant or the main market. Monday was the main market day, and there was a smaller market every Friday as well. He went to them regularly, because it was a good way to meet his customers.

Because of his health, Nicolas did not drive – the magistrate knew that. It was Andrée who drove the Citroën to Triant every Thursday to purchase goods from various wholesalers.

Every other Thursday, she stayed in town all day, adding a visit to the hairdresser's.

'You must have run into her often, during those four years?'

'A certain number of times, yes. One always meets people from Saint-Justin in Triant.'

'Did you usually speak to each other?'

'In greeting.'

'At a distance?'

'At a distance, or more personally, it depended.'

'There were no other contacts between you?'

'I must have asked occasionally how her husband was, or how she was doing.'

'Without any designs on her?'

'Excuse me?'

'This inquiry has revealed that in the course of your professional comings and goings you indulged in a certain number of amorous adventures.'

'Yes, like everyone else.'

'Often?'

'Whenever I could.'

'Among others, with Françoise, your brother's maid?'

'Once. For fun. It was more like a joke.'

'What do you mean?'

'She'd dared me, I no longer remember the pretext, and one day when I met her on the stairs . . .'

'It happened on the stairs?'

'Yes.'

Why did they sometimes look at him as if he were a cynical monster and at other times, freakishly naive?

'Neither of us took it seriously.'

'Still, you did have intercourse?'

'Of course.'

'You never felt like doing it again?'

'No.'

'Why not?'

'Perhaps because, right after that, there was Andrée.'

'Your brother's maid didn't resent you for this?'

'Why would she?'

How different life is when one is living it from when one picks through it later on! In the end he was unsettled by the feelings they ascribed to him, no longer knowing how to tell the true from the false, wondering what separated right from wrong.

That encounter in September, for example! A Thursday, probably, since Andrée had gone to Triant. She must have been delayed, at the hairdresser's or elsewhere, because she was going home later than usual, and it was growing dark.

As for him, he had been obliged to have a few glasses of the local wine with some clients. He tried to avoid drinking but in his job he could not always refuse a friendly round.

The Blue Room

He was feeling fine, light-hearted, as he had been when standing completely naked in front of the mirror in the blue room, staunching the bleeding from his lip.

He had just turned on his headlights when he spotted Andrée's grey Citroën by the side of the road, and Andrée, in light-coloured clothing, signalling him to stop.

Quite naturally, he had.

'It's a lucky thing you were passing by, Tony . . .'

Later they would ask him, as if it were an indictment against him: 'You were already on familiar terms?'

'Ever since school, of course.'

'Continue.'

Whatever could the magistrate have been writing on the typed sheet of paper in front of him?

'She said, "I end up with a puncture the *one* time I haven't room for the jack and leave it at home! You've got one, right?"'

He hadn't needed to take off his jacket because it was still so hot that he wasn't wearing one. He remembered that his open-necked shirt had short sleeves and that his trousers were of blue twill.

What else could he do but change the tyre?

'Have you a spare?'

While he was working night fell, and Andrée stood near him, handing him the tools.

'You'll be late for dinner.'

'You know, in my line of work, that's not unusual.'

'Your wife doesn't say anything?'

'She knows it isn't my fault.'

'You met her in Paris?'

'In Poitiers.'

'She's from there?'

'From a village close by. She worked in Poitiers.'

'You like blondes?'

Gisèle was a blonde, with delicate, pearly skin that flushed pink at the slightest emotion.

'I don't know. I've never thought about it.'

'I was wondering if brunettes scared you.'

'Why?'

'Because years ago, you kissed almost all the girls in the village, except me.'

'I probably just didn't think of it.'

He was kidding around, wiping his hands off with his handkerchief.

'You want to try, for once, to kiss me?'

He had looked at her in amazement, tempted to say it again: *Why?*

He couldn't see her clearly in the darkness.

'You want to?' she had repeated, in a voice he had hardly recognized.

He remembered the little red lights at the back of the car, the scent of the chestnut trees, then the smell, the taste of Andrée's mouth. With her lips clinging to his, she grabbed his hand and guided it to her breast, which he was astonished to find so round, so heavy and alive.

And he had thought of her as a statue!

A lorry was coming, and, to avoid its headlamps, they drew back, still locked together, towards the ditch by the edge of the wood, where Andrée suddenly began to tremble the way no other woman he had known had ever done, leaning on him with her whole body and saying over and over: 'You want to?'

They had found themselves on the ground, in the tall grass and nettles.

He told neither the policemen nor the magistrate. Only Professor Bigot, the psychiatrist, dragged the truth out of him, bit by bit: she was the one who had pulled her skirt up over her belly and bared her breasts, commanding him in a voice as hoarse as a death rattle: 'Fuck me, Tony!'

In fact, it was she who had possessed him, and her eyes had gleamed with as much triumph as passion.

'I'd never suspected she was like that.'

'What do you mean?'

'I'd thought she was cold, haughty, like her mother.'

'Afterwards, she wasn't at all upset?'

Lying still in the grass with her legs wide apart, as on that afternoon in the hotel room, she had said, 'Thank you, Tony.'

She had seemed to mean it. She had looked humble, almost like a little girl.

'I've wanted to for so long, you see! Ever since school. You remember Linette Pichat, the girl with one eye a little crossed? It didn't stop you from running after her for months!'

Linette now taught at a school in the Vendée region and every year came home to spend her holidays with her parents.

'I caught you together, once. You must have been fourteen.'

'Behind the brickyard?'

'You haven't forgotten?'

He laughed.

'I haven't forgotten because it was the first time.'

'For her too?'

'I haven't a clue. I was too inexperienced to notice that.'

'I hated her! For months, in bed at night, I racked my brain for ways to make her suffer.'

'Did you find any?'

'No. I settled for praying that she'd get sick or be disfigured in an accident.'

'We'd better be getting back to Saint-Justin.'

'Wait a moment, Tony. No! Don't get up. We have to find a way to meet somewhere else. I go to Triant every Thursday.'

'I know.'

'Maybe your brother . . .'

The magistrate would later conclude: 'In short, as of that evening, it was all settled?'

It was hard to tell if he was being ironic.

On 2 August, the magistrate had not yet entered his life, and Tony drove on home. Night had not yet fallen, as it had in September. The sky was only just beginning to glow red in the west, and he had to dawdle a long time behind a herd of cows before he could pass them.

A village in a hollow: Doncœur. Then a gentle slope, more fields, meadows, a vast stretch of sky and, after a rise in the road, the sight of his brand-new house, of pink brick, with the sun reflecting off one window, his daughter Marianne sitting on the doorstep and, at the far end of the property, the silvery shed where he stored farm machinery had his name emblazoned on it, just as it was on the van, which Marianne had already spotted in the distance.

Twisting around, she must have been announcing into the house, 'It's Pop!'

She refused to say 'papa' like the other children and sometimes as a game (and perhaps because she was jealous of her mother) she called him Tony.

2

Halfway up a hill on the left was his house, surrounded by its garden, separated by a field from the old, grey, slate-roofed house of the Molard sisters. Beyond it were the smithy and finally, a hundred metres further down, the village, with real streets, terrace houses, shops and small cafés. The local people preferred to call it a market town, however, a large one of 1,600 inhabitants, not counting the three adjoining hamlets.

'You been fighting, Pop?'

He had forgotten Andrée's bite.

'Your lip's all swollen.'

'I bumped into something.'

'What?'

'A lamp-post, in Triant. That's what happens when you forget to watch where you're going.'

'Mama! Pop bumped into a lamp-post . . .'

His wife came out of the kitchen in a small-checked apron and carrying a saucepan.

'Is that true, Tony?'

'It's nothing, as you can see.'

Mother and daughter looked so much alike that, when they stood side by side, it sometimes startled him.

'It wasn't too hot for you today?'

'Not really. Now I have to finish some work in the office.'

The Blue Room

'Can we eat at 6.30?'

'I hope so.'

They ate early because Marianne went to bed at eight o'clock. She had her own apron with little blue checks. She had just lost two front baby teeth, and the gaps gave her an almost pathetic expression. It was as if, for a few weeks, she were a child and a little old woman at the same time.

'Can I come with you, Pop? I promise not to make a noise.'

The office, with its pine shelves full of green boxes and piles of brochures, looked out on the road, and Tony was anxious to see the Citroën go by.

Next door was what the architect had called the living room, the largest room in the house, intended to serve as both dining and sitting rooms.

During the first week they had discovered that it simply wasn't practical for Gisèle to shuttle back and forth with the dishes, leaving the table to check food on the stove, and they had decided to eat in the kitchen.

That room was large and cheerful. The scullery was used for washing and ironing. Everything was well planned, remarkably clean, never untidy.

'Your wife, I take it then, could be called an excellent housekeeper?'

'Yes, Your Honour.'

'Is that why you married her?'

'When I married her, I didn't know that.'

Things had developed in three stages, actually, if not four. The first in Saint-Justin, in his house, when the police sergeant, then the lieutenant, had hounded him with questions he found baffling. Then it was Inspector Mani's turn, in Poitiers: he specified dates, compared times, reconstructed Tony's comings and goings.

At first no one was interested in his thoughts and outlook – especially not the police, or perhaps they simply found his private life unsurprising and basically like their own. With Diem and then the psychiatrist, even his lawyer, all that would change. Whenever Tony appeared before the examining magistrate, for example, he arrived from prison, in the police van that would soon ferry him back there, whereas the magistrate went home for lunch or dinner.

It was Diem who made him the most uneasy, perhaps because they were about the same age. The magistrate was a year younger than Tony and had been married for a year and a half. His wife had just had their first baby. The magistrate's father, not a rich man, worked as an office manager in the Social Security Department, and Diem had married a typist. They lived in a modest apartment, three rooms and a kitchen, in the newest neighbourhood in town.

Shouldn't they have been able to understand each other?

'What was it, exactly, that frightened you that night?'

What answer could he give! Everything. Nothing in particular. Nicolas hadn't turned the shop over to his mother and taken the train for no good reason. He hadn't come to Triant just to sit at a little table on the terrace of the Hôtel des Voyageurs and drink some lemonade.

The Blue Room

When Tony had left the blue room, Andrée was still naked on the bed and showing no sign of going anywhere soon.

'Did you consider Nicolas a violent man?'

'No.'

He was, however, a sick man who had been morose and withdrawn ever since childhood.

'Did you wonder, in Triant, if he might be armed?'

He hadn't thought of that.

'Were you afraid for your family?'

They weren't managing, he and Diem, to use words that meant the same thing to them both, to place themselves on the same footing. They were always a little out of step with each other.

Pencil in hand before a pile of invoices, he pretended to work, now and then placing a meaningless cross next to a number to look busy.

Sitting at his feet, his daughter was playing with a toy car that had lost a wheel. Beyond the lawn and the white fence, he could see the road about twenty metres away and, across a meadow, the backs of some village houses, their yards and small gardens where dahlias were in bloom. In one spot an enormous yellow sunflower with its black heart stood out brightly against a grey wall, near a barrel.

When he had come home, he had automatically checked the clock: 5.45. At 6.20, Gisèle came to ask him, 'Can I start serving now?'

'Maybe a little later. I'd like to finish this before dinner.'

'I'm hungry, Pop!'

'It won't take long, my pet. If I'm late, you'll sit down to eat with Mama.'

It was around then that he felt flooded by a panic unlike what he had felt earlier, when clutching his clothes and dashing upstairs in the hotel. This was a heart-wrenching, bodily anguish, an abrupt rush of fever that forced him to go and stand by the window.

When he lit a cigarette, his hand trembled. His legs felt shaky. A presentiment? He spoke to the psychiatrist about it – or, rather, Professor Bigot persuaded him to discuss it.

'That had never happened to you before?'

'No. Not even when by some miracle I survived a car accident unharmed. And yet that time, when I came to, sitting in a field without a scratch, I began to cry.'

'Were you afraid of Nicolas?'

'I always found him disturbing, somehow.'

'Even back in school?'

As luck would have it, just before 6.30, the Citroën appeared at the top of the rise. It drove past the house with Andrée at the wheel, her husband beside her, and neither of them looked in his direction.

'Ready when you are, Gisèle . . .'

'Then dinner is served. Go and wash your hands, Marianne.'

They had begun their evening meal as usual: soup, a ham omelette, salad, a camembert and some apricots for dessert.

Outside the windows lay the kitchen garden the couple tended together, where Marianne crouched for hours, pulling up weeds.

The Blue Room

The runner beans had reached the top of their poles. Behind the wire fencing of the hen-house at least a dozen white Leghorn hens were pecking away, and there were shadowy forms in the rabbit hutches.

The day seemed to be winding down like any other summer day. A mild breeze came in through the open window, with an occasional breath of cooler air. Fat Didier the blacksmith was still busy at his forge. Nature was calm and settling in for the night.

Professor Bigot's questions almost always came out of the blue.

'Did you have the feeling, from that evening on, that you had lost her?'

'Who? Andrée?'

He was nonplussed, because he hadn't thought of that at all.

'You'd been caught up, for eleven months, in what can certainly be called a grand passion . . .'

And that was not how he would have described it. He desired Andrée. After a few days without her, thoughts of their tumultuous, ardent hours together would haunt him with memories of her smell, her breasts, her belly, her boldness. Sometimes he lay awake next to Gisèle for hours, tortured by incredible fantasies.

'What do you think about going to the cinema?'

'What day is it?'

'Thursday.'

Gisèle was a little surprised; they usually went to the cinema once a week, in Triant, just twelve kilometres away.

On other evenings, Tony would work in his office while his wife washed the dishes, then joined him to sew or darn socks while he worked. Now and then they would pause to chat briefly, almost always about Marianne, who would be starting school in October.

Once in a while, they would sit in front of their house, gazing out at the gathering dusk, the red and grey roofs in the moonlight, the dark mass of the trees with their barely whispering leaves.

'What's showing?'

'An American film. I saw the poster, but can't remember the title.'

'If you want to go . . . I'll tell the Molards.'

When they went out in the evening, one or both of the Molard sisters came to stay with Marianne. The eldest, Léonore, was thirty-seven or -eight; Marthe was a bit younger, but they seemed of no particular age and would turn into old maids without anyone even noticing.

Both had round, moonlike faces with indistinct features and wore the same dresses, the same coats, the same hats, as some twins do.

Often they were the sole worshippers at the seven o'clock mass, where they took communion every morning, and they never missed vespers or benediction.

It was they who helped Father Louvette in the church, putting flowers on the altars, tending the cemetery, and they again who sat up with the dying and laid out the dead.

They were seamstresses, and passers-by could see them

The Blue Room

working through their front window, where a big caféau-lait cat often lay napping on the sill.

Marianne did not like them.

'They smell bad,' she said.

They did indeed have a particular odour about them, the one found in churches and dry-goods stores, plus a hint of the smell in sickrooms.

'They're ugly!'

'If they weren't here to take care of you, you'd be left alone in the house.'

'I'm not scared.'

Gisèle smiled her own little smile, a faint one that barely curved her lips, as if she were trying to keep it to herself.

'You ascribe that to her sense of discretion?'

'Yes, Your Honour.'

'What do you mean by that? Able to keep a secret?'

More words!

'That's not how I think of it. She didn't like to be noticed. She was afraid of taking up too much room, of disturbing people, of asking them any favours.'

'Was she already like that as a child?'

'I believe so. After a film or a dance, for instance, she would never have admitted that she was thirsty, so that I wouldn't have to spend more money.'

'Did she have women friends?'

'Only one, a lady neighbour older than she was, with whom she took long walks.'

'What attracted you to her?'

'I don't know. I never asked myself that.'

'Did she seem safe and reassuring?'

Tony stared at the magistrate's face, trying to understand.

'I thought she would make . . .'

He couldn't find the right word.

'A good wife?'

That wasn't quite it, but he sighed and said, 'Yes.'

'Did you love her?'

And when there was no answer: 'Did you want to sleep with her? Did you go to bed with her before your marriage?'

'No.'

'You didn't desire her?'

He must have, since he married her.

'And she? Do you think she loved you or that it was the marriage itself that appealed to her?'

'I don't know. I think . . .'

What would the magistrate have replied if he had asked *him* the same question? They made a good couple, that's all. Gisèle was tidy, energetic, unassuming, the perfect housewife in their new house.

He was glad to come home to her in the evenings and until Andrée he had never had any serious affairs, even if he did take advantage of the odd opportunity.

'You maintain that you never considered a divorce?'

'It's the truth.'

'Not even during these last few months?'

'Not for one moment.'

'Yet you told your mistress . . .'

Then Tony suddenly raised his voice, even banged his fist on the little magistrate's desk without realizing it.

The Blue Room

'But that's just it, I never actually said anything! She was the one talking! She was naked on the bed. I was naked in front of the mirror: we'd just, the two of us . . . I mean, you know this as well as I do. In such moments, who worries about words? I could barely hear what she was saying. Listen: for a good long while, I was watching a bee . . .'

He suddenly recalled the bee: he had even opened the shutters wider to let it fly out.

'I was nodding or shaking my head while thinking of other things . . .'

'What, for example?'

It was too discouraging. He couldn't wait to get back to his prisoner cage inside the police van, where no one asked him any questions.

'I don't know.'

While Gisèle dashed next door to alert the Molard sisters, Tony put Marianne to bed, then showered and changed his underwear, as he did whenever he had seen Andrée in Triant. There were three bedrooms and a bathroom upstairs.

'If we have more children, we can put the boys in one bedroom and the girls in the other,' Gisèle had said when they were discussing the new house.

After six years, they still had only Marianne and had used the third bedroom just once, when Gisèle's parents had visited Saint-Justin during the holidays.

They lived in Montsartois, six kilometres from Poitiers. Germain Coutet, journeyman plumber, was a heavy man built like a gorilla, with a ruddy face, a booming voice, and he began every sentence with: 'I've always said . . .' or 'What I think is . . .'

From day one it was easy to see that he envied his son-in-law, envied him his bright, orderly office, the modern kitchen and especially the gleaming shed where the machinery was kept.

'Me, I still think it's a mistake for a workman to branch out on his own . . .'

He opened his first bottle of red wine at eight in the morning and drank all day long. He could be found loudly holding forth in all the village bistros and, although never drunk, would become increasingly categorical, even aggressive, as the day wore on.

'Who goes fishing every Sunday morning? You or me? So there! Who has three weeks of paid holidays? And who doesn't need to come home at the end of the day and bust his brain over a bunch of numbers?'

His wife – fat, passive, with a prominent stomach – never challenged him. Could that explain why Gisèle was so shy?

Towards the end of their stay, there had been some heated arguments, and the Coutets spent no further holidays in Saint-Justin.

After speaking to the Molard sisters, Gisèle had time to put away the dishes and even change her clothes. She barely seemed to move yet never appeared to hurry as she went about her chores, which got done as if by magic.

A last goodnight to Marianne, in the warm shadows

The Blue Room

of her room. Downstairs, the Molard ladies were already bending over their sewing.

'Have a good time.'

It was all very familiar, a scene so frequently repeated that they paid no attention to it any more.

The engine started. Side by side in the front seat of the van, they left the village behind, where someone was working late in his garden while most others, sitting on chairs in front of their houses, were taking quiet advantage of the cool evening air, a few listening to a radio playing somewhere behind them in an empty room.

They drove in silence at first, lost in their own thoughts.

'Tell me, Tony . . .'

When she paused, he felt a pang in his heart and wondered what would come next.

'Don't you think that for some time now Marianne has been looking a touch pale?'

Their daughter had always been thin, with long arms, long legs, and her complexion had never been rosy.

'I spoke to Dr Riquet about it earlier today, when I ran into him coming out of the grocery store . . .'

Hadn't she been surprised to see that Nicolas had vanished, leaving his mother behind the counter? Hadn't she thought it strange?

'As he says, we have nice fresh air, but children need change. He suggests that, when we can, perhaps next year, we should take her to the seaside.'

He startled himself with the speed of his reply.

'Why not this year?'

She hardly dared believe it. Summer was Tony's busiest

season, so they hadn't taken a single holiday since their move to Saint-Justin. They'd spent their savings on the property, but they would be paying off the house and machinery shed for a few years yet.

'You think we could?'

Once, the first year of their marriage, while they were still in Poitiers, they had spent two weeks at Les Sables-d'Olonne, renting a furnished room from an old woman, where Gisèle cooked their meals on an alcohol stove.

'It's already August. I'm afraid there won't be anything left.'

'We'll go to the hotel. You remember that hotel, at the very end of the beach, a little before the pine woods?'

'Les Roches Grises. No! Les Roches Noires!'

They had dined there one night on an enormous sole to celebrate Gisèle's birthday, and the Muscadet had made her a little tipsy.

Tony was happy with his decision: he would be cutting off contact with Andrée and Nicolas for a while.

'When do you want to . . .'

'I'll tell you later.'

Before being absolutely sure about this holiday and choosing specific dates, he would have to speak to his brother. It was in order to see Vincent, in fact, that he was taking his wife to the cinema. He drove past the Hôtel des Voyageurs without stopping and turned into Rue Gambetta, where he found a parking space right outside the Olympia. On the pavement, one could tell the Parisians from the local people by the way they dressed, the way they walked and gazed at the lighted shop windows.

The Blue Room

Tony and Gisèle always took the same seats, in the balcony. During the intermission after the newsreels, documentary and cartoon, he suggested, 'How about a beer at Vincent's place?'

The terrace tables were almost all occupied, but Françoise found one for them and wiped it with her cloth.

'Two beers, Françoise. Is my brother here?'

'At the bar, Monsieur Tony.'

Inside the café, men were playing cards in the yellowish light, regulars whom Tony had seen a hundred times sitting in the same corner, with the same customers to watch and comment on each play.

'Well?'

His brother answered in Italian, which was unusual, for they'd been born in France and had spoken Italian only with their mother, who had never managed to learn French.

'I'm not exactly sure what happened. I have the feeling that everything's fine. He was there, on the terrace . . .'

'I know. I saw him from upstairs.'

'Ten minutes after you left, she came down, relaxed, as if she hadn't a care in the world, and crossed the café calling out: "Do thank your wife for me, Vincent . . ." She was speaking loudly enough for her husband to hear. She left the same way, carrying her handbag. Just as she reached the corner of Rue Gambetta, she suddenly seemed to notice Nicolas: "Well! What are you doing here?"

'She sat down across from him, and I didn't hear the rest of their conversation.'

'Did they seem to be arguing?'

'No. At one point, she opened her bag and calmly applied fresh powder and lipstick.'

'How did he seem?'

'With him, it's hard to tell. You ever see him laugh, hmm? If you ask me, she got away with it, but if I were you . . . Is Gisèle here?'

'On the terrace.'

Vincent went to say hello to her. The air was mild, the sky clear. An express train went through the station without stopping or slowing down. In Rue Gambetta, Gisèle placed her hand on her husband's arm, as she always did when out walking with him.

'Is your brother pleased with how things are going?'

'It's been a good season so far. There are more and more tourists every year.'

Vincent had not had to buy the building, but only the business, because the landlord, who had run the hotel before him and had retired to La Ciotat, did not want to sell.

Starting with nothing, the two brothers had managed quite well for themselves and had already come a long way.

'Did you see Lucia?'

'No. She must have been in the kitchen. I didn't have time to go and see her.'

He felt vaguely uneasy, and not for the first time. Gisèle knew he had been in Triant that afternoon, yet had not asked him if he had seen his brother.

At times he would have preferred that she ask him questions, painful though they might prove. Since she helped him with his bookkeeping at the end of every month, and thus knew all about his business, why wouldn't she be interested in what he did when he was off at work?

Did she have suspicions she preferred to keep to herself?

They hurried back, for they could hear the bell inside the cinema signalling the end of the intermission, and others poured out of the little bar next door to join them.

It was only on the way home, in the darkness of the car, as the headlamps flared across black-and-white landscapes like the ones in the film, that he suddenly announced, 'Today is Thursday.'

The word alone made him blush. Did it not evoke the blue room, Andrée's voluptuous body, her spread thighs, her dark sex slowly oozing semen?

'We could go on Saturday. I'll phone Les Roches Noires tomorrow. If they have two rooms, or even one, and could supply a little bed for Marianne . . .'

'Can you leave your work now?'

'I could dash back here once or twice if necessary.'

He felt saved, realizing only now the danger from which he had escaped.

'We'll stay there for two weeks, the three of us, lounging on the beach.'

Filled with a sudden wave of tenderness for his daughter, he blamed himself for not having noticed her pallor. He had wronged his wife, too, but through sins of omission. For example, he would never have been able to stop the car by the side of the road, take Gisèle in his arms, press his face close to hers murmuring, 'I love you, you know!'

And yet, the thought had crossed his mind, he had often considered it. He had never done it. What was he ashamed of? Wouldn't he have seemed like someone guilty and begging for forgiveness?

He needed her. Marianne needed her mother, too. And he had betrayed them both when Andrée had asked him her questions. True, he had listened to them only distractedly, patting his lip with the damp towel. They were coming back to him now anyway, with cutting clarity, and he could even weigh the silence of her pauses.

'You have a beautiful back.'

It was ridiculous. Gisèle would never think of going into ecstasies over his back or his chest.

'Do you love me, Tony?'

In the overheated room smelling of sex, such a question was only natural, whereas now, in the quiet night, as the van hummed along, the words and intonations became unreal. He had thought himself clever to reply grudgingly, 'I think so.'

'You're not sure?'

Did he think he was playing a game? Didn't he realize that for her, it was so much more than that?

'Could you spend your whole life with me?'

She had asked that question twice in the space of a few minutes. Hadn't he already heard it during their previous encounters in the same room?

'Sure!' he had replied, flying high, light in body and spirit.

She had sensed so strongly that he wasn't speaking from his heart that she had come at him again.

The Blue Room

'Really sure? . . . Wouldn't you be afraid?'

What a fool he had been to say, with a clever glint in his eye: 'Afraid of what?'

The whole conversation was coming back to him, word for word.

'Can you imagine what our days would be like?'

She hadn't said *nights*, but *days*, as if she meant for them to spend all their time in bed.

'We'd get used to it in the end.'

'Used to what?'

'To us.'

And it was Gisèle who sat next to him in the darkness, watching the same stretch of road, the same trees, the same telegraph poles surge out of the night only to hurtle into nothingness. He was tempted to take her hand and he didn't dare.

He would admit that one day to Dr Bigot, who preferred to visit him in his cell rather than the prison infirmary. Although the guard brought him a chair, he sat on the edge of the bed.

'If I understand correctly, you loved your wife?'

Tony spread his hands wide but simply said, 'Yes.'

'Only, you were unable to reach her . . .'

He had never suspected that life could be so complicated. What did the psychiatrist mean, exactly, by 'reach her'? They lived together like any married couple, didn't they?

'Why did you have no more children, after Marianne?'

'I don't know.'

'You didn't want any more?'

On the contrary! He would have wanted six, a dozen, a houseful of children, as in Italy. As for Gisèle, she had talked about two or three boys and a girl, and they'd taken no precautions against a pregnancy.

'Did you often have sex with your wife?'

'Mainly at the beginning.'

He spoke freely, without trying to hide anything. He had got caught up in this investigation and was as anxious as his interrogators to get to the bottom of it all.

'There was a period while she was pregnant, of course, when . . .'

'Was that when you began seeing other women?'

'I would have done that anyway.'

'Is it some need you have?'

'I don't know. All men are like that, aren't they?'

Professor Bigot was around fifty, with a grown son studying in Paris and a daughter recently married to a haematologist, for whom she worked as a lab assistant.

The psychiatrist was untidy, wore loose-fitting, shabby clothes, on which a button often hung by a thread, and he was always blowing his nose as if suffering from a perpetual cold.

How could he make this man understand that drive home in the night? Nothing special had happened. He and Gisèle hadn't said much to each other. At that time he had been certain that she knew nothing – nothing about that afternoon's events, at least, and probably nothing about his affair with Andrée, even if she had heard rumours about a few other escapades.

Yet it was while driving those twelve kilometres that

The Blue Room

he had felt the closest he ever had to her, the most deeply bound to her. It was on the tip of his tongue: 'I need you, Gisèle.'

Needed her with him. Needed her to believe in him.

'When I think of the years you cost me.'

It was not his wife's voice, but Andrée's, a little hoarse, from deep in her heaving chest, reproaching him for leaving the village when he was sixteen to learn a profession elsewhere.

He had gone to Paris and had worked in a garage until called up for military service. He had never paid any attention to Andrée: she was too tall, she lived in the chateau, and her father was a local hero.

A cold, stuck-up girl. A statue.

'Why are you laughing?'

For he was driving along laughing, and not very pleasantly.

'I was remembering the film.'

'Did you think it was good?'

'As good as the rest of them.'

A statue that came strangely to life and asked him, with a faraway look in its eye:

'Tell me, Tony: if I became free?'

Everyone knew that Nicolas was ill and would not make old bones, but that was no reason to talk about him as if he were as good as dead! He had pretended not to have heard her.

'Would you free yourself too?'

The train whistle had blown a furious blast.

'What did you say?'

'I'm asking if, in that case . . .'

What would he have replied if he hadn't recognized Nicolas in the crowd from the station, coming across the square?

The lights were on downstairs in their house. Keeping track of the time, the Molard sisters must have put away their sewing and got ready to go home, for they were usually in bed by nine o'clock or even earlier.

'I'll put the van away.'

She got out and walked around to the back of the house to go in the kitchen door, while he went to park the van next to the massive, bright red and yellow machines in the shed.

As he came up to the house, the two sisters were leaving.

'Goodnight, Tony.'

'Goodnight.'

Gisèle was taking a last look around to see that everything was in order.

'Want something to drink? Are you hungry?'

'No, thanks.'

Later he would ask himself if at that moment she might have been waiting for some sign, some word from him. Was it possible that she had sensed a threat hanging over them?

After they had been to the cinema, she usually went directly up to check on Marianne's breathing.

'I know it's silly,' she had admitted to him one evening. 'I only do it after I've been away from the house. When I'm here, I feel I'm protecting her. That we're protecting

The Blue Room

her,' she added quickly. 'When I'm not with her, she seems so helpless to me!'

She would actually lean anxiously over her daughter until she could see her breathing evenly.

He could think of nothing to say. They undressed facing one another, as they always did.

Gisèle's hips had broadened after childbearing, but she was still thin, otherwise, and her pale breasts sagged a little.

How could he make others understand that he loved her, when that evening, longing to pour out his feelings to her, he hadn't been able to make her understand that?

'Goodnight, Tony.'

'Goodnight, Gisèle.'

She was the one who turned out the bedside lamp, on her side, because she was always the first one up, and in the winter it was still dark.

Wasn't she hesitating a moment, before turning it off? He held his breath.

Click . . .

3

He wasn't the nervous type. They had put him through enough tests in Poitiers to find that out: first the prison doctor had examined him, then the psychiatrist, and that strange woman, a psychologist with eyes like a gypsy, who seemed comical at times but frightening at others.

People tended instead to be amazed and even shocked at how calm he was, and someone in the courtroom – the assistant public prosecutor or the counsel for the plaintiff – would later describe his composure as cynical, even aggressive.

It was true that he was usually in control of himself, more inclined to a wait-and-see attitude, preferring to remain on his guard instead of being more outgoing, more enterprising.

Hadn't it been a happy time, those two weeks at Les Sables-d'Olonne? Happy and a bit sad, with sudden rushes of anxiety he couldn't always hide from his wife and daughter.

They were living like most summer holiday-makers, having breakfast on the terrace, with Marianne already in her red bathing suit, and by nine all three of them were at the beach, where they had quickly claimed their own private spot.

In two days they had established their habits and

The Blue Room

rituals, meeting their neighbours in the dining room of Les Roches Noires, smiling at the elderly couple at the table opposite theirs, who would wave affectionately at Marianne. As for Marianne, she was fascinated by the old gentleman's beard.

'If he leans any lower, his beard will land in his soup.'

She spied on him every evening, waiting for the inevitable.

Every morning and afternoon the same people would settle in under beach umbrellas all around them: the blonde lady who spent so much time putting on suntan oil before lying on her stomach, reading all day with her shoulder straps down, and the bad-mannered kids from Paris, who stuck their tongues out at Marianne and pushed her, out in the water . . .

Gisèle, unused to being at leisure, was knitting a sky-blue pullover for their daughter to wear on her first day at school, her lips moving as she counted stitches.

Was this holiday at the beach really turning out to be such a good idea? He played with Marianne, teaching her to swim, waist-deep in the water with his hand under her chin. He had tried to teach his wife, too, but as soon as she lost her footing she would panic, flailing around and clutching at him. Once a wave had suddenly knocked her over and she had shot him a look of – was it fear? Not fear of the sea. Fear of him.

For hours, he stayed calm, relaxed, playing ball, walking with Marianne to the end of the pier. They would all stroll together along the narrow streets of the town, visiting the cathedral, taking photos of the fishing boats at the docks, the local fishwives at the market in their pleated skirts and varnished wooden shoes.

There were perhaps ten thousand tourists all doing the same things, and whenever a storm broke, they would snatch up their belongings to rush off to the hotels and cafés.

Why, at times, did he seem to absent himself? Was he regretting having left Saint-Justin, where Andrée might be trying in vain to signal him?

'Now about this signal, Monsieur Falcone . . .'

After a few weeks in Poitiers, he was losing track of which questions had been Diem's and which the psychiatrist's. Sometimes they asked the same thing, with different words, in a different context. Weren't they getting together to compare statements between interrogations, hoping he would contradict himself in the end?

'When did you and your mistress establish this signal?'

'That first evening.'

'You mean in September, by the side of the road?'

'Yes.'

'Whose idea was it?'

'Hers. I already told you. She wanted us to meet again somewhere else and thought right away of my brother's hotel.'

'And the towel?'

'Her first suggestion was to put a specific item in a corner of a shop window.'

There were two front windows displaying a jumble of groceries, cotton cloths, aprons, rubber boots. The Despierre store was on the main street, a few steps from

The Blue Room

the church, and everyone going through town had to pass it.

It was dark inside, with barrels and crates piled against the walls, both counters stacked high with merchandise, shelves brimming with bottles and cans, drill trousers, wicker baskets and hams hanging from the ceilings.

The smell of this shop was the strongest, most evocative scent of his entire childhood, with that high note from the cans of kerosene, for the isolated farms and hamlets did not yet have electricity.

'What item?'

'She'd thought of a packet of starch. Then she was afraid that her husband might move it without her noticing while she was off in the kitchen.'

How could they hope to learn in a few hours a day, over weeks or even months, everything they needed to know about a life so different from theirs? Not only his life, and Gisèle's, but the lives of Andrée, Madame Despierre, Madame Formier, the life of the village, the back-and-forth between Triant and Saint-Justin. Simply to understand the blue room, they would have had to . . .

'In the end she decided that on the Thursdays when she could join me in the hotel she would set a towel out to dry on her window-sill.'

Their bedroom window, hers and Nicolas'! For they did sleep in the same room. It was over the shop, one of the three narrow windows with safety bars, the one in which a lithograph in a black-and-gold frame could be glimpsed in the dim light, hanging on the muddy-brown wall.

'So that every Thursday morning . . .'

'I passed her house.'

Who knows whether, while he was living in a bathing suit on the beach, perhaps Andrée was signalling him for help, and the towel was permanently draped on the safety bar... True, he had seen her and Nicolas driving home from Triant in the Citroën, but he knew nothing about their state of mind.

'I wonder, Monsieur Falcone, whether, in suggesting that holiday to your wife...'

'She had just mentioned Marianne's poor colour.'

'I'm aware of that. You did seize the opportunity: a chance, perhaps, to reassure her, to play the good husband, the loving father, to allay her suspicions. What do you think of that explanation?'

'It isn't true.'

'You continue to claim that your intention was to get away from your mistress?'

He hated that word, yet he had to put up with it.

'That's about it.'

'You'd already decided not to see her again?'

'I hadn't any definite plan.'

'Have you seen her again during the intervening months?'

'No.'

'She never signalled to you again?'

'I have no idea, because from then on I avoided going by her house on Thursday mornings.'

'And you did so simply because one afternoon you saw her husband walk from the station to the hotel terrace to sit there drinking lemonade? She is the only woman, by your own admission, with whom you have experienced

The Blue Room

the fulfilment of physical love. You described it, as I recall, as a revelation . . .'

That was true, even if he hadn't used that particular word. At Les Sables-d'Olonne, sometimes he found himself thinking about the blue room against his will, gritting his teeth with desire. At other times he could be unreasonable, impatient, scolding Marianne for a trifle or withdrawing into himself, with a hard look in his eye. Gisèle and her daughter would look at each other, the mother seeming to tell her child, 'Pay no attention, your father has things on his mind.'

A moment later, were they not just as uneasy when he abruptly became exaggeratedly patient, gentle and affectionate?

'Are you ambitious, Monsieur Falcone?'

He had to think about that, since he never had before. Are there really people who spend their lives looking at themselves in a mirror and asking themselves questions – about themselves?

'Depends on what you mean by that. At twelve I worked after school and during the holidays to buy myself a bicycle. Later I dreamed about having a motorbike. I went to Paris. When I married Gisèle, I started thinking about having my own business. In Poitiers, the firm I worked for assembled agricultural machinery shipped in pieces from America, and I was earning a good living.'

'Your brother set up on his own, too, after trying out several trades.'

What connection could there be between their two careers?

It wasn't Diem, but Professor Bigot speaking, slowly, as if musing aloud.

'I wonder if the fact that your parents were Italian, so that you were both foreigners in a French village . . . I've been told your father was a bricklayer?'

The magistrate had spent an entire afternoon questioning the elder Falcone, seeking him out in his cottage in La Boisselle.

'What do you know about your father?'

'He came from Larina, a very poor village in the Piedmont region, about thirty kilometres from Vercelli. Out there, where the mountains can't support everyone, most boys emigrate, and my father did the same, when he was fourteen or fifteen. He came to France with a crew that dug a tunnel, I don't know which one, somewhere near Limoges; then he travelled around, worked on other tunnels . . .'

It was difficult to talk about Angelo Falcone, whom everyone in Saint-Justin called old Angelo, for he was different, somehow, from other men.

'He travelled a lot in France – north, south, east, west – and finally settled down in La Boisselle.'

Even now, Tony remembered it as an astonishing place. Two or three kilometres from Saint-Justin, La Boisselle had been a monastery built on the site of an ancient fortress and constructed from its very stones. One could still see sections of the old walls among the rampant weeds and remnants of the moat, filled with stagnant water, where he had fished for frogs.

The monks had probably practised agriculture, for

The Blue Room

around the large courtyard there remained buildings of all kinds, stables, workshops and winepress sheds.

The Coutant family occupied most of the area, with about a dozen cows, some sheep, two draught horses and an old billy goat that chewed tobacco. They rented out whatever buildings they didn't need, if they were still habitable, and these formed a motley little colony comprising, aside from the Falcones, a Czech family and some people from Alsace with their eight children.

'Your father wasn't that young any more when you were born.'

'He was forty-three, forty-four when he returned to his Piedmontese village and brought my mother back with him.'

'In other words, he decided it was time for him to marry and he went home to find a wife?'

'I believe that's what happened.'

His mother's maiden name had been Maria Passaris, and when she arrived in France she was twenty-two years old.

'Were they a happy couple?'

'I never heard them argue.'

'Did your father keep working as a bricklayer?'

'That was all he knew, and it never occurred to him to do anything else.'

'You were born first, and your brother Vincent came along three years later.'

'Then my sister Angelina.'

'Does she live in Saint-Justin?'

'She died.'

'At an early age?'

'At six months. My mother had gone to Triant, I don't know why. Before she came to France, she had never left her village. Here, in a country where she didn't speak the language, she rarely left the house. That day, in Triant, it's thought that she opened the wrong door by mistake and got out of the train on the wrong side. She and the baby in her arms were run down by an express.'

'How old were you?'

'Seven. My brother was four.'

'Was it your father who raised you?'

'Yes. When he got home from his job, he did the cooking and housework. I didn't know him well enough from before to know if the accident changed him.'

'What do you mean?'

'You know perfectly well. Didn't you speak with him?'

There was an edge in Tony's voice now.

'Yes . . .'

'And what do you think? Are the people around here right? Is my father simple?'

In Saint-Justin, no one said 'simple-minded': just 'simple' was enough. Embarrassed, Bigot merely gestured vaguely in reply.

'I don't know if you got anything out of him. For years, we never heard him speak, my brother and I, unless it was absolutely necessary. At seventy-eight, he lives alone in the house where we were born and still does a little brick laying here and there.

'He refuses to come live with me or Vincent. His only distraction is building a miniature village in his tiny

The Blue Room

garden. He began working on it twenty years ago. The church is less than a metre high, but it's complete to the last detail.

'You can see the inn, the town hall, a bridge over a stream, a water mill, and every year he adds a house or two. Seems it's a faithful reproduction of Larina, that village he and my mother came from.'

He did not say what he really thought. His father was an uncouth man of limited intelligence who had been content to live alone until he was past forty. Tony could see pretty well why he had gone back to Larina to seek a wife.

In his way, Angelo Falcone had loved Maria Passaris, who was young enough to be his daughter. Not with words, or grand shows of affection, because he was a man who kept things to himself.

When she had died along with his daughter, Angelo Falcone had withdrawn into himself for good and had soon begun building his strange toy village in the garden.

'He isn't crazy!' exclaimed Tony fiercely.

He could guess what some people must think, including, perhaps, this Professor Bigot.

'And I'm not crazy either!'

'There has never been any question of that.'

'Then why are you still grilling me for the sixth or seventh time? Because the newspapers are calling me a monster?'

But this still lay in the future . . .

At Les Roches Noires people lived on the beach, with the taste of sand in their mouths and sand in their beds and pockets.

It rained only twice in two weeks. The sun dazzled everyone's eyes and skin to the point of vertigo, especially if they stared a long time at the white-crested waves rolling slowly in from the open sea, one after another, until they crashed into a spray of a myriad sparkling drops.

Marianne got a touch of sunburn. After a few days, Tony was brown enough that when he undressed at night, his pale skin showed the shape of his bathing suit. Only Gisèle, who stayed under the beach umbrella, still looked the same as always.

What was happening in Saint-Justin, in the Despierres' gloomy shop? And in the evening, in the bedroom where Andrée and Nicolas undressed in front of each other?

The pink-edged towel: wasn't it draped over the guard rail as a signal of alarm? And Nicolas' stony-faced mother: had she not crossed the garden to take the situation in hand – and take revenge, at last, on her daughter-in-law?

They thought, all these people in Poitiers, policemen, magistrates, doctors, even that unnerving lady psychologist, that they were going to establish the truth, when they knew almost nothing about the Despierres, the Formiers and so many others who were important in their own ways.

And Tony: what did they know about him? Less than he did, right?

Madame Despierre was certainly the most important and imposing personage in Saint-Justin, eclipsing even the mayor, a wealthy cattle merchant in his own right. In a village where men and women of the same generation

The Blue Room

had all gone to the same school together, few dared call her Germaine, much less address her familiarly. To everyone, she was Madame Despierre.

Tony must have been mistaken, for she was barely thirty when he had begun purchasing things for his parents at the grocery store, but he remembered her hair being just as grey then as it was now. Behind her counter, she wore a grey smock, leaving her chalk-white face as the only pale spot.

He had known her husband, a puny man with a hesitant manner and a timorous expression, wearing a pince-nez and a smock that was too long for him.

Sometimes he would start swaying, and his wife would hustle him into the room behind the store, closing the door on the customers glancing knowingly at one another and shaking their heads.

Tony had been hearing talk about the falling sickness well before he understood that Despierre suffered from epilepsy and that, behind the closed door, he was thrashing convulsively, lying on the floor with his jaws clenched and drool streaking his chin.

He could recall the man's funeral and following his procession with all the other schoolchildren in little rows, save for Nicolas, who was with his mother at the front of the mourners.

They were said to be very rich and very stingy. Not only did they own several houses in town, but two large farms as well, worked by tenant farmers, plus the hamlet of La Guipotte.

'Monsieur Falcone: why did you choose to settle in

Saint-Justin, which you had left more than ten years earlier?'

Hadn't he already answered that question? They repeated the same things to him so often that he just didn't know any more. He must be contradicting himself at times, for he himself did not have the answers to these 'whys' and 'hows'.

'Maybe it was because of my father.'

'You hardly saw him.'

About once a week. Old Angelo had come to his house two or three times but had seemed ill at ease. Gisèle was a stranger to him, and he was uncomfortable around her. Tony preferred to go to La Boissière every Saturday evening.

The door would stay open. They did not light the lamp. They listened to the frogs croaking in the marsh, and the two men, sitting on straw-bottomed chairs, let the time pass without a word.

'Don't forget that my brother was already established in Triant.'

'You're sure you didn't come back for Andrée?'

'That again!'

'You were aware of her marriage to your former classmate Nicolas?'

No! That had come as a surprise. There was a vast gulf between the Despierres and the Formiers, and the two mothers, although close in age, came from different worlds.

While Madame Despierre was the very model of a nouveau riche peasant, the wife of Dr Formier was typical of a certain provincial bourgeoisie fallen on hard times and refusing to lose face.

Her father had been a notary at Villiers-le-Haut, and the Bardave family men, from father to son, had been socializing with the local gentry for so long, hunting and playing bridge with them, that they'd come to think of themselves as gentry too.

Andrée's grandfather had bequeathed nothing to his children, and neither had her father. Dr Formier had left his wife and daughter an annuity so modest that, although they still lived in the chateau and dressed like townspeople, they did not always have enough to eat.

Which of them, Madame Despierre or Madame Formier, had proposed this marriage to the other one? Was it the proud, spiteful widow with her grocery store? Or the bourgeoise anxious to see her daughter safe from want, knowing that she would be rich one day – and probably before long, at that?

'At school, Nicolas seems to have been bullied by his classmates . . .'

True and false, like all the rest of it. Sickly, often plagued by stomach aches, unable to join his classmates' games, Nicolas had been fated to become a laughing stock for the other boys. They called him a sissy, a fraidy-cat, accused him of clinging to his mother's skirts. Even worse, unable to defend himself, he reported to the principal all the tricks the kids played on him.

Tony hadn't belonged to the gang that harassed him. He wasn't any better than they were, perhaps, but as a foreigner he was a bit of an outsider himself. Once during their break time, and once more, when school was letting out, he had come to the defence of Nicolas, whom he did not yet know was ill.

The boy had had his first fit at the age of twelve and a half, out of nowhere, in the middle of a class. There had been the sound of a body falling to the floor, and as his classmates began turning around, the teacher had slapped his desk with a ruler.

'Nobody move!'

It was spring. The chestnut trees in the playground were in flower. There had been swarms of maybugs that year, and all eyes had been on them as they flew clumsily around the classroom, bumping into windows and walls.

In spite of the teacher's order, the children stared at Nicolas, their faces blanching, and some were so frightened they began to feel sick.

'Everybody go to the playground!'

There had been a general stampede outside, but the bravest kids soon crept up to the windows to watch the teacher force his handkerchief into Nicolas' mouth.

One of them had raced to the grocery store, and it wasn't long before Madame Despierre arrived in her eternal grey smock.

The children outside pestered those at the window.

'What's going on?'

'Nothing. They're leaving him on the floor. He must be dying.'

There were a lot of guilty consciences that day.

'You think he ate something bad for him?'

'No. Seems his father had the same fits.'

The Blue Room

'Are they catching?'

Fifteen or thirty minutes later – they had lost track of time – Madame Despierre left through the playground, holding the hand of her son, who looked bewildered but otherwise the same as usual.

He had never had another fit at school. As far as Tony knew, he could almost always sense one coming, sometimes several days in advance, and his mother would keep him home.

No one ever spoke of this in front of Madame Despierre, and certainly not in her store. Without knowing why, everyone considered the malady something to be ashamed of. Nicolas had not gone to upper school in Triant, nor had he done any military service or even gone to any dances. He had never had a bicycle or a motorbike and he did not drive the Citroën.

Sometimes he wouldn't speak for a week. Sullen, suspicious, he would look at people as if they wished him harm. He drank neither liquor nor wine, and his stomach could tolerate only bland food.

Hadn't Tony been disturbed by the thought of him that September evening, there with Andrée half-naked by the roadside?

'Weren't you more or less aware of resenting him, because he was rich?'

He shrugged. Naturally, before he had learned that Nicolas was ill, before that first fit in school, he had envied him in a childish way: he had dreamed of jars of rainbow-coloured sweets and the biscuits in the glass-topped tins that Nicolas, he imagined, could simply raid at will, whereas *he* could afford just the cheapest sweets, and only now and then.

'When you learned of his marriage, didn't you think that he had in some way bought Andrée, or that his mother had bought her for him?'

Perhaps. He had felt a little contemptuous of 'the statue', because he refused to believe that she had married for love.

After thinking about it, he had felt sorry for her. As a child, he had sometimes gone hungry, too, but he hadn't lived in the chateau or felt obliged to keep up a front.

He had no idea how the marriage had been arranged. From what he knew of the two mothers, each must have imposed her own conditions. They lived almost across from each other: the chateau was to the right of the church, near the presbytery; across the square, on the corner of Rue Neuve, the Despierre grocery store was backed by the town hall and the school.

Although people still talked about the elaborate white wedding and the banquet at the inn, the newlyweds had not gone on a honeymoon but spent that night, and every night thereafter, in the bedroom over the shop.

As for Madame Despierre, she had moved into a small cottage next to the garden, about twenty metres from the couple's home.

At first the two women worked behind the counter, and the mother continued to do the cooking. An elderly local woman, wearing men's shoes, came every day to clean.

The whole town was watching Madame Despierre and

Andrée, and soon it was obvious that they spoke to each other only about business matters.

Later, the mother began eating her meals in the cottage. Finally, after a few months, she ceased to appear in the store or the house, and her son began going through the garden two or three times a day to see her.

Did this mean that Andrée had won the battle? Had she resolved, when she got married, to gradually supplant her mother-in-law?

Tony had been with Andrée in the blue room eight times, and he had never thought of asking her about it, preferring not to know, not to think too much about this other life of the naked and wanton woman he knew so well.

He vaguely sensed a vital truth he could not manage to express. It informed, he felt, what was said on 2 August, that fatal August day he had experienced so simply, never suspecting how much would later be made of it, including fodder for front-page news.

A reporter from a major Parisian paper would even launch a phrase adopted by all his colleagues: 'The Frenzied Lovers'.

'Would you like to spend your whole life with me?'
'Sure.'

He had said that, he did not deny it. He was the one who had reported that conversation to the magistrate. But the important thing was his tone of voice. He was just talking, without meaning anything by it. It wasn't real. In the blue room, nothing was real. Or rather, its reality was of a different nature, incomprehensible anywhere else.

He had tried to explain this to the psychiatrist, and at the time Bigot had seemed to understand, but a bit later, through some question or remark, he had shown that he hadn't understood at all.

If Tony had been thinking about living with her, he wouldn't have said, 'Sure!'

He hadn't the slightest idea what he would have replied, but he would have found other words. Andrée had rightly sensed that, for she had pressed him on it.

'Really sure? . . . Wouldn't you be afraid?'

'Afraid of what?'

'Can you imagine what our days would be like?'

'We'd get used to it in the end!'

'Used to what?'

Was that real life? Would he have spoken like that to Gisèle? Andrée, sprawled sated on the bed, was playing the game, along with him.

'To us.'

Precisely. They were 'us' only in a bed, in the blue room they strove in a kind of frenzy – to use that journalist's word – to impregnate with their odour.

They had never been a couple elsewhere, except when they made love the first time, in the tall grass and nettles beside Bois de Sarelle.

'If you didn't love her, how do you explain . . .'

What did they mean by love? Could Professor Bigot – who prided himself on his scientific credentials – have defined that word for him? His daughter had just got married: how did she love her husband?

And the little magistrate, Monsieur Diem, with

his halo of unruly hair ... His wife had recently given him his first child, and, like all young fathers, he must have had, like Tony, to get up at night to bottle-feed the baby. What kind of love did he feel for his wife?

To answer their questions, Tony would have had to tell them things that don't bear talking about, moments like those he had experienced at Les Sables-d'Olonne.

'Why choose Les Sables over some beach in Brittany or the Vendée?'

'Because that's where we went during the first year of our marriage.'

'So your wife may have thought that it was a pilgrimage, that this spot had some sentimental value for you? Isn't that exactly what you would have done if you were trying to allay her suspicions?'

All he could do was bite his tongue and boil with anger inside. It was useless to fight back.

Could he tell them about the last day at the shore? First, that morning ... Lying under the beach umbrella, sometimes he would glance through half-closed eyelids at his wife, sitting in a striped deck chair, hurrying to finish the sky-blue pullover.

'What are you thinking about?' she had asked him.

'You.'

'And just what are you thinking?'

'That I was lucky to meet you.'

It wasn't the whole truth. Behind him, he could hear Marianne pretending to read the text of a picture book, and he had been reflecting that, in twelve or fifteen years, she would be in love, she would get married, she would leave them to share the life of a man.

Of a stranger, in effect, because it takes more than a few months, or two or three years, for a married couple to really know each other.

That's how he had arrived at Gisèle: he was watching her knit, relaxed, focused.

Just when she had asked her question, he had been wondering what *she* was thinking.

To tell the truth, he did not know what she thought of him, how she saw him, how she judged his actions.

They had been married for seven years. So he had then tried to imagine their life to come. They would gradually grow old. Marianne would become a young lady. They would attend her wedding. One day, she would tell them that she was expecting, and when the baby arrived they would take second place behind the father.

Wouldn't that be the moment when he and Gisèle would truly love each other? Don't couples take long years to learn how to know each other, sharing many memories, ones like those of this very morning they were living now?

They must have been thinking along the same lines because shortly afterwards, his wife murmured, 'It feels strange to think that Marianne is already heading off to school . . .'

And he was all the way up to her wedding!

Their daughter sensed that she could get away with anything at the beach and was taking complete advantage of her father – that afternoon more than ever. She

The Blue Room

never left him alone for a minute. The tide was out, the distant sea beyond reach: for more than an hour, he had to help Marianne build an enormous fortress in the sand, or, rather, he had to follow her orders. And, like old Angelo in his garden, she kept demanding one more thing: a moat, a ditch, a drawbridge.

'Now let's go and find shells to pave the courtyard and the paths outside.'

'Watch out for the sun. Put on your hat!'

They'd bought her a Venetian gondolier's hat in a seaside shop.

Gisèle didn't dare add, 'Don't wear your father out!'

Each carrying a red pail, they had traipsed the entire length of the beach, father and daughter, heads down, eyes peeled for the gleam of a shell in the brown sand, sometimes tripping over the leg of a stretched-out sunbather or nimbly avoiding a beach ball.

Did he feel he was fulfilling a duty, earning forgiveness for some failing, atoning for a fault committed? In all honesty, he would not have known. What he did know was that this walk in the sunshine, accompanied by the fluting voice of his daughter, was both melancholy and sweet.

He was happy, and sad. Not because of Andrée, or of Nicolas. He didn't remember giving them a thought. He would freely have said: happy and sad like life itself.

When they turned around, to the sound of the music from the nearby casino, the way back looked long, and their goal distant, especially to Marianne, who began dragging her feet.

'Tired?'

'A little.'

'You want me to carry you on my shoulders?'

She had laughed, revealing the gap in her teeth.

'I'm too big!'

When she had been two or three, that had been her favourite game. He had always carried her up to bed at night that way.

'People will laugh at you,' she added, sorely tempted.

He had hoisted her up and, since she was holding on to his head, he carried both the pails.

'I'm not too heavy?'

'No.'

'Is it true I'm skinny?'

'Who says so?'

'Roland.'

He was the blacksmith's son.

'He's a year younger than me and he weighs twenty-five kilos. Me, I only weigh nineteen. I got weighed before we left, on the scale at the grocery store.'

'Boys are heavier than girls.'

'Why?'

Pensively, Gisèle watched them approach, perhaps with a pang in her heart. He set his daughter down on the sand.

'Help me add the shells.'

'Don't you think you're overdoing it, Marianne? Your father is here to rest. He has to go back to work the day after tomorrow.'

'He's the one who wanted to carry me!'

Their eyes had met.

The Blue Room

'It's the last day of holiday for her, too,' he had said lightly in her defence.

Gisèle had said nothing further, but he thought he had glimpsed a grateful look in her eye.

Grateful for what? For having devoted himself, for two weeks, to both of them?

It seemed only natural to him . . .

4

Sometimes he had to wait in the corridor outside the magistrate's door, sitting handcuffed on a bench between two gendarmes, different ones almost every time.

He no longer felt humiliated, had stopped raging inside. He watched people pass by, prisoners and witnesses going to wait in front of other doors, robed lawyers flapping their big sleeves like wings, and he didn't flinch when anyone glanced at him curiously or turned around to stare.

Once inside the magistrate's chambers, after removing his handcuffs, the guards would leave at a sign from Diem, who would apologize for being late or having been detained then automatically hold out his silver cigarette case. It had become a ritual.

The chambers were old-fashioned, not all that clean, as in train stations and administrative buildings: greenish walls, a black marble mantelpiece topped with a clock – also black – that had probably been showing 11.55 for years now.

Sometimes the magistrate started by saying, 'I don't think I'll be needing you, Monsieur Trinquet.'

The clerk with the brown moustache would leave, carrying some work he would go God knows where to do, which meant that they would not really be talking about the facts of the matter.

'I suppose you have understood why I ask you questions

The Blue Room

that don't seem to have any bearing on the case. I am trying to establish, in a way, a certain foundation, a personal file on you.'

They could hear the noises of the town, see the open windows across the street and people in their homes going about their daily business. The magistrate allowed Tony to stand up whenever he needed to stretch his legs, walk up and down, go and spend a moment watching the bustling street.

'I would like you to describe, for example, the course of your day at work.'

'Well, that depends on what day of the week it is, and in which season. Most of all, it varies with the fairs and market days.'

Realizing that he had spoken in the present tense, Tony caught himself with a wan smile.

'At least it used to . . . I'd follow the fairs within a radius of about thirty kilometres, the ones at Virieux, Ambasse, Chiron. Do you want the entire list?'

'That isn't necessary.'

'On those days, I'd leave early, sometimes at five in the morning.'

'Did your wife get up to fix you breakfast?'

'She insisted on it. On other days, I'd have appointments out at various farms, to demonstrate some machinery or carry out repairs. Sometimes customers would come to me, and we'd be out in the shed.'

'Let's take an average day.'

'Gisèle would get up first, at six.'

She would slip quietly out of bed, taking along her

salmon-pink dressing gown, and he would soon hear her lighting the fire in the kitchen range, just below him. Then she would go out to the garden to throw cracked corn to the hens and feed the rabbits.

Towards 6.30 he would simply run a comb through his thick hair and go downstairs without washing or shaving. The table was set in the kitchen, without a cloth, because it had a Formica top. They would eat together while Marianne slept on, as late as she liked.

'Until she started school. Then we had to wake her up at seven.'

'Did you drive her there?'

'Only for the first few days.'

'You did so yourself?'

'My wife drove her, and then did her shopping. Otherwise, she would go to the village towards nine, going to the butcher's shop or the grocery store . . .'

'The Despierres' store?'

'It's more or less the only grocery in Saint-Justin.'

During the mornings in particular, a half-dozen women were always gathered in the shop, chatting under the low ceiling while awaiting their turns. One day, he had compared the place to a church sacristy, he no longer remembered why.

'Did your wife ever send you on errands?'

'Only when I went to Triant or some other town, for things we couldn't find in the village.'

He realized that these questions were not as innocent as they seemed, but he still answered them frankly, trying to be precise.

The Blue Room

'Did you ever go inside the Despierre grocery store?'

'Once every two months, maybe . . . When my wife was doing a thorough housecleaning, say, or if she had the flu . . .'

'On what day did she clean the house?'

'Saturday.'

That was typical. Monday was wash day, while Tuesday or Wednesday, depending on the weather and if the laundry was dry or not, would be spent ironing. It was the same in most of the village houses, and on some mornings the yards and gardens were completely decked out in laundry pinned to clotheslines.

'What time did your mail arrive?'

'It wasn't delivered to the house. The train goes through Saint-Justin at 8.07 in the morning, and the bags are taken straight to the post office. Our place is at the far end of the village, so we're at the end of the postman's round – he'd only get to us around noon. I preferred to go to the post office, where I often had to wait for them to finish sorting. Otherwise, they held my letters for me.'

'We'll come back to that. Did you walk there?'

'Usually. I only took the van if I had something to do outside the village.'

'Say, every other day? A few times a week?'

'More like every other day, except in the middle of winter, because I didn't drive around as much then.'

He would have had to explain his profession in detail, the rhythm of the seasons, the crops. For example, when they had returned from the seaside the fairs were at their height. Then the grape harvests had followed, and fields were ploughed in the autumn in readiness for spring, so that he was overwhelmed with work.

That first Thursday, he had avoided taking Rue Neuve to see if Andrée had put the towel in the window. He had already said that to Diem, who had gone over it anyway.

'You'd decided not to see her again?'

'"Decided" isn't the right word . . .'

'Wasn't that because you'd heard from her through some other channel?'

This time, he had made a mistake and he had realized it the moment he opened his mouth. Too late: the words, already prepared, were leaving his lips.

'I received no news from her.'

He wasn't lying for himself. And he wasn't aware of lying for Andrée, either. It was from some sort of fidelity, or male honesty.

On the day of that interview, Tony remembered, it had been raining, and Monsieur Trinquet, the clerk, was at his end of the table.

'You came home from Les Sables with your wife and daughter on 17 August. The first Thursday, contrary to your usual routine, you did not go to Triant. Were you afraid of encountering Andrée Despierre?'

'Perhaps. But I would not use the word "afraid".'

'Let's continue. On the following Thursday you had an appointment at ten that morning with a certain Félicien Hurlot, the secretary of a farming cooperative. You met him at your brother's hotel. You had lunch there with your client and you drove home to Saint-Justin without showing yourself on Place du Marché. Still to avoid any possibility of finding yourself face to face with your mistress?'

He found it impossible to reply. He truly did not know. For weeks he had been in a fog, confused, not asking himself any questions and, above all, not making any decisions.

What he could honestly say was that he felt a new distance between himself and Andrée, and that he stayed more at home, as if he needed to be close to his family.

'On 4 September . . .'

While the magistrate was talking, Tony tried to remember what that date could mean.

'On 4 September, you received the first letter.'

He had turned red.

'I don't know what letter you mean.'

'Your name and your address, on the envelope, were written in block letters. It was postmarked Triant.'

'I don't remember.'

He kept on lying, since it seemed too late to change his story now.

'The postmaster, Monsieur Bouvier, made a comment to you about that letter.'

Diem pulled a page from his file and read it aloud.

' "I told him: Tony, it looks to me just like an anonymous letter. People who send anonymous letters write like that."

'That still doesn't refresh your memory?'

He shook his head, ashamed of lying, because he lied badly, flushing red, staring into space so that no one could see the misery in his eyes.

Although it bore no signature, the letter was still revealing in its own way. The text, quite short, was also written in block letters.

Everything is fine. Don't be afraid.

'You see, Monsieur Falcone, I am convinced that the person who wrote to you and went to mail this letter from Triant was disguising the writing for fear of being identified not by you, but by the postmaster. That would suggest someone from Saint-Justin, whose normal handwriting is familiar to Monsieur Bouvier. The following week, there was a second envelope, just like the first, addressed to you.

'Making light of it, the postmaster said to you, "Well, well! I may have been mistaken. There may be some love story behind all this."'

The text was no longer than the first message.

I haven't forgotten. I love you.

He had been so shaken that he hadn't dared go anywhere near Rue Neuve and had detoured around it to go to the station, where he often received machine parts sent on the high-speed train.

He had spent several anxious weeks going off to the markets and farms or working in overalls at home in the shed.

More often than in the past, he would cross the field to the house to find Gisèle busy peeling vegetables, washing

The Blue Room

the tile floor in the kitchen or tidying the bedrooms upstairs. With Marianne in school, the house seemed emptier. When she came home at four, he felt impelled to come and see them in the kitchen, sitting across from each other having their afternoon snack, each with her own pot of jam.

Later they would go over that again as well, and more than once. Marianne liked only strawberry jam, whereas strawberries, even when cooked, gave her mother a rash, so she preferred plum jam.

At the beginning of their marriage, Gisèle's tastes in food had amused him, and he had teased her about them.

Because of her blonde hair, pale skin and oval face, people often said there was something angelic about her.

Actually, she liked only strong flavours: pickled herring, salads with lots of garlic and vinegar, and strong cheeses. It wasn't unusual, when she was working in the kitchen garden, to see her munching on a big raw onion. Yet she didn't touch sweets and never ate dessert. He was the one fond of pastry.

There were other peculiarities about their married life. His parents, as good Italians, had raised their sons in the Roman Catholic religion, and his childhood memories were filled with the sounds of church organs, with women and girls coming out of mass on Sunday mornings in silk dresses, wearing the rice powder and perfume they used only on that day.

He knew every house, every stone in the village and could still recall, coming home from school one day, having retied a shoelace with his foot on a particular milestone, but it was the church that loomed the largest, with its three stained-glass windows behind the chancel and its burning tapers. The other windows were of clear glass. The chancel windows bore the names of their donors, and one on the right, the name of Nicolas' grandfather or great-grandfather: Despierre.

He still went to Sunday mass with Marianne; Gisèle stayed at home. She had never been baptized. Her father was a professed atheist and in his entire life had read only a few books, four or five novels by Zola.

'I'm an ordinary working man, Tony, but I'm telling you, that *Germinal* . . .'

In other families it was the reverse: the men would escort their women to the church door before heading to the nearest café to bend their elbows until the end of the service.

'Would you insist on claiming, Monsieur Falcone, that during that particular October you were not expecting something to happen?'

Nothing specific. It was more like the uneasiness one feels before an illness. They'd had an unusually rainy October. Tony had worn his winter outfit from dawn to dusk: jodhpurs, high laced boots, brown sheepskin jacket.

Marianne found school exciting and chattered about it at every meal.

'You no longer recall anything about the third letter, either? Monsieur Bouvier has a better memory than you do. He says you received it on a Friday, like the others, either before or after the 20th of October.'

It had been the briefest, the most disturbing.

Soon! I love you.

'I suppose you burned these notes and those that followed?'

No. He had torn them into little pieces that he then threw into the Orneau. Swollen by the rains, the brownish water swept along tree branches, dead animals and all sorts of debris.

'My experience tells me that you will soon change your tune. You seem to have answered with complete candour on every other point. I would be astonished if your lawyer did not advise you to take the same attitude with regard to these letters, which would allow you to tell me about your state of mind late in October.'

It was impossible. His state of mind changed every hour. He tried not to think, and felt Gisèle watching him with curiosity – perhaps even worry. She no longer asked him, 'What are you thinking?' but would remark, as if tired, 'You're not hungry?'

He had no appetite. Three times, at dawn, he had gone to pick mushrooms in the meadow between them and the blacksmith's, at the highest spot, near the big cherry tree. He had sold several tractors, including two to the agricultural cooperative at Virieux, which leased them to small farmers, and they had also ordered a reaper-binder for the coming summer, for the same purpose.

It had been a good year, and he would be able to pay off a significant part of what he owed on the house.

'We've arrived at 31 October. What did you do that day?'

'I went to see a customer in Vermoise, thirty-two

kilometres away, and I worked for part of the day on his broken-down tractor. I was having trouble finding where the problem was and had lunch at the farm.'

'Did you return via Triant? And stop to see your brother?'

'It was on my way, and I usually chat with him and Lucia for a moment.'

'You never spoke to them of your apprehensions? Or a possible – perhaps probable – change in your circumstances?'

'What change?'

'We'll come back to that. You went home and had dinner. After which you watched television, one you'd bought two weeks earlier. That is what you told the police inspector from Poitiers, whose report I have in front of me. You went upstairs to bed at the same time as your wife?'

'Of course.'

'You were unaware of what was happening that night, less than half a kilometre away?'

'How could I have known?'

'You're forgetting the letters, Falcone. You're saying they don't exist, true, but I am taking them into account. The next day, All Saints, you went off to church at around ten o'clock, holding your daughter's hand.'

'That's correct.'

'So you went past the grocery store.'

'The shutters were closed, as they are on Sundays and holidays.'

'The upstairs ones as well?'

'I did not look up.'

'Does your indifference mean that you considered your relationship with Andrée Despierre at an end?'

'I believe so.'

'Or, if you did you not look up, wasn't it because you already knew?'

'I didn't know.'

'Several people were standing on the pavement in front of the shop.'

'People gather every Sunday on the square before and after high mass.'

'When did you learn that Nicolas had died?'

'At the beginning of the sermon. As soon as he reached the pulpit, Abbé Louvette invited the faithful to pray with him for the soul of Nicolas Despierre, who had died during the night at the age of thirty-three.'

'What was your reaction?'

'I was stunned.'

'Did you notice that, after the priest had spoken, several people turned to look at you?'

'No.'

'I have here the testimony of the tinsmith, Pirou, who is also a local constable and who swears to this.'

'It's possible . . . I don't see how anyone in Saint-Justin could have known.'

'Known what?'

'About my relations with Andrée.'

'You went straight home from church without visiting your mother's grave.'

'My wife and I had agreed to go the cemetery that afternoon.'

'Along the way, the blacksmith Didier, your closest neighbour, joined you and walked a bit of the way with you. He said, "It was certainly bound to happen eventually, but I wasn't expecting it to come so soon. There's one woman who's going to be pleased!"'

'Perhaps he did say that. I don't remember.'

'Perhaps you were too overwhelmed to notice?'

What could he say? Yes? No? He had run out of words. He was numb. All he remembered was holding Marianne's little hand in its woollen glove and the rain starting up again.

The phone rang on the magistrate's desk, interrupting the interrogation with a long conversation about someone named Martin, a jewellery store and a witness unwilling to say what he knew.

From what Tony could hear, the public prosecutor was on the other end of the line, a self-important man whom he had seen for only half an hour and who frightened him.

Diem did not frighten him; it was a much different feeling. Tony felt that it would have taken so little for them to understand each other, even become friends, but it never quite happened.

'Please excuse me, Monsieur Falcone.'

'Not at all.'

'Where were we? Ah, yes: your return from high mass. I suppose you told your wife the news?'

'My daughter did. At the front door she let go of my hand and ran in to the kitchen.'

The house had its Sunday smell, the aroma of the roast

The Blue Room

Gisèle was basting with meat juices, crouching in front of the open oven. They ate roast beef every Sunday, studded with cloves, served with peas and mashed potatoes. On Tuesdays it turned into pot-au-feu.

He hadn't realized, at the time, how comforting these homey traditions were.

'Do you remember what your little girl said?'

'She was all excited and blurted out, "Mama! Important news! Nicolas is dead!"'

'How did your wife react?'

'She turned to me and asked, "Is it true, Tony?"'

He was lying again, leaving something out, and would not look the magistrate in the eye. Gisèle had actually gone pale and almost dropped her wooden spoon. He had been as upset as she was. It was a good moment before she had murmured, almost to herself, 'He was the one who served me, only yesterday . . .'

That was something he could tell the magistrate. Although there wasn't anything really dangerous in what followed, he preferred not to mention it in front of him. Marianne had spoken up.

'I'll be going to the funeral?'

'Children don't go to funerals.'

'Josette did!'

'Because it was her grandfather who died.'

Marianne had gone in to the next room to play, and that's when Gisèle had asked, without looking at her husband, 'What will Andrée do?'

'I've no idea.'

'Shouldn't you go and pay your respects?'

'Not today. There'll be time enough the morning of the funeral.'

'It must have happened yesterday evening or last night . . .'

She hadn't been herself for the rest of the day.

'How about the next few days?' asked the magistrate pointedly.

'I was hardly ever at home.'

'You didn't try to find out how Nicolas had died?'

'I did not set foot in the village.'

'Not even to pick up your mail?'

'I went just to the post office, no further.'

Diem consulted his file.

'I see that, although the grocery store was closed on All Saints, it opened its doors the morning of All Souls' Day.'

'It's the village custom.'

'Who was behind the counter?'

'I've no idea.'

'Your wife didn't buy anything at Despierre's that day?'

'I don't recall. She probably did.'

'But she said nothing to you?'

'No.'

What he did know was that it was raining, the trees were flailing in the wind, and Marianne was grumpy, the way she always was when bad weather kept her from playing outside.

'I will tell you what transpired in the grocery store. For several days, Nicolas Despierre had been taciturn, on edge, which usually happened before a fit.

The Blue Room

'In such a case, on the orders of Dr Riquet – who has confirmed this – he would take a mild sedative.

'On 31 October, his mother came to see him towards eight in the evening, after dinner, while Andrée was doing the dishes, and she complained that she was coming down with the flu.'

Tony had already heard about this.

'Do you know, Monsieur Falcone, that on that evening, most unusually, Dr Riquet had gone to Niort to see his sister, who was ill, and that he would not return to Saint-Justin until the following morning?'

'I did not.'

'I suppose that he was also your family doctor. So you know that he almost never left the village and did not take many holidays. Late on the afternoon of the previous day, he had come to the store to see Nicolas and inform him of this brief trip.'

With his bushy beard, the doctor looked like a water spaniel and was not at all above playing a few hands of cards and downing a few drinks at the Café de la Gare.

'Madame Despierre's flu; Dr Riquet out of town: you see what I'm getting at? At three in the morning, your friend Andrée phoned the doctor as if she hadn't heard of his absence. Only the maid was there, for Madame Riquet had accompanied her husband.

'Instead of calling a doctor in Triant, she went in her dressing gown to awaken her mother-in-law in her cottage, and when the two women returned to the upstairs bedroom, Nicolas was dead.'

He listened, acutely uncomfortable, uncertain how to respond.

'Since it was too late in any case, Madame Despierre did not see the point of summoning a doctor unfamiliar with the village, and it was only at eleven the following morning that Dr Riquet arrived at Nicolas' bedside.

'Given the patient's history, after a brief examination, he signed the death certificate. Later on, Dr Riquet explained the medical reasons why the overwhelming majority of his colleagues would have done the same.

'Nevertheless, rumours were rampant in the village the next day. You knew nothing about them?'

'No.'

This time, he meant it. It was only much later that he had learned, to his amazement, that in Saint-Justin he and Andrée were already an item of interest.

'You know the countryside better than I do, Monsieur Falcone. So you shouldn't be surprised that those involved rarely learn of such rumours, and of course the authorities are the last to know.

'It took months and further developments for tongues to begin to wag. Even then, Inspector Mani and I have had a lot of trouble obtaining viable statements.

'With patience, we did compile this thick dossier, a copy of which has been sent to your lawyer. Maître Demarié must have discussed this with you.'

He nodded. In reality, he still did not understand. For eleven months, he and Andrée had taken every imaginable precaution to keep their affair a secret.

Not only had Tony done his best to stay away from the

grocery store, but when he had to go there, he would speak to Nicolas, not his wife. If he saw Andrée among the crowd at the market in Triant, he would simply nod at her in greeting.

Aside from their encounter in September, at the roadside, they had met only in the blue room and would arrive there separately, each by a different door, leaving their respective cars at some distance from the hotel.

Neither his brother nor his sister-in-law had talked, he was sure of it. And he had equal confidence in Françoise's discretion.

'You two were so linked in the public's mind that, at the funeral, everyone was watching you and feeling sorry for your wife.'

He had sensed that, and it had terrified him.

'It's hard to say how these rumours spring up, but, once they have, nothing can stop them. The first gossip was that Nicolas had died at a good time and that his wife must feel relieved.

'Then someone mentioned the doctor's absence that night, so convenient for a person hoping to rid herself of the grocer under the cover of his fits.

'Had he been called earlier, when Nicolas was still alive, Dr Riquet would doubtless have made a different diagnosis.'

All this was true. He could say nothing in reply.

'It was also widely remarked that at the burial you stood at the very back of the throng, as if to keep as far as possible from your mistress, and this behaviour was seen by some as a ruse.'

He wiped his face with his handkerchief, because he was in a sweat. For months he had lived without ever suspecting that people were spying on him and that everyone in Saint-Justin knew he was Andrée's lover and was wondering what was going to happen.

'Really, Falcone, do you think your wife could not have known what was common knowledge? That she wasn't waiting, as they were, for what would come next?'

He shook his head, feebly, for he no longer knew quite what to think.

'Supposing she had learned of your affair with Andrée: would she have talked to you about it?'

'Perhaps not . . .'

Certainly not. It was not in her nature. For she had never mentioned other adventures that she had known about.

Not for anything in the world would he have lived through that winter again, and yet he had never felt so strongly bound to his family, to the feeling that the three of them formed a whole, a sensation of almost animal intimacy, as if he were huddled deep in a den with his mate and their offspring.

The atmosphere in the house, painted in the cheerful colours they had chosen, had become heavy, oppressive. When he had to leave on business, he did so unwillingly, conscious of some danger that might threaten while he was away.

'You did not see your mistress at all over the winter, Monsieur Falcone?'

The Blue Room

'I may have caught a glimpse of her at a distance. I swear that I did not speak even one word to her.'

'You did not go to meet her again at your brother's hotel?'

'Absolutely not.'

'Did she not, several times, put out the signal?'

'I saw it only once. I was careful, particularly on Thursdays, to avoid Rue Neuve.'

'So you did go by there one Thursday. When?'

'Early in December. I was going to the station and I took the quickest route. I was startled to see the towel up in the window and wondered if it was intentional.'

'You did not go to Triant that day?'

'No.'

'Did you see the Citroën go by?'

'Only on her way home. I was in my office when I heard her honk her horn two or three times as she went by.'

'Did your brother tell you about her visit?'

'Yes.'

'And he told you that she had gone directly to the blue room, that according to Françoise, she'd undressed there and waited for you, on the bed, for more than half an hour?'

'Yes.'

'What message did she give Françoise for you?'

'That it was vital that we talk.'

'Did Françoise describe the state she was in after waiting for that half-hour?'

'She confessed that Andrée had frightened her.'

'What did she mean?'

'She couldn't explain it.'

'Did you talk to your brother about this?'

'Yes. He advised me to drop the whole thing. Those were the words he used. I told him that I'd broken the affair off a long time ago. Then he said, "It may be over for you, but not for her!"'

The autumn rains had lasted until mid-December, flooding low-lying fields, followed by a serious cold snap and then, on 20 or 21 December, by snow. Marianne was beside herself with joy and rushed to the window every morning to make sure the snow hadn't melted.

'I want so much for it to last until Christmas!'

She had never yet been treated to a white Christmas, for earlier years had brought only rain or frost.

Now that she was a big girl, as she proudly claimed after starting school, she had helped her father decorate the Christmas tree and had herself placed the plaster shepherds and sheep around the manger.

'You insist you knew nothing of what was happening in the Despierre family?'

'I knew, through my wife, that the mother had returned to the counter in the store, but that the two women were still not talking to each other.'

'Wasn't there some mention of a lawsuit?'

'I overheard a conversation about that in a café.'

His job sometimes involved spending a certain amount of time in small village cafés, most of them dimly lit, where men simply sat nursing beers, their discussions growing louder as the hours went by. There were six cafés

The Blue Room

in Saint-Justin, although three of them did good business only on fair days.

'And did you expect as well that the two women would wind up going to court?'

'Your Honour, I tell you I paid no attention to all that.'

'Still, you were aware of the situation?'

'Like everyone else. The word was that old Madame Despierre, crafty as she was, had made a bad bargain, and that Andrée had come out the winner in the end.'

'You didn't know if that was true?'

'How could I have?'

'Your mistress, during your eleven-month liaison, did not tell you that she and her husband owned everything in common?'

'We never discussed her marriage.'

They had spent so little time talking that they might better have not talked at all. And the magistrate proved it by returning once more to that last Thursday in the blue room.

'Still, you did speak of your future together.'

'Those words were just air, we didn't take them seriously.'

'She didn't? You're sure about Andrée? Allow me to remind you that two months before the death of her husband, she was anticipating that event.'

He was about to protest, but Diem kept talking.

'Perhaps not specifically, but she was alluding to his disappearance when she asked you how you would feel when she became free.'

He would have given anything – an arm, a leg, an

eye – if only certain words had never been spoken! He was ashamed to have heard them without protest and hated that other Tony standing before the mirror, dabbing at his bloody lip, proud of his nakedness in the sunlight, of being an admired, handsome male, of seeing his seed dripping from any female's vulva.

'*Would you like to live with me always?*'

And a little later, '*Are you still bleeding?*'

She was pleased at herself for having bitten him, obliging him to go home and show his wife and daughter the mark of their lovemaking!

'*What will you say, if she asks about it?*'

She: that was Gisèle, and he had spoken of her so carelessly, as if she were of no importance.

'*I'll tell her I bumped into my windshield, say, from braking too suddenly.*'

He felt the treachery of those words so deeply that when Marianne, not Gisèle, had asked him about his swollen lip, he had changed his explanation and turned the windshield into a lamp-post.

'*Would you like to spend your whole life with me?*'

What would have happened if the train hadn't whistled, as if to shout at him in warning, when she was saying in her throaty voice, '*Tell me, Tony. If I became free . . .*'

Now he hated those words!

'*Would you free yourself too?*'

Could he admit to the magistrate that he had heard those words throbbing in his ears all winter, that they haunted him at the table in the kitchen with its steamed-up windows, that he was even saying them over to himself at the very moment when his daughter was discovering the toys under the Christmas tree?

'The grocery store on Rue Neuve,' continued Diem implacably, 'the houses, the farms, the hamlet of La Guipotte now belong to the two women, and Andrée Despierre has the right to force the public auction of the entire estate in order to collect her part of the inheritance.'

He paused for a long moment.

'There's been a lot of talk about this in Saint-Justin, hasn't there?'

'I believe so. Yes.'

'Was it not felt that old lady Despierre would never accept having part of her property fall into the hands of strangers? Isn't that why she returned to the store, beside the daughter-in-law she detests and to whom she refuses to speak? Everything depended on Andrée, and her decision depended on yours . . .'

He gave a start and couldn't help opening his mouth as if to object . . .

'I'm telling you what everyone was saying. That's why they watched you, wondering whose side you would take. Old lady Despierre belongs to the village, she's one of them, even if they resent her stubborn greed.

'As for Andrée, they've never liked her grand airs and only tolerated her out of respect for her father's memory.

'And you: not only were your parents foreigners, but you abandoned the area for ten years, and people wondered why you had returned.'

'What are you getting at?'

'Nothing in particular. The betting was on. Many people expected that Andrée would have everything sold, going to court if necessary, and that once in possession of the spoils she'd leave Saint-Justin with you.

'The person everyone felt the sorriest for was your wife, despite her lack of strong ties to the villagers. Do you know what some of them called her? "The sweet little lady who tries so hard".'

Diem smiled as he placed an index finger on one of the files.

'Everything I've told you today is in here, in black and white. They all talked in the end. Your lawyer, I repeat, has a copy of this file. He could have been present during these interviews. He decided, with your approval, to leave you on your own.'

'I asked him to.'

'I know. Although I still don't understand why.'

What use was it to explain that, when he went to confession, the priest behind the grille didn't bother him, but a third person would have turned him mute. And although Diem feigned astonishment, he knew this so well that, whenever he tackled a difficult point, a delicate matter, he was careful to send away his clerk.

'And now, Monsieur Falcone, shall we discuss the two last letters, the ones sent at the end of December and on 20 January?'

5

His lawyer, too, kept on at him about the letters.

'Why don't you tell the truth about them as you did about everything else? You definitely received those letters. The postmaster in Saint-Justin could not possibly have invented them.'

Like a kid who has lied and is too proud to admit it, he would say over and over, 'I don't know what you're talking about.'

In his case, it wasn't pride, but perhaps a remnant of loyalty to the blue room. He had never intended to marry Andrée. Even if they had both been free, if neither of them had been married, it would never have occurred to him to make her his wife.

Why? He didn't know.

'Admit that her passion unnerved you,' Professor Bigot had suggested. 'It must have been a shock when you discovered, that September evening next to the little wood, that the woman you'd thought of as a statue, calm and aloof, could change into a sexually voracious female.'

'It did surprise me.'

'Flattered you, too, probably. Because it now seems that she was sincere in claiming to have loved you ever since you were in school together.'

'I felt somewhat responsible.'

'Responsible for this passion?'

'That isn't the right word . . . It seemed to me that I owed her something. This isn't quite the right comparison, but when a lost cat starts following you, meowing pitifully, and then camps out on your doorstep, you feel responsible for what might happen to it.'

Bigot seemed to understand. This interview took place during the second or third week of Tony's imprisonment. The first time he had left his cell had been to go to the courthouse, and exceptional precautions had been taken on account of the reporters, photographers and eager onlookers packing the main staircase there.

Just as he had been about to climb into the Black Maria, the prison warden had rushed up, alerted by a phone call from the public prosecutor, and he had been returned to his cell for almost an hour.

When they had brought him out again, he was no longer escorted by gendarmes but by Inspector Mani and a plain-clothes policeman. The police van was not in the prison courtyard, having been sent on with two relatively unknown detainees to mislead the crowd.

He had gone off in an ordinary car without special markings, which had pulled up near a small door at the back of the courthouse.

They had played the same game for two weeks. Stirred up by the press, the public had turned against him to the point of threatening violence.

Two months had passed. Most of the journalists from Paris and other big cities had left Poitiers, leaving the job

The Blue Room

of following the case to local correspondents and press agency representatives.

Now and then he had come across images in magazines and newsreels of defendants being hustled through crowds to get to court or prison, protected by policemen and trying to hide their faces.

Now he was like them, except that he did not cover his face. Did he look like them? Like someone already excluded from human society and unable to understand why?

He kept himself under control. Before the examining magistrate, he did not behave like a hunted man. He answered questions as best he could, like a good schoolboy, proud of his sincerity and attention to detail, except on the subject of the letters. He was convinced that if he gave in on that point, he would never see the end of it.

He had received the December letter on New Year's Eve. The frozen snow crackled underfoot. People were beginning to call out 'Happy New Year!' when they met.

'And a Happy New Year to you, too!'

The sky was clear, the air crisp. Some kids were taking turns sliding down the middle of Rue Neuve. The postmaster had made no comment when handing over his mail, which Tony usually glanced through off in a corner of the post office.

Happy Our Year.

The blow to his heart, the pain, had been more violent this time. He sensed some mysterious menace in this message. The words had been carefully chosen, that was obvious, and he struggled to understand them. Wasn't that 'our' the core of Andrée's thinking?

He had burned it, this last letter of the year, for the banks of the Orneau were sheathed in ice, and the river was down to a trickle.

The next morning, he had gone with his wife and child to wish old Angelo a Happy New Year. His father had hardly said a word, not looking even once at Marianne, and Tony thought he knew why. Didn't she remind him of both his dead wife and daughter?

As they did every year, they had gone that afternoon to see his brother, who had to keep the hotel and café open for the holiday.

Early that morning he had found his wife alone in the kitchen and had hugged her tight for a long time, her head leaning against his shoulder.

'Happy New Year, Gisèle.'

Had she sensed the special intensity of his emotion? Had she understood how worried he was, how afraid that this new year would not be a happy one for them?

'Happy New Year, Tony.'

Then she had looked up at him and smiled. She could never really manage a big smile, though, so it had made him feel more wistful than relieved.

Ever since Marianne had started school, he and his wife had eaten their midday meal together. Since many children attended from farms several kilometres away and hadn't the time to go home for lunch, the teacher had set up a canteen. Marianne, who loved being at school, had begged her parents to let her eat there.

The Blue Room

'She's going through a phase,' Gisèle told him. 'I'm sure that next year, she'll change her mind.'

It wasn't always easy for Tony to sit across from Gisèle while trying to hide all his worries from her. What did they say to each other? Silence made them both uneasy, and they would talk lightly about anything at all, meaningless chitchat, and be startled whenever they both simply ran out of words.

The last letter had made things still worse. Andrée was practically giving him an order and reminding him of what she considered a promise. The message was only two words, written in big letters that took up the whole page.

Now you!

He had opened the envelope, as always, in the post office, on the desk with the violet ink, a broken pen and the forms for telegrams and postal orders. He could not have said afterwards how he had behaved; strangely, no doubt, because, behind his little window, Monsieur Bouvier had been concerned and asked him if he had received bad news.

'I'd never seen him like that before,' the postmaster would later tell the magistrate. 'He looked like a man who'd just received a death sentence. He didn't answer, just looked at me, but I'm not sure he even saw me. Then he rushed outside without stopping to close the door.'

Fortunately, he had been planning to visit some farms and had his car with him that day. He drove aimlessly, staring hard at the road, without a thought for the customers awaiting him. He went wherever the road took him, trying desperately to see those two words in some reassuring light yet knowing it was hopeless. They could mean only one thing: 'Your turn!'

'When I think of the years you cost me . . .'

She wasn't going to waste any more time. Now that she had taken possession of him, she would finally see her childhood dream, still alive after all those years, come true.

Could she really have waited so long for Tony without anything breaking that spell?

The psychiatrist seemed to think so. Perhaps he had seen similar cases.

Andrée was telling him, in no uncertain terms: 'I've done my part; now you do yours.'

Or else? Because the threat was understood. He had not protested when she had said, behind his back, *'Tell me, Tony. If I became free . . .'*

And free she had been, for two months now, after developments he refused to think about. Free and rich. Free to do as she liked with the rest of her life without answering to anyone.

'Would you free yourself too?'

He had not replied. Didn't she know, in her heart of hearts, that he had deliberately avoided answering her? True, there had been that strident, outraged whistle from the train . . . Andrée might have imagined that he had said yes, or had nodded in reply.

Now you!

If she truly wasn't expecting him to refuse, what did she think he would do?

Divorce his wife? Go to Gisèle and tell her point-blank . . .

Unthinkable. He had nothing against his wife. He had known what he was doing when he married her. He didn't want an impassioned mistress for a wife but a woman exactly like Gisèle, and her shy modesty had not displeased him – on the contrary.

One doesn't spend one's life in a bed with someone, in a room glowing with sunshine, in the naked embrace of bodily passion.

Gisèle was his companion, Marianne's mother, the first one downstairs in the morning to light the fire, the one who kept the house clean and cheerful, welcoming him without any questions when he came home.

They would grow closer together as they grew old together, for they would have more and more memories to share. Sometimes Tony imagined the conversations they would have in later years, when they began to feel their age.

'You remember that grand passion of yours?'

Who knows? Gisèle's smile might ripen with time into its full glory. And flattered, a touch ashamed, he might reply, 'Oh, that's a bit of an exaggeration.'

'If you could have seen yourself, when you came home from Triant!'

'I was young . . .'

'Luckily, I already knew you rather well by then. I had faith in you, although sometimes I did feel afraid. Especially after Nicolas died. Then she was suddenly free . . .'

'She tried . . .'

'To get you to ask for a divorce? Sometimes I even wonder if she didn't love you more than I did.'

He would take her hand, in the twilight. Because he imagined them together in front of their house, in the summer, with night coming on.

'I pity her. Even back then there were days when I felt sorry for her.'

And now he was being ordered, in two words, to have done with Gisèle!

Now you!

The more he considered those words, the more sinister they became. Andrée had not divorced Nicolas. He had died. In the bedroom above the grocery store, she was the only one who had witnessed his death agony. She had waited until he was gone before crossing the garden to alert her mother-in-law.

Was it really a divorce she had in mind for him?

Now you!

Driving around without knowing where he was, sometimes he screamed in rage: 'Now you! Now you! Now you! Now you . . .'

How could he awaken from this nightmare? Go to Andrée's house and tell her straight out: 'I will never divorce my wife. I love her.'

'What about me?'

Would he dare reply, 'I don't love you'?

'But . . .'

She was capable of cutting right to the heart of his thoughts with a glare of defiance.

'But you let me kill Nicolas.'

The Blue Room

He had suspected her right away. So had Gisèle. Along with most of the villagers. It was only an intuition. People didn't know what had happened. Maybe she had simply let him die by not sending for help.

He had had nothing to do with it.

'You know perfectly well, Andrée, that . . .'

He couldn't even run away from her by leaving Saint-Justin with his family. He had not yet finished paying off his house, the shed, the equipment. He was only just beginning to enjoy a certain prosperity and provide his family with a comfortable life.

It was unbelievable, it made no sense. He wound up stopping at an inn for a drink. Tony's sobriety was so well known that the woman who served him, while keeping an eye on her baby playing on the floor, began worrying about him, too. She would give evidence later on as well.

Undaunted by the stubborn silence of these country people, Inspector Mani had kept returning to the attack for however long it would take.

'Shall I read you the testimony of the postmaster regarding that last letter?'

'There's no need.'

'You mean that he lied, that he imagined the incident of the door left wide open?'

'I don't mean anything.'

'One of the farmers you were supposed to meet that morning telephoned your house to see if you'd been delayed or were not coming. Your wife told him that you were on your way. Is that correct?'

'Probably.'

'Where did you go?'

'I don't recall.'

'In general, you have a remarkable memory. At the Auberge des Quatre Vents, you drank, not wine or beer, but brandy. You rarely drink spirits. You had four brandies in quick succession, then looked at the clock behind the counter and appeared surprised that it was already noon...'

He had driven very fast, hoping to get home before lunch-time. Gisèle had realized he had been drinking, and for a moment he resented her for it. Just because he had married her, did that give her the right to spend her time watching him? He had had enough of being spied on! She wasn't saying anything, true, but that was worse than if she had scolded him.

He was free! A free man! And whether his wife liked it or not, he was the head of the family. He was the one who earned their living, slaving away to bring them up in the world. Everything depended on him!

She kept quiet and, at the other end of the table, so did he, glancing at her furtively now and then, a little abashed, for he knew deep down that he was wrong. He should not have had those drinks.

'You know, it isn't my fault. With the customers, it's rude to refuse.'

'That reminds me, Brambois called.'

Why did people force him to lie? It was humiliating, and he bitterly resented it.

'I didn't have time to go to his farm because I was delayed somewhere else.'

Now you! Now you! Now you!

She was right there in front of him, eating he didn't even know what, doing her best not to look at him because she could tell he was annoyed.

What did Andrée want of him? That he kill her?

There! He had done it. He was finally daring to confront the thoughts that had been seething in his mind. Hadn't Professor Bigot, by drilling ever deeper with his careful questions, helped him to reach this point?

He hadn't told him everything, of course. Against all evidence, he still denied knowing anything about the letters.

The fact remained: on that day, the day of the last message and the four brandies (a local 65 proof *marc* that burned its way down), he had asked himself that question while having lunch with his wife.

Was this what Andrée was demanding of him? That he kill his wife?

Abruptly, his inebriation turned maudlin: he was to blame. He felt impelled to ask for forgiveness. He reached across the table to take his wife's hand.

'Listen! Don't be angry at me. I'm a little drunk.'

'You'll have a rest after lunch.'

'It upsets you, doesn't it?'

'No, really . . .'

'I know it does. I am not behaving the way I should.'

He had the feeling he was going out on a limb.

'Are you angry at me, Gisèle?'

'For what?'

'You do worry about me, admit it.'

'I like it better when you're happy . . .'

'And you think I'm not? Is that it? Don't I have everything? I have the best wife ever, a daughter just like her whom I adore, a beautiful house, a thriving business. So why wouldn't I be happy? All right! I do worry about some things at times. When you're born in a shack without electricity or running water out in La Boisselle, it isn't all that easy to set up on your own. Think how far we've come since I met you in Poitiers. I was only a common working man then . . .'

He talked, talked, growing more and more wound up.

'I'm the happiest man in the world, Gisèle, and if anyone claims otherwise, you can tell him from me he's lying. The happiest of men, you hear me?'

He was weeping now, choking back a sob as he dashed upstairs to lock himself in the bathroom.

Gisèle never said a word to him about this.

'Forgive me for asking you this question yet again, Monsieur Falcone. It will be the last time. Did you receive those letters?'

Tony shook his head as if to say that all he could do was say no. Diem expected this and turned to his clerk.

'Please bring in Madame Despierre.'

If Tony flinched, it was barely visible. In any case, he did not show the emotional reaction the magistrate expected – because for everyone in Saint-Justin, 'Madame Despierre' meant Nicolas' mother, not his wife, whom no one would ever have called by that name. Andrée was the daughter-in-law or, for the older villagers, the Formier girl.

The Blue Room

He was wondering how the old woman could ever shed any light on the letters. He didn't relish the idea of having to face her, but that was all. He had stood up automatically and was waiting, half turned towards the door.

And when that door opened abruptly, he was staring at Andrée. A corpulent man with the air of a bon vivant followed her in, as well as one of the gendarmes, but Tony saw only her, only her white face, which seemed even paler against her black dress.

She was staring at him as well, serenely, her features softened by a faint smile, and one might have thought that she was calmly taking possession of him, engulfing him.

'Hello, Tony.'

That throaty voice of hers, a touch hoarse, enveloping him. He did not return her greeting. He could not have spoken and did not want to. He nodded brusquely to her and turned towards Diem as if seeking his protection.

'Remove her handcuffs.'

Still smiling, she held her wrists out to the gendarme, and he heard the double click he knew so well.

In Saint-Justin, he had not noticed, the few times he had seen her since her husband's death, that she was in mourning. Her face had grown plumper in prison, and her body as well, just enough to make her clothes fit more tightly. It was the first time he had ever seen her wear black stockings.

After the gendarme left, there was an instant of uncertainty. They all stood there in the tiny office, with the sun shining directly in. The clerk was the first to sit down again, in front of his papers at the end of the table, while the fat man with Andrée remarked, surprised, 'My colleague Demarié isn't here?'

'Monsieur Falcone does not wish him to be – unless he changes his mind, for this particular confrontation. In which case I should not have to look far, as he has informed me that he will be in the building until six o'clock. What shall it be, Monsieur Falcone?'

The question startled him.

'Do you wish me to summon your lawyer?'

'What for?'

Diem and Maître Capade then walked to the window to have a quiet discussion of some legal matters. Still standing, Tony and Andrée were hardly an arm's length apart; he might almost have touched her. She was still gazing at him with the dazzled eyes of a child given an unexpected toy.

'Tony . . .'

It was barely a murmur; her lips moved simply to form his name. As for him, he looked away from her, relieved when the conversation at the window ended and the magistrate drew up a chair for the young woman.

'Sit down. You, too, Monsieur Falcone. There is another chair, Maître.'

With everyone seated, Diem rummaged through his files to pull out a small diary bound in black oilcloth, the kind sold in the grocery store.

'Do you recognize this object, Madame Despierre?'

'I have already told you, yes.'

'That you have. I am obliged to ask you a certain

number of questions that I have already put to you and I remind you that your replies are a matter of record, which does not prevent you from reconsidering or correcting them.'

Perhaps because of the lawyer's presence, the magistrate's manner seemed more formal than it was with Tony, almost pompous.

'The notations here have mostly to do with shopping lists, appointments with the dentist or dressmaker,' he said softly, skimming through the book. 'This is last year's diary, and the dates of your meetings with Tony Falcone are underlined.'

He had no idea that this diary would play a decisive role in his fate, or that – had he known of its contents earlier – he might have escaped at least one of the accusations against him.

'The last time we spoke, I asked you the meaning of these little circles I see in every month.'

'I told you that they marked the dates of my periods.'

She spoke without any false modesty. A few weeks earlier, Tony, too, had been asked equally intimate questions.

'Everyone in Saint-Justin,' Diem had told him, 'thought Nicolas was sterile, if not impotent, and the fact is that after eight years of marriage, his wife has had no children. Dr Riquet, moreover, has confirmed that he was probably sterile. Did you know this?'

'I had heard it said.'

'Fine! Now remember the extremely detailed account you gave me of your meeting on 2 August in what you call the blue room of the Hôtel des Voyageurs, from which we may conclude that during your amorous encounters with your mistress you took no precautions to avoid pregnancy.'

When he did not reply, the magistrate continued.

'Did you behave the same way during your other extra-marital affairs?'

'I don't know.'

'Do you recall a certain Jeanne, who is a farm worker employed by one of your customers? Inspector Mani questioned her, promising that her name would not appear in the case file or be introduced in a public hearing. You had sexual relations with her three times. The first time, during the act, when she seemed frightened, you whispered in her ear, "Don't be scared, I'll pull out in time."

'From this I deduce that this was your habit in such situations. If you deny this, I will have other persons with whom you have had relations identified and questioned.'

'I do not deny it.'

'In that case, tell me why, with Andrée Despierre and with her alone, you never took even any basic precautions.'

'She's the one who . . .'

'Did she bring up the subject?'

No. But the first time, she had held him close when he had tried to withdraw. Surprised, he had almost asked her, 'Aren't you afraid?'

There at the roadside near Bois de Sarelle, he had concluded that she would take the necessary steps when she

The Blue Room

got home. Later, at the Hôtel des Voyageurs, he had realized she was doing nothing of the sort.

If he hadn't immediately grasped the connection between the magistrate's question and the accusation brought against him, he soon would.

'Is that not the way you would both have behaved if you had decided to live together, no matter what happened? To be unconcerned about Andrée's possible pregnancy, Monsieur Falcone, means that such an eventuality would have changed nothing, except perhaps to force you to accelerate your plans, isn't that so?'

He had left that session utterly demoralized, wondering if the magistrate had ever in his life had a mistress.

Today, however, Diem did not seem inclined to revisit the point.

'I see here, on 1 September, a cross followed by the number 1. Would you tell us what that means?'

Still completely at ease, she looked at the magistrate, then at Tony, smiling at him in encouragement.

'It's the date of my first letter.'

'Be more precise, would you? To whom did you write that day?'

'To Tony, naturally.'

'Why?'

'When my husband took the train to Triant, on 2 August, I realized that he was suspicious and I didn't dare return to Vincent's hotel.'

'So you were no longer using the agreed-upon signal?'

'That's right. Tony had been quite shaken when he saw Nicolas on Place de la Gare. I didn't want him to keep fretting because he thought some drama might be taking place.'

'What do you mean by that?'

'He might have thought there had been violent scenes between me and my husband, that Nicolas had told his mother and that they were making life difficult for me, or who knows what, when in reality I had managed to come up with a plausible explanation for my presence at the hotel.'

'Do you remember what you wrote?'

'Perfectly. "Everything is fine." I added, "Don't be afraid."'

Diem turned towards him.

'Do you still deny this, Monsieur Falcone?'

Andrée turned to him in perplexity.

'Why would you deny it? Didn't you get my letters?'

He was baffled, even wondered if she might actually be unaware of her situation and not suspect the trap into which they were leading her.

'Let's continue. Perhaps you will soon change your mind. Second cross, 25 September this time. What did the second letter say?'

She did not need to search her memory. She knew the letters by heart, the way he knew everything that had been said in the blue room on that afternoon of 2 August.

'It was simply a greeting. "I haven't forgotten. I love you."'

'Let me point out that, according to your own recollection, you did not write "I haven't forgotten you" . . .'

'No. I hadn't forgotten.'

The Blue Room

'What hadn't you forgotten?'

'Everything. Our love. Our promises.'

'The 10th of October was three weeks before your husband's death. During an earlier interview, you provided the text of this third letter: "Soon! I love you." What did you mean by "soon"?'

Still imperturbable, she replied, first darting a reassuring glance at Tony.

'That we would soon be able to renew our rendezvous.'

'Why?'

'I had succeeded in allaying all Nicolas' suspicions.'

'Wasn't it rather that you knew he would not live much longer?'

'I have already explained this to you twice. He was very ill, and might well have lingered on for a few years – or suddenly passed away, and his mother and I had just been reminded of that by Dr Riquet, a few days earlier.'

'When?'

'When he had had one of his fits. They were becoming more frequent, and he was having increasing trouble with his digestion.'

Tony listened in disbelief. At moments he found himself thinking that Diem, Andrée and her lawyer, nodding his head in approval, had banded together to put on this show for him. The questions flooding his mind should have been asked by the magistrate – who was taking pains to avoid them!

'We now come to 29 December. The New Year is around the corner. A small cross in your diary.'

She immediately provided the text of her message.

' "Happy Our Year." '

With a touch of pride, she added, 'I spent a long time coming up with that. It might not be good French, but I wanted to emphasize that this year would be ours.'

'What did you mean by that?'

'Have you forgotten that Nicolas was dead?'

She was the first to mention this, placidly, with that same unnerving composure.

'You mean that you were free?'

'Obviously.'

'And in that case, there was no longer anything to prevent the coming year from being yours, meaning yours and Tony's?'

She nodded, more coolly self-satisfied than ever. Once again, instead of challenging her assertions, Diem let them stand and picked up another diary, similar to the first.

Only now did Tony realize that he was not the only one to have spent long hours in this room over the past two months. His lawyer had, of course, informed him of the arrest of Andrée, ten or twelve days after his own. She had been interrogated, obviously, but he hadn't really thought about what that meant. He had never imagined that her testimony could have as much weight, if not more, than his own.

'There is one letter left, Madame Despierre, the shortest but most significant one, consisting of only two words.'

Andrée crowed defiantly, ' "Now you!" '

'Would you explain to us, as clearly as possible, what you meant by that?'

'Isn't it plain enough? As you said yourself, I was free. Once I was out of mourning . . .'

'Just a moment! Was it because you were in mourning that you did not resume your meetings at the hotel after your husband's death?'

'That was part of it, but also because I was in litigation with my mother-in-law, and if this had led to a lawsuit, our liaison might have been damaging to me.'

'So you did not set the towel in the window after All Saints' Day?'

'Once.'

'Did you see your lover?'

'No.'

'Did you go up to the room?'

'I undressed as usual,' she announced boldly, 'convinced that he would come.'

'Was there anything you needed to talk over with him?'

'If there had been, I wouldn't have waited there naked.'

'Did you not have any matters to discuss with him?'

'Such as?'

'Among other things, how he was going to get himself free.'

'That had been decided long before.'

'On 2 August?'

'That wasn't the first time.'

'You'd agreed that he would get a divorce?'

'I'm not sure that exact word was used, but that's what I understood.'

'Do you hear that, Falcone?'

Turning to him, she opened her eyes wide.

'You haven't told them?'

Then she turned back to the magistrate.

'I don't see what's so extraordinary about this. People get divorced every day. We love each other. I loved him already when I was just a little girl and if I resigned myself to marrying Nicolas, it was because Tony had gone away, and I was convinced he would never return.

'When we found each other again, we both realized that we belonged to one another for ever.'

He wanted to protest, to stand up and shout: 'No! No! Stop this! It's all a lie! It's all fake!'

He just sat there, too confounded to make a move. Could she really believe what she was saying? She was speaking simply, dispassionately, as if all this were perfectly normal, with nothing inexplicable or tragic about it!

'And so, when you wrote "Now you", what you were thinking was . . .'

'That I was waiting for him. That it was up to him to do what was necessary . . .'

'To ask for a divorce?'

She paused a moment – was it deliberate? – before replying, 'Yes'.

Now it was Tony the magistrate glanced at in complicity before continuing to question Andrée, as if to say, 'Listen to this, it will interest you.'

And in an even voice, without a trace of irony or sarcasm, he asked her, 'Did you ever give a thought to the misery this would bring to Gisèle Falcone?'

'She would not have cried for very long.'

'How do you know? Didn't she love her husband?'

'Not the way I did. Women like that aren't capable of real love.'

'What about her daughter?'

'Exactly! Her daughter would have been a consolation to her and, as long as they received some small income, they would have had a nice little life.'

'You hear that, Falcone?'

The magistrate must have regretted having pushed things that far, for Tony's face was terrifying, almost inhuman with hatred and pain. He rose slowly from his chair, his features frozen, his eyes staring, like a sleepwalker.

His fists were clenched; his arms seemed abnormally long. The fat lawyer, who had turned casually to look at him, now jumped up to stand between him and his client.

Diem signalled urgently to the clerk, who ran to the door.

Although this scene lasted only a few seconds, it seemed to take much longer. The gendarmes came in; one of them roughly slapped handcuffs on Tony, then waited for orders. The magistrate hesitated, looking back and forth between his prisoner and Andrée, who seemed simply surprised.

'I don't understand, Tony, why you . . .'

But at a sign from the magistrate she was the one removed from the room. Her lawyer held her arm and pushed her firmly towards the door. She turned around once more to exclaim, 'You know very well that you said yourself . . .'

The rest was cut off when the door closed behind them.

'I apologize, Falcone. I had to do that. In a few moments, as soon as the coast is clear, you'll be taken back to prison.'

That evening, Diem told his wife about the episode as he was finishing dinner.

'Today I had to proceed with the cruellest confrontation of my entire career and I hope never to preside again over anything that painful.'

As for Tony, back in his cell, he lay awake all night.

6

He spent two days in a kind of stupor, emerging only now and then in a brief burst of rebellion that set him pacing in his cell as if he were going to hurl himself headfirst against the walls.

It was a weekend, and everyone must have gone off to the countryside.

Surprisingly, he had got used to prison life almost immediately, obeying its rules and the guards' orders without protest.

It wasn't until the third day that he felt abandoned. No one came to see him. There was no mention of taking him to the law courts. He listened impatiently to the footsteps in the corridor and stood up whenever someone stopped at his spy hole.

Only later did he realize that the street outside was silent, with almost no traffic, and one of the jailers confirmed at around four that afternoon that that Monday was a holiday.

At ten o'clock the next morning, a sunburned Demarié arrived to see him in his cell. He took his time setting out the papers he removed from his briefcase and getting comfortable, then offered Tony a cigarette and lit one himself.

'I suppose the past three days must have dragged on for ever for you . . .'

He gave a little cough, since Tony hadn't bothered to reply and was waiting with discouraging indifference.

'I've received a copy of the transcript from your last interrogation and the confrontation with Andrée Despierre.'

Did he believe in his client's innocence? Was he still making up his mind?

'I'd be lying if I said things look good for us. This business of the letters is a disaster and will have an even worse effect on the jury in that you've been denying their existence. The messages as reported by the Despierre woman, are they correct?'

'Yes.'

'I would like you to answer, truthfully, one question. When you stubbornly denied receiving those letters, was it to avoid implicating your mistress or because you thought the messages were dangerous for you?' What was the use of trying any more? Men like to think that they act, in all circumstances, for a definite reason. The first time the letters had been mentioned, he hadn't really thought about it and had never imagined that someone would go and question the postmaster.

It had taken weeks for him to realize how unbelievably hard Inspector Mani and his colleagues had worked, how many people were visited day after day – until they gave in and started talking.

Was there a single person in Saint-Justin, a single local farmer, any regular visitor to the fairs, especially the one in Triant, who hadn't said his piece?

The Blue Room

The reporters had got in on the job as well and churned out whole columns of interviews in the newspapers.

'I met briefly with Diem, and he gave me to understand that the confrontation was particularly upsetting for you. It seems you lost your head at the end. Andrée, on the contrary, kept up her cool self-confidence. I presume she will behave the same way in court.'

Demarié was making a real effort to rouse him from his apathy.

'I tried to find out what the magistrate thinks, although his opinion will be far from decisive once the judicial inquiry is over. He doesn't conceal a certain sympathy for you, yet I would swear that in the almost two months now since he began his inquiry, he still hasn't managed to make up his mind.'

Why all this nattering, this tedious talk?

'By the way, I happened to run into Bigot, too, on Friday night, at a bridge party given by friends, and he took me aside to tell me he'd learned something rather interesting but, unfortunately, too late for us.

'You have essentially admitted that with Andrée you did not take the usual precautions you did with the other women and that you were not worried that she took none herself, which will lead the jury to conclude that you were not concerned about making her pregnant.'

Tony listened, curious to see where this was going.

'Andrée, as you know, kept track of her periods in her diary. Bigot was intrigued enough to compare the dates with those of your meetings in Triant during the eleven months of your affair. Diem hadn't thought of that, and neither, I admit, had I.

'Do you know how those dates matched up? In absolutely every case, the meetings took place when your mistress was not fertile.

'In other words, Andrée Despierre was taking no chances, a detail that would have been in your favour – without those earlier statements. I'll use it anyway, but it won't have the same impact.'

Tony sank back into indifference, and the lawyer soon gave up.

'I believe you'll be going to the courthouse this afternoon.'

'Will she?'

'No. Just you this time. You still don't want me there?'

What for? Demarié was like the others. He understood no more than they did. His interventions would only complicate things. Still, Tony was glad to know that the little magistrate liked him . . .

He saw him again at three o'clock in his chambers. It was drizzling outside, and an umbrella stood dripping in the corner, the clerk's, probably, since the magistrate came to the courthouse in his black Renault 4CV.

Diem had not been out in the sun, for, as he soon explained: 'I took advantage of the long weekend to review the entire dossier. How do you feel today, Falcone? I should warn you, this interview may last some time, because we've reached Wednesday, 17 February. Will you go over your movements on that day in as much detail as possible?'

The Blue Room

He had been expecting this. Each time they had taken him away after a meeting, he had wondered why they hadn't reached this point yet.

The 17th of February was the end, the end of everything, an end he had never foreseen, not even in his worst nightmares, and which he had later realized, however, was logical and fated to happen.

'Would you like me to help you by asking specific questions?'

He nodded. On his own, he would not have known where to begin.

'Your wife got up at the usual time?'

'A little earlier. It had rained all Tuesday morning, so the laundry hadn't dried until mid-afternoon. She was planning to spend the entire day ironing.'

'And you?'

'I came downstairs at 6.30.'

'Did you eat breakfast together? Was there any discussion of your appointments that day? Try to be as accurate as possible.'

Diem had spread out the transcripts of his other statements, the first ones, from interrogations by the lieutenant at Triant – Gaston Joris, with whom Tony had often had an aperitif at his brother's place – and Inspector Mani, a Corsican.

'I'd told her the evening before, that's Tuesday night, that I would have a full day, that I would not be back for lunch and might even be late for dinner.'

'Did you tell her where you'd be as the day went on?'

'I mentioned only the fair at Ambasse, where some

clients were expecting me, and a repair job over at Bolinsur-Sièvre.'

'Wasn't that outside your area?'

'Bolin's only thirty-five kilometres from Saint-Justin, and I was beginning to extend my territory.'

'Did you know at the time that your itinerary was inaccurate?'

'It wasn't completely wrong.'

'You went upstairs at seven to awaken your daughter. Did you often do that?'

'Almost every morning. I'd wake her up before having my wash and shave.'

'You selected your best suit, a blue suit you saved for Sundays.'

'Because of my appointment in Poitiers. I wanted to look prosperous when I saw Garcia.'

'We'll get back to him later. When you came downstairs, your daughter, in the kitchen, was getting ready for school. Before heading for Ambasse and Bolin-sur-Sièvre, you had to drop by the post office, then the station, where you were expecting a package.'

'A piston I'd ordered for my client in Bolin.'

He had glanced automatically a few times at the empty chair in front of Diem's desk and finally realized it was the one Andrée had used the week before.

Although just an ordinary chair, it seemed to have remained in the same place since that Friday – and to be bothering Tony, so the magistrate, as he walked up and down the room, set it back against a wall.

'You offered to drive your daughter to school in the van.'

The Blue Room

'Yes.'

'Wasn't that unusual? Did you have no reason, that morning, to be particularly affectionate with her?'

'No.'

'Didn't you ask your wife if there were any errands to run in the village?'

'No. And I told the inspector that. I was on my way out when Gisèle called me back. She said, "Would you drop by the grocery store to pick up a kilo of sugar and two packets of soap powder? That way I won't have to change clothes." Those are her exact words.'

'You often did that sort of thing?'

Did he have to go through their complete household routine yet again? He had already done that with Mani. Almost every day, as in every household, there were different purchases to make in different places, including the butcher's shop or the charcuterie. Gisèle avoided sending him there, where customers almost always had to wait.

'She used to say that it wasn't a man's job.'

That Wednesday she wanted to get to her ironing as quickly as possible. Since they'd had a leg of mutton the previous evening, there were leftovers for that day's supper, and there was only the one errand to run.

'So you left with your daughter.'

He could still see, in his rear-view mirror, Gisèle at the front door, wiping her hands on her apron . . .

'You dropped Marianne off at the school and headed for the post office. Then?'

'I went inside the grocery store.'

'How long had it been since the last time?'

'Perhaps two months.'

'You hadn't been back there since the last letter, the one that said simply, "Now you!"?'

'No.'

'Monsieur Falcone, were you nervous? Excited?'

'It wasn't that. I would rather not have been in Andrée's presence, especially while several people were watching.'

'Were you afraid of giving yourself away?'

'I was uncomfortable.'

'Who was in the store when you came in?'

'I remember a child to whom I paid no attention, one of the Molard sisters and an old woman with a squint whom everyone calls La Louchote.'

'Was old Madame Despierre there?'

'I didn't see her.'

'Did you wait your turn?'

'No. Andrée immediately asked me, "And what can I get you, Tony?"'

'She waited on you before the others? No one objected?'

'It's customary. Just about everywhere, they serve the men first.

'I said, "A kilo of sugar and two packets of soap powder." She fetched them from the shelves, then said, "Wait a minute, I got in the plum jam your wife's been asking after for two weeks." She disappeared into the back room and returned with a pot of jam of the same brand I usually saw at home . . .'

'Was she gone long?'

'Not very long.'

'One minute? Two?'

'The time seemed normal to me.'

'Long enough to pick up a pot of jam and bring it into the shop? Or to look around for it among other piles of things?'

'Between the two. I don't know.'

'Did Andrée Despierre show any emotion?'

'I avoided looking at her.'

'Still, you saw her at some point. You heard her voice.'

'I think she was glad to see me.'

'She said nothing more to you?'

'When I was opening the door, she called out after me, "Have a good day, Tony!"'

'Did her voice sound natural?'

'At the time, I wasn't paying any attention. It was a day like any other.'

'And afterwards?'

'Perhaps her voice sounded more affectionate.'

'Did Andrée ever behave affectionately towards you?'

Wasn't he obliged to tell the truth?

'Yes. It's hard to explain. With a particular kind of affection, like the kind I show Marianne on certain days, for example.'

'Maternal affection?'

'That's not it either. "Protective" might be closer.'

'So, the first coincidence: your wife asks you, rather exceptionally, to go to the grocery store in her place. Second coincidence: the kitchen has been out of a certain jam, which only she eats, for several weeks. There's been a delivery at the store, and you're given a pot. Third coincidence, which Inspector Mani did not fail to point out: that day you did not go straight home but stopped by the station.'

'I'd had the piston sent to me express mail and—'

'That's not all. The station at Saint-Justin, like most buildings, has four sides: one facing the tracks; the one on the opposite side, through which passengers come and go; and a third, on the left, with the stationmaster's door. The fourth side, to the north, has neither door nor window. It's a bare wall, a blind wall, and it's beside this wall that you parked your van.'

'If you've been there, you must know it's the logical place to park.'

'The stationmaster, busy with paperwork, told you to get your package yourself from the freight room.'

'All the local people did that.'

'How long were you in or near the station?'

'I didn't look at the time. A few minutes.'

'The stationmaster has said that he heard your car leave only after a rather long time.'

'I wanted to make sure that they'd sent me the right piston, because they make mistakes fairly often.'

'You opened the package?'

'Yes.'

'In the van?'

'Yes.'

'Where no one could see you? Let's add this coincidence to the others. Home again, you place your purchases on the kitchen table. Your wife, in the garden, was taking the laundry off the lines and putting it in a basket. Did you go outside to her? Kiss her before leaving again?'

'That wasn't our way. I wasn't going off on a trip. I called to her from the doorway, "See you this evening!"'

'You didn't tell her that the jam had arrived?'

'Why would I? She'd find it on the table.'

'You didn't linger in the kitchen at all?'

'At the last moment, I saw the coffee pot set at the side of the burner and poured myself a cup.'

'If I'm not mistaken, that makes at least the fifth coincidence.'

Why was Diem making such a big point of all this? Tony could not change what had happened. What did they want from him? Protests, outrage? He had got past all that long ago. Now he answered their questions impassively. The weather was as dreary and damp as it had been on that 17 February, with its flat grey sky, its dull light, the empty-looking countryside, the puddles left by a recent downpour.

'Why did you go through Triant?'

'Because it was on my way.'

'You had no other reason?'

'I wanted to talk to my brother.'

'To ask his advice? Did you often do that, even though you are the elder brother?'

'I'd talk to him now and then about my business. Besides, he was the only one who knew of my difficulties with Andrée.'

'So you admit that there were problems?'

'Her letters worried me.'

'Isn't that rather an understatement, given what you admitted to Mani?'

'Let's say that they frightened me.'

'And you came to a decision? That's what you wanted to talk to Vincent about? It so happens, Monsieur Falcone, that while you were talking with him, your sister-in-law was out doing her shopping, and Françoise was upstairs cleaning the rooms.'

'It's like that every morning. When I walked into the café, Vincent wasn't there either. I heard the clinking of bottles in the cellar and saw the trap door open behind the counter. My brother was bringing up the day's wine, and I waited for him.'

'Without telling him you were there?'

'I didn't want to interrupt him. And I had time to wait. I sat near the window and thought about what I would say to Garcia.'

'You'd come to ask for your brother's advice, but you'd already made up your mind?'

'More or less.'

'Explain yourself.'

'I expected Garcia to hesitate, because he's a cautious man who retreats easily. Which meant that it was a toss-up for me.'

'You were gambling with your future and that of your family?'

'Yes. If Garcia could be convinced, I would sell. If he refused to risk the venture, I'd stay put.'

'And your brother in all this?'

'I wanted to let him know how things stood.'

'Without any witnesses, not even your sister-in-law, so that, aside from Vincent and you, no one can tell us about

The Blue Room

that conversation. You're very close to your brother, aren't you?'

Tony remembered the time when he used to take his little brother to school along muddy or frozen roads. They wore heavy pea-jackets. In the winter it was dark when they left home and still dark when they returned. Tired, Vincent often dragged his feet in their hobnail shoes and had to be tugged along. Tony would keep an eye on him from a distance during play time, and back at La Boisselle, waiting for their father, he was the one who made his brother's bread-and-butter snack. But such things, such simple things, cannot simply be explained with words: one must have personally experienced them. And Diem had not.

Vincent was certainly the person with whom he felt the closest bond of understanding, and Vincent in turn appreciated the way he did not lord it over him as the older brother. Speaking Italian to each other was another tie between them, linking them to the days when, as children, they spoke only that language with their mother.

'Vincent, I'm afraid that if I stay, I'll never have any peace.'

'She didn't say anything to you, this morning?'

'We weren't alone in the store. I expect I'll get another letter in two or three days, and God knows what will be in it!'

'How will you explain things to Gisèle?'

'I haven't thought about that yet. If I tell her that there

are no opportunities to expand my business in this area, she'll believe me.'

They had had a vermouth together, talking across the bar counter, and when a delivery man had arrived with some bottled lemonade, Tony had headed out of the door, which was still standing open.

'It's in God's hands!' Vincent had called after him.

Diem found it hard to believe that the brothers had talked things over so matter-of-factly; perhaps it was because they had experienced so much misfortune, even when they were little children.

'He didn't try to dissuade you?'

'On the contrary, he seemed relieved. He'd been unhappy about my affair with Andrée from the start.'

'Go on with your schedule on that day.'

'I spent hardly any time at Ambasse, which was just a small winter fair. After handing out a few brochures, I went on to Bolin-sur-Sièvre, where I had an appointment with my customer.'

'One moment. Did your wife know his name?'

'I don't remember telling her that.'

'When you went off on your rounds, didn't you let her know where you'd be, in case she had to contact you?'

'Not necessarily. For the fairs, it was easy, because I always went to the same cafés. When I visited farms, she had a general idea where I was and could telephone around for me.'

'You didn't mention Poitiers to her?'

'No.'

'Why not?'

'Because nothing was definite yet, and I didn't want her worrying for nothing.'

'It never occurred to you simply to confess the truth and tell her how worried you were about your affair with Andrée Despierre? Since this affair was over, according to you, wouldn't that have been best? You never considered that?'

No. An absurd, foolish answer perhaps, but it was the truth.

'At Bolin-sur-Sièvre I had lunch with my customer, Dambois, who has a good-sized farm, and I finished the repair job by two o'clock, so I wasn't in a rush when I drove off to Poitiers.'

'How had you set up your appointment with your friend Garcia?'

'I'd written to him the previous Saturday to let him know I'd pick him up after work. Garcia was my foreman when I worked at the main warehouse. He's about ten years older than I am, with three children, including a son at the local lycée.'

'Go on.'

'I was quite early. I could have visited the assembly workshop, but I'd have had to talk to everyone I knew there and I didn't have the heart. The factory is two kilometres from the city, on the Angoulême road. I went on to Poitiers and went to see a newsreel.'

'At what time did you leave the cinema?'

'Half past four.'

'When did you leave your brother that morning?'

'A little before ten.'

'In other words, most unusually, from ten in the morning until half past four, no one, not your wife or anyone else, knew where to reach you?'

'It never struck me that way.'

'Suppose your daughter had had a serious accident . . . Well, let's get on with it! You went to wait for Garcia outside the factory gate.'

'Yes. My letter had interested him. We considered going to the café across the street, but we'd have known too many people there. Since Garcia had his motorbike with him, he followed me into Poitiers as far as the Brasserie du Globe.'

'So no one knew you were there, either? Not even your brother?'

'No. Garcia and I exchanged news about our families, after which I explained my offer to him.'

'Did you tell him why you wanted to leave Saint-Justin?'

'Only that it had to do with a woman. I was aware that he had money set aside and that he'd spoken several times about setting up on his own. I was presenting him with a complete package: house, shed, equipment, plus an already thriving business and customer base.'

'Was he tempted?'

'He didn't give me a definite answer, wanted a week to think about it. Above all he had to discuss it with his wife and oldest son. What bothered him the most was having to leave Poitiers, especially because of the boy, who had friends there and was doing well at his studies. I pointed out that there was a good school in Triant. He shot back,

"With a fifteen-kilometre roundtrip, unless we board him there!"'

'How long did this discussion last?'

'Until about seven. Garcia invited me to dinner, but I told him my wife was waiting.'

'If Garcia had taken you up on your offer that following week, what were you planning to do?'

'I'd have asked the company to make me a representative in the north or east, in Alsace, for example, as far as possible from Saint-Justin. And they'd have done it, because they value my work. One day, perhaps, I might have set up on my own again.'

'You'd have left your father alone out at La Boisselle?'

'Vincent is close by.'

'Would you like to take a short break, Monsieur Falcone?'

'May I open the window?'

He needed air. He had felt suffocated right from the start of this interrogation, which appeared quite banal, but there was something threatening and unreal about having to speak so precisely about things rooted in a tragedy that was never mentioned.

'Cigarette?'

He took one and stared out at the street, at the windows and wet roofs across the way. If only this were the last time! But even if Diem never mentioned it again, he would still have to start all over in court.

He sat down heavily.

'We're almost at the end, Falcone.'

With a sad smile, he nodded at the magistrate, in whom he thought he sensed a certain compassion.

'You came directly home to Saint-Justin? Without stopping anywhere?'

'Suddenly, all I wanted was to get home to my wife and daughter. I think I drove very fast. Normally it takes about an hour and a half to cover the distance, and I did it in less than an hour.'

'Had you had anything to drink with Garcia?'

'He had two aperitifs, I had a single vermouth.'

'As with your brother.'

'Yes.'

'You drove past his place. You didn't stop to tell him how your appointment had gone?'

'No. Anyway, at that hour the café was always crowded, and Vincent would certainly have been busy.'

'It was dark out. You saw the lights of Saint-Justin in the distance. Did you notice anything?'

'I was surprised to see all the windows of my house lit up, which we never did, and I felt sure something awful had happened.'

'What did you think that might be?'

'My daughter . . .'

'Not your wife?'

'The way I saw it, Marianne was naturally the most fragile, the most at risk of an accident.'

'Without trying to drive your car to the shed, you left it some twenty metres from the house.'

'Half the village was gathered in front of our gate, so I knew it was bad.'

'You had to make your way through the crowd.'

'It made way for me, but instead of looking at me

The Blue Room

sympathetically everyone was angry, glaring at me, and I didn't understand. Didier, the fat blacksmith in his leather apron, even stepped in front of me with his hands on his hips – and spat on my shoes.

'While I was crossing the lawn, I felt threatened by the muttering behind me. The door opened as I reached it, and I knew the gendarme standing there, I'd often seen him at the market in Triant. "In there!" he barked at me. He pointed to the door of my office.

'I found Sergeant Langre sitting at my desk. Instead of calling me Tony, as he always did, he said nastily, "Sit down, you bastard!"

'That's when I shouted, "Where's my wife? Where's my daughter?" And he said, "Your wife? You know as well as I do where she is!"'

He fell silent. He couldn't get the words out any more. He was not upset, but uncannily calm.

Diem stopped questioning him; the clerk studied the tip of his pencil.

'I just don't know, Your Honour, it's so mixed up . . . Langre told me at some point that Marianne had been taken away by the Molard sisters, so I stopped worrying about her.

'Then he yelled at me, "Admit it, you knew and you didn't expect to find them alive! Fucking foreigner! You sonofabitch!"

'He'd stood up, and I saw he was just itching to hit me. I shouted again, "Where is my wife?"

'"In the hospital at Triant," he snapped, "as if you didn't know!"

'Then he looked at his watch: "Only, by this time, I doubt she's still alive. We'll know soon. And where were you, all day long? Hiding, eh? Didn't want to see it! We were wondering if you'd come back or if you might have run away."

'"Did Gisèle have an accident?" I asked. He said, "Accident? That's a good one! You killed her, that's what you did! And were careful not to be around when it happened."'

By this time, the lieutenant had driven up.

'What does he say?'

'He's playing the innocent, as I expected. Champion liars, these Italians. To listen to him, he hasn't a clue what happened here.'

The lieutenant was no less hostile than the sergeant, but he tried to stay calm and professional.

'Where have you been?'

'Poitiers.'

'What did you do all day? We tried to reach you just about everywhere.'

'At what time?'

'From 4.30 on.'

'What happened at 4.30?'

'Dr Riquet telephoned us.'

Tony suddenly lost control of himself.

'Lieutenant, tell me exactly what's happened! Has my wife had an accident?'

Then Lieutenant Joris had looked him in the eye.

'Are you playing games with us?'

'No, I swear, on my daughter's head and I'm begging you, tell me how my wife is! Is she alive?'

Joris looked at his watch, too.

'She was alive until forty-five minutes ago. I was at her bedside.'

'She's dead?'

He could not believe it. The house was full of strange noises, heavy footsteps upstairs . . .

'What are all these men doing in my house?'

'Searching, although we've already found what we were looking for.'

'I want to see my wife.'

'You'll do as we tell you. As of this moment, Antonio Falcone, you are under arrest.'

'What for?'

'I'm asking the questions here.'

Collapsing into a chair, he put his head in his hands. Still without knowing exactly what had happened, he had then been obliged to tell the police about his entire day from the moment he had awakened.

'You admit that you were the one who brought home this pot of jam?'

'Yes, of course.'

'Had your wife asked you to?'

'No. She'd asked me to buy some sugar and washing powder. It was Andrée Despierre who gave me the jam that Gisèle, it seems, had been expecting for a fortnight.'

'Did you come here directly from the grocery store?'

The package at the post office . . . The replacement piston . . .

'Is this the same pot of jam?'

They thrust it at his face. The pot had been opened, and a large amount of jam was gone.

'I think so. The label is the same.'

'You personally handed it to your wife?'

'I put it on the kitchen table.'

'Without mentioning it?'

'I didn't see the need. My wife was busy getting laundry off the line.'

'When were you last inside your shed?'

'This morning, shortly before eight, to get my van.'

'You took nothing else from there? You were alone?'

'My daughter was waiting for me in front of the house.'

All that was so recent – yet so long ago! The entire day, going here and there, was becoming unreal.

'And this, Falcone: you recognize it?'

He looked at the tin, which he knew well, since it had spent the last four years sitting on the top shelf in the shed.

'That looks like mine, yes.'

'What's in it?'

'Poison.'

'Do you know what kind?'

'Some arsenic or strychnine. That's from the first year we lived here. Where the shed is now, that used to be landfill, where the butcher dumped his rubbish. The rats had got used to coming around, and Madame Despierre—'

'Wait. Which? The old lady or the other one?'

'The mother. She sold me the same poison she sells all the farmers. I don't remember any more if it's . . .'

'It's strychnine. How much of it did you mix with the jam?'

Tony did not go crazy. He did not scream or howl,

either, but he did clench his teeth so fiercely that one of them cracked.

'At what time, normally, would your wife have had some of the jam?'

He heard himself reply, as if from a great distance.

'Around ten o'clock . . .'

Ever since they had moved to the country and she began rising early, Gisèle had made herself a mid-morning snack. Before Marianne had started school, they had eaten one together, the way they still had a snack when she came home in the afternoon.

'So you knew!'

'Knew what?'

'That she would be eating jam at ten o'clock. Do you know what a fatal dose of strychnine is? Two centigrams. And you probably know that ten or fifteen minutes after ingestion, the poison takes effect with the first convulsions. Where were you at ten o'clock?'

'Just leaving my brother's place.'

'Well, your wife was lying on the kitchen floor. She remained alone in the house, without help, until your daughter came home from school at four. So she lay dying for six hours before anyone could come to her aid. Very well organized, don't you think?'

'You mean she's dead?'

'Yes, Falcone. I believe you know all this already. After the first crisis she probably felt some relief. That's what Dr Riquet thinks. I don't know why she didn't immediately call for help. Later, when the convulsions returned, they would be relentless until the end.

'Coming home soon after four, your daughter found her mother lying on the floor in a state I would rather not describe to you. Hysterical, the girl ran in terror to pound on the door of the Molard ladies. Léonore came here to see for herself and called the doctor. Where were you at 4.15?'

'In a cinema in Poitiers . . .'

'Riquet diagnosed poisoning and sent for an ambulance. It was too late for a stomach pump; all they could do was sedate her.

'Riquet also called me and told me about the pot of jam. While waiting for the ambulance, he'd nosed around the kitchen. Bread, a knife, a cup with the remains of some café au lait and a plate with smears of jam were still on the table. He tasted the jam with the tip of his tongue.'

'I want to see her! I want to see my daughter!'

'As for your daughter, now is not the moment, because you might be torn to pieces by the crowd: Léonore Molard had nothing better to do than run door to door with the news. Out in the shed, my men found this tin of strychnine, and I contacted the public prosecutor at Poitiers.

'Now, Falcone, you will come with me. The police station would be more suitable for continuing this interrogation properly. Since you will doubtless not be returning here for a long time, I advise you to pack a suitcase with some clothes and personal effects. I will go upstairs with you.'

With question after question, Diem made him retell this story, describing his departure from Saint-Justin-du-Loup, suitcase in hand, through the throng of onlookers muttering angrily as he passed, while some stared wild-eyed at him, as if the discovery of a murderer in the village meant that any one of them could have been the victim.

'The law requires that you identify the body.'

He had had to wait out in a corridor of the hospital with the lieutenant and a gendarme. He was already in handcuffs but not yet used to them, and they hurt him whenever he moved too suddenly.

Studying him with particular attention, Diem observed, 'When they let you see your wife's body, after they'd finished laying her out, you stood a few steps away from her, completely still, without a word. Isn't that what a guilty man would do, Monsieur Falcone?'

How could he explain it to the magistrate? At that moment, in his heart, he had indeed felt guilty. He tried to tell him so, in a way . . .

'She died, after all, because of me.'

7

That interrogation, in the chambers of Examining Magistrate Diem, proved to be the last. The magistrate may have intended to question Tony again on certain points, or to confront him another time with Andrée, but what he was told about the prisoner's condition persuaded him to abandon any such thought.

Two days later, visiting him in his cell, Professor Bigot had already found a man indifferent to words, indifferent to everything, who appeared to have lapsed into a vegetative state.

His blood pressure had dropped significantly, and the psychiatrist had sent him for observation to the infirmary, where, in spite of intensive treatment, his state did not really improve.

He slept, ate, made a semblance of replying when spoken to, but in a colourless, impersonal voice.

His brother's visit had not awakened him from his prostration. Tony looked at him in amazement, surprised, it seemed, to see Vincent – as he knew him, as he was in his café in Triant – suddenly appear within the alien world of the infirmary.

'You mustn't let yourself lose heart, Tony. Don't forget that you have a daughter and that your family's all with you.'

What was the use?

'Marianne's settling in quite well with us. We'd sent her away to school, at first.'

'Did they tell her?' he'd asked dully.

'There was no way to prevent her classmates from talking. One evening she asked me, "Is it true Pop killed Mama?" So I reassured her, told her absolutely not.

' "Is he still a murderer anyway?"

' "Of course not, since he didn't kill anyone."

' "Then why's his picture in the paper?"

'You see, Tony? She doesn't really understand, so she isn't suffering . . .'

Was it the end of May, or the beginning of June? He no longer counted the days, or even the weeks, and when Demarié came to tell him that he had been charged, along with Andrée, with the murders of Nicolas and Gisèle, he showed no reaction at all.

'They decided against separate trials, which will make it harder for the defence.'

His condition remained unchanged. Sent back to his cell, instead of rebelling against the monotony of prison life, he adapted with impressive docility.

Then overnight all visits ceased; the days were empty, the guards themselves less numerous. The judicial recess had coincided with summer holidays, and hundreds of thousands of people were out on the roads, hurrying to the beaches, the mountains, the cottages tucked away in the countryside.

The newspapers had picked up the scent of a quarrel

that would dominate the trial, they hinted: the battle of the expert witnesses.

After an anonymous letter and the subsequent investigations in Triant, which had confirmed the liaison between Tony and Andrée, Nicolas had been exhumed. The first forensic tests had been carried out by a specialist in Poitiers, Dr Gendre, who reported finding a massive amount of strychnine in the body.

Twelve days after Tony's imprisonment, an arrest warrant had been issued for Andrée Despierre.

The lawyer she had chosen, Maître Capade, had called in a world-famous Parisian specialist, Professor Schwartz, who severely criticized his colleague's work and reached far less damning conclusions.

In three months, Nicolas had been exhumed two times and there was talk of a third, for the police forensic laboratory at Lyons, consulted in turn, demanded fresh evidence.

Discussion centred as well on the mild sedatives taken every evening by the grocer of Saint-Justin if he felt a fit coming on. When questioned, the pharmacist at Triant who had supplied them had confirmed that since the two halves of the capsules were not solidly joined, they could easily be opened and filled with something else.

What did all this have to do with Tony? He no longer even cared whether he was found guilty or not, or, if guilty, what the sentence would be.

On 14 October, the crowd in the courtroom of the Assizes and the many lawyers gathered there seemed startled by his attitude, while the newspapers claimed he was both heartless and shameless.

They were sitting on the same bench, he and Andrée, with a gendarme between them, and Andrée had leaned a little forwards to say, 'Hello, Tony!'

He had neither turned nor winced at the sound of her voice.

The defence lawyers and their clerks were fussing over their papers on a bench in the well of the court. In addition to Capade, Andrée had hired one of the great orators of the Parisian bar, Maître Follier, at whom the spectators gawped as if he were a film star.

The presiding judge had silky grey hair; one of his associate judges, a very young man, seemed nervous, while the other spent his time doodling.

Tony observed all this in a detached way, almost as if he were in a train staring out of a window at the landscape streaming past. The jurors fascinated him, and he studied each in turn for so long that, by the second session, he was familiar with the slightest detail of their faces.

Standing with a respectful demeanour, he answered the preliminary questions reluctantly, with the same neutral tone he had taken way back in catechism class. Here, too, was he not reciting by heart answers he had supplied many times before?

The first witness called was La Louchote, and it turned out that she had been the first, on a day when she was leaving the train station at Triant, to see Andrée going inside the Hôtel des Voyageurs via the little door on Rue Gambetta.

As chance would have it, she had been in Rue Gambetta two hours later just as Andrée was leaving, and when she had gone inside the café to wait, as she was too early for her train home, who should be there but Tony.

That was how it all started, all those rumours Falcone had learned about only much later. It was Inspector Mani who had finally, so patiently, tracked her down.

One after another they came and went, men and women he knew, many of whom he called by their first names, some of whom he had known since school. They had all dressed in their Sunday best and sometimes their responses, or their unwittingly comical behaviour, provoked ripples of laughter in the court.

Motionless and impassive, old Angelo was there in the second row, where he would sit in the same seat all through the trial. Vincent would join him after giving his evidence; until then, he had to wait in a room with other witnesses, among whom were Françoise and old Madame Despierre.

'You are the brother of the accused and, as such, you cannot be placed under oath.'

The courtroom was very warm and smelled of unwashed bodies. A young and pretty woman lawyer, Capade's assistant, kept handing peppermints to him. Once she turned around to offer one to Andrée and then, after a moment's hesitation, to Tony.

Again, his impressions were of jarring images, of noses, eyes, smiles, yellowed teeth in half-open mouths, the startling red of a woman's hat, and snatches of sentences he did not bother lining up to find out what they meant.

'You say that about once a month your brother Tony would join the Despierre woman in a room in your hotel, room 3, which you called the blue room. Was it your habit to thus welcome such couples in your establishment?'

Poor Vincent, publicly insulted like that, when from the beginning he had begged his brother to break off the affair!

There was something else the presiding judge had said, during Tony's interrogation.

'You were so passionately in love with Andrée Despierre that you didn't hesitate to hide your guilty lovemaking beneath the roof of your brother and sister-in-law.'

It was a hotel, wasn't it? At times he could not help smiling, as if it were all happening to someone else. Playing to the audience, the presiding judge made harsh or sardonic comments the eager journalists could feed to their papers.

And then Andrée's famous barrister from Paris, stung, would rise to deliver his own trenchant ripostes.

Demarié had advised Tony to get a second lawyer as well, but he had refused.

He just didn't see the point. The long-drawn-out tale already pieced together in Diem's chambers would now be retold for the jury and the public.

The atmosphere was more solemn, with more ritual formulae and flourishes, more actors and bit players, but it was basically the same old story.

The dates were rehashed one by one, along with the

comings and goings of all concerned, but when the letters came up there was a general commotion, with squabbling not only between the prosecution and the defence but within each team itself. Every word was dissected and Follier even brandished one volume of Littré's dictionary to list the various meanings of certain words used every day by everyone.

Andrée, dressed in black, took a more intense interest in the proceedings than Tony did and leaned forwards sometimes to smile at him or give him a knowing look.

The battle of the expert witnesses broke out only on the third day.

'Until now,' said the presiding judge, 'I had always thought that the sale of poisons was strictly regulated and that a doctor's prescription was required to obtain them. But what do we see in this case?

'An old cocoa tin containing more than fifty grams of strychnine, which toxicologists estimate would kill some twenty people, sits in a shed that is open all day long.

'And on the shelves in the back room of the Despierre grocery store, next to the food supplies, we find two kilos – you hear me, two kilos! – of the same poison as well as an equally substantial amount of arsenic.'

'We all deplore this situation,' replied one of the expert witnesses, 'but unfortunately, that is the law. Although in pharmacies the sale of poisons is tightly controlled, those used as pesticides are freely sold in agricultural cooperatives, drugstores and some village shops.'

Day in and day out there they all were in their appointed spots: the magistrates, jurors, barristers, gendarmes, journalists and even the onlookers, who must have had some way of retaining the same seats and whom the witnesses, one after the other, would join after their brief turn in the witness box.

Now and then one of the lawyers near the little side door would slip out to defend a client in another court, and during any adjournment the room buzzed like a school playground.

At such times Tony was escorted to a dark room where the only window was three metres high on the wall, and Andrée was doubtless in a similar place. Demarié brought him soft drinks; Tony supposed the magistrates must have had something to drink as well. Then a bell would summon everyone back to their places, as in the theatre or the cinema.

Her complexion more chalk-white than ever, old Madame Despierre made a spectacular entrance. And with her, the judge took a softer tone, for she was, in a way, one of the victims.

'I never encouraged my son in this marriage, as I knew no good would come of it. Unfortunately, he loved the woman, and I hadn't the heart to oppose . . .'

Why did he remember some words but not others?

'I am obliged, madame, to remind you of unhappy events and to speak of your son's death.'

'If she hadn't pushed me out of my own house, I would have watched over him, and nothing would have happened. She never loved him, you see. All she wanted was our money. She knew he wouldn't live long. When she took a lover . . .'

'You were aware of her affair with the accused?'

'Like everyone else in Saint-Justin, except my poor Nicolas.'

'In August of last year, he seems to have grown suspicious.'

'I was so hoping he would catch them in the act and would throw her out – but she managed to twist him around her little finger.'

'What was your reaction upon finding your son dead?'

'I felt right away that he hadn't succumbed to one of his attacks and that his wife was somehow involved.'

'Of course, you had no proof.'

'I waited for them to go after his wife.'

She pointed at Tony.

'It was only a matter of time. And I was right.'

'Was it not you who, two days after the death of Madame Falcone, sent an anonymous letter to the public prosecutor?'

'The experts have not formally identified my writing. The note may be from anyone.'

'Let's talk about the pot of jam. Who took delivery of it in the shop?'

'I did, the day before it happened, meaning Tuesday, 16 February.'

'Did you open it?'

'No. I knew from the label what it was and I set it aside in the back room.'

This was one of those rare moments when Tony paid attention. He was not the only one to show particular

The Blue Room

interest in this testimony: his lawyer had risen and moved several steps closer, as if intent on hearing better, perhaps – but in reality in the vain hope of disconcerting the witness.

The answers Madame Despierre was about to give would largely determine Tony's fate.

'That morning, at what time did you go to the store?'

'The morning of the 17th? At seven o'clock, as always.'

'You saw the package?'

'It was still in the same place.'

'Was the string intact and the sealing tape unbroken?'

'Yes.'

'You remained at the counter until 7.50, when your daughter-in-law took your place, and you went home for a bite to eat. Is that correct?'

'It is the truth.'

'How many people were in the shop when you left it?'

'Four. I had just served Marguerite Chauchois when I saw that man come across the street towards us. I went home through the garden.'

She was lying. And unable to help herself, she looked defiantly at Tony. If the package was open at that moment, as it certainly was – and all the more obviously if it had been open overnight, as was quite probable, then Andrée had had more than enough time to mix the poison into one of the jam pots.

If, on the contrary, the package was intact, then she could not possibly have poisoned the jam during the minute or two he had stood waiting in the shop.

It was not enough for old Madame Despierre that

Andrée should pay for killing Nicolas. Tony had to pay for it as well.

'May it please Your Honour, I should like—' began Demarié, as murmuring swelled in the room.

'You will have ample time to present your case in due course to the jury.'

Tony was not looking at Andrée, but the newspapers claimed that at that moment she had smiled, with what one article described as a "greedy" expression.

For the first time, Tony noticed the Molard sisters sitting way at the back of the courtroom, to the left of the exit, in similar hats and dresses, with identical handbags in their laps, their faces even more moonlike in the dreary courtroom light.

Andrée had preceded Tony in the witness box, where she had proudly declared or, rather, proclaimed to the court and the public, as if making a profession of faith, 'I did not poison my husband, but if he had taken too long to die, then perhaps I would have. I loved Tony and I love him still.'

'How did you mean to get rid of Madame Falcone?'

'That had nothing to do with me. I wrote so to Tony. I told him: "Now you!" I had confidence, and waited.'

'Waited for what?'

'Waited for him to free himself, as we'd decided he would as soon as I gained my freedom.'

'You did not anticipate that he would kill her?'

Then, holding her head high, she had exclaimed in her rich, throaty voice, 'We love each other!'

So great was the uproar that the judge had threatened to clear the court.

The Blue Room

The die had been cast on the very first day. And that was not the day Nicolas died, or the day of Gisèle's agonizing death.

The first day had been 2 August of the previous year, when Tony, naked and self-satisfied in the scorching heat of the blue room, stood in front of a mirror showing him Andrée lying as if splayed wide open.

'Did I hurt you?'

'No.'

'Are you angry with me?'

'No.'

'Is your wife going to ask you any questions?'

'I don't think so.'

'Does she ever ask any?'

Gisèle was still alive, and, shortly after those words were spoken, he would go home to her and Marianne in their new house.

'You have a beautiful back. Do you love me, Tony?'

'I think so.'

'You're not sure?'

Had he loved her? A gendarme was sitting between them, and at times she leaned forwards to look at him with that same expression she had worn in the room at Triant.

'Would you like to spend your whole life with me?'

'Sure!'

The words had lost all meaning, yet they were what everyone was carrying on about now with ridiculous solemnity. About things that did not exist. And a man who did not exist, either.

The public prosecutor spoke all afternoon long, finally demanding, his face streaming with sweat, the death penalty for both the accused.

The lawyers for the defence spent the entire next day delivering their closing speeches, and it was eight o'clock when the jury retired to deliberate.

'We still have a chance,' insisted Demarié, pacing restlessly around the little room, where Tony was the calmer of the two.

Did the lawyer believe in his innocence? Had he any doubts? It didn't matter. He kept looking at his watch. By 9.30, the bell that would summon them back to the courtroom had not yet echoed along the corridors.

'A good sign. When deliberations drag on, it usually means that . . .'

They waited for another half an hour before being recalled to their places. One of the ceiling lights had burned out.

'I remind the public that I will tolerate no disorder.'

The foreman of the jury rose, holding a sheet of paper.

'In the matter of Andrée Despierre, née Formier, the verdict of the jury on the first count is: yes. On the second count: yes. On the third and the fourth counts: no.'

She had been found guilty of the murder of her husband, with premeditation, but innocent of the death of Gisèle.

'In the matter of Antoine Falcone, the verdict of the jury . . .'

He was found innocent of the murder of Nicolas, but guilty of murdering his wife and in his case, too, the charge of premeditation was considered proven.

While the presiding judge was speaking quietly with his associates, leaning in turn from one to the other, the silence that fell was tense with impatience.

At last the judge pronounced sentence. On the recommendation of the jury, the death penalty for the two accused was commuted to life in prison with hard labour.

In the ensuing tumult, while everyone stood up at once and people shouted to one another all across the courtroom, Andrée rose as well and turned slowly towards Tony.

This time, he was so fascinated by her face that he could not turn away. Never, even when they had been the most closely united as one flesh, had he seen her so radiant and beautiful. Never had her voluptuous mouth smiled at him as it did now, in the triumph of love. Never, with one look, had she possessed him so completely.

'You see, Tony?' she exulted. 'Nothing can part us now!'

« *Certes, ils préfèrent que je ne voie pas certaines choses. Mais ce qu'il ne faut surtout pas, c'est que je leur en raconte d'autres* ».

« – *Vous direz tout?*
– *Et vous?*
– *J'essaierai. Si je n'y parviens pas, je m'en voudrais toute ma vie* »

Peuples qui ont faim, 1934